Jo Spain has worked as a party advisor on the economy in the Irish parliament. Her first novel, *With Our Blessing*, was shortlisted for the Richard and Judy 'Search for a Bestseller' competition and became a top-ten bestseller in Ireland. Jo lives in Dublin with her husband and their four young children.

# Sleeping Beauties

## JO SPAIN

Quercus

First published in Great Britain in 2017 by Quercus
This edition published in 2018 by

Quercus Editions Ltd
Carmelite House
50 Victoria Embankment
London EC4Y 0DZ

An Hachette UK company

A CIP catalogue record for this book is available
from the British Library

PB ISBN 978 1 78648 394 2
EBOOK ISBN 978 1 78648 393 5

10 9 8 7 6 5 4 3 2 1

Typeset by Jouve (UK), Milton Keynes

Printed and bound in Great Britain by Clays Ltd, St Ives plc

For Julie and Maureen, two beautiful ladies

# PROLOGUE

## Fiona, 2012

*How could I have been so stupid?*

*Such a pathetic, moronic idiot.*

*I'm that woman, the one I used to scorn. I believed him when he said he didn't mean it, when he said he was sorry. The first time. The second time. Every time. I thought he'd change.*

*But he's gone too far.*

*He'll kill me if I don't end things.*

*No. This stops now.*

*I won't be a dumb victim.*

This is what Fiona tells herself, bravely and resolutely, as she slowly limps along the lonely, narrow, hedgerow-lined road that leads to her home.

The sun is setting but still retains some heat, the evening hazy with it. Her bared arms are pale; the flimsy yellow cardigan hanging loosely from her fingers is almost trailing on the ground. The string strap of her vest slips down with every other step, coming to rest on an ugly four-finger-shaped bruise before she roughly pulls it back onto her shoulder, wishing it would stay put.

She's nearing the river. Angry midges swarm at her face and she swats them away. She accidentally swipes her mouth with her finger and winces. Her split lip still stings.

She'll stop at the bridge, rest a little on the stone wall her grandfather built with his own hands using rocks from their land. She's always loved that spot. She can make herself look respectable, wash away the worst of the blood and the mascara tears before she returns to her mother and father. She'll be safe then. Fiona inhales the sweet smell of pruned cherry laurel bushes and starts to relax.

A horn blares behind her and she jumps, her heart pounding in her chest. She hadn't even heard the car as it approached, despite the near silence of the countryside, the only sounds the late melody of the song thrush and leaves whispering in the gentle breeze.

Frightened, she turns to see who's approaching. Is it him?

There's little room for a car to pass; she has to stand flat against the hedge. Its sharp branches scratch her back.

It's the blue Ford that belongs to the neighbour from two miles up. An older man who has just moved in to renovate the house vacated by his recently deceased mother.

He doesn't observe rural custom. He doesn't wave, doesn't stop to offer Fiona a lift. He tries to not look at her at all, which is difficult considering she's inches away from his bonnet as the car edges by. When he does glance sideways, she can see the shock register on his face.

He's wondering, she realises, as the car passes but doesn't pick up speed, if he should stop. But, no. He shifts gear. That girl looks a mess, he's likely thinking. What if she claims he did that to her? He's hardly here a wet week, but perhaps he already knows all about Fiona Holland. What type of girl she is.

What she doesn't know is that later, he won't come forward and say he saw her on that road. He will be afraid that as a single, childless, older man and the last witness to her whereabouts, they'll try to pin something on him. He'll keep quiet all the while they're searching.

She drops her head in shame as the car moves past, belching exhaust fumes into the shimmering hot air in its wake. Then, defiantly, knowing he won't be able to resist peeking in his rear-view mirror, she raises her middle finger.

'Fuck you very much,' she mouths at the departing vehicle. Her ribs hurt from where they were punched, her heels are blistered from shoes designed for aesthetic, not practical purposes. She would have gratefully accepted the offer of a ride.

A single tear meanders a lonely path down her cheek and she continues on her way.

She's at the river when she hears the next car. This time, she's aware of it. Alarmed because she'd started to relax, she's on full alert now, her pulse that bit quicker, her senses heightened. Silly, really. Her boyfriend is far too wasted to drive. And yet she's on edge, fearing danger in every unexpected sound, each sudden movement. He's done that to her; he's made her this nervous, jittery person.

The vehicle crawls to a halt and despite herself, she feels relief. She's weary. She needs a cool shower and her soft, downy bed – her mother bringing her strong tea and bread toasted the right shade of golden-brown, smothered in real butter to the edges. No judgement, always loving her little girl no matter what. This car could belong to Jack the Ripper and she'd still take a lift. She thinks that, but Fiona knows there's no risk. She left the real danger back in the village, downing whiskey shots from a mug, admiring his grazed knuckles and feeling like a big man.

The driver waves, but the sun's glare on the windscreen means she can't see his face, only the friendly movement of his hand.

Does she want to get in?

Bloody right she does. She opens the car door and slides into the passenger seat, pulling the seatbelt across and turning to smile at her knight in shining armour.

He doesn't look at her. Instead, he keeps his eyes focused on the road ahead. The anger radiates from him, filling the small car with menace. She hears a click. He's locked the car doors. She won't be getting out.

Only then, too late, does she realise her mistake.

# CHAPTER 1

'He won't let me see my mother.'

'What?'

'Sean. He won't let . . .'

June McGuinness let the rest of the sentence trail off.

'Sorry, what was I saying, dear?'

Louise Reynolds frowned, knowing what she'd heard but unable to repeat it. She continued to brush the older woman's hair, gentle strokes with an old-fashioned soft-bristle brush.

'Never mind that,' she said, lifting June's chin so she could see herself in the mirror. 'Now, look how beautiful you are. We'll go down and show the boys, shall we?'

June's eyes lit up as she beheld her neat bob. She reached out for the make-up bag on the dressing table.

'Not without some lippie, dear.'

They found Tom and Sean in the conservatory at the back of the house, conversing in hushed tones.

'Well, what do you think?'

June did a little twirl for her audience, patting her grey do and smiling.

Her husband of almost half a century smiled back, the strain barely evident.

'You look really elegant, love,' he exclaimed, his thick Kerry accent full of forced jollity for his wife's benefit. 'Now, a drink. What's it to be, lads and lassies? Tea or coffee?'

'For heaven's sake, Sean. It's a beautiful summer's afternoon. Why don't we crack open the white wine? I'll get the glasses.'

June glided off in the direction of the kitchen, a petite ticking time bomb, followed by her six-foot strapping husband, quivering with nerves in her wake.

Louise joined Tom on the rattan two-seater, resting her head on his shoulder. The heat-regulating glass panes were working extra hard to keep the room bearable in the hot midday sun.

Tom took his wife's hand.

'Tough going?' he asked, concerned.

Louise pursed her lips.

'Horrible,' she replied. 'It seems to come in waves. One minute she's completely lucid, the next she's telling me Sean won't let her see her mother. Didn't her mother die thirty years ago? I don't know how he's coping.'

Tom sighed.

Sean McGuinness, up until very recently, had been the Chief Superintendent of the National Bureau of Criminal Investigation. Tom Reynolds headed up the murder investigation unit, a Dublin-based specialist team under the NBCI's remit, and Sean had been the detective inspector's boss. They were also long-time friends.

Which had made it all the harder when the previous year June had been diagnosed with early onset Alzheimer's.

Her condition had deteriorated more rapidly than expected and the chief, a man who lived for his work but loved his wife more, had taken early retirement to care for her. Not for one second had he considered placing her in a home. He was sixty, after all; it was time to go. It didn't matter that the entire force had expected Sean to be carried out of his office in a box long after he should have headed for the hills, such was his dedication to the job.

Louise cupped her husband's face in her hands, noticing the worried look in his usually smiling green eyes. He'd cut his hair tight this summer because the longer it grew the greyer it looked. She thought the short style suited him better – she didn't even mind that he appeared to be sneakily growing a long-wished-for beard. He looked very handsome, in fact.

'He seems to be just getting on with it,' Tom said, quietly. 'It's his new norm. Having to repeat everything, remind her of things, expect the unexpected.'

'Sorry that took so long.' June led the way back into the conservatory, carrying a wooden board laden with mixed cheeses, chutney, fruit and crackers. 'He hid the wine glasses.'

Sean followed, bearing the tray of glasses and a bottle of Riesling, his expression resigned.

'I didn't hide them,' he corrected her, resting his load on the table.

'Oh, your begonia is stunning.' Louise diverted June's attention.

'Yes, the whole garden is beautiful this year,' the older woman replied. 'Actually, would you like to see what I found buried down the end the other day?'

Louise tried to look enthusiastic. She followed June out through the double doors and the two women made their way down a winding stone path towards the trees and wilderness at the bottom of the garden.

The conservatory was awash with scents from outside, the sweet fragrance of gardenia and dianthus and freshly mown grass filling the air. Tom watched the women as they strolled, wine glasses in hand. The scene was so peaceful and relaxed he could almost imagine it was just a normal, lazy Saturday afternoon, like they used to have.

'So, how are you getting on with Joe Kennedy?' Sean asked, breaking the spell. He needed a distraction from the daily struggle with June's illness.

Tom sighed.

'Chief Superintendent Joe Kennedy, to give him his full title,' Sean continued with a smile. 'Which he makes me use, as it happens.'

'You're joking.'

'He doesn't want people to get confused or imagine I'm still the boss.'

Tom cursed under his breath. In his humble opinion, the new chief wasn't fit to lick McGuinness' boots. He knew Sean felt the same. The inspector also knew that if he got stuck into Joe Kennedy, Sean would reprimand him and remind him he must show his new boss the respect his title deserved.

This was his old boss's way of chiding him for not taking on the role himself.

It had been offered. The assistant commissioner, Bronwyn Maher, had summoned Tom that spring just after Sean had dropped the bombshell about leaving, and told him the job was his for the taking.

'People in high places hold you in strong regard,' she had said.

'Forcing your hand, are they?' Tom had quipped.

She'd smiled.

'Not at all. I'm your biggest advocate. How on earth do you know the new Taoiseach, anyway?'

'Jarlath O'Keefe? Oh, we go way back. Well, back to that case in Leinster House last autumn anyhow.'

'Ah. You were the making of him, so. He's pushed hard for you, Tom. He'll be giving you my job next. Can't say I'd mind. Look, I'd be happy to have you in as head of the Bureau. But only if you're willing to put your heart and soul into the job. You can't half do this role.'

And that had been the problem. The inspector didn't want the added responsibility and pressure that being Chief of the National Bureau would bring. He liked his job and it was already demanding enough. And when he'd turned fifty the previous year, he'd begun to realise that he wanted to spend more time with his family, not less.

So he'd resisted the promotion and Joe Kennedy was appointed.

Kennedy was a master of spin. He'd cultivated a persona that was at once serious, intelligent and comforting. He wore period-rimmed spectacles and an expression of constant concern for the safety of the Irish public. He came into his own at press conferences, when reassuring rhetoric dripped from his lips like honey.

He was a complete remove from the man sitting across from Tom now, with his frenzied bushy black eyebrows and shock of grey hair, the wine glass looking dainty in a hand so large it could pull up a small tree by the root. McGuinness was brusque and intimidating, but he ran deep, as the saying went.

The decision to replace Sean with Joe Kennedy was so clichéd it made Tom nauseous.

'It's all quiet on the western front,' he said, keeping his thoughts on his new boss to himself. 'This weather's too hot to be off killing people.'

'I wouldn't go planning any holidays, Tom. You might be on hiatus now, but this heat . . . it gets people feverish. A man can go from being mildly irritated at his wife nagging him to do the garden or stoke the barbecue, straight to feeling murderous.'

'We've already been away,' said the inspector, thinking wistfully of the trip they'd taken to Cuba in May. It had been hotter there, but they'd been better prepared for it. Not like in Ireland, where people reacted with joyous wonderment to the first proper sunny day, but after two weeks of heat couldn't understand how on earth anybody was supposed to live in such a climate, let alone work. 'But you're right. It's too quiet. I think if Louise suggests one more time I paint our shed, I'll bury her under it.'

'What are they up to down there?' Sean asked distractedly, perching on the edge of his chair to peer down the garden. Barely five minutes had passed and already he was uneasy about his wife.

Louise and June were kneeling beneath a late blooming Judas tree.

'We'll join them, shall we?' Tom suggested, curious himself.

As the two men approached, they could hear June chattering excitedly. Louise leaned back on her heels and turned to face them, her face pale.

'Oh, June,' Sean said in dismay. 'Look at your lovely hands. They're all mucky. Come up to the house and we'll wash them.'

'I was just showing Louise the treasure,' his wife protested.

Sean helped June up and guided her back to the conservatory, ignoring the items spread out on the grass beside the disturbed soil.

Tom raised a puzzled eyebrow.

'She's been burying cutlery,' Louise said, gathering up the knives and forks.

Tom opened and closed his mouth, lost for words.

His phone buzzed in his pocket, jolting him back to reality.

'D. I. Reynolds,' he answered, without checking the number on his screen.

'Tom? It's me, Laura. Sorry, I know you're off today, but a body has been found up in Glendalough. Myself and Ray are en route, but the buzz in headquarters is that it might be that girl who went missing last week in Meath. Early reports indicate it's a young female.'

'They're sure it's not suicide?' the inspector asked, thinking of the lakes at the scenic mountain spot.

'They're adamant it's not.'

'Ask Willie Callaghan to collect me, will you, Laura? Tell him I'm at Sean McGuinness' house. I'll be with you as soon as I can.'

'Sorry,' he said, helping Louise to a standing position. 'Willie will pick me up, so you can take the car home at least.'

'Can't be helped. I'll stay with them for a while. Get a wash on for Sean and tidy a bit.'

'You're an angel.' Tom kissed her cheek tenderly.

Sean had been right about the peace not lasting.

But just how badly was it about to be shattered?

# CHAPTER 2

The visitors' car park at Glendalough was chaotic. Elongated tourist coaches and saloon cars packed with sweating, stressed families competed to reverse, u-turn, and extricate themselves from what was rapidly turning into the seventh circle of hell for the single guard on traffic duty. The old monastic site, set in a spectacular glacial valley with two lakes, was a popular tourist spot and on this, a fine summer's day, it was humming with activity.

'To think, the missus suggested we come up here this weekend,' Willie Callaghan remarked. 'What a lucky escape.' Tom's driver stroked his pristinely trimmed moustache, shaking his head in amazement at the close call.

Tom ignored the obvious retort, which was that Willie was now, in fact, in Glendalough.

'Why wouldn't you bring her?' the inspector asked, as his driver honked the horn repeatedly at a busload of startled pensioners.

'Glendalough on a sunny Saturday in July?' Willie exclaimed. 'What kind of mad bastard would you be to inflict that on yourself? Besides, there's sport on. Which I'm bloody missing now.'

His driver spotted the area of the car park that had been marked out for official vehicles and left his hand on the horn until they reached it.

'Jesus Christ!' Tom said, as the car pulled up. 'We'll have to get you treatment for road rage.'

Detective Sergeant Ray Lennon, Tom's deputy, was waiting inside the cordon for his boss's car. He was wearing a short-sleeved white shirt, his tie knot pulled loose at the neck. Unlike Tom, Ray had decided to grow his hair this summer. He was taunting his boss with his naturally dark mane, not a grey strand in sight. The extra couple of inches in a heatwave seemed masochistic, and was probably, Tom suspected, something akin to Bikram yoga for his super-fit deputy.

A few feet away, a small group of women in their early twenties were whispering and giggling as they gazed at the tall detective adoringly. Ray had that effect on women and was, as usual, oblivious to it.

'We heard you before we saw you,' he greeted Tom.

'Where's the scene?' the inspector asked. 'And what's going on with that crowd? Haven't they been told the valley is off limits?'

'The body is in woodland close to the lower lake. We've been trying to clear the two car parks for the last hour but new vehicles keep arriving. It's gone out on the radio bulletins now, so people will stay away, hopefully. The normal ones, anyhow.'

'Who found her?' Tom asked, as they began walking.

'A couple of kids and their dog. Aged ten and eleven.'

'Oh, shit.'

'No, it's okay. The mother and father are traumatised, for sure. But the kids were thrilled. It's like something from their favourite show – The Walking Dead – apparently. I think they'll survive.'

Tom cast a backwards glance at the car park and the people still milling around. They'd all have a great story to tell about their trip to the Wicklow beauty spot today, each of them shivering and remarking with shocked awe: 'It could have been me, I could have found her . . . to think, how close we were!'

'Who's up here?' he asked.

'Laura Brennan came out with me and a couple of the team are en route. She's organising the ground search. We've set up a quarter-mile radius, but we're concentrating on the main route of approach, along the path we're taking. We're working on the assumption that whoever brought her here used this car park. It would have been a twenty-minute hike if he'd left his car near the monastic ruins entrance. We've about ten uniforms assisting. We'll need more. Moya and Emmet are taking care of the body and the scene.'

Tom felt a shiver, despite the burning afternoon sun. That was ominous. Moya Chambers was the new Deputy State Pathologist and Emmet McDonagh was the Chief Superintendent of the Technical Bureau, the Garda Síochána forensic unit. For both department heads to be at the same crime scene was unusual.

It took them about ten minutes to reach the site – a section of the wooded area below the main trail between the monastic settlement and the valley's lower lake.

'He wouldn't have been able to get his car any closer to this spot,' Tom observed, before they left the path.

'I know. That's why we're walking.'

'That's my point. If he killed her at the site, she trusted him enough to walk along this path with him and go off the public trail. He couldn't have forced her all this way and if he dragged her down to the wood, somebody might have spotted it. If he didn't kill her here, he had to carry her body all the way from the car park. So, in that scenario, we're talking about somebody fit, or two people. Could you carry a dead body this distance?'

Ray was a decent benchmark of what could or couldn't be achieved, strength-wise.

His DS shrugged. 'It would depend on her weight and how I was carrying her. Over my shoulder, a regular-sized woman, yeah – just about. But surely somebody would spot you lugging a body over your shoulder?'

'Not if it was the dead of night. Is it her, do you think?'

'Fiona Holland? I don't know. I haven't seen her yet. Emmet and Moya were just securing the scene and the body when we arrived.'

Neither of them said anything more. What was worse – for the missing girl to be found dead, or for her to still be missing, fate unknown, and this to be some other poor woman?

They made their way down into the woods, negotiating their footing over awkward paths scarred by ancient tree roots, rocks and sprawling moss. It was darker down here, the tall trees obscuring the natural daylight. But as they approached the crime scene the greenery overhead thinned and they found themselves in a small glade.

A perimeter cordon had been established: tape stretched from tree to tree around the clearing and a low tent had been erected over the body.

Tom and Ray stepped into crime-scene gear before joining their colleagues.

The affectionate term for the coupling of Moya and Emmet was Little and Large. Almost at retirement age, the Tech Bureau chief, though a handsome man, was at least four stone overweight and on the tipping point of diabetes, heart disease and all other kinds of obesity-related illnesses. Moya, by contrast, was a petite woman in her forties. Her bleached blonde hair was set in a perm straight out of an eighties soap opera. That, along with her ample bust, gave her a passing resemblance to Dolly Parton, though none of her colleagues would ever make that observation to her face. Sharp, focused and authoritative, Moya suffered no fools. She was Boudica reincarnated.

'Tom, wait a moment,' Emmet called over. He was sweating profusely. His glasses hung on a chain around his neck, unable to keep their grip on the sweat-slicked surface of his nose. His dyed brown hair was damp from the exertion of just turning up to work on such a hot day.

The inspector was expecting Emmet to launch into a full-blown tirade railing against being summoned to work on a weekend and was preparing a response that involved the words 'Piss' and 'off'. The Tech Bureau chief had a reputation for being crotchety, but it was better to meet his rudeness with good-natured chutzpah, rather than fawning capitulation.

But Emmet wasn't himself today. He appeared uneasy, rattled, even.

Tom wondered what the hell was under the tent. It took a lot to put that look on his colleague's face.

'Just walk in a straight line to the middle here,' Emmet instructed the two detectives. 'Avoid the edges.'

Tom and Ray, seasoned in forensics protocol, obeyed the order.

The four shook hands.

'What have we got?' the inspector asked, directing the question to Moya. 'Is it the Meath girl?'

The pathologist shook her head, thin lips sucked in to make them even thinner.

'Absolutely not. The state of decomposition would indicate that this woman has been in the ground for approximately a year. It's difficult to be exact – the ground here is damp, which speeds up the process.'

'A year?' Tom parroted. He went through a list of names in his head. Who'd gone missing this time last year? He couldn't recall any cases last summer that had dominated the news headlines for more than a day or two, enough to make them memorable. 'Will you need a post-mortem to determine cause of death?'

'Definitely, but she doesn't appear to have been stabbed or shot. By the looks of it, though, you won't need to worry too much about getting an ID on this one.'

'What do you mean?'

'She's wearing the clothes she went missing in. Well, what's left of them. We think it's Una Dolan.'

'Una Dolan,' Ray repeated. 'Una . . . that was spring of last year, wasn't it?'

'That's right,' Tom said. 'I remember. Twenty-four, never made it home from a nightclub. But you're saying she was only murdered last summer, maybe later? Does that mean . . .?'

'He kept her?' Moya finished the sentence. 'Possibly. I won't be able to give you a definite date but I'll be closer to the exact period of death when I've done a full examination.'

'Can we take a look?' The inspector indicated the ground. Emmet's uncharacteristic silence was putting Tom on edge.

The two experts stood clear and the detectives crouched down beside the small tent. They unzipped one of the flaps and took in the sight of the woman's remains.

The body lay on top of plastic sheeting. The tattered remnants of tight blue jeans and a black velvet hoodie clung to its frame, clothing immortalised in the last CCTV footage of Una Dolan – the still image that had been used by all the media outlets for weeks. She was recognisably female, some long black strands of hair still evident on her scalp. But no – they wouldn't be asking the family to identify her. DNA analysis would confirm if this was indeed Una.

'She'd been disturbed,' Emmet said, breaking the silence. 'Prior to being found by the dog and the kids, I mean. If she'd been buried originally that close to the surface she'd have been discovered before now, and there'd have been little left after the wildlife was done. I'd guess she was dug up and reburied, but in a shallower grave the second time.'

That was enough for Ray. He rose abruptly, hand across his mouth, and turned away from the tent.

'Do not vomit!' Emmet barked at the detective.

Tom stood up to offer some moral support to his infamously weak-stomached deputy.

'Give the man a break,' he said. 'It's not a pretty sight. And you're looking a little peaky yourself, truth be told. What's on your mind?'

'There's somebody I want you to talk to. Mark!'

Tom recognised Mark Dunne, the man Emmet had summoned with his roar. He had worked with the Tech Bureau for a few years and was a friendly chap, good at his job. He was a big rugby player in his spare time, from what the inspector recalled, and had the cauliflower ears and misshapen nose to prove it.

'Tom, you know Mark, don't you? Right, well, as it turns out, my assistant is a bit of a nature expert.'

'Ok-ay.' Tom drew out the word, one eyebrow raised quizzically. 'What's the relevance?'

'Do you know much about Glendalough?' Mark asked.

'Tourist facts.'

'Okay, so, before I went into forensic science, I studied botany. I'm familiar in particular with the flora and fauna of the Wicklow Mountains National Park.'

Tom and Ray stared at him blankly.

'Eh, let me give you some context. You see these trees around us? They're mainly oak trees. Centuries ago, the trees in Glendalough were coppiced – cut down and regrown from their stumps. It was good practice for managing woodland, but they overdid it here and lost a lot of the trees. Around the mid-eighteenth century they replanted but there are still little glades like this one here and there, a legacy of the coppicing. In the main, though, Glendalough is filled with deciduous woodland – that means the trees are so thick overhead that there's competition for light and space to grow. So the plant life in these woods has adapted. It has stratified.'

'Go on,' said Tom, still at a loss as to where this was heading.

'Well, you've the trees at the top – the canopy layer. Then there's the shrub layer, holly mainly. There's a ground layer of mosses. The grass-height plants are called the herb layer. These have to be clever to survive in such a fierce environment. You still with me?'

'So far, and kudos for your extensive knowledge of Glendalough greenery,' the inspector replied, wryly. 'What's the point, though?'

Mark produced an evidence bag and withdrew from it a delicate blue flower. Soil still clung to its roots.

'This, in layman's terms, is blue-eyed grass. I found it amid the loose soil covering the victim. It was a genius choice.

Whoever planted it here knew their flora. Blue-eyed grass will thrive in damp soil and we're near a lake, but this plant is native to marshes and wetlands in the west of Ireland. Not here in the east and not in Glendalough.'

'So, somebody brought it here and placed it on the grave?'

'No. As I said, it was planted,' Mark replied.

'But you said . . .'

'Look at the ground around us, Tom,' Emmet interrupted.

The inspector frowned and examined the earth under the trees. As he scanned the glade, his stomach lurched.

One, two, three, four. Five, counting the mound of earth disturbed under the tent.

Tom counted five separate patches where the same delicate blue flower was blooming. And then he saw it. The unnatural plots, too tidy, too cultivated compared to the unruly foliage that covered the forest floor beyond the circle. In some areas, the blue flowers had taken hold and were spreading, and yet they still appeared contained, as though they were being cared for.

Somebody had cleared the earth of its natural layer and sown their own flowers.

In five places.

Five graves.

# CHAPTER 3

*Una, 2011*

The effects of the alcohol were starting to wear off.

Una realised now how stupid she'd been, but she still thought there was a way out of all this. She clung to it.

She didn't realise that, while it was her first time being kidnapped, it wasn't his first time to kidnap.

She didn't know about the others. Yet.

It had all started with one careless decision. She'd stormed out of the nightclub determined to walk home on her own. Una wasn't used to rejection, which, as it turned out, tasted bitter. And to come second to Mairead Towell . . . Jesus. They were friends and all, but what had Mairead got over her? Minus the three inches of slap and Wonderbra, she was a dozy cow with no bloody eyebrows and an A cup.

Not that dozy, though. It wasn't Mairead trapped in this car.

Underneath it all, Una had just been hurt. She'd fancied the newcomer, even though he was older. She'd flirted outrageously, worn her lowest top and highest heels. The men had fallen over themselves trying to get into her knickers, as usual. But all she'd wanted was him.

So, when he'd so overtly chosen Mairead, ramming his tongue down her throat in the middle of the dance floor, it had been like a punch in the gut. Una knew from the sideways glance he gave her that he was playing mindgames, looking to provoke a reaction.

Una refused to play and stomped out of the venue, gasping for the fresh air at the front door and shrugging off her friends' concerns. Zipping up her hoodie, she'd started off through the town. She knew she was being reckless and silly, but didn't give a shit. She needed to pound off the embarrassment.

Some lads had leered at her on the main street as she tottered along it in increasingly painful heels, her skinny jeans chafing her thighs. They had given her a fright, reminding her that, angry as she was, she was vulnerable. She'd turned down a quiet side street to avoid the catcalls.

When the car had pulled up, she'd been grateful to see it. The fresh air had sobered her up and she wanted to go home.

She hadn't been alarmed at the start. He'd driven in the direction of her house, while she rested her head on the cool glass of the window and berated herself for her over-reaction. A heady mix of vodka and her bloody ego. She needed to calm the hell down and stop going out so much. Even her friends were getting pissed off with her these days. They hadn't a clue. They all had something going for them. College degrees, job prospects, relationships. All she had was her looks and she had to make them work for her. Her parents were sick of her living at home, tired of her dropping out of courses and frustrated that she couldn't hold down even crappy jobs in shops and offices.

She needed a bloody man earning a decent salary who considered it a privilege to take care of her. What was the point of being a looker if she couldn't secure that basic necessity?

Una had looked up when the car passed the entrance to her housing estate and pointed out that he'd missed the turn.

He didn't answer. So she said it again, louder, this time with a little fluttering of butterflies in the bottom of her stomach. Still, she didn't think she'd anything to be really nervous about. He was probably just chancing his arm.

'Hey!' she cried. 'I said you missed my turn. Stop the car, will you? I'm not interested in going anywhere with you. Just bring me home.'

But he didn't. So she'd tried to open her door, even with the car moving. He'd locked it from his side.

'Where are you taking me?' she pleaded, quietly, panic building. And he continued to ignore her.

It was like she was already gone.

She'd stopped talking then, trying to figure out what to do. Slowly, she reached her hand into her bag, praying he wouldn't notice. Her phone was at the bottom. If she could dial a number – anybody – and start talking, they'd know she was in trouble. Maybe they could trace her mobile.

Without even looking at Una, he'd slapped the bag from her hands, then held her firm against the seat with one hand as she strained to reach it. When she'd bit him hard on the arm, he stopped the car and thumped her in the face. Once the shock of the pain subsided, she'd fought him, yelling and scratching at him with her nails.

'You won't be getting out of the car,' he spat in her face, and clamped his hand around her throat until she stopped resisting.

Now she was numb, watching the passing woods, wondering what the hell was happening. If he was going to rape her, she'd go along with it. She'd let him do whatever he wanted as long as she could get out of this car and survive this ordeal.

She'd figure a way out.

# CHAPTER 4

They worked late into the night.

All involved, from the ordinary uniforms to hardened senior officers, were shocked at the scale of the discovery.

Tom stayed on site, overseeing operations and offering his unit leadership and support. As the hours wore on and fatigue set in, he and Laura made their way to the café by the lake to source coffees for the team. Its owner had stayed on with the kind offer of supplying the guards with sustenance.

They stood on the shore, the water lapping at their feet, as they waited for the order to be made up. Laura's long chestnut curls lifted softly in the gentle, early evening breeze.

'I can't get my head around this,' she said, hushed and appalled. 'This is Ireland! I still remember when one murder could keep the public horrified and enthralled for months. I know things have escalated since then, but a serial killer? Here?'

In her early thirties, Laura was the youngest member of Tom's team. She'd already seen far too much for her years but nothing came close to what they'd found this day.

'We've had cases before of people who killed multiple times,' he answered. 'Remember Kilcross? But, no, there's been nothing like this. Not that we didn't suspect it was coming. Too many women have vanished into thin air over the years.'

He reached down to pick up a smooth stone from among the pebbles at their feet and tossed it into the water, watching the ripples before looking up at the mountains that met at the top of the lake, still visible in the half light of the summer night.

'When we were children, we used to come up to Dublin to see the Kerry footballers playing in Croke Park on match day Sundays,' Laura said. 'When Dad could get a Saturday off, we'd make a weekend of it. Our parents would take us here or to Powerscourt. I remember this great sense of freedom. Running up and down hills, climbing trees, ice creams if we were lucky. Being here as an adult . . . well, you realise how peaceful it is, don't you?'

She let out a sigh and pulled her cardigan closed against an imaginary chill.

'It's hard to imagine violence here. You can see why the monks chose this spot as a centre for prayer. It's like –'

She paused.

'What?' The inspector asked.

'I . . . I was just thinking it's so magnificent, it's like God pressed his thumb on the earth to mark this place out.' She flushed red.

Tom smiled at her candour, thinking he couldn't have articulated it better. And he was as much, if not more, of an atheist.

Her words had stirred an idea into being.

'Hmm,' he said.

'What are you thinking?'

'I was wondering, why here? Why not some place where he could have gotten the car that bit closer, even if it was nighttime when he buried them? Maybe the religious resonance of Glendalough is important to him.'

'There's a cemetery down at the monastic ruins, isn't there?'

Tom nodded. He'd been there many times, squinting at the names on the old stones, trying to make out dates, marvelling at the similarities in the inscriptions for those who died in 1750 and those in 1950. Earth to earth, ashes to ashes. Everyone equal in the end.

'So, he made his own graveyard, nearer the lake,' Laura remarked, icily. 'Maybe it was his way of making peace with what he'd done. Bastard.'

Chief Superintendent Joe Kennedy arrived shortly after they returned to the site. Tom had been expecting him sooner, but he'd forgotten his boss had been attending a meeting with his counterpart in Belfast.

'How the hell did it go unnoticed?' Kennedy asked, as he rocked on his heels, hands clasped tightly behind his back. 'Five bloody graves in Glendalough. How come they weren't disturbed over the years?'

'It seems like the rumours were true,' Tom shrugged.

'What do mean?'

'That there's a serial killer operating in Ireland. I suppose nobody wanted to believe it. And now . . .'

'And now it transpires that the Garda Síochána have been letting a dangerous individual operate with impunity for all these years, without the first clue of what was happening, who he is, or how to stop him.'

Tom bristled and flashed his boss a sharp look.

'If any of one of those bodies had been discovered, we would have thrown everything at finding the killer. We can't launch murder investigations into missing persons.'

Kennedy raised an eyebrow.

'It's not what I think, Inspector Reynolds. I'm just saying

out loud what the talk-show hosts and op-eds will be spouting for weeks and months to come. We're facing a media onslaught.'

*No shit, Sherlock,* Tom retorted silently.

'I presume you'll be looking at the ground staff,' Kennedy continued. 'People who know the area and have frequent access? We have to say we're following definite leads.'

The inspector nodded, trying to suppress his growing irritation. Sean McGuinness would have pointed out the obvious course too, but he'd earned the right. Kennedy was a few years short of Tom's fifty and had gone into the desk-jockey end of policing early. He had very little on-the-ground experience, the sort that mattered.

'We'll look at the staff,' Tom said, patiently. 'But this is a public park. There's no entrance fee, no teams of security guards patrolling at night. The priority is to establish the victims' identities and then trawl through the details of their lives to see if anything connects them.'

'Hmm,' was Kennedy's reply, dissatisfaction coming off him in waves. The inspector wasn't being reassuring enough. The new chief superintendent wanted his lead man to be confident to the point of arrogance and to promise a speedy result. He didn't mind hearing Tom bullshit if it sounded convincing and could be then parsed and delivered to the press in comforting sound bites.

As the night wore on, the thorny issue of resources arose. The chief was in the middle of outlining what he thought he could get, versus what Tom needed, when Emmet McDonagh approached. Kennedy gave him the briefest of nods and left. The two department heads didn't see eye to eye and Emmet was winning in the war of cool looks and snarky asides. Tom should have felt sorry for his boss; Emmet was a formidable foe. But Kennedy's knack for rubbing people up the wrong way meant he must have done or said something to the Tech Bureau chief to warrant such treatment.

'We've done all we can here,' Emmet said, his wide shoulders sagging. 'The bodies have all been removed from the ground and will be transferred to Moya's lab shortly. She's flying over a couple of colleagues from London to assist. We need to date them. None of the cadavers are fully decomposed, so we reckon they go back a few years, not decades.'

It was to Emmet that Tom voiced the concern that was plaguing him.

'Where's Fiona Holland? She's not one of those bodies, but has he struck again? Has she been taken by a serial killer?'

Emmet sighed. He wasn't the most tactile person, but he patted the inspector's back in solidarity as the two men stared in the direction of the clearing where the five bodies lay.

'I don't know, *chara*. Maybe she's run off with a fella. Maybe she's done herself in. Who knows . . .?'

They left the rest unsaid.

'You need to go home,' Emmet insisted. 'Get some rest.'

Tom glanced at his watch. It was nearing midnight. To give Kennedy his due, he'd stayed there all day, refusing to deal with the massive media presence outside the car park until they had a handle on the number of bodies and could make an informed statement.

Tom didn't want to leave. He knew he wouldn't sleep. How could he when there was the possibility they were working against the clock to save Fiona Holland's life? His team would work alongside him without stop, if he asked them to.

Yet he knew that was the least sensible course. After a few

hours' rest, they would all meet in HQ, their brains more alert, ready to begin this unprecedented investigation.

'You should, you know,' Emmet said, about to launch into a lecture about the need for sleep.

Tom smiled grimly and cut him off.

'I know. I've delivered that advice often enough myself, old friend. You go, too. Let your team finish up here and come at it fresh tomorrow. We're all going to need our wits about us for this one and the site will be secured for as long as we want.'

'Do me a favour, Tom?'

'What?'

'Say a prayer with me.'

Tom blinked, surprised at the Tech chief's request. He hadn't pegged Emmet as a religious man. But standing there now, the bodies of the murdered women yards from their feet and the hour late, the inspector suddenly felt that praying was absolutely the appropriate reaction.

So he bowed his head and closed his eyes as Emmet intoned a Hail Mary, summoning the mother of Christ to help them find a killer. And when he'd finished, Tom, feeling like an utter hypocrite, silently made his own plea to a God he'd long stopped believing in. He prayed for the families of the murdered women and then he prayed that he'd never have to live through the grief that they were about to experience.

Willie drove the inspector home to his house on Blackhorse Avenue, a road that ran along one side of the sprawling Phoenix Park in west Dublin. They didn't speak. Tom rested his head against the back of the seat. He felt like he'd been holding his breath all day and now, away from the scene, he was exhausted.

Willie sat erect in the driver's seat, every now and again shaking his head and coughing to clear his throat. He'd chain-smoked as he hung around Glendalough, giving up his spare time to be on call in case Tom needed him. He too had been horrified as the news filtered out about the multiple bodies.

At home, Tom looked in on his daughter and granddaughter before going to bed.

Maria had taken Cáit in with her. The two faced each other on the pillow, one small head nose-to-nose with a bigger one, their features a mirror image bar their size. His daughter's auburn hair fanned out on the pillow behind her. His granddaughter's fairer hair was stuck to her head in sleep-damp curls.

The inspector felt his throat constrict as he looked at his sleeping beauties. They were safe and happy, oblivious to the evil that existed outside their dreams, unaware of the malevolence that he felt clung to the threads of his clothes after where he'd been.

Maria was twenty-one. They didn't know the ages of the women they'd found today but Tom expected them to be all of a grouping. Late teens, twenties, maybe early thirties. Una Dolan was twenty-four. Fiona Holland, nineteen.

There was usually a type.

Tomorrow they'd start with the lists of missing women and the process of identifying their victims.

There were five families out there, six if you included Fiona Holland's, waiting for news of a daughter, a sister, a girlfriend. Each of the victims had been loved by somebody, had been held at some point with the same devotion that Maria felt for Cáit and Tom felt for both of them. When each woman vanished, the loss and anguish felt by their parents and loved ones must have been indescribable.

Now, five families would receive the worst possible news.

Tomorrow, Tom sighed. Tomorrow.

# CHAPTER 5

The bodies had been taken to the Mater Hospital in Dublin's city centre, under the direction of the state pathologist. The Victorian-fronted complex housed a large mortuary and a state-of-the-art forensics laboratory. Moya Chambers had summoned both of her deputies and had been joined by two colleagues from the London Metropolitan Police Service. Several senior laboratory staff members had also been reassigned to supplement her team.

The pathology unit had worked through the night and the Mater was the inspector's first point of call that Sunday morning.

'You've brought in the real experts, then.' Tom nodded at the new foreign personnel.

'They flew in last night. Sure, all I know about serial killings of this nature is what I've picked up watching CSI.'

'Jesus. I was kidding. You look tired.' He handed the pathologist a coffee offering.

'Do you want an award for stating the blindingly obvious?' Moya retorted, lowering her facemask. She winced at the scalding hot styrofoam cup in her hand. 'Christ. They used to have little cardboard yokes you could put around these things so you wouldn't burn the hand off yourself. How much do you think the monkeys in accounts saved by getting rid of that luxury? Tight bastards.'

'I'd have bought everybody a cup but at €2.50 a pop it seemed a bit over and above.'

Moya waved her hand dismissively at her team.

'Don't worry about the minions. I'm letting them go up for breakfast now, anyhow. Rubber sausages and burnt toast that'll probably cost half a day's salary. Come on, I'll talk you through what I've found so far.'

The lab cleared out at her command, leaving just the pathologist, the inspector and five cadavers in varying states of fetid decomposition.

'Our biggest problem,' Moya said, 'is that they were buried in damp soil. He wrapped them in plastic sheeting, but that wasn't enough to keep the little critters out. You can see yourself – the maggots have had a field day with the earliest victims.'

'I'm trying to digest my own breakfast,' Tom groaned. He'd taken the precaution of rubbing Vicks under his nose before entering the lab. There was no way anybody would be mistaking him for a hard-as-nails copper who wasn't fazed by the smell of rotten, putrid corpses freshly dug out of the ground and cut open.

She shrugged. 'I can't sugar-coat this for you, my love. Anyhow, between the insects and the damp, it's impossible to put definite dates on the deaths more specific than the approximate year for some of them. I can tell you for certain that Una Dolan was killed less than twelve months ago. So, you were right. He kept her for a while. That must be his M.O.'

'Most likely,' Tom said. 'Go on.'

'We've extracted DNA samples and made dental X-rays, so you can use those to ID them. I'd estimate that we're going back about five or six years to the first victim. There's still some residual flesh and membranes; none of the bodies are entirely skeletal yet. We can confirm they're all women and make an educated guess that they were all young enough. Under forty, in any case. That's a guess, mind. And I'm pretty sure they're all of Caucasion race. I gave that lass on your team that bit this morning to help with the missing persons match-ups. Again, I'm confirming as I go. If you put a rush on the DNA and get names, some of this will become redundant.'

'Five years for five victims,' Tom remarked, through gritted teeth. 'So, what – Fiona Holland is number six in year six?'

'That's how it appears, but you don't sound convinced.' Moya liberated her peroxide perm from its tight knot, massaging the point on her head where a clip had held the curls fast.

'Linda McCarn is coming in to help,' the inspector answered. 'But I suspect she'll say it's unusual for a serial killer to be so structured and controlled. They usually escalate their acting out, if they're not caught.'

Linda was the State's leading criminal psychologist. The inspector had worked with her on numerous occasions and had always respected the woman, even if he found her eccentric personality a little excessive. But bringing her in on cases wasn't without its difficulties. She and Emmet McDonagh had once been engaged in an affair that had ended terribly. For a long number of years now, they'd been treating each other with open contempt and were more than happy to drag unwilling bystanders into battles of 'whose side are you on?'

Tom had previously taken an embarrassingly stereotypical approach, siding with his fellow man. Last year, though, he had discovered the tragic truth behind their break-up and knew Linda hadn't had it easy.

'I think it would be wise to consult her,' Moya observed. 'The London crew suggested you bring in a criminal psychologist. Anyway, back to the here and now. Just because I can't give you exact dates of death doesn't mean I'm completely useless. Come over here.'

She led him to the most recent body, the one they assumed was Una Dolan.

'We think we've established cause of death and – bearing in mind that most serial killers repeat methods – it was probably the same M.O. for the rest of them. Look here.'

Moya sipped from her cup while poking at the neck of the cadaver with a gloved finger.

Tom crouched down to see what the diminutive pathologist was trying to show him. He didn't have her medical eye. Nothing leapt out at him.

'What am I looking at?' he inquired, too long in the tooth to feign an expertise he didn't have.

'Even with the decay, you can see the discolouration of the skin at the neck,' Moya replied. 'And the trachea is crushed. See?' She prodded at some moveable lump beneath the skin.

Tom recoiled.

He stood up.

'He strangles them?'

'Yep. Manually. Violently. Like this. Jesus, bend down again, we're not all genetically modified giants.'

The inspector leaned forward and Moya pulled off her gloves and placed her hands around his neck, thumbs on his vocal cords. Up close, he smelled coffee and the bitter tang of cigarette smoke on her breath.

'Her killer throttled her with so much force, he broke her windpipe,' Moya explained. 'She was probably unconscious at that stage, anyway. She would have fought for breath when he started and used up most of her oxygen struggling against him. The pain and burning in her lungs would have passed after a few seconds and she'd have felt light-headed. Then she'd have blacked out. But he'd have kept squeezing. If her eyes hadn't been eaten out of their sockets, they'd be bulging right now. It's a very nasty way to murder somebody. Very intimate. And it takes real strength. I couldn't strangle you even if I was off my face on crack cocaine. It's more likely my thumbs would break as you resisted. Of course, she may have already been unconscious when she was strangled, which would have made it easier.'

Moya released her grip and Tom, even though the pathologist's fingers had been placed on his neck gently, immediately lifted a hand to caress it.

'By the way,' she said, one eyebrow raised. 'Is that beard some form of birth control for you and your wife? You wouldn't get near me with that. No shave, no sex.'

'I had to do something to keep the other women away,' he countered, dryly. 'Can we tell if the victims were sexually assaulted?'

'It will be difficult, unless he was very violent and left them damaged internally. Especially with the older cadavers.'

'Lovely. I've got to head back to HQ and conduct a team meeting. When can we expect the DNA and dental results?'

'Any minute now. What would any of us background team need with food or sleep or any of that lark?' She smiled, grimly. 'Don't worry. Myself and Emmet got calls from a VIP. We'll go hard on this until we have what you need.'

'A VIP like Joe Kennedy?' Tom asked.

Moya raised an eyebrow.

'Tom, really? Sean McGuinness was on. Trust me, there are very few men I'll jump for and Joe is not one of them. If ever there was a case of a man being promoted to his level of incompetence . . . Oh, shit. I nearly forgot. The most important thing.'

Moya crossed the room to a table where five plastic bags had been placed beside numbered cards. She pulled on fresh gloves, handed Tom a pair, then opened up the first bag and withdrew a delicate bracelet.

'Do you recognise this?' she quizzed the inspector.

He took the tarnished silver charm bracelet from her, turning it over to examine the little hearts that hung from its clasp.

'Should I?' he asked in return.

'I wouldn't have thought so. I pulled up Una Dolan's file early this morning to check her *last seen wearing* description. There was no mention of a charm bracelet. These are her belongings.'

'Okay, but maybe her family didn't know she had it or was wearing it – a boyfriend or friend had given it to her, something like that. It wouldn't be unusual.'

'Not at all. But here's what is.'

Moya made her way along the table, opening each bag and retrieving the same item from each – a silver charm bracelet.

'Jesus,' Tom said, when the five bracelets were all laid out on the table.

'Yep,' Moya nodded. 'It looks like he gave them little keepsakes.'

# CHAPTER 6

The major incident room they'd been allocated in headquarters was twice the usual size, impressing upon its new residents the magnitude of the job at hand. Desks and IT equipment had been provided for the additional personnel and brand-new glass evidence boards stood at the top of the room. They'd been recently secured by Joe Kennedy to replace the white display boards previously used by the teams in the NBCI. Tom couldn't get to grips with the see-through effect. He had bemoaned their arrival to Louise one night, sniping that Kennedy had probably got the idea from one of the Swedish detective series he fantasised about starring in.

'Don't they always solve their cases in those shows?' his wife had responded, before retreating behind the pages of her latest Scandinavian thriller.

The boards were being put to use now.

Detective Sergeant Michael Geoghegan was writing down names called out by Laura Brennan. She was making her way through a stack of files on the desk beside her, pausing every so often to fan herself with a redundant folder. Laura was dressed in a light cotton blouse and pleated skirt, stylishly cool but still too hot. Michael, casual at the best of times, was wearing a pair of Nike shorts and a blue polo shirt, a sweat patch visible under his raised arm.

Tom made his way across the room, nicking a bottle of chilled water from Ray Lennon's desk en route. He'd walked from Moya's lab to headquarters, but by the time he left the Mater the late-morning sun was already belting out higher than average temperatures. He too was sticky with perspiration.

'Boss, we need air-conditioning in here,' Michael griped. 'The ink is nearly sliding off the board.'

'I'll get some fans sent up,' Tom said. 'They're not going to shell out for a state-of-the-art air-conditioning system because of a once-in-a-century heatwave, Michael. This is Ireland. We'll probably be building snowmen next week. Right, are we ready to start?' He'd spotted Ray ushering the last of the squad into the room.

The inspector's usual team was all present. Twenty rank-and-file gardaí had also been assigned.

Natasha McCarthy, the head of the Sexual Assault unit, had turned up to listen in. They'd no idea yet if the killer was also a rapist, but the inspector welcomed her presence nonetheless. Natasha was an impressive operator, dogged in her approach to her work. She'd overseen a large increase in the number of sexual assault cases brought to trial. Unfortunately, the justice and legislative systems had yet to catch up with her progressive drive. Most of those she caught either walked free or were handed down sentences that were an insult to their victims. Still, she persisted.

Her determination and ambition were necessary, from a personal perspective as much as anything. Natasha's father was from Mali and she was one of the few mixed-race members of the force, and one of the only senior gardaí of colour.

Linda McCarn was there too. Tom had become quite adept at

not overtly reacting to the psychologist's unconventional attire. In fact, at this stage, he'd be more surprised if she arrived wearing an outfit that could be considered normal. Today she'd donned a white toga-like dress, tied at the waist with a rope-belt, and Grecian sandals. Her brown corkscrew curls were swept up in a patterned gold headscarf. She looked like she'd popped in en route to the Colosseum.

In fairness, of all of them, she was the best dressed for the weather.

'Settle down,' Tom yelled over the noise.

He gave the room a moment or two to come to order.

'Now,' he said, 'I'm glad to see so many of you here and I've no doubt we'll end up being supplemented by guards from around the county and beyond when we establish the victims' identities and origins. The workload for this investigation will be immense, so let your loved ones know the summer holidays are over.

'Folks, what we're dealing with is something we all hoped we'd never encounter. We've five victims and the only conclusion we can draw is that a serial killer is operating in Ireland. Maybe even killers, plural. Pathology has brought in specialists from London and the crime scene unit is also consulting with international experts. We have the State's leading criminal psychologist, Linda McCarn, with us today, and she'll give us some guidance on the sort of individual or individuals we might be dealing with. I'll be referring to the murderer as *he*, but in reality we don't yet know the gender or the number of perpetrators.

'Now, we've a lot to get through and it's hot as hell, so I'm going to bring you up to speed on pathology's findings so far and then I want us to start talking crime scene, IDs and suspects.'

When Tom had finished updating the room on Moya's work, Michael raised his hand.

'Boss, are we working under the assumption he's taken Fiona Holland? Her parents are in a right state. They've turned up at their local station looking to know if we've found their daughter's body.'

'We haven't,' Tom answered. 'Make sure the family liaison officer is with them. As to whether our killer has her or not, I do not want anybody to mention outside this room the possibility of her being the latest victim. The media will make its own assumptions but we're not speculating for the sake of their headlines. Let's be conscious of her family. However, amongst ourselves, we must consider that he might have her. Everything about her disappearance is alarmingly similar to Una Dolan's last year, bar the time of day.

'And considering it appears that this man keeps his victims for a period before killing them, there is the further possibility that she might still be alive. I'll go see the Hollands myself and discuss her missing persons case with our colleagues in Meath. Now, back to potential IDs. Laura?'

The detective sergeant stood up beside the list of names on the board.

'Right, so, we're being assisted by the Garda Missing Persons Bureau in compiling these names. The guys over there are terrific. It's unbelievable the volume of cases they deal with. In 2011 alone, they compiled over eight thousand files. By the end of the year, they had it down to twenty-three outstanding cases. Most files close themselves – the report was a mistake, somebody returned home, that kind of thing. Sometimes, the missing person was in an accident. And then there are the suicides.'

She paused. They all knew the statistics for suicide in Ireland were amongst the highest in Europe.

'Since the Bureau was founded, back in the early eighties, it's built up an open caseload of over fifteen hundred missing persons. They're the people who never came home, or whose bodies weren't discovered. In the last few years, a fair proportion of that number is speculated to be young migrant women and children sold to sex traffickers.'

Out of the corner of his eye, Tom could see Natasha McCarthy nodding. She was familiar with the facts and figures.

'Myself and DS Geoghegan worked with the Bureau to narrow down the number of missing adult females reported over the last ten years aged forty and under at the time of their disappearance, whose cases were never solved. We cast the net as wide as a decade in case the perpetrator kept some of his victims for lengthy periods before he killed them. We're working on the assumption that they're all relatively young, based on the pathologist's advice so far, but forty seemed like a good starting point.'

She turned to the board.

'This is what we're left with. Eighty women between the ages of seventeen and forty, missing since 2002, who never turned up again. These are the high-profile cases, but we're running a secondary list. Fiona Holland is the most recent name. The name before hers is one we're familiar with – Una Dolan.

'There are a few on the list that we think we can rule out, for example, women with a history of depression or suicidal tendencies. One woman, Pauline O'Hara, was apparently in an abusive relationship. It was her partner who reported her missing, not her family, who were satisfied she'd left him and was safe somewhere. Even leaving those examples aside, we're still left with a lot of names and we only have five bodies. Also, these are all white females, on the basis of what Moya Chambers has advised. If it turns out one of the victims is of a different race, that number will increase.'

Tom scanned the list. Some of the names were familiar and he could recall their faces and those of their worried relatives at the missing persons press conferences. Women who'd just vanished with no warning, no signs that anything was amiss.

'Patterns,' he said. 'If he is taking them in spring and keeping them for a few months – does that narrow it down?'

Laura and Michael exchanged a glance that said the inspector had hit on something.

Michael stood in front of the board and began to write something beside several names, underlining as he went.

When he'd finished, he moved aside. There was a collective intake of breath as everybody absorbed the new information.

The detective had pinpointed five names. Beside them, he'd written their age at the time of their disappearance, the county they'd gone missing in and the date they'd vanished.

Una Dolan, 24, Waterford, April 29th, 2011
Eimear Johnson, 20, Kerry, February 26th, 2010
Treasa Lee, 33, Cork, May 2nd, 2009
Mary Ellen Lehane, 25, Cork, April 17th, 2008
Geraldine Lougheed, 30, Tipperary, March 25th, 2007

'In amongst so many missing persons, it's not as obvious,' Laura added. 'In those two-page spreads the tabloids run about a potential Irish serial killer, they usually lump in a fair few of the women listed here, even names that the Missing Persons Bureau says we can discount. But these five definitely fit a pattern. Young women who went missing in spring months and were concentrated in a specific geographic area.'

'It seems a bit convenient for us that we've got it down to five names already,' Tom observed. 'Are there really no other cases of women who disappeared over those months in each year? February to May is a long period.'

Laura nodded.

'That's the secondary list I mentioned. There are, of course, but these are the names that jumped out. For example, a woman went missing in March last year, forty-two, three teenage children. The family say her disappearance was out of the blue and not in character. But her file shows she went missing twice previously and had a history of mental health issues. The woman I mentioned earlier – Pauline O'Hara – went missing in February of 2006, but for the reasons I outlined, we haven't included her. Until we've DNA and dental confirmation, we should probably assume that any of the women who are named here could be one of our victims. These five are leading the race.'

'If he sticks to those months and that region, should that give us comfort then on the Fiona Holland front?' Bridget Duffy asked. 'It's July and she went missing in Meath – that's a fair distance from the Munster province.'

The inspector had been wondering that himself and he looked to Laura and Michael expectantly. Laura cocked her head at Ray, who stood up with an air of apology, and Tom knew he was about to say something that would put everybody in the room back on edge.

'Once Laura and Michael had established the pattern, I had the lads downstairs look up reports of attempted abductions during the spring months of this year. Back in April, a woman claimed that a man tried to lure her into a vehicle outside a pub in Clare, but apparently another car pulled up and he sped off. She was drunk and couldn't give a description of the man or the car, and the pub's CCTV camera was broken. Our colleagues down there took the report seriously because she's the daughter of a local guard. The driver of the car that apparently scared the man off said he saw a vehicle speeding away but it was too dark to see its colour or make.'

Tom rolled his shoulders to relieve the tension that had built up. A trickle of sweat made its way down his neck between his shoulder blades. To cap it all, his fledgling beard was itching like crazy.

'So,' he sighed, 'you think he tried to take a woman in keeping with his habits, but was scared off, and the next opportunity that presented itself was last week with Fiona Holland?'

Ray shrugged.

'That's a possibility. The other being that she's not connected at all. He might have somebody we don't know about yet, or maybe he's stopped.'

'What do you think, Linda?' Tom asked. 'Enlighten us as to what we're dealing with here.'

The inspector perched on the edge of his desk, giving the criminal psychologist the floor.

Linda stretched both her arms above her head, exhaling loudly as she considered her contribution.

'Well, darling,' she drawled, in her husky upper-class Dublin accent. 'I can tell you what the research would indicate. It's highly unlikely you're dealing with a woman, or at least a woman acting alone. We know that more than eighty percent of serial killers are male and in their twenties and thirties, and physically, strangling would be beyond most female perpetrators.

'So, as you say, you're most likely looking for a man or men. Serial killers tend to target Caucasian women, which fits with your victims. But in terms of anomalies, it is unusual for a serial killer to remain so organised over such a long period of time. The discipline required would lead me to believe you have a single killer. If it were a pair, one of them would most likely have broken ranks at this stage. Most repeat murderers, as many of you know, tend to escalate their crimes – seeking the rush of the kill more frequently. But that's if they've taken their victim with the sole intent of ending their lives. If this man is abducting women and holding them captive for a period, their deaths might not be the end goal. He might want something else from them – sexual gratification, torture, or even just their company. The deaths might come about because they've served their purpose or refuse to comply.'

Linda stood, her tall, thin frame striding over to the display wall. She held out her hand for Michael's marker.

'May I?' she asked Tom, indicating the board.

'Go ahead.'

'Right, then. The crime scene you've found shows signs of careful planning and organisation. That would indicate the killer is older and has a high IQ. He's most likely burying them in that same spot for a reason. Maybe he works there and can visit their graves regularly?'

Linda turned to the board and wrote:

*Single Caucasian male*

*Older 35+?*

*Strong/fit*

*Glendalough resonates*

'We have a theory as to why he's chosen that location,' the

inspector said, and explained the idea that had struck him when he'd stood at the lake with Laura.

'Yes, the religious symbolism of Glendalough could be relevant,' the psychologist agreed. 'His way of making peace with the victims and himself. The proximity of the actual cemetery might mean something. Also, there's a round tower in the monastic settlement. That has fairytale connotations – sleeping princesses, that sort of thing. The fact that he gave them all gifts, the bracelets that you mentioned, would imply that he does care for his victims, in his own warped way. Perhaps they remind him of somebody and that time of the year is the key.'

This time she wrote:

*Lost a loved one in spring? – Abandoned? Divorced? Murdered? Accident?*

'It's unlikely that he managed to forcibly abduct all of these women without anybody spotting some sort of commotion,' she resumed. 'That would lead me to believe he either spied on his victims for a period to establish their routines and then snatched them when they were alone, or he was able to entice them to go along with him. You should speak to the woman you think was an attempted abduction earlier this year and see if her being outside that pub on her own late at night was a regular occurrence. Did she go there every Friday and usually walk home alone, that kind of thing?

'He's probably handsome, or has a harmless appearance. He might wear glasses. Women tend to find men wearing spectacles less threatening. Or perhaps he's a professional of some kind – a doctor maybe, somebody who can get his hands on a uniform that women find reassuring.'

Linda hesitated, her writing hand poised mid-air.

'If Fiona Holland was taken to compensate for him missing out on that intended sixth victim last spring, then he has deviated from his usual routine. Acting on opportunity as opposed to planning – I would consider that escalation. However, he's not grabbing women off the street willy-nilly, so he's still controlled and we have to assume he functions quite normally – even when he has his victim in situ.'

'Does he live in the region he's abducting them from?' Tom asked. 'Or closer to Glendalough where he buries them?'

Linda frowned.

'Hmm. Now there's a question. It's more likely that the Munster region is his hunting ground and he buries them close to where he lives so he can keep an eye on them, visit them, that sort of thing. So you're looking at Dublin and its surrounding counties for his home – Wicklow, Kildare. I'd pay special attention to Meath, where Fiona lived. It would fit with the escalation theory that he would take somebody from near his home, possibly somebody he's known for a long time. He might be a man who travels a lot and especially to the south – a sales rep, something like that. Most serial killers are occupationally mobile. It's entirely in keeping with the facts that he would kidnap and kill in one place and dispose of his victims in another.'

She turned and wrote: *Geographically mobile.*

'Why does he do it?' This was Ray. He'd crossed over to where Tom was sitting and reclaimed his half-empty bottle of water, throwing his boss a dirty look.

'I can give you all the clichés, and unfortunately they're usually true. It's most likely, unless we have an extremely rare, utter psychopath on our hands, that the killer comes from an abusive background and that he was either abandoned young by a parent, or later by his wife. But none of that will be apparent in his day-to-day behaviour. What you should also be on the alert for is a groupie. Somebody who wants to be involved with the case.'

As she was writing this, she continued to speak over her shoulder.

'You should keep an eye, too, for a direct link to one of the victims – most likely the first or second. It's highly probable that he was consumed with the desire to kill one specific woman and he's been trying to recreate that feeling ever since. I say first or second because he may have killed a stranger first so he could be sure he was capable of doing it.'

Tom had been listening so intently he'd completely forgotten that he'd been sweating prior to Linda standing up. In fact, his body temperature seemed to have plummeted. It didn't help that the psychologist was describing the most horrific things in such a polite, matter-of-fact way.

'At the scene,' he said, wanting to squeeze every last drop of valuable knowledge from her, 'Emmet said that the body we think is Una Dolan appeared to have been dug up and reburied, shallow enough that she was easily found by the dog. The other bodies were much deeper. What motive could the killer have had for digging her up?'

Several officers in the room turned a distinct shade of green – including Ray, despite being already aware of the grisly fact.

'Do you remember, Tom, a couple of years ago we got into a conversation about that book your wife loves – *Wuthering Heights*?'

The inspector had to scan his memories. Jesus, Linda McCarn forgot nothing. He had it now. A cosy sitting room in a convent in Limerick, the psychologist picking up the discarded favoured book of one of the nuns central to a case at the time.

'I do,' he confirmed for Linda.

'And do you recall, we talked about that horrific but beautifully poignant scene when Heathcliff digs up Cathy because he needs to see and hold her one last time?'

'That's disgusting!' Ray exclaimed.

Linda shrugged.

'There is one other explanation, if it indeed was her killer who dug her up.'

'Which is?' Tom prompted.

'He wanted her and the others to be found. He's tired of doing this without you knowing. He's either inviting you onto his dance floor or . . .'

'What, Linda?'

'Or he wants to be stopped.'

# CHAPTER 7

'We have to start talking to these women's families as soon as possible.'

Tom was back in his office, the Sunday papers spread out in front of him. Kennedy had kindly sent them down, a reminder of what they were up against.

'This lot are already speculating about the victims and revisiting all their cold case articles. They'll be hounding the relatives.'

'Some of the families will be happy with that,' Ray observed. 'This one here is about a woman who vanished fifteen years ago. The family is probably glad to see her name in the papers again. It gets the public re-engaged in her case.'

'Sure,' the inspector agreed. 'They'll all want their loved ones mentioned in the hope it jogs somebody's memory or inspires a missing woman to return. But they won't want any of the victims to be their daughter or sister or wife. They'll become hysterical if the uncertainty around the victims' IDs persists. We'll have to send out a memo to stations around the country that we're focusing on particular cases, so they have something to tell the families who approach them. We'll keep working closely with the Missing Persons Bureau as well. They'll be inundated.'

'Yeah. How are you splitting up the team?'

Ray's tone was casual and he didn't look up from the paper he was scanning. The inspector wasn't fooled. His deputy was praying Tom would send him off to do interviews with Laura.

The dynamics of his team had changed utterly.

For years, Laura had been carrying a torch for Ray, of which he, in his usual oblivious way, had been entirely ignorant. But then he'd started spending more time with the younger detective. When she eventually took up with another bloke, Ray finally sat up and noticed her.

Laura had since dumped the boyfriend and the inspector had assumed that she and Ray would get it together. But Laura was playing it cool. Either she'd gone off Tom's deputy, or she was making him work for it.

The inspector had consulted his all-seeing, all-knowing wife for her opinion.

'She's probably just nervous,' Louise had stated, decisively.

'Nervous? Why would she be nervous? It's obvious that Ray is smitten with her. Jesus, Louise, even I can see that and you know my vision is 2D when it comes to affairs of the heart.'

'It mightn't be obvious to her,' his wife snorted. 'And even if it is, she was badly burned by him when he went after that poor girl Ellie Byrne that time, wasn't she? Laura's got no self-esteem issues. If he wants her, he'll wait until she's ready.'

Tom wasn't unmoved by Ray's plight. But he was the boss; he had no intention of being his deputy's wingman, or putting Laura in an uncomfortable situation.

'You can team up with me,' he said. 'We'll take Fiona Holland and Una Dolan's files. I'll assign two to Laura and Michael and the last two to Bridget and Brian. That's the six priority files covered and uniforms can take the other names. The travel distance poses a problem. We'll get Laura and Michael to do the two Cork cases – Mary Ellen Lehane and Treasa Lee. The others can take Geraldine Lougheed in Tipperary and then go down to Eimear Johnson's family in Kerry. We'll organise those interviews as soon as we get the DNA and dental results back and make matches. We'll be visiting the families informed, then. You and I can go speak to the Hollands later, they're only up the road.'

Ray opened the office door just as Natasha McCarthy was raising her hand to knock.

'Have you got five minutes?' she asked Tom.

'Sure.' He beckoned her in and pointed to his deputy's vacated chair. 'Thanks for sitting in downstairs. What are your feelings about the case?'

'Aside from revulsion?' Natasha shrugged, fiddling with a gold chain that graced her long, elegant neck. 'I'm not sure, Tom. I don't know if I'll be much help to you in this one. Oh, this weather!'

Tom watched amused as she removed her pale pink cardigan and dabbed at her underarms with a Kleenex from the box on his desk.

'Don't look at me like that – I bet you've changed your shirt twice already today.'

He smiled.

'Good detective work. So, do you think our killer is a rapist?'

'Who knows? We know rape and murder often go hand in hand. Especially when strangulation is the cause of the death. The perpetrator will keep his hands on his victim's throat to control her during the attack, sometimes with the intent to kill but, more often than not, unaware that he's actually choked her to death. Both types will come to associate the rush of murder with the climax of sexual intercourse and are likely to seek it out again. Linda would tell you that they're 'lust' serial killers. Ted Bundy, John Wayne Gacy – they met that description. But I'm not sure that's what you have here.'

'How so?'

'Well, those who kill for lust tend to do it more frequently than once a year. The Americans think Bundy had over one hundred victims. The only possible anomaly you have is the digging up of the body. Bundy would sometimes have sex with his victims' corpses. But if your killer did that up in Glendalough, Moya would have picked up something from the most recent cadaver.'

Tom placed his elbows on the desk and rested his chin on his hands.

'I never thought I'd have to deal with something like this,' he said, his voice thick. 'I've seen all sorts of depravity in this job – but necrophilia?'

Natasha raised her eyebrows.

'Ah, Tom, if you knew what I'd seen in terms of sex crimes . . . let's just say that the dead can't feel anything. But look, if it brings you comfort, I really don't think that's what you're up against and I think Linda McCarn agrees. The care that he's showing his victims would indicate that he's not abusing and disposing of them, as most sex murderers would. I'm happy to be of any assistance, but I don't think you'll need me for this one.'

The inspector sighed. He sincerely hoped not.

No sooner had Natasha left than Tom's phone erupted. He always felt that when Joe Kennedy dialled, the ring tone got more shrill.

'Sir,' Tom answered. It was childish but it jarred to use the term 'Sir' for somebody that bit younger than him.

'I'm disappointed you've finished your team meeting already, Inspector. I was going to pop in and say a few words.'

Tom had guessed that would be Kennedy's plan and had deliberately organised the meeting to start and finish before the chief was done with that morning's gathering of top brass. The priority was getting work underway, not listening to a half hour 'go get 'em' lecture peppered with cringe-worthy buzzwords.

'My apologies,' he lied. 'I just wanted us out of the blocks. Chief McGuinness rarely came to team meetings.' That was another stretching of the truth. It wasn't usual for Sean to sit in on an incident room but in a case this big, he'd have made an exception and Tom would have welcomed him there.

Kennedy began to say something, then stopped. The inspector wondered if he'd been about to correct Tom's use of 'Chief McGuinness'.

'I imagine you're feeling a little at sea, without your former colleague here to guide you on this one,' Kennedy said. The remark, and its generous tone, was so unexpected that Tom was thrown. Just for a moment, he pictured the man in the office upstairs, sitting at his desk alone – trying to assert himself in unfamiliar terrain with not overly friendly colleagues. It stirred something in the inspector. He felt a little ashamed of himself.

'Inspector?'

'I'm here. That's not an issue, Sir. Of course, I miss working with Sean, but he wouldn't have been that involved in my day-to-day casework. You might want to run things differently and I've no objection to you wanting to sit in on the odd team meeting.'

'That's all I ask. I appreciate I'm not long in the job but in a case this big, it's important we all put our shoulders to the wheel and pull together.'

The words might have formed the sort of banal utterance the inspector was used to hearing from Kennedy, but he appreciated the sentiment.

'I agree.'

'Good. Get a quick report up to me so I have something for the press – nothing too juicy, just enough to keep them going.'

'No problem. You'll have that shortly.'

'And Inspector, one more thing.'

Tom waited.

'If the former chief superintendent does try to become involved in this case, you will remember that he's no longer in situ? My heart goes out to Mr McGuinness and his wife, but there's only room for one head of this department.'

It was like being crept up on and slapped in the back of the head. Kennedy had reeled Tom in, then thrown a dig at Sean.

'Somebody's here to see me,' the inspector said. 'I'll check in later.'

He ended the call and stared at the phone like it was contaminated.

Kennedy was an idiot.

The only thing that mattered right now was finding this serial killer and establishing whether or not he'd taken Fiona Holland. Kennedy should have been asking the inspector to use his friendship with Sean to avail of his experience and advice. But his insecurity and pride were more important to him than the case at hand.

More and more, Tom disliked his new boss.

# CHAPTER 8

Summer suited the Meath countryside.

Tom and Ray had driven west through the picturesque town of Trim, with its ancient castle and narrow streets. They were now in the more rural end of the county. The hedgerows that lined the roads were pruned to perfection, the grassy fields beyond the knee-high stone walls a rich, fertile green. Meath was known as the Royal County, having once been the ancient seat of the High Kings of Ireland. As they drove, Tom could see the royal colours in the green and gold bunting that locals had hung out in support of the county's Gaelic footballers, who were playing a championship match in Croke Park that Sunday afternoon.

The combination of the tranquil scenery, the humming of lawn mowers and the smell of weekend barbecues was almost enough to make Tom feel relaxed. Almost.

'I wish we'd taken my car,' Ray moaned, rolling up his window to keep out the smoke billowing from the exhaust of his boss' Citroën. 'You need to get that seen to.'

'It was in the garage last week,' Tom said. 'It's just the system cleaning itself out, nothing to worry about. Diesel engines get a bit clogged up.'

'All diesels, or just yours?'

Ray fiddled with the air conditioning, turning the cold air

up as high as it would go. The car was struggling to keep the heat of the day at bay.

'Anyhow,' Tom snapped irritably. 'I want to get out to this family today. At the speed you drive, we'd still be in the car park back at headquarters.' He was hot, and tired of having the various minor issues with his car pointed out to him by all and sundry. Louise hated the Citroën and had been at him to get rid of it since he'd bought it.

'There's the stud farm Willie told us to look out for,' his deputy said, pointedly ignoring his boss. 'We should pass through Luttrell village shortly and then we just keep going straight. We come off the main road at the sign for their landscaping business. That will bring us to their house.'

Sure enough, within minutes they were driving through a one-street village. They passed three pubs, a post office, a hardware store and a garage with a Centra supermarket.

'Hello and goodbye, rural metropolis,' Ray murmured, as the car swept down the main street in less than a minute.

Tom soon spotted the sign for Holland's Garden Centre and Landscaping.

The road they turned onto was narrow, bordered by high cherry laurel bushes. Further along, they crossed a little stone bridge over a river and took the right fork towards the Holland estate.

'I think that's it,' Ray said, pointing at a set of black and gold wrought iron gates that lay open ahead. 'Looks like these folks have a few bob.'

Tom nodded in agreement as he cruised slowly along the cypress-tree-lined drive. They emerged onto a large gravel parking area beside a plush green lawn.

'Would you look at that,' his deputy whistled. 'It's a mansion.'

Ray had grown up on a council estate. He lived in an apartment now, bought in the boom and in massive negative equity following the recent recession and property crash. While it was a step up from the three-bed terraced houses in his former estate, he could only dream of owning a sprawling home like this one.

The building that faced them was Tudor-style – white-fronted with a heavy external chimney to one side and steep-pitched roofs. The sills of the mullioned windows were hung with boxes ablaze with summer blooms.

Tom parked the car beside a brand-new silver BMW and they got out, feet crunching on the pebbles underfoot.

The front door opened as they approached, a frazzled-looking woman hurrying out onto the porch to greet them. She was rake thin – so tiny she looked like a collection of sticks that had been thrown together and covered in a spotty blue dress. A small dog rushed past her ankles, barked at the new arrivals, then dashed onto the perfectly manicured lawn like it was possessed. The woman opened her mouth as though to call the dog, but then decided not to bother. There were more important things to think about than whether the terrier was going to shit on the grass.

'Are you the detectives from Dublin?' she asked, her hands balled into little fists at her side. 'I'm Caroline Holland. Fiona's mother.'

The inspector had seen several photos of Fiona Holland. Although fuller in figure, she bore a remarkable resemblance to her mother – small, light blue eyes; skinny frame and pale skin; long, strawberry-blonde hair with a flicked Farrah Fawcett fringe. On a good day, Caroline could probably pass for her daughter's sister. But after a week of worry and the shock of the

JO SPAIN | 60

discovery yesterday, the woman looked haggard. Her neck was covered in nervous red splotches, her forehead was creased in a permanent frown and her eyes carried the haunted look of the insomniac.

The detectives introduced themselves and made to follow her into the house.

'Do you want me to get the dog?' Ray asked, before she shut the hall door.

Caroline looked at him blankly for a moment.

'Oh. No. Don't worry. The heat is driving him mad. I'll leave him out there a while.'

She led them to a comfortable, pleasantly cool sitting room. It was on the opposite side of the house to the sun and was further shaded by a Japanese maple tree outside. The room had been painted olive and its white couches were dotted with cushions in various shades of green. The designer had brought the garden inside.

Caroline had laid a wicker table with a tea service in anticipation of their arrival.

They'd just sat down when the door opened and a man entered.

Richard Holland was tanned and weather-beaten. His coarse brown hair framed dark, almost black eyes. He crossed the room and shook both the detectives' hands firmly before joining his wife on the two-seater facing them.

'I'm just back from the local cop shop,' he said. 'I'm glad to see you here. They won't tell us anything. Is it our girl? Did he . . . did that monster who buried those girls up in Glendalough take her?' His voice was throaty and he squeezed his wife's hand as he spoke, her eyes already bubbling with tears.

'Mr and Mrs Holland, Fiona's was not one of the bodies discovered in Glendalough yesterday,' Tom said, annoyed that this fact hadn't already been communicated to them. 'I can absolutely confirm that.'

A spring in Caroline Holland's body seemed to uncoil and she collapsed against her husband, a sound somewhere between a sob and a groan freeing itself from her lips. He placed his arms around her and buried his face in her hair.

'It's okay,' he murmured. 'It's not our baby.'

She shuddered. The inspector was willing to give them a minute, but Caroline recovered herself fairly quickly.

'I'm sorry, Inspector. I don't know why I'm crying. It must be the relief. I feel like I haven't breathed since the news broke about the bodies last night. We kept waiting for somebody to ring and say one of them was Fi. Oh God, the parents of those poor girls. I can't imagine . . .'

She shook her head.

Her husband was staring at Tom and Ray, intense eyes darting from one to the other.

'If Fi hasn't been found – why are you here, Detectives? I mean,' he pointed to Tom, 'you're that chap, aren't you? The head of the murder squad. The Glendalough thing is your case, isn't it? Why have you come out here to talk to us?'

The inspector glanced down at his hands, needing to break eye contact with the concerned, astute man sitting across from him.

It was Caroline who voiced what her husband had already pieced together.

'You think he might have her, don't you?' Her voice was small and shocked.

'We don't know,' Tom said, honestly. 'But it is something we have to consider. I want to give you some confidential information, but I need to be able to trust your discretion.'

Both parents nodded, eyes wide.

'One theory we are exploring is that the man who murdered the women we found may have held them captive for a short time beforehand.'

Caroline Holland looked like her heart had stopped beating. Her husband sat forward, his elbows resting on knees spread apart, all the appearance of somebody about to vomit.

'It is still entirely likely that Fiona has gone off of her own accord,' the inspector continued. 'That's the situation in the majority of missing persons cases, as I'm sure you're now aware. But, as a precaution, we want to intensify the search for your daughter and to do that, I need to familiarise myself with her case. That's why we're here.'

'She wouldn't have just gone off,' Richard said, his voice raspy. 'We keep telling them that, down at the station. I love my girl, Inspector. But Fi and Caroline have a bond. She's the sort who needs to be mothered. Nineteen, but still a child. Fi thinks she's strong and mature, but she's not. She gets herself into situations and there's the –'

'No, Richard,' Caroline snapped. 'I won't have a bad word said about my daughter.'

'I'm not having a go at her, sweetheart. I'm just trying to tell the inspector what he needs to know. It's better coming from us than from somebody who doesn't know her.'

'It is absolutely vital,' Tom interjected, 'that you are completely frank with me. For Fiona's sake. Time may be of the essence here.'

Caroline looked from her husband to Tom. The branches of the tree outside the window swayed softly, causing a shadow effect to ripple over her face. She blinked away tears and sighed.

'I know,' she said. 'I know. I just don't want anybody to think that if something's happened to her, it's her fault. She's young. We all do stupid things at that age. We're supposed to live long enough that they become an embarrassing memory.'

'Why would anybody think it was her fault?' Tom asked, his voice gentle.

Richard stood up.

'Give me a moment,' he said, leaving the room.

Caroline watched him go.

'He's barely holding up,' she said, when the door closed. 'Yet he thinks I'm the one who needs all the support. Richard travels a lot with his job. He feels guilty that he wasn't here when she disappeared. He worships Fiona, even if at times they butt heads.'

'Why is that?' Tom asked.

'My daughter has what some narrow-minded people would describe as a "reputation",' she said, in a tone that challenged the two men to react. When they remained impassive, she continued.

'Richard is her father – that's always going to be difficult for him to deal with. She's not a bad girl. Just a bit wild. At first, it was bunking off school and failing in exams. We argued with her over it, but we didn't come down like a ton of bricks. Neither Richard nor I were angels as kids and we won't be hypocrites as parents. I always said to Richard, it's our job to put our kids on the right path and show them they're loved, but we must respect them as individuals. We couldn't beat Fiona into being responsible. And I knew she'd grow out of whatever little phase she was going through, she always did. Her brother is very different. In some ways, he's harder work. Fi has always been fun-loving and affectionate. She's always trying to work her way round us with mischievous cheek. Fergus tends to sulk.'

'Aside from skipping school,' Ray queried, 'what else was she doing that concerned you? Was she mixing with a bad crowd?'

Caroline sighed. 'She started drinking when she was fifteen, going into larger towns like Navan for the nightclubs. We cut her pocket money, even took away her phone at one point. But Fi is good at winding people around her little finger. She's the sort of girl who doesn't have to put her hand in her pocket to buy a drink. There's always a man there, ready to fork out. She made people jealous with that and in turn, it made them spiteful.'

'People are wont to do that,' the inspector nodded. 'So, she has a way with men, like a lot of young, pretty girls. Does she have a boyfriend?'

Caroline bristled.

'She's had a few. She doesn't tell me about all of them. Even though we're very close, Fi likes her secrets. I always know if she's seeing a nice chap because she's all hugs and kisses and "I love you, Mam". If she's with somebody she's not happy with, she just comes home at night and heads straight to her room. She'll have a face on her for a while until he dumps her.'

'Why wouldn't she dump him?' Ray asked.

'I don't know,' Caroline shrugged. 'For all the love we give Fiona, she has an awful tendency to pick the bad lads. She's seeing some guy at the moment; I don't know his name. But I know she's not happy.'

Caroline stared at her hands, then looked up at Tom. 'I should have asked more questions, shouldn't I? I know I should have. I've been too distracted. This last year, Fiona has been making sillier and sillier choices. I should have been more involved. It's just . . . I had somebody else to take care of.'

The door to the sitting room opened and Richard came back in. He was carrying an infant, no more than twelve months, a little boy with red hair and sleepy eyes. He'd just woken from his nap.

'Is this your son?' Tom asked, confused. He'd been under the impression the other Holland sibling was older.

'*Our* son?' Caroline said, puzzled. 'No, Fergus is out back.'

Tom turned back to Richard, confused.

'He may as well be our son, Caroline,' he said, shifting the baby around to face them. 'This is Cían. He's Fiona's. We've no idea who his dad is. She's never told us. And she doesn't bother with him much, either.'

'It's still no reason, is it?' Caroline said. 'Just because a girl is a little wild, that's no reason for something to happen her?'

The inspector shook his head and looked back to the baby.

He'd had no idea that Fiona Holland was a mother. None of the news items had mentioned a child. He'd scanned her file – if it was in there, he hadn't spotted it.

And now there was another, even more important person he had to find her for. Her baby.

Fergus Holland was burning cuttings at the far end of his family's back garden.

'What do you think of the parents?' Ray asked, as they walked down the long lawn.

'They seem terrified,' Tom said. 'I've no doubt they love that girl. By the looks of things, they're rearing her child for her, and unquestioningly. Daddy's princess and Mammy's pride and joy.'

'Could it be that she's just fled the family nest? Got sick of the pandering and fussing? Didn't want to be stuck with the kid, a reminder of having to be thankful to the folks?'

'I'd prefer that to the alternative. Look, she's a young woman who has vanished with no indication that she was planning to leave. We won't jump to conclusions, but considering we now know there's a serial killer operating in the State targeting young women, I'm not taking any chances. Let's step up the investigation into Fiona's disappearance and if she turns up of her own volition, well, that's a win. But we'll sleep easier at night, knowing we acted.'

As they drew nearer to the small bonfire, a young man rounded it, carrying branches. He flung them into the fire, then stood watching them burn as he rubbed his hands together to rid them of the detritus.

While Fiona was the carbon copy of her mother, Fergus could have been carved from the hipbone of his father. He was as tall as Tom or Ray, his shoulders broad and his neck thick. He had the same weather-beaten colouring, a mixture of tan and red. He didn't come to meet the approaching men, but instead walked back around the bonfire, presumably to fetch more kindling.

'What's he at?' Ray said. 'I know the heat is going out of the day a bit but why on earth would you light a fire?'

'He's got control of it,' Tom answered. 'It's a good distance from the surrounding trees. He'll let it burn down, then extinguish it. He's getting rid of dead wood that could cause an actual wildfire.'

Fergus emerged into view with his arms full again. They were near enough now to call out a greeting.

'I know who you are,' he grunted, nodding up at the house. 'The mother texted me. Still haven't found her, then?'

Tom shook his head.

Fergus threw his load into the flames, then put his hands on his hips, feet planted wide apart. His jeans and T-shirt were dirty from the garden and smoke, but beneath his workman's appearance – the stance and his obvious strength – he was quite baby-faced. Richard had said Fergus was four years older than his sister, which made him twenty-three.

'Don't come any closer,' he said, nodding at the fire. 'And don't inhale too deeply.'

'Why's that, then?' Ray asked.

'Cherry laurel,' Fergus answered. 'When it's cut, that sweet smell you get is actually poisonous. They say when you burn it, the fumes it releases are akin to cyanide.'

The frown on the young man's face hadn't lifted and his tone was confrontational.

'You must be very worried about your sister?' Tom probed, thinking if Fergus got any closer to the fire, the chip on his shoulder might ignite.

He shrugged.

'She'll be back. She's just making some sort of point.'

'Why would she do that?'

'Dunno. Looking for attention or something. Fi is never happy unless we're all running around after her. Cleaning up her mess. She doesn't give a shit about how her carry-on affects us.'

'How does it affect you?' Tom asked. Beneath the harshness, he could hear a quiver in Fergus' voice.

'It's not easy being the brother of the town slut.'

The inspector was taken aback. He turned to Ray, whose expression was just as shocked.

'Aren't you concerned that something might have happened

to your sister?' Ray asked, unable to keep the incredulity from his voice. 'Do you really think she's capable of running away, of leaving her son like that? Did she say anything to you to make you think she was planning that, the last time you saw her?'

'Her son?' Fergus snorted. 'She might have squeezed him out from between those legs she can't keep shut, but she's no more his mother than I am. That pair of idiots up at the house are his mammy and daddy. Hopefully, they don't make as much of a balls with him as they did with Fi. And to answer your question, when I last spoke to my sister, she was telling me to keep my, and I quote, "fucking fat nose out of her fucking business". She has a way with words.'

'So, you argued,' the inspector said. 'Over what?'

'Yeah, we argued. And then we went our separate ways, just in case you're getting any notions. It was the same old row. What man she was screwing this week and how humiliated I should be the next time I was in the pub.'

Neither detective said anything.

Fergus grimaced.

'I wasn't . . . I didn't start out trying to fight with her. Not that time, anyway. I'd noticed she was coming home with the odd bruise. I asked her what was going on and she just laughed in my face. But whoever she was with, he was hitting her. I mean, how stupid can you get? As angry as I was with her, if she'd been scared of some bloke, I'd have sorted it, you know. She only had to ask.'

'Your mother said she thought Fiona was unhappy in her current relationship but she didn't know who she was seeing. Do you know?'

The inspector watched as the fire danced in the young man's

eyes. He could feel the heat from the blaze where he was standing, but Fergus was closer. So he didn't know if the man was tearing up from the smoke or from sadness.

'No, I don't know. But if I find him and he hurt my sister – I'll kill him.'

# CHAPTER 9

They drove in silence for the best part of the journey back to Dublin. The inspector felt a dull thumping behind his temples, the length and stuffiness of the day bringing on a headache.

'Fancy a quick one in your local before finishing up?' Ray suggested, mindreading. 'I can stroll back through the park to get my car from headquarters.'

The dashboard clock said 8:00 p.m.

'Go on, then,' the inspector nodded, his arm twisted.

They parked at Tom's house and walked up to the Hole in the Wall, a long, narrow pub that nestled against the outer wall of Phoenix Park. The owner had set up an outdoor seating area so his customers could enjoy the balmy evening. Tom and Ray opted for indoors, where it was cooler and quieter.

'What are you having?' Ray asked, as the inspector slipped into a recently vacated oak-panelled snug.

'Get me one of their craft beers. Surprise me.'

His deputy returned with two tall glasses and packets of scampi fries and nuts.

'What am I drinking?' Tom asked, taking a sip from the cool, refreshing ale.

'8 Degrees Howling Gale ale. Mine's a Galway Hooker. I think my subconscious is trying to tell me something about my single state.'

They sat in companionable silence and let the stress of the day seep away.

'Any progress on the Laura front?' the inspector pried, as Ray shredded his beer mat.

'None whatsoever. I don't get it,' he said, and took a swig of his drink. 'She was into me for years, apparently, but she doesn't seem to have any time for me nowadays. What am I doing wrong?'

Tom shrugged. Relationship advice wasn't his forte. He thought of what Louise had said.

'Have you told her you like her? Straight out?'

Ray snorted.

'What? Like we're teenagers down the back of the disco? "I like you, Laura. Do you like me?"'

'Fair enough,' Tom conceded. 'Well, have you asked her out on a date? I don't mean popping along to the pub with everybody else after work.'

'Yeah, I mean, sort of. Actually, no. Not on our own. I don't want to be in her face. She seems sort of angry with me. Like I'm the reason she's single – yet she's not giving me any signals at all.'

'Ah, Ray.' Tom shook his head. 'You really are a muppet!'

'Here, Grandad. It's the twenty-first century. She could ask me out if she wanted.'

'That might be something women feel they *can* do, but it doesn't mean they all *want* to. No wonder she's annoyed at you. She dumps her boyfriend and goes back to waiting for you and you do nothing. Don't you think if she were the sort to take the initiative, she'd have done it long before now? I don't know. How do you manage to get yourself dressed and out the door in the morning?'

Ray furrowed his brow, pondering what Tom had said.

The inspector's phone rang and he pulled it out of his pocket, expecting it to be Louise asking why his car was home but not its owner. It was Laura.

'Speak of the devil,' he said. 'Laura. What's happening?'

He listened for a couple of minutes, making acknowledging sounds, while Ray sipped his drink and waited.

'I see,' Tom said. 'Okay. Make sure somebody speaks to the women's families tonight and tells them we'll see them tomorrow. Where was that first victim from? Hm. Right. We'll go out to her family, then. We'll be in that neck of the woods anyway to see Una Dolan's family. Let Brian Cullinane and Bridget Duffy know too, will you? They can make the trip to County Kerry. Thanks.'

The inspector hung up and took a mouthful of ale.

'We have IDs,' he told Ray, when he'd swallowed.

'That was quick. Did we get the five right?'

'No. We were one out.'

Ray raised his eyebrows.

'Shit. Which one was wrong?'

Tom rifled through the pockets of his suit jacket until he found the small notepad he'd used at the team meeting earlier. He flicked to the page with the five names Laura and Michael had come up with.

'Geraldine Lougheed isn't one of the bodies. The rest were right. Una Dolan in 2011. Eimear Johnson in 2010. Treasa Lee in 2009 and Mary Ellen Lehane in 2008. It seems he didn't start in 2007. His first victim was taken in 2006. Unless he's buried Geraldine somewhere else, which seems unlikely. We're searching the surrounding area, anyway.'

'Who was his first victim, then?'

'Believe it or not, Laura mentioned her at the meeting. Remember she spoke about a Pauline O'Hara?'

Ray nodded. 'Yeah. Yeah, I do. Didn't she say the boyfriend or husband had reported her missing, but the family hadn't?'

'That was it. Because allegedly he was abusive and they thought she'd left him. Well, as it turns out, she hadn't. Not of her own free will, anyway. It's interesting, though, isn't it? That she was in an abusive relationship.'

'And Fergus Holland thought his sister was seeing a man who was hitting her,' Ray added. 'Interesting indeed. He could have been giving them those charm bracelets while he was dating them.'

A new theory had formed in the inspector's head, one that caused a shadow to cross over his face.

'What is it?' his deputy asked.

'I just had a disturbing thought,' Tom responded. 'Our killer. Think about it – either he waited two years before he killed again or we're missing a body for 2007, possibly Geraldine's.'

'Or?' Ray prompted, sensing there was more.

'Or . . .' Tom swallowed. 'He kept Pauline O'Hara alive for a very long time before he murdered her.'

# CHAPTER 10

*Eimear, 2010*

He'd expected Eimear to be one of the slower ones; he thought she was one of those bitches who abandoned their children with the folks so they could go around drinking and screwing, but he'd got her wrong. When he'd got her into the car she'd been pissed, but he'd been surprised at how quickly she sobered up when she realised what was happening.

And then she started screaming for her kid.

Her baby. She would fight for her baby.

The car shuddered to a halt and Eimear prepared herself. It had taken her a few minutes to come to after he'd knocked her out. When she'd regained consciousness she hadn't realised where she was, as she was bumped up and down in the dark. She felt around the small space with her hands, the panic building. She suffered a little with claustrophobia and was struggling to breathe in the tight space.

She could smell petrol and hear an engine – she was in the boot of the car. She tried to get her breathing under control. She needed to be strong, to be ready. For her little Lily.

When he opened the boot she'd catch him by surprise. He

probably thought she was still out of it. But she'd kick and bite and slap and then run as fast as she could.

And when she reached safety and got home, she'd never leave it again. She would hold Lily tight, inhaling her, loving her. She'd be a proper mother. No more booze, no more dancing, no more men. It would just be Eimear and her daughter, and the comfort of her parents.

Why had she got into the bloody car with him? She could have walked home. It wasn't far, drunk or not. But they lived in a village in rural Kerry, for God's sake. It was safe. You could trust people.

Eimear had no idea how long he'd been watching her, studying her movements. She thought, even now, that this had all been unhappy chance. If she'd turned left instead of right coming out of the pub. If she'd stayed in that night. If she'd gone home with one of the locals.

This was like something you read about, something that happened to other women. Not to her. Eimear was normally sharp. Fair enough, she'd got caught with Lily, but by Jesus, she didn't regret that for a second. As soon as they'd placed her little angel in her arms, she'd known she'd love her forever.

Eimear was young, though, and it was hard work being a full-time mother. Every day started with a few hours' sleep and became just one more endless cycle of feeding and washing and walking Lily. There was nothing left for her at the end of it. Her mother gave her lots of advice and stepped in to babysit sometimes, but her favourite phrase was, "You've made your bed, now you have to lie in it". Ironic, really. Lily hadn't been conceived in a bed. Eimear had been bent over the bonnet of a car, six West Coast Coolers in, believing the man behind her was wearing a condom.

She'd learned a harsh lesson then and she was getting another one now.

The boot opened suddenly and Eimear was shocked to see it was light outside. How long had she been in the car? She felt woozy. The surprise morning sun assaulted her eyes and added to the feeling of being stunned, but then she remembered her plan and lashed out at her kidnapper.

It was futile. He was like a tree trunk, completely unfazed by her attack. He lifted her out of the car, throwing her over his shoulder as she hammered at his back and tried to kick him between the legs. She used everything – her nails, her teeth – nothing stopped him. Even as she was resisting, she noticed the white and grey pebbles on the ground, the dew on the grass, the daisies unfurling their petals after the night's hibernation. Why, she wondered in the days to come, had those little things made such an imprint on her brain? Had she known it would be the last she'd see of God's beautiful earth?

Then they were in a house and there was a hole in the floor. He started to climb down steps, even as she flailed and struggled on his shoulder.

He was bringing her into a cellar.

No, she screamed, but realised the sound hadn't come out of her mouth. It was like a bad dream. She was yelling, but her lips weren't cooperating. They wouldn't open. Everything had stopped. Her limbs had ceased fighting, her voice refused to engage. All that was working was her mind and that was in overdrive – crying, pleading, begging – please, please, don't leave me down here. Take me to Lily. Lily needs me. I'm her mammy.

He dumped her on the floor and climbed the stairs.

As the door slammed shut and the light disappeared, she

conjured up the image of her little baby's face – her green eyes and blonde curls, her tiny nose and rosebud lips, the pudgy, dimpled cheeks and soft chin. How had she not known that was all she'd needed?

And now, Eimear realised, she would never see Lily again.

# CHAPTER 11

Laura and Michael left for Cork early on Monday morning. The plan was to visit Mary Ellen Lehane's family first on the western side of the county. Then they would make their way across to east Cork to see Treasa Lee's family in Cobh. If it got too late, they'd stay the night and return to Dublin the following day.

There had been a moment, when Tom let them know who was pairing up with whom, when Laura had hoped she might be teamed up with Ray Lennon. But he'd been chosen to go with their boss, as usual. She didn't regret her decision to finish with her boyfriend Eoin last year. It wasn't fair on him, when she had feelings for someone else. And she'd really thought that Ray was starting to give out signals. Yet again, though, she'd been wrong. She was completely bloody invisible to him.

'I might have hated you at 6 a.m., but good call on the early start,' Michael said, interrupting her thoughts. 'It's going to be another stonker of a day; better we get the driving done early. How long will it take, again?'

'They say four and a half hours, but I can do it in four. We might need a bathroom break, mind. Unless you want to use one of the water bottles.'

Michael smiled.

'I've never been to West Cork.'

'You're shitting me.'

Laura glanced sideways at her colleague. He was as respectably dressed as it got for him – a short-sleeved shirt and pair of Levi's. They were en route to meet grieving families, so he'd left the sports tees at home. But he'd shaved his spiky brown hair recently and, with his sunglasses on, looked more like a drug dealer than ever. She estimated that she dressed ten years older than him, in her sharp suits and labelled clothes, when in fact, he had a few birthdays on her.

'I was thinking about bringing Anne and the baby down this summer.'

'You should,' Laura said, amused. As a Kerry woman, she'd spent a lot of time in the neighbouring county of Cork. She still couldn't get her head around Dubliners, who'd quite happily hop on a flight to Spain but wouldn't think of venturing to other parts of their own country. They seemed to consider the capital's M50 ring road as some sort of demarcation line.

They made good time and arrived on the Beara Peninsula just after 11 a.m., even managing to stop for a quick breakfast along the way.

'Do you need the satnav for this last bit?' Michael asked. 'The address is Glendale village, but I don't think the family live slap bang in the middle.'

'The satnav!' Laura snorted. 'What should I type in? *The Lehanes' house*? Don't worry, we'll find it.'

They were almost at the village when Laura spotted a farmer ushering the last of his sheep into a gated field. She slowed the car to a halt and wound down the window.

'Pleasant day,' she said.

''Tis.' The man rested one arm on the gate and looked curiously at the car. 'Down from Dublin, are ye?'

'We are today. I'm from just over the way, originally. The Kingdom.'

Michael noticed with amusement that Laura's Kerry accent got thicker the further they travelled from Dublin.

The farmer raised a sardonic eyebrow.

'Not going too well for your footballers this year, is it?' he teased.

'We're looking for the Lehanes,' Michael said, leaning across. He didn't want to bear witness to a Kerry and Cork slanging match about Gaelic sports.

'The Lehanes. Is that right now? What would you be wanting them for?'

'Mary Ellen,' Laura said. 'We're gardaí.'

'Ah.' The man's demeanour changed as he straightened. 'Turn left before you enter the village. Go up the hill, give or take a mile. Through the crossroads. You'll see their gate on the left. It needs fixing.'

They thanked him and set off again, following his directions.

'Does everybody around here know where everybody else lives?' Michael asked.

'Michael, everybody around here knows everything about everybody.'

They drove for what seemed like an age along what appeared more like a long weedy entrance to someone's house than a road. It was a bucolic scene, fields sloping in either direction, some dotted with grazing animals, others filled with golden crops swaying softly in the light breeze.

'He said a mile,' Michael griped. 'We must have missed it.'

Laura didn't even respond. A country mile was a world away from a Dublin measure.

Moments later they drove through the crossroads. The

Lehane house wasn't hard to find. A woman was standing at the part of the gate that was still attached to its hinges. She waved at the approaching car.

'You found us alright, then,' she said, as Laura pulled into the drive. 'John rang from the next farm over to say you were on your way.' Her voice was harsh, her tone unwelcoming.

The woman was in her thirties and bore a strong resemblance to her missing sister – black, curly hair and tiny eyes, a pert nose and small mouth. Local officers had visited the family the previous night to inform them that Mary Ellen's body had been found, so Laura and Michael didn't have to break the news. Thankfully.

'We're very sorry about Mary Ellen,' Laura said, offering her hand. 'You must be her sister, Elizabeth.'

The woman looked down at the proffered hand but didn't take it. Her eyes were bloodshot.

'I'm her sister. I can't say the news didn't come as a relief. We knew Mary Ellen was dead. Four years is too long to go without finding her, though. It's near destroyed Mammy.'

'That's Nora, isn't it?' Michael asked. 'Have you more family?'

'No, it's just us two. Our brother's in England and Daddy died ten years ago. Farming accident. At least he was spared all this. Come in, then. I suppose you'll be wanting tea?'

'Just water will be grand,' Laura said, following the woman as she strode purposefully into the ramshackle old farmhouse. The heat was intensifying as they approached midday and neither detective believed the perceived wisdom that drinking hot tea could regulate the body's temperature.

Elizabeth brought them through to a small parlour at the rear of the house, just off the kitchen.

The room they entered was dark and gloomy. It had one small window, divided in half by a lace net curtain and faced onto a semi-enclosed yard. A couple of fat bluebottles buzzed lazily against the cracked pane of glass.

A wooden dresser was heaped with old crockery and photos. Beside it, an older woman sat on a hard-backed chair, hands clasped on her breast, rosary beads entwined in her fingers. She wore a pale green blouse stretched across an ample bosom. Legs mapped by varicose veins poked out from under a matching green skirt.

She opened her eyes and made to stand as they entered the parlour.

'You're grand, Mrs Lehane,' Laura said. 'Not on our account, please. We're very sorry about your daughter.'

Nora sniffed and bowed her head.

Michael took a seat beside Laura, echoing her words, receiving as little acknowledgement.

Elizabeth sat with her mother, their elbows touching, bodies leaning towards each other almost defensively.

'I knew she was dead,' Nora said, resignedly. 'I felt it. In here.' She pointed at her chest, where her heart lay broken. 'Even when they said she wasn't. They said she'd run off. But a mother knows. When you bring a life into this world, you're bound, you see. There's a thread that connects you to your child. They're part of you, your flesh and your blood, forever. Until you die or they do. You feel light when they're happy, you feel heavy when they're sad. Ask any woman. I think that's what hurt the most – when the other mothers in the village tried to tell me she'd just left. Like I wouldn't have known.'

Nora closed her eyes and shuddered. Any stoicism she'd been trying to project deserted her.

The pain in the room was suffocating.

'Did she . . . did she suffer?' Elizabeth sounded almost embarrassed to have to ask for information. 'The guards who came up didn't know anything. They just said her body had been found and we wouldn't be needed to identify her.'

Nora stayed silent as her remaining daughter spoke, but Laura could see her body tense.

'We don't know,' the detective answered, honestly. 'They're examining all the bodies we found. We think he may have kept her for a while and we believe she was . . . that he strangled his victims.'

'I'll be going up to see her.' Nora broke the uncomfortable silence that followed.

The two detectives exchanged a glance. Nora caught it. Breathing heavily, she reached across Elizabeth and took a picture from the dresser. It was of a child, a smiling little girl, maybe seven years old. It had been taken on a summer's day in a field not unlike the one outside. White vest and shorts over tanned arms and skinny, grazed legs, a smile from ear to ear under a shock of dark curls that looked too big for her tiny body. She stood in front of an apple tree with a swing hanging from its branches and you could tell she'd just leapt from its seat to pose. So full of life.

'That's Mary Ellen,' her mother said. 'That's my baby. Whatever you saw up in Dublin, whatever he left of her, this is how she'll always be to me. Lord, she hated school because it kept her indoors. All she needed to make her day was the sun shining. She would be out there making daisy chains and chasing bees, eating jam sandwiches. She was more tomboyish than her brother but pretty enough to charm the wings off a butterfly.

'You know, she slept in my arms every night until she was three. When I reported her missing, your lot said she was an adult and was allowed off to do her own thing. I told them she'd been taken. I *knew* she had. If the man who took her didn't kill her straight away then maybe she could have been saved, if anybody had taken me seriously. You wouldn't help me find my baby, but you will allow me to see her. I don't care if it's only her bones. I'll hold her one more time.'

Great big tears spilled down the woman's cheeks, her face crumpling in despair.

'We'll see what can be arranged,' Laura said, gently. 'But it might be better, Mrs Lehane, if that's the image you keep of Mary Ellen in your head.' She pointed at the picture. 'If you remember her like that, not as a body that's been taken from the ground.'

Silence descended again, bar the sniffs of the distraught mother. Nora had no more words.

'You wanted water,' Elizabeth said, standing abruptly. 'Come out to the kitchen with me and I'll get you a glass. Mammy, I'm going to open the back door and let a bit of air in. It's stifling in here.'

She patted her mother's shoulder and led the two detectives from the room.

'We'll go outside,' Elizabeth said. She filled a jug with water from the tap, begrudgingly threw in some ice cubes, and grabbed two glasses.

They followed her out to a garden overlooking the rolling plains. An old bench was positioned just outside the back door and they sat on that, taking in the view, as the comforting smell of fabric softener from the sheets hanging on the washing line drifted in their direction.

'I can't say what I'm about to tell you in front of Mammy. It will get her all riled up and she'd think I was wasting my time. She reckons you're all the same. But you're from Dublin and I don't know – maybe you're a bit more open-minded up there.'

'Who's all the same?' Laura asked. 'The guards?'

'Aye.'

'Because the gardaí didn't take you seriously when you reported that Mary Ellen had gone missing?'

Elizabeth looked at her sharply. Laura held up a conciliatory hand.

'It's okay,' she said. 'We're open to anything you want to tell us. Mary Ellen was murdered, so everything is relevant now. Anything you have to say will be listened to with the utmost gravity, I promise you.'

Elizabeth hesitated, studying Laura.

'Aye, well. Let's see if you close ranks on this one. It wasn't just that the guards didn't take Mary Ellen's disappearance seriously. They *ridiculed* us when we went to report it, wouldn't even write it down. She was missing for a month before we could get them to log it with that – what is it you call it?'

'The Missing Persons Bureau?'

'Yeah. That.'

'Sorry, are you saying a whole month passed before her disappearance was logged?' This was Michael. 'What date did she go missing?'

'The 17th of March, 2008. St Patrick's Day. A month later, they decided they'd finally open a file on her.'

'Why?' Laura asked. Considering Mary Ellen had been twenty-five, she could imagine how the family might have met with sceptical reassurances when they'd first turned up at their local station. But there was no excuse, after some time had passed and it was obvious she was indeed missing for the guards not to have logged the report quicker. Even if they had thought she'd gone off of her own volition.

Elizabeth stared out at the rural vista, her eyes sad. She shrugged.

'You're going to hear things about my sister,' she said. 'They'll tell you that she was . . . that she'd go off with anybody. That's what they said to us when we went down to the station. Laughing and joking while my mother sobbed her heart out. It's all lies. Mary Ellen was no convent girl. She drank like a trooper and smoked like a chimney. And yes, she had a boyfriend or two. But she wasn't a slut. She wasn't some selfish party girl who would have just abandoned Mammy and me. My sister used to bring her boyfriends up here. She didn't keep dirty little secrets. And she'd got herself into enough dodgy situations to know how to take care of herself.'

'She was your younger sister?' Laura asked.

Elizabeth bristled.

'Yes. By five years. But that doesn't mean I was soft when it came to her. If I thought she'd just run off, I'd have told Mammy and saved her the worry all this time.'

'Elizabeth, did your sister ever go with a man who was treating her badly? A chap who might have hit her? Did you get the impression she was hiding anything from you?'

'I just told you; she didn't keep secrets from us. And more – Mary Ellen wasn't stupid. No matter how drunk she was, she never forgot where she lived. She didn't take drugs or get pregnant. And she wouldn't come home late at night without being accompanied.

'She went with a few oddballs, but nobody I can think of who would have laid a hand on her. She wouldn't have stood for it anyway. But somebody took her, and I think it was someone she knew. You know what the worst thing was at the time she went missing?'

'What?'

'Sergeant Doyle. He's the most senior guard in the area. He came up here last night and it was all I could do not to spit in his face. Back then, he spoke about Mary Ellen like she was something you'd pick off your shoe. He got angry at Mammy because she kept going down and harassing him. I couldn't go with her every time; I was trying to keep on top of the farm work. But she came back once and wouldn't speak for days after what he said to her.'

'What did he say?' Michael asked.

Mary Ellen's sister made a choked, angry sound.

'He said that if – and he stressed "if" – something had happened to Mary Ellen, she had it coming.'

She turned to the two detectives, her face livid.

'But I know the real reason why he didn't bother to look into my sister's disappearance.'

# CHAPTER 12

'I think you've made a dreadful mistake. I said as much to the guards who called this morning. Pauline wasn't taken. She left. Steve was knocking her about and she got away from him. It was all planned.'

The news had yet to sink in properly with Barbara Gavan, Pauline O'Hara's sister. Tom and Ray had driven to Waterford that same Monday morning, a couple of hours after the local guards had broken the news to her that Pauline's body had been located. Barbara's husband brought them through to the kitchen of the terraced house, where his wife sat, puffing her way through a pack of Marlboros, lighting one cigarette from the other. She kept insisting he go to work, further proof that she was in denial.

The back door was open, but still Tom could feel the secondary smoke burning his lungs and seeping into the fabric of his shirt. Two small children were playing outside, climbing all over a Wendy house and throwing grass and small stones into the neighbour's back garden. Their mother cast them an occasional worried glance, but it was no more than habitual reflex. She had other things on her mind.

'So, that's why her partner reported her missing but you didn't? What's his full name?'

'Steve Moore. He came around here a week after she left. I'd only been let out of hospital the day before. I'd just given birth to my eldest, so I remember the date. The 24th of February. He said Pauline had gone missing a few days after Valentine's Day, on the 17th. "She hasn't gone missing," I told him. "She's left you, arsehole." '

Barbara adopted the same fierce tone she'd used on the man when he called. She paused to tap some ash and chew one of her fingernails. Tom estimated her age to be around twenty-nine, the age her sister had been when she'd gone missing six years ago. So she'd have been roughly twenty-three at the time. Young, to be fronting up to a man her sister claimed could be violent.

'Why were you so certain Pauline had left him? How long had they been together?'

'They started seeing each other the year I finished nursing training. I'd just turned twenty-one, so . . .' She counted on her fingers. 'Two years. That's how long they were together. He was all smiles at first. Friendly, like. Used to drive around to our dad's house to collect her, loaded down with flowers and chocolates. He worked in a wholesalers that delivered to supermarkets, got everything on the cheap. Pauline was still living at home then, because Dad wasn't well and she didn't want to leave him on his own. He died a couple of months after she started seeing Steve. That was when he started to show his true colours.'

'Your dad lived alone – where was your mam?' Ray asked.

'Oh, she died when we were little. Lung cancer.'

The inspector couldn't help but glance at the mounting pile of butts in the overflowing ashtray. Barbara caught his eye. She tucked her short red hair behind her ear, cheeks flushing.

'I know, I know. I don't normally smoke like this. Would you believe I took it up when I started nursing? It's such a bloody stressful job, you need some sort of release.'

Still, the little reminder had had a powerful effect. Barbara gave her children another cursory glance, but this time her gaze lingered. She stubbed out the cigarette.

'You said you thought Steve's behaviour changed after your dad died,' Tom remarked. 'How so?'

'I don't know how to say it. I'm not good with words. He changed how he acted towards Pauline. I mean, I never liked him to begin with. There was something – I don't know – *forced* about him. He had to be the centre of attention, the life and soul of the party, or he got stroppy. When Dad died, everybody was making a fuss over Pauline and me. We were two orphans. I mean, we were in our twenties, but still. It's unusual to lose both your parents before you've turned thirty. Steve was all right at first – happy to be getting a share of the sympathy as Pauline's boyfriend, everybody saying it must have been hard on him too. Jesus, they'd only been going out a few months. But he revelled in it. Couldn't do enough for the pair of us.

'Then people went back to their own lives and I think he realised that Pauline was going to be on her own and that she was vulnerable. I'd started in the hospital at that stage, working night shifts, so I wasn't around much. It was months before I noticed the bruises. By that stage he'd stopped giving a shit about where he was leaving his mark.'

'And you're absolutely sure that he was being violent towards her?'

Barbara raised a finely plucked eyebrow.

'Inspector, I don't just mean she had the odd little bruise on her arm. He busted her lip open. Gave her black eyes. Near strangled her at one point. I lost the plot that first Christmas, when I found out. She arrived for dinner black and blue. I was going to bleeding kill Steve. My boyfriend at the time talked me down. Said Pauline had to figure it out for herself or she wouldn't thank me. But he had a quiet word with Steve and things seemed to ease off.'

'But not for good?'

She shook her head.

'Did she ever report him to the guards?'

'No. And he kept on, all through the following year. What is it, love?'

One of the children had come in, and stared at the two detectives, awestruck.

'Drink,' he said, without taking his eyes off the strange men in the kitchen.

'Ask your . . . oh, he's gone to work. There are juice bottles in the fridge. Grab two.'

The child sourced the purple bottles from the refrigerator, still eyeballing Tom and Ray.

'Are you policemen?' he asked, eyes wide.

'Yes,' Ray said.

'Do you have guns?'

'Eh, yeah.'

'Do you shoot people dead? Do you blow their heads off? Could you beat Captain America in a fight? Could . . .'

'Outside!' Barbara barked at the child, waiting until he'd gone before resuming her story.

'Sorry about that. He's obsessed with Marvel heroes. Anyway, where was I? Oh, yeah. See, Steve – he picked just the right time in Pauline's life. That's what they do, isn't it? Abusers. Steve must have seen something in her. My sister and I were alike in many ways. We both have the caring gene, that's for sure. She stepped into minding Steve after Dad had gone without pausing for breath. But we were chalk and cheese in other respects. If my husband ever raised a hand to me, I'd lob his mickey off in his sleep.'

The inspector had only spent a short time in Barbara's company, but he didn't doubt her.

'Steve knew Pauline needed to mother somebody and that she was devastated when we lost our father. He took advantage of those things. He'd drink, hit her, then start sobbing about how shit his life had been.'

'And had it been shit?' Tom asked.

Barbara shook her head dismissively.

'Not at all, from what I knew. He said his dad drank when they were kids, but from the sound of it he was a few-nights-a-week drinker, not a bottle-in-the-pocket-of-his-anorak type. I don't know what shite he was feeding my sister, but she ate it up. Until that second Christmas, anyway.'

'What happened then?'

'She wanted to have a family Christmas. I was nearly due that little git you just met – I know, I was only a year in my shagging job and I got pregnant by a night porter. Couldn't even land a junior doctor. We're still together, mind, so it's not all bad news. Anyway, Pauline wanted to fuss over me and had bought all these pressies. We knew I was having a boy and she'd got every blue baby blanket and teddy bear she could lay her hands on. Then Steve got pissed on Christmas Eve, tore her flat asunder, ripped the gifts to bits and left her with two cracked ribs.'

'Did she try to leave him then?' Ray asked.

'No. I begged her to, obviously. We turned up on Christmas morning and she opened the door with the latch on and said she had an upset stomach. I had to be restrained. You should have heard the abuse I was yelling through the gap in the door. And me seven months pregnant. He was probably sleeping it off, but it made me feel better. She begged me to go, but that night she rang and said she had a plan. She was going to leave him, but first she wanted to separate their bank accounts and make sure she'd somewhere to go. I offered to put her up – we'd just bought a three-bed house – but she point-blank refused. Said she wouldn't, not with the baby coming. She was going to leave him on Valentine's Day. That's what she said.'

'So, when she went missing that February, you assumed she'd followed through,' the inspector said. They'd been sitting here talking all this time and Barbara still hadn't acknowledged that her sister was dead. She was using the past tense, sure, but only because she hadn't seen her sister in so long.

'Tell me this,' he continued. 'Didn't you think it was odd that she left and didn't contact you? With you having a baby and everything? It sounds like you were very close.'

Barbara nodded and frowned.

'All through January, any time we talked, she kept telling me she had everything nearly ready so she could leave him. She wouldn't tell me where she was going to go, though. It was like she was afraid if she told me he might get it out of me. I was concerned for her, but I didn't push for information as much as I should have. I got pre-eclampsia at the end of my pregnancy and I was distracted.

'When she left, well, time went on and I heard nothing from her, but I told myself that she was probably too afraid to come home. I mean, it took eighteen months to leave him after the violence started.'

'I'm sure you had a lot on your mind, with a new baby to mind,' Tom said. Barbara's eyes were wet with tears. The reality of what had happened was starting to sink in and it was being followed at a pace by guilt.

'Yes, I did. And I told myself that maybe it was because of the baby that she didn't want to stay and risk having Steve hanging around. I thought maybe he had threatened me or something.'

The inspector took a deep breath. The situation was so tragic. Barbara's sister hadn't got away. She hadn't been avoiding her family. She'd been taken and murdered and nobody had even missed her.

'This Steve Moore. Is he still around?'

She shook her head.

'Not in Waterford City. I'd know. We're well liked here, the husband and me. Somebody would have told us if he'd come back. He left a few months after Pauline disappeared and we were glad to see the back of him.'

'Do you know where he went?'

Unconsciously, Barbara had removed and lit a fresh cigarette from the pack.

She waved the smoke away and raised the chewed nail to her mouth again. It was bitten to the quick. Any more worrying at it and she'd draw blood.

'I'm sorry, I can't take this in. I mean, I did worry about Pauline. Not at the start. But as the years went by I wondered why she wasn't getting in touch. Especially why she wasn't checking up on her nephew. She was going to be his godmother. She is, as it happens. We had somebody stand in for her at the baptism.

'When I gave birth to my little girl, I really missed Pauline.

She would have loved having a niece. I kept accepting scam friends when I first got my Facebook account, the ones without profile pictures, because I thought one of them might be her, trying to make contact. Sometimes I was angry with her for making me worry. But you're saying now that all this time . . .'

Barbara placed her hand on her chest as though to calm herself and her eyes widened. Her voice when she spoke again was shrill.

'Wait a minute. Are you sure it's even her? How do you know? Nobody's asked me to identify a body.'

'Barbara, I'm afraid the DNA samples given at the time of Pauline's disappearance match one of the bodies found in Glendalough. It's definite.'

'But the guards went to Steve for Pauline's DNA samples,' she protested. 'He gave them her toothbrush and a hairbrush or something. I didn't give them anything. I didn't think anything had happened to her. He's not a man to be trusted; maybe he got the hair from another girl or something. Steve could easily have been having an affair.'

Tom held Barbara's gaze and leaned across the table towards her, speaking gently but firmly.

'We've also checked the dental records. It's Pauline.'

Barbara slumped again, her shoulders hunched, cigarette forgotten in the ashtray. She massaged the side of her head. After a long pause, she looked straight at Tom.

'I don't know where that bastard went. Did he do it? Did he kill her?'

The inspector kept his features composed. They had no proof of that, yet. Just a theory about a man who dated and abused the women he ultimately murdered. The anomaly in this instance was that Steve had actually reported Pauline missing. But that could have been a sick attempt to put himself at the centre of the investigation into her disappearance.

He jumped as Barbara emitted a howl so loud, so full of rage and anguish, that both children in the garden froze and dropped the drinks they'd been squirting at each other.

'He killed her, didn't he?' she sobbed. 'That man killed my sister.'

She covered her mouth with her hands, shocked at what had just come out of it. Then the tears came. Tom stood up and fetched some kitchen roll from the counter, offering it to her as a poor substitute for a handkerchief.

'What can I do?' she asked, dabbing at her eyes and cheeks. 'What can I do to help you catch him?'

'First, I need you to look at something. Did Steve ever give your sister a bracelet like this one?' The inspector pulled out his phone and located the image of the charm bracelet.

Barbara studied the photograph.

'I don't know. Was she found with this?'

'Yes,' Tom said, though he didn't know if this had been Pauline's or one of the others.

'He was always buying her gifts after he hit her,' Barbara said, her mouth set in a hard line. 'Little tokens to say sorry. Except they weren't olive branches, not really. He could have given her that, yeah. He'd have used it to reel her back in for more violence. That was what he did. The evil bastard.'

# CHAPTER 13

'Right, that's the hotel booked and I've let the wife know I won't be back tonight. Do you reckon Sergeant Doyle is back from lunch yet?'

Michael slid his phone onto the table, just as Laura finished tapping out a text update for Tom. They were sitting in the courtyard of a pub in Glendale village, half-eaten sandwiches and recently replenished glasses of sparkling lemonade on the table in front of them. The ice cubes were already melting.

It was a pretty drinking spot. Each of the wooden tables had fresh, scented posies in its centre and the owner had kitted out the cobbled yard with old-fashioned gas lanterns and barrels bursting with blooms. Customers had a pleasant view of a peaceful brook that trickled by at the back of the premises.

Laura checked the time on her phone. It had been an hour since the guard at the station had told them they'd just missed Sergeant Ultan Doyle. He had to be back by now, surely.

'Let's go see,' she suggested to Michael. 'I have no appetite. It's too bloody hot. We can get a decent meal in Cobh when it cools down later. Make the most of our little holiday.'

They walked the couple of hundred metres to the station. The guard they'd met earlier passed them on the way.

'The boss is back,' he informed them. 'I'm just nipping out for an hour.'

Doyle greeted the two detectives amiably when they sauntered into the converted house that served as the village's garda headquarters. He was a good-looking man, early fifties, a full head of silver-grey hair. Slim, smart in his uniform, with sculpted cheekbones and a jaw that gave him a touch of the Frank Sinatra.

'Nice to meet you, folks,' he said. His handshake was firm and self-assured. 'Sorry it's in these circumstances. We were shocked when we got the call last night from Dublin. 'Twas awful to have to bring that news up to Nora. But at least she knows now. There's some small mercy in that. Can I get you something to drink?'

'No, thanks,' Laura said. 'We've just come from lunch.' She was struggling to get to grips with Doyle in person, given what Elizabeth had told them. He was perfectly welcoming and friendly. Guilt, she decided. He knows he's messed up.

'Of course, of course. Sorry you had to wait for me; I didn't know when you'd be here and had to get something myself. There are only two of us manning the station, so you take your breaks when you can. The chap who just left wasn't here in 2008 so I figured you wouldn't be interested in talking to him anyway. But listen, I know you need to be getting on. How can I help you?'

He offered them seats and took one himself, his posture relaxed and open.

'We want to have a chat with you about Mary Ellen,' Michael said. 'About what happened when her mother came in to report her missing.'

They'd decided that Michael would do most of the talking with Doyle. Laura's gut told her he'd respond better to a male detective.

'Ah, I see. It's only natural that they'd think we didn't do enough, but I really thought she'd just run off. Everybody did, at the time.'

'Except her family,' Michael said. 'And now we know she didn't. Look, we don't have time to pussyfoot around – the Lehanes say that they reported Mary Ellen missing on 17th March but you didn't open an official file on her until April. Why the delay?'

Doyle had the good grace to look embarrassed. He rubbed the back of his neck and leaned forward.

'Can we speak frankly – colleague to colleague?'

Michael shrugged, a non-committal gesture. If it turned out Doyle had botched the investigation into Mary Ellen's disappearance, the family would be entitled to pursue it. His only concern at the moment was establishing the facts around the time she'd gone missing and whether they held any clues as to who'd taken her.

'You've been up with the Lehanes and I know they've an axe to grind with me.' Doyle had taken Michael's silence as tacit agreement they were now off the record, as such. 'Fair enough. Now that we know what we know, I absolutely should have taken their concerns more seriously at the time. But everybody has twenty-twenty vision in hindsight. Back then, I was fully convinced Mary Ellen had just gone up to Dublin or . . .'

'What?' Michael prompted.

'There was a rumour about the village that she'd got the boat to England for – you know.'

Michael frowned.

'No. I don't.'

'An abortion,' Doyle explained, his voice hushed. 'Mary Ellen had a bit of a reputation. She was referred to as the village bike, if you know what I mean. Everybody was getting a ride on her. She was a good-looking girl, but Jaysus, I'd say she was riddled.'

Laura raised her eyebrows. What a nasty thing to say. And there was something in Doyle's face that implied he enjoyed the salacious gossip about Mary Ellen.

'People talk,' Michael responded. 'But it was your job to get to the facts, surely?'

'Hell, of course.' Doyle nodded his head in agreement. 'It's just, when you live and work in a tight-knit area like this, you get to know people. Nora and Elizabeth Lehane aren't known for facing up to reality.'

'How do you mean?'

'Well, look, I guess they told you that the father had died in a farming accident. Yes? There you go – the *accident* happened when old man Lehane, who began most days with a whiskey breakfast, decided to mix slurry while he was pissed as a fart. He was overcome by the fumes and died. The man was a danger to himself and everybody who worked with him on that farm. And I imagine the women mentioned the brother who's gone to England?'

Michael nodded.

'Aye. Well, I'll tell you this much – he didn't go in search of work. That fella owes money to every sod in this townland. His name is dirt around here. They're in denial about that one, too.'

'I see,' Michael said.

Doyle rubbed his hands on his trouser legs. The man was nervous, Laura realised.

'I'm not comfortable, hanging their dirty washing out like this,' he said. 'I don't want you getting the wrong idea about me. But you need to know the family to know why I made the judgement I did. Nora and Elizabeth would tell you Mary Ellen was whiter than white, that she just had the odd boyfriend. That wasn't the case. Not only was she sleeping with everything that moved – including, I might add, married men – but the apple hadn't fallen far from the tree where drink was concerned. She was down here most nights knocking it back in any pub that would serve her. Maybe I'm a little traditional, but that kind of behaviour in a young lass – it was always going to lead to trouble.'

'I see,' Michael said, edging the man along. 'But none of that explains why you didn't take her disappearance seriously. Even if all those things are true, even if the girl had upped and left herself, you didn't know that for certain.'

Doyle's eye twitched and for a moment, there was a hint of something behind the façade of affability.

'I didn't just dismiss her family.' He shook his head, indignant. 'The story they told me didn't add up. And I figured that they were so embarrassed by Mary Ellen's departure they were creating a fiction to mask it.'

'What was their story?'

'They claimed she hadn't come home the night before. Now, this was only the next day and I knew for a fact that there had been plenty of nights when Mary Ellen hadn't made it home. They'd never called to the station to report her missing before. But this night, as it happens, she'd got a taxi home. The man insisted he brought her to her gate and we had about twenty witnesses to say he was back in the pub fifteen minutes later and stayed there for the night.

'That man was hounded by the Lehanes. The two women confronted him in the village, claimed he was lying, that a gang of local men had done away with Mary Ellen and he was covering up for them. All sorts of fantastical notions, they had. He was mortified. He hadn't even charged the girl, she'd been so out of it. Somebody else had to give him directions to get her home; he'd only moved to the area a short time before. He was trying to be a Good Samaritan and look where it got him.'

'You're positive he did nothing wrong?' Michael asked. 'Did he know Mary Ellen before he gave her a lift that night? Was he one of the men she'd had a relationship with?'

'No, absolutely not. The fella was a quiet man. Mary Ellen liked the party animals. And here's something else her mother and sister won't have told you. We checked the fella's house and everything. Nobody believed he'd done anything, but we had to be seen to be acting. A few days later I went up and searched the place. Absolutely nothing – no sign there'd ever been a woman in the house. He couldn't get over the smear, though. He moved away a few months later.'

'And do you know where he went?'

Doyle shook his head. 'He said he had relatives in England. He'd moved here originally because he'd had some stressful job up in Dublin, at a bank I think – and he had a minor heart attack. It was a wake-up call for his health. He packed it in, bought a taxi licence and moved down here for the peace. When it all kicked off – well, it wasn't exactly the calm life he was looking for.

'So, you see, we had several witnesses who saw Mary Ellen get into the taxi. The man himself, with no previous record – yes, I checked – drove her to her home and went straight back to the village. Where the hell could she have gone missing? The only thing I can assume is what I thought at the time: Mary

Ellen went home pissed, told the clan she was leaving and why, and was gone the next morning. Okay, we know something happened to her now, but she could have been anywhere when she was taken. I should have logged her with Missing Persons earlier. I accept that. But I checked the family's story and there was no cause for concern. I only put her on the register the following month because they wouldn't let up.'

Laura sat forward.

'Sergeant, we believe the man who killed Mary Ellen had a hunting ground. His victims are all from the southern region. Cork, Kerry, Waterford. This is a tourist village. He may have been passing through when he grabbed her. Maybe that taxi driver wasn't telling the truth or maybe Mary Ellen went back out again that night. Either way, there's nothing to indicate – so far anyway – that she was seen after March 17th, 2008, so when the family say she went missing, we have to presume she went missing. The thing is, we believe this man kept his victims for a period before he killed them. Do you understand what that means? Mary Ellen was probably alive that whole month when you didn't issue a national alert through the Missing Persons Bureau.'

Doyle baulked, his face a picture of panic.

'I didn't know,' he said. 'I mean, how could I have? How could any of us?' He looked accusingly from one to the other of the detectives, as though they had been complicit in his dereliction of duty.

'As you say,' Laura continued. 'Hindsight is a wonderful thing. We do have one other concern, though. Michael?'

'We do, yeah.' Her colleague picked up the baton. 'Mary Ellen's sister believes that you had a personal reason for not looking into her disappearance.'

'What was that, now?' The sergeant's tone was even, but his eye twitched furiously.

Michael leaned forward.

'She says Mary Ellen accused you of trying to rape her.'

'Should we call back to the Lehanes?' Michael asked, as they pulled out of the village of Glendale.

Laura shrugged.

'I don't think so. I don't want to be caught in the middle of "he says, she says" with Elizabeth and Doyle. It doesn't matter how her father died or why her brother emigrated to England. Nor does it matter who Mary Ellen was shagging. That's Doyle trying to create a defence for his poor police work. And I'm not charging in there accusing them of lying about Mary Ellen not coming home that night – not the day after they've been informed of her death.'

'It mightn't have been intentional on Doyle's part,' Michael mused. 'Sloppy, maybe. But the whole point of having a local guard is to have local knowledge and we can't dismiss the value that brings.'

Laura stared at her colleague, aghast.

'It brings no bloody value if it creates a bias that leads to ineffectiveness,' she snapped. 'And anyway, none of that is the reason he didn't treat the report seriously, if Elizabeth is to be believed. It was because he was glad to see the back of a woman who was causing trouble for him. Nobody else in the village knew about the accusation against him at that stage, bar Mary Ellen's sister, so Doyle was relieved she was gone.'

'*If* you believe he's guilty of what she claimed,' Michael ventured.

His colleague tutted.

'It doesn't matter whether he is or isn't. Well, it matters, but you know what I mean. I'm not presuming the woman is always telling the truth, Michael. Mary Ellen said he'd tried to rape her and true or not, that was going to cause Doyle a lot of bother. As it happens, I'd be inclined to believe that he did try something on with her. He gave me the creeps. The things he said about her shouldn't have come out of a professional police-man's mouth. It was vindictive – the "village bike" and saying she was "riddled". And telling us about the abortion rumour – it's all a bit accusatory, isn't it? Like she was asking to be murdered.'

Michael considered his response carefully. He wanted to be on the same page as his colleague. But Doyle's denial of the accusation had been spirited and Michael had perceived him as frank in his analysis of Mary Ellen's disappearance, not biased. The man had screwed up, that was for sure, but deliberately so? Michael didn't know. Then again, was he seeing the situation from a blinkered male perspective?

Laura stopped the car.

'I'm serious, Michael. I'm not happy with this whole affair. I can't see how it's not black and white for you. A woman went missing and because she wasn't challenging for the role of the Virgin Mary our colleagues down here made certain assump-tions. Jesus, we know full well that the institutions of the State have always been stacked against women in Ireland, and I'm including the gardaí in that. Things might have changed, but in some parts of the country they've changed faster than others. So you've Sergeant Doyle happy to see the back of her and the villagers whispering. And all the while those derogatory con-versations were being had, Mary Ellen was being held captive in some bloody house or basement somewhere, with her kidnapper doing God knows what to her. Don't you think Doyle has something to answer for?'

'All I'm saying is that I can see things a little from his point of view,' Michael said, defensively. 'It's a small place and you said yourself, everybody knows everybody's business, so he knows the family. It also seems like a safe place. You'd never make the leap that Mary Ellen had been snatched, especially if you had a witness who brought her virtually to her door. Not to mention she was a grown woman.

'I'm not fighting with you, Laura. There's no excuse for Doyle not logging her disappearance properly. And if he treated the family as badly as they claim, well, they have him by the balls. But – and hear me out – you know what it's like to be a guard. Sometimes, you can't do right for doing wrong in the eyes of the public. The Lehane family had their problems and Doyle factored those in. Look at the inconsistencies he had to deal with – the fact they reported her missing the next day, even though she'd been out all night on previous occasions. And it's not like he did nothing. They searched the taxi driver's house. Ultimately, Doyle made a mistake. But perhaps it was an understandable one.'

'Unless he did try to rape her,' Laura said, her features hard. 'Then he's not just a friendly, bumbling guard. He's a dangerous arsehole. And I'm really surprised that you'd take his word as verbatim that she had stayed out on other nights. Is he telling the truth, just because he's a guard?'

Michael was about to say that yes, that would be his understanding, but instead he just shrugged, trying to be conciliatory. This was one he wasn't going to win and he didn't want to make the drive to Cobh any longer than it had to be.

'Anyway, at least we have a bit of a lead,' he said.

'What?' Laura started the car again, her cheeks flushed from the exchange.

'That taxi driver that dropped her home. Cormac Ryan. Unless the Lehanes are lying and she did go home that night, he was the last person to see Mary Ellen before she disappeared. Where are you going? I thought we were heading straight to Cobh.'

Laura had turned the car around and was heading back into the village.

'I can't let this go, Michael,' she said. 'I need to know if Doyle was just inept or purposely not doing his job because he didn't like Mary Ellen. Let's ask around. It's 2012. Not all country people think single women should be nuns and they certainly don't think all guards are saints.'

Their first port of call back in the village was the pub they'd had lunch in. The afternoon trade had died off and the place was quieter. They found the landlord out in the courtyard, reading a paper and drinking coffee.

'Would you mind terribly if we disturbed you for five minutes?' Laura asked, flashing her most appealing smile.

Michael hung back. He was smarting a little from the exchange in the car. If you'd asked him prior to today, he'd have imagined that he was more liberal and open-minded than Laura. It wasn't a man/woman thing. More an urban/rural divide. Michael was a dyed-in-the-wool Dub and Laura, while having lived in Dublin since her teens, was from somewhere in the arse end of Kerry. In Michael's mind, the capital's natives were more progressive. But he was being challenged this afternoon.

The landlord gestured to the other chairs around the table.

'No bother at all,' he said, with a smile. 'You'll be the detectives from the Big Smoke, so?'

Laura nodded.

'We've been up to see the Lehanes and in with Sergeant Doyle, but we just wanted to chat with some local people about Mary Ellen's disappearance. Did you know her at all?'

The landlord stroked his jaw, nodding.

'I did, aye. I'm born and bred here, like the Lehanes. Know the family all my life. It's an awful lot of tragedy poor Nora has had to deal with.'

'This wasn't the pub that Mary Ellen went home from the night she went missing, is it?'

'No. She'd been drinking in Murphy's, up the road. It's closed down now. It was in a fierce state of disrepair, couldn't compete for the tourists and the locals were getting tired of old Murphy never cleaning his glasses properly. Walking across the floor was like stepping through treacle. It was already on the downturn when Mary Ellen was drinking there, but . . .'

'What?'

'Ah, you know. My old mammy, God rest her soul, used to say you never speak ill of the dead.'

'Please,' Laura said, already noting how much tact this man was showing, in contrast to Doyle. A bit of class cost nothing. 'It's important that we get a full picture of Mary Ellen's life. It could help us with our investigation.'

'Aye, I suppose you're right. God bless her, but she liked to have a good time, did Mary Ellen. She was barred from a couple of places. Temporarily, like. A small village like this, you can't go writing off custom. Tourists only come in the summer. Mary Ellen enjoyed herself. Probably nothing out of the norm for you lads and lassies in the city, but in a quiet village – well, people are cruel. Frustrated housewives with their curtains twitching, worried about a pretty cailín flashing a bit of leg and leading the husband or son astray.'

'Did she have many boyfriends?'

'I wouldn't say that, now.' The landlord shook his head. 'Just because she liked a flirt didn't mean it was leading anywhere. I didn't believe everything they said about her. She helped out here one summer, collecting glasses for me, and I got the impression it was a bit of a front with the lass.'

Laura flashed Michael a triumphant glance. Doyle's analysis was starting to crumble and they'd only had to speak to the first local they met.

'When she disappeared, do you feel it was taken seriously?' she asked, on a roll now. 'Did the guards put any effort into finding her? Please, be honest. We need to know what happened at the time.'

The landlord looked puzzled.

'I'd have said so, yes,' he said. 'They put the effort in. I know this is a bone of contention between Nora and Ultan Doyle but to be honest, I thought that Mary Ellen had just upped and left as well. Who'd have blamed her? But after a couple of days Ultan started asking around about who'd seen her that night. Then he questioned the lad who was doing the taxi at the time. Cormac, I think his name was. Even searched his house. I think the guards took it more seriously than the rest of us. I suppose Ultan had to prove a point once Nora started pointing fingers and claiming he wasn't doing his job.'

Michael had sat back and let Laura do the talking, but now he leaned forward.

'Was there ever any talk of Ultan Doyle and Mary Ellen having a relationship?' he asked. 'Of him fancying her, anything like that?'

'Ultan and Mary Ellen?' The landlord's voice had risen a pitch. 'Good God, the man had twenty years on her. Mary Ellen wouldn't have touched him with a barge pole. She hung around with lads her own age, despite the gossip. And sure, the good sergeant is too busy fancying himself to fancy anybody else. Not to mention, he has a wife. No. I think Doyle would have steered clear of Mary Ellen. She'd a tendency, with a few drinks in her, to get a bit argumentative sometimes. She'd . . . claim things. Any man with sense would know to stay away from that.'

'Did she make any allegations against Doyle?'

The landlord shook his head.

'No. But she did say one or two other lads in the village had got a bit heavy, so to be honest, if she'd claimed something about Doyle I'm not sure anybody would have believed her.'

When they left the pub, Laura turned in the direction of the car.

'Don't you want to talk to more people?' Michael asked.

She stopped.

'What's the point? I imagine his opinion is as nuanced as we'll get. Fair enough, I concede the point to you. Doyle investigated her disappearance. But it's clear that what he had to say about Mary Ellen was based on opinion, not necessarily fact. Glendale is just one of those villages. A girl sleeps with a man or two and suddenly she's a raging slut who can't be trusted or believed. It looks like I was wrong about things having changed.'

Laura looked so distressed that Michael felt immediately ashamed at how satisfied he'd felt when the landlord confirmed the guards had indeed made enquiries about the disappearance.

'You know what it is, Michael,' she continued. 'I can't stop thinking of Mary Ellen holed up somewhere while everybody in that village was telling one another she'd done a flit. Nobody deserves to be forgotten and be left to suffer like that, no matter what people thought of her. It bugs the hell out of me – the notion that a woman could be held responsible for the actions of her rapist or killer just because she acted a certain way or walked home alone at night.'

'But not everybody thinks like that,' Michael said. 'Look, you were right. The sergeant was wrong to speak about Mary Ellen like that. Especially now we know what happened to her.'

Laura had been fussing at a stone on the ground with her shoe.

'Forget it,' she said. 'I'm not annoyed at you. You're just trying to be fair to everybody. I shouldn't have driven us back down here. I wanted to make a point.'

'Well, if it makes you feel better, everyone in this village who had a bad word to say about Mary Ellen when she went missing will be feeling like right shits now, when they hear what happened to her. Come on, let's get on the road to Cobh to interview Treasa Lee's family. The best thing we can do for all these women now is find their killer. Once we've that sorted, we can send a report up above about Sergeant Doyle and the accusations that were made against him. It will all come out in the wash, Laura.'

# CHAPTER 14

'You know I'm dropping Maria and Cáit down to my parents later, don't you?'

Louise poured fresh grapefruit juice into two glasses. Tom was poking at the fruit and Greek yoghurt in the small bowl in front of him. So far, none of it had made it into his mouth. His wife had put the healthy dish on the table minutes after he'd sat down, her expression brooking no dissent.

'Aren't you going to thank me for making you breakfast?' she asked, handing him his glass.

'When you offered to make me brekkie, I thought you meant something fried. This is dessert.'

'Tom Reynolds, have you looked at your tummy lately? Do you know that where you're carrying those extra few pounds is the most dangerous place in the body and a big indicator you could be making yourself a candidate for heart disease?'

His wife had been watching *a lot* of healthy eating shows recently.

'And don't think I haven't noticed your diminishing supply of cigars. I mean, you brought *boxes* back from Cuba. How fast are you smoking them?'

He sighed dramatically.

'Anyhow,' she continued, 'I was thinking I'd stay down with them in Wicklow for a while. It's a little cooler by the sea and – don't think I've lost the plot – but I kind of don't want to let Maria out of my sight at the moment. With what's going on and everything. I know you won't miss us here, I'm only telling you because I won't be around to pop in to help Sean with June.'

This time, Tom sighed for real.

'What's up?' Louise asked, force-feeding him a grape. 'Aside from having to investigate five murders and a missing girl.'

He swallowed, distractedly.

'I thought Sean would have been on to me by now. He rang Moya Chambers and I'd lay money he's talked to Emmet McDonagh. Probably Linda, too. I don't feel like I can ring him about work but I miss his advice.'

'He's just giving you space,' Louise said. 'Call him, why don't you?'

Her husband nodded, silently mulling as his wife poked a spoon of yoghurt into his mouth.

'Jesus, Louise,' he said, coming to. 'I'm not the baby.'

'Well, stop bloody acting like her, then. Eat your breakfast, fatso. I'm off for a shower. What time is your meeting?'

'Not until eleven. Laura and Michael stayed in Cork last night. I'm giving them a chance to get back.'

'Can we have a chat?'

'Snap.'

Laura and Brian had both intercepted Tom as soon as he entered headquarters.

'Can't it wait until after this meeting?'

'Eh, I want to talk to you about the guards who handled the investigation in Cork,' Laura said. 'I'm not sure it's for everybody's ears.'

'Interesting. I want to talk to him about the investigation in Kerry,' Brian added. He blinked several times. He'd recently taken to wearing contact lenses but the heat was making his eyes dry. He was happy, however, to stick with vanity over comfort. Although not yet forty, Brian was already balding; he had to at least dispense with the glasses. Not to mention the fact that far more blokes had come on to him in the last three months than in the last three years.

'As they say in the hip shows you kids watch, let's walk and talk,' the inspector said, breaking into a stride.

By the time they arrived at the incident room, his growing sense of unease had become a whole ton of concern.

'Right,' he said. 'Give this lot in here the salient facts about the investigations at the time, but maybe leave out some of the more colourful commentary. It's relevant because it paints a picture of how the women were perceived and the responses to their disappearances, but terms like the village bike are not something I want bandied around. Even if it's just reporting what somebody else said, you can't presume that every officer in here is going to dismiss it. I don't want that kind of rubbish seeping into people's heads.'

Laura and Brian nodded and followed Tom into the team meeting.

Somebody, most likely Ian Kelly, the sergeant in charge of rank and file, had managed to source a few fans and had placed them strategically around the large room, blowing welcome gusts of air. The windows were opened as wide as they could go. It was makeshift air conditioning, but it would have to do.

Pictures of the five confirmed victims, taken when they were alive, had been pinned to the boards beside the recent snap of

Fiona Holland. Smiling women, all unaware of the tragic fate their futures held.

'Thank God I have a buddy who works in electrical supplies,' Ian said, handing Tom a report of the uniforms' activity from the previous day. 'Seeing as we blew all our funds on those poxy see-through boards. Great investment, what?'

'But they're so shiny,' Tom said, drily. 'Okay, boys and girls, let's call this meeting to order. I imagine we all want to get back out into the field quickly, if just so we can be a few degrees cooler. Let's get updates on how informing the families went first. We also have the final reports from pathology and crime scene. Then we've the interviews with staff in Glendalough. What else?'

'The woman who says she was almost abducted in April of this year,' Ian said. 'The one that got away.'

'That's it. Right, Ray, you lead off. Bring everyone up to speed on the interviews with the Holland, O'Hara and Dolan families.'

Tom propped himself against a window as his deputy ran through his update. How long could this heatwave last? It had to break at some stage.

'There are marked similarities in the circumstances of the Una Dolan and Fiona Holland cases,' Ray said, arriving at the final part of his report. 'A single young woman, making her way home from a nightclub alone, not seen again – though she went missing at night and Fiona vanished in broad daylight. The family doesn't know if Una was seeing anybody at the time; apparently her and the folks were going through a bit of a rough patch. They thought she needed to grow up and move out, so it was hardly surprising she didn't tell them everything. Her friends claim there was nobody special but they also say that Una was the secretive type. The consensus is that she was a man's woman, not a girl's girl, if that makes sense.

'Anyhow, they did say she was chasing some chap the night of her disappearance but he got off with another in their circle, so Una stormed off in a huff. The girl he went with can't even remember his name – she said she was with him the once and never again. The guy moved on. He was only doing casual work in the town.'

'Where was Pauline O'Hara last seen?' Laura asked.

'She was shopping in Waterford City the day she went missing,' Ray responded. 'She was last seen waiting for her bus home that evening with a few Superquinn shopping bags.'

'Thanks, Ray,' Tom said. 'Laura and Michael?'

Laura gave the room the rundown on Mary Ellen Lehane and Treasa Lee.

'Treasa is the oldest victim, that we know of,' she concluded. 'She was thirty-three and in a relationship. According to her family, the boyfriend was serious but she didn't see it like that. She was a beauty, as you can see from her picture, and she was popular. The guards in Cobh weren't quite as blunt as the sergeant who looked into Mary Ellen's disappearance, but they did assume at the outset that Treasa was off partying and would eventually turn up with the mother of all hangovers.

'Her father gave that no quarter. He was adamant she had come to harm. Said she rang him every day without fail and wouldn't dream of just going off the radar. Apparently, when she was younger, she'd suffered from depression. After that, she made it her job to check in regularly, so her folks wouldn't worry. The father was right to be concerned, of course. She was last seen walking out of a small industrial estate on the outskirts of the town after leaving work. She was off the next day and told her colleagues she planned to go clothes shopping. There was nothing out of the ordinary.'

'Boyfriend's name?

'Eric Weber, a German. He moved back there at the end of 2009. We're checking to see if he has returned to Ireland since.

'Brian and Bridget?' Tom called the remaining detectives' names.

Brian stood up, forehead furrowed in concern.

'We made one trip – to Eimear Johnson's family in Kerry. There are worrying similarities in how people reacted to her disappearance. Eimear was twenty and a single mother. She lived with her folks outside Steppingtown in south Kerry – more of a village than a town. Last seen going home after a night out, walking alone. Her case was investigated thoroughly, we checked up on that. It was mentioned to us a couple of times, however, that Eimear had a reputation. People assumed she'd done a runner. We were told nobody knew who the child's father was, that sort of thing. Her parents are devastated. They were adamant she wouldn't have left the baby willingly. Said she doted on her. They did say that she was young and liked her nights out but her mother said Eimear never neglected her daughter. Even after a few drinks, she'd be up the next morning getting her breakfast and so on.'

Brian shrugged, to indicate that was all he had.

'Okay,' Tom said.

He walked over to the boards and picked up a marker.

Underneath each victim he began to fill in the corresponding facts, speaking as he wrote.

'There are similarities between all the victims. For the purposes of this room only, I'm including Fiona Holland in our analysis. Each girl was making her way home alone from somewhere when she went missing. They're all in a tight-ish age range, nineteen to thirty-three.'

The inspector stood back and looked at the pictures again.

'Their features are different,' he continued. 'But they all have small frames, going by these photos and their files. Could that mean a woman did take them? I know Linda said probably not, but let's not rule it out.'

He wrote 'female abductor' with a large question mark beside it.

'Several times the word "reputation" has come up, with the exception of Pauline O'Hara, who was, we believe, in an abusive relationship. She was kidnapped in 2006 and then there was a gap until 2008. Had she not been buried in the same place, I'd have been inclined to think that somebody else had murdered her. But perhaps, after his first victim, the killer changed his M.O.

'We know for certain two of the victims had boyfriends. This is where I want us to look closely, keeping those charm bracelets in mind. We need to check up on Treasa's bloke – Eric. And Pauline O'Hara was living with a Steve Moore. He's an interesting character. Violent, an attention seeker, and the sister said he worked in a wholesalers delivering to regional supermarkets, which gives him mobility. We need to track him down and get his work records. Let's see where he was when the other women went missing.

'On top of that, Fiona Holland's family believe she was seeing somebody who was hitting her. They don't know who it was but we'd better make sure it's not Stevie-boy from Waterford. Pauline O'Hara's sister told us she thought Steve Moore was twenty-six in 2006, making him approximately thirty-two now. She didn't know his exact age, but apparently he and Pauline used to joke about her having a toy boy because he was a few years younger. Perhaps he moved to Meath and maybe Fiona's into older men.'

Tom paused to cap the marker.

'What we haven't got,' he said, turning to the room, 'is anything that links all these women. Their killer is the common denominator, but how did he target them? There are too many likenesses, bar with Pauline, for them to have been picked at random. It can't have been through their jobs. Fiona doesn't work. Pauline worked part-time in a doctor's clinic as a receptionist, Mary Ellen on her family farm. Treasa worked for a computer manufacturer. Eimear had no job. Una worked part-time in a clothes shop. They weren't all members of the same club, nor do there seem to be any shared interests outside of drinking and partying, again, Pauline being the notable exception. So how did he choose them? Did he move from town to town – is that how he got to know them? Yet, Linda thinks he probably lives closer to where he buries his victims. So does he have a family home up this end of the country and rentals in the southern region?'

Tom perched on the edge of a desk and waited for his team to make suggestions.

'He lives near them for a while,' Laura suggested. 'That's how he gets to know their backgrounds. Most of them come from villages or small towns and neighbours talk. As we've already discovered.'

'So we're looking for somebody who moved in and out of the area in a relatively short period before the women disappeared,' Tom said. 'That makes your taxi driver in Glendale a real person of interest.'

'Yep,' Michael said. 'Barring the fact he dropped her home and was back in the pub within fifteen minutes and stayed there for the night.'

'How do we know he dropped her home?' Ray asked. 'What if he brought her somewhere?'

'They searched his house,' Michael responded. 'If he brought her there, he moved her again very quickly. Where to?'

'I want that house checked again,' the inspector said. 'Make sure the local guards didn't miss a hidey-hole of sorts. It might have been a cursory search, something to appease the family. Where did the taxi driver come from and where did he go afterwards? We need all of that information.'

Michael nodded, though he didn't relish the thought of the long haul back down to Cork.

'Right, that's what we have on the victims,' Tom said. 'And there's a lot to follow up on. Let's look at these reports.'

'Pathology,' Ray said, getting another nod from his boss. He hated being pitched into the spotlight but was getting a little better at it. Up until the last few months, that was. Now, he worried about what Laura was thinking while he was talking, whether he was spitting as he spoke, if his shirt was tucked in and lots of other entirely irrelevant things.

'Moya has confirmed, as best she can given the decomposition of the earlier victims, that asphyxiation was the cause of each woman's death. There are no bullet or stab wounds. Also no blunt force trauma, which poses the question of how he gets the women to go with him. The boyfriend angle is the most convincing in that scenario.'

'Did she pick up any traces of chemicals he might have drugged them with – is that possible after time?' Laura asked.

'Una Dolan was the best bet for that,' Ray answered. 'And no. There was nothing traceable in her system. In fact, Moya says each of the women appeared to be in tiptop condition. There was no damage to the sexual organs. She didn't find any evidence of post-mortem intercourse on Una, so if it was him who dug her up and reburied her, it wasn't for that reason.'

Tom shook his head, both in relieved disgust and also amazement that Ray had got that bit out without gagging.

'There was one injury on Una that you could read as being consistent with resisting the final attack. A fractured little finger. Aside from that, the bodies aren't giving us much. Oh, one other thing: none of them were emaciated. Moya was able to check that based on the bone density. He was feeding them while they were in captivity.'

'So, we've a compassionate murderer,' the inspector said, his voice hard. 'Thanks, Ray. Okay, moving on to forensics. Ah, Emmet, thanks for coming in.'

'You've not a lot to thank me for, I'm afraid,' Emmet barked in his usual affable way as he planted his wide bottom on a straining chair. 'Aside from Mark's little moment of genius down at the site with those flowers, we've nothing for you. The sheets the victims were wrapped in were clean and there were no foreign fibres on the bodies. He might have given them different things to wear while he held them captive, but the fabrics in the graves correspond to the colours and designs matching the items each woman was wearing when she disappeared.'

Emmet sighed as he removed his glasses to clean the lenses.

'The only lead we have for you, Tom, is something that, from what I hear, is fairly obvious. Those flowers he planted would have been likely to come from the south-west of the country and Cork or Kerry would be a good bet. So, perhaps he's from there? And, as Mark said, he knows his plants. You've discussed flexibility – maybe he's a sales rep for a gardening company?'

'The Hollands own a landscaping business,' Ray said. 'Does he work for them?'

'Is it one of the Hollands?' Laura followed up, her eyebrow raised.

Tom nodded, thoughtfully. They'd plenty of avenues to pursue but little actual evidence.

'Thanks, Emmet. Ian, bring us up to speed on what the rest of the team have been up to.'

Ian loosened his tie and ran a handkerchief over his bald head to wipe away the visible sheen of sweat.

'No problem. Okay, first off, Glendalough has been reopened to the public. The burial site remains cordoned off. For now, anyway. The media are mad to get inside the "valley of horror", as they've named it. I think it will attract a different sort of pilgrim from here on.

'We're making our way through the interviews with the staff. Strangely enough, so far we don't have a single sighting over the course of the six years of somebody carrying a body through the place. People do camp in Glendalough and the car parks tend to have vehicles in them, even at night. Nobody would have considered it out of the ordinary to see a car or van there out of hours.'

Ian sipped some water before continuing.

'Anyhow, there are a lot of people who work in the park, over one hundred and fifty in total and that's not including the volunteers. You've rangers, general operatives, the Visitor Centre staff, workers from the hotel at the entrance . . . the list goes on. We can't ask people for alibis for any date in particular because we don't know what nights the bodies were buried. The only dates we have for certain are the kidnap dates, so we're going with Fiona Holland's, last week. Of the people we've spoken to in the last twenty-four hours, over a quarter have no alibi for when Fiona went missing. They were either working on their own in various sections of the park or were alone at home.

'We haven't spoken to those in the hotel yet, which amounts to seventy-odd of that one hundred and fifty I mentioned, but we are going to be asking them to go over their guest register for anybody who checked in each year around spring/summer since '06.

'One more thing. We looked into those bracelets found with the victims. They're all sterling silver and part of a range that's readily available in Debenhams nationwide. They sell thousands every year, both here and in Britain. The chances of us tracking down the buyer are slim to none.'

'More good news,' Tom said. 'What about the young woman we think he tried to abduct in Clare earlier in the year, the daughter of the guard?'

'I spoke to her father,' Ian said. 'There's no new information on the car she said pulled up beside her – he looked into that himself. But, after a little coaxing, he admitted that she drinks in that pub regularly and he's always on at her for making her own way home. He didn't say anything about her being a handful, nowt like that, mind, but I got the impression he's not happy with her lifestyle.'

The inspector winced. 'A handful.' And Ian meant nothing by it.

He would delegate tasks for today and then he would seek out Chief Kennedy to have a word about the original garda responses to the missing women reports.

Kennedy had retained most of the furniture in Sean McGuinness' old office but had added a flat-screen TV, which he kept tuned to the national broadcaster's twenty-four-hour news channel. McGuinness would have thought that a ridiculous expense. The new chief had also installed a special orthopaedic chair that had cost another small fortune. Kennedy insisted he had back problems, which, in his less charitable moments, Tom imagined came from bowing to lick the boots of his superiors.

'Inspector, come in. Good to see you.'

Kennedy did indeed seem pleased to see him and again Tom felt ashamed for thinking such mean-spirited thoughts about the man.

'I'm trying to get proper air conditioning sorted out for the incident room,' he said, pulling out a chair for the inspector. 'But you know what the civil service mandarins are like. I'm banging my head off a wall. They're just short of suggesting I go down there and flap my arms to create a breeze.'

'We're managing,' Tom smiled, feeling more contrite by the passing second. He'd spent the morning cursing the lack of cool air downstairs, blaming his boss. Ian's fans were a poor substitute and Tom was sick of having to change his shirt after every team meeting.

'It's not good enough in this day and age. I'll get our offices in this building modernised if it kills me. The job is hard enough without having to deal with continuous budget cuts. Anyway, don't mind me. How can I help?'

'Well, it's to do with modernising, as it happens. I'm getting some curious reports as to attitudes towards the Glendalough victims by some of our colleagues.'

Kennedy's face transformed from its normal docile expression to one of alarm. He sat forward, elbows on the desk.

'What do you mean?'

'The woman who went missing in West Cork, for example,

Mary Ellen Lehane. She told her family that the sergeant down there had tried to rape her. When she was reported missing, he didn't officially record her disappearance for a full month. He appears to have conducted an investigation of sorts, but the Lehanes claim he was quick to dismiss their concerns at the time. His conversation with Laura and Michael would lead me to believe that. He used some choice words to paint a picture of her as promiscuous and said he believed she'd run off of her own accord.'

Tom hesitated. Kennedy's face was getting redder. This must be a nightmare for the man – the thought that the gardaí hadn't done their jobs properly. He was all about procedure. The lads in West Cork were about to be landed in a ton of shit.

'There's a similar story in Kerry,' the inspector continued.

When he'd finished, he paused and waited for Kennedy's response. The man seemed lost for words. He got up from his chair and stood in front of the window, his back to Tom, hands clasped behind him.

'I'd be concerned,' Tom added, observing the epaulettes on Kennedy's narrow shoulders, 'that some of our colleagues had an attitude towards these women that may have negatively affected the original investigations into their disappearances. And given what we suspect – that this man held his victims before he killed them – that really worries me. I think it's something we will need to address. I thought we'd moved on from that sort of carry-on. I mean, Mary Ellen Lehane disappeared in 2008. There's enough training nowadays to knock that kind of prejudice out of officers.'

Kennedy returned to his seat and sat down wearily.

'This is very concerning,' he said, picking up a pen and fiddling with its lid. He seemed unnaturally calm.

'I agree,' Tom answered. 'What will you do?'

'I'll have to think about it for a while. This has to be dealt with carefully. We have to make sure we don't overreact.'

'Well, I don't think we should be jumping up and down, making this the focus rather than the actual case. But if these disappearances weren't investigated properly, the chance to save one or more of these women may have been missed. We can't let that go.'

Kennedy adjusted his glasses and pushed back into place the fringe that had fallen onto his forehead.

'Of course not, Inspector. But, in all our responses to allegations of garda impropriety, we must remember what this force is up against. Gangland crime is on the rise. Guards are risking their lives every day to protect the citizens of this state, with fewer and fewer resources. We need people to respect their local guards. Fear them a little, even. Not think that if they drop a scurrilous word here or there, the force will start turning on itself.

'You said it yourself; the sergeant in West Cork investigated the girl's disappearance. We have to accept he had local knowledge and work with him – not against him.'

Tom was disappointed. He'd expected more from the chief. Moreover, he felt like he was being lectured on something about which the man in front of him had very little actual experience.

'I'm well aware of the dangers officers face,' he said, his voice steady. 'There isn't a member of my team who hasn't had direct or indirect threats made to them in the course of murder investigations related to gang feuding, including me. But in all my years working for this force, I've learned that the way to earn the respect of citizens is to do my job and to ensure that the people who work for me are doing theirs. I fail to see how ignoring or airbrushing incompetence and lack of professionalism serves that aim. It certainly hasn't worked for us in the past.'

Kennedy sat back in his chair and crossed his arms.

'It's good to see there are still some idealists in the force, Inspector. And I'm not saying you're not correct in your assessment of this situation. I will look into this, as I said, but let's concentrate on the job in hand. Your goal is finding a serial killer, not reviewing the performance of your colleagues around the country. Let me worry about whether the missing persons investigations were hampered by any undue prejudices. And, Tom, before you go, I want an assurance that this exchange won't go beyond this room. It's for your own good. People might misunderstand your intentions. You know as well as I do that we have to be seen to be team players.'

The chief's voice was even. But the threat in what he'd said was implicit. The inspector had never felt so belittled by an immediate superior. It was the opposite reaction to the one he'd been expecting and it was deeply worrying.

There was no point arguing with Kennedy.

There was one person the inspector wanted to talk to, though.

Sean McGuinness.

# CHAPTER 15

Sean and June's daughter opened the door and appeared relieved when she saw the inspector standing there.

'Ah, Tom. Perfect timing. Take him for a walk and a few jars, will you? I've been trying to explain to him that there's absolutely no point him being here when we are. He needs to take the respite when he can get it. Bloody stubborn git. Come in and sit with Mam while I get him.'

The inspector followed Mary into the sitting room at the front of the house. The blinds had been partially drawn to shade the room from the late afternoon sun.

June sat on a red-and-beige-striped sofa, staring absentmindedly out the window while she picked at the stitching on the seam of one of the cushions.

'Oh, Mam, will you stop worrying at that?' Mary removed the cushion. 'You'll have all the stuffing out. Give me a minute, Tom. Dad's on a call.'

The inspector sat at the other end of the sofa. June peered at him with vague curiosity. She didn't seem to recognise him.

'Hello, June,' he said, loudly. 'It's me, Tom.'

The older woman blinked.

'I know who you are. Why are you shouting at me like I'm some decrepit old bat? I'm losing my sanity, dear. Not my hearing.'

She gave him her most schoolmarmish glare.

Tom squirmed.

'My apologies. I was being silly. And I'm sorry I forgot to bring you something. I came over in a rush.'

'Were you meant to bring me something?'

'No. I just mean flowers, or chocolates. That sort of thing.'

'Oh, no,' June straightened her pale cream skirt over her knees. 'My mother wouldn't like you bringing me favours. That's not proper. Not when Sean is courting me.'

Tom opened and closed his mouth, not sure what to say next. It was just like Louise had said. One moment she was June, as he had always known her. The next, it was like the last forty years of her life had never happened.

'Where's my cushion?' June sought around her for the familiar object, eventually retrieving it from the pile in the corner where Mary had placed it. She tutted.

'Don't have children, Tom. That Mary one, she's always fussing around me. Telling me what I can and can't eat. Saying I need fresh air. I don't know who she thinks she is. I'm the mother. And why isn't she in school? That's what I want to know.'

June stopped fiddling with the stitching. She looked so desolate. Tom put his hand on her elbow. She snatched it away, but dropped her guard when she saw the hurt look in his eyes.

'Oh. I'm sorry, Tom. I've so much on my mind at the moment. And I've such a terrible headache.'

The inspector felt a lump in his throat. He was going through a torrent of emotions, the overriding one being guilt. June was his old friend and her husband and family had to cope with this every day. The living death they called it, when the person you loved was still there but no longer themselves. And Tom was glad – yes, he was glad – that he would be out of this uncomfortable situation in a few minutes and not have to deal with the pain of it.

He hadn't realised he could be so selfish.

'Is there anything I can get you?' he asked her. 'Would you like a glass of water? It might be the heat giving you the headache.' Tom spoke to her like everything was absolutely normal, in the fond, familiar voice he always used with June.

'No,' she replied, looking down. 'It's not the heat. It's my head. It feels like it's exploding inside. Maybe it's better this way. The other way would have been so drawn out.'

'What?'

June leaned across and grabbed his arm; her fingers gripped so tight it was painful. He tried not to react. Instead, he placed his hand over hers.

She stared at him, her gaze intense.

'Promise me, Tom. Promise me you'll look after him. He's going to struggle when I'm gone. Everybody thinks he's this big lump of a man, all brains and brawn and no heart. But he's a big softie, my Sean. I mind him, not the other way round. This will break him, watching me go through this.'

Tom swallowed.

'Of course I will, June. But you're not going anywhere for a long time.' He smiled reassuringly. She studied his face, then, after a long pause, smiled back.

'Of course,' she replied.

The door opened and Sean appeared.

'Tom. Summoned to get me out of the house, were you? Fine, then. I give in. Come on, we'll go for a walk down the seafront.'

The inspector kissed June on the cheek.

'I'll see you soon,' he said. 'We miss you.'

She nodded. 'Absolutely. Maybe we'll have a dinner party? Oh, that would be lovely. Tell Louise not to worry about bringing anything. Just yourselves.'

Tom cast a final glance back into the sitting room as he and Sean were leaving and saw that June had already resumed staring out the window. It was like he hadn't even been there.

'I'm surprised you've the time to be calling out to babysit me,' Sean said, as he strode purposefully down the quiet street. Never had a man moved so swiftly away from a situation he allegedly didn't want to leave. 'Not that I'm not grateful to get out. Our bloody family is using all this as the perfect opportunity to step in and take over our lives. June's ill, not me. You know what I've realised in the last few months, Tom? I'm a misanthrope. I hate being around other people. Even my own kids.'

The inspector's silence alerted something in his companion. Sean stopped abruptly and turned to study his friend's face.

'Nobody rang you, did they?

Tom shook his head.

'You were coming to see me anyway . . . about the case?'

The inspector sighed.

Sean arched an eyebrow.

'Ah. That's the sound of a man dealing with unnecessary drama. You want to talk about my replacement.'

'Eh . . . yeah.'

'To hell with the seafront, then. It'll be full of noisy families enjoying themselves. Let's go somewhere we can be miserable in peace.'

They strolled on for another few streets, landing at Sean's favourite watering hole. They took stools at the bar, increasing to five the grand total of customers scattered throughout the establishment.

'Grape or grain?' Sean asked.

'I suppose I can have a wine. Willie is coming back for me.'

'Good. I hate drinking alone. Derek, two glasses of the good Malbec you've got stashed under the counter.'

The old man behind the bar looked up from the betting slips he'd been checking and sighed, moving laboriously to fetch two wine glasses and the bottle.

'Jesus, careful you don't strain yourself there, now,' Sean tutted impatiently, nosing over the counter at the racing dockets.

'Haven't missed you much,' Derek grumbled. He placed the glasses in front of the two men, then scrunched up his betting dockets so Sean couldn't see how much he'd lost. 'Here, the wife made this up for your better half.' He reached under the counter again and produced a small hamper of sweets, wrapped in cellophane with a long yellow ribbon curled around its neck.

'Lovely. Don't suppose the drink is on the house, no? Seeing as I don't get out much these days?'

Derek held out his palm for the money, while Sean made a show of searching his pockets for his wallet.

'Tight bastard,' he said, as the other man limped down to the till at the far end of the counter. 'Polio as a kid,' Sean added, catching Tom's eye. 'Made him bitter.'

'I see.'

'So. Are you going to tell me what Joe Kennedy has done or do I have to get there through a series of guesses?'

'It's what he hasn't done,' Tom sighed. 'Or won't do, to be more accurate.' He twirled the stem of his glass between his fingers. 'I take it you know what we're dealing with up in Glendalough?'

'I have my sources. Can't say I'm surprised. We've had too many women vanish into thin air over the years. It was either a massive coincidence or a serial killer at work. He had to slip up sometime.'

'There's something not right, though. I don't know if we'd have ever discovered those bodies if one of them hadn't been buried as shallow as she was. The rest were a good six feet down. Has he slipped up or is it intentional?'

'You think he's challenging you? Sick of the dozy, plodding coppers not knowing what he's capable of?'

Tom shrugged.

'We won't know what his game is until we catch him, or until he communicates with us in some way. I'm petrified for that girl, Fiona Holland. You know she has a baby?'

Sean shook his head. This was new information, something even the media were unaware of.

'Maybe he's giving you and her a chance,' he mused.

'Maybe. Anyway, we met with the victims' families. Most of the women seem to fit a profile. Single, outgoing, independent. That's how I'd describe them. Others have used . . . different words.'

'Ah.' Sean sipped his drink. 'Not prim and proper little girls, is that what you're getting at?'

'Pretty much. Some of our colleagues didn't exactly rush to launch investigations into the disappearances at the time. They presumed the women had just run off. The families' concerns were dismissed.'

'You raised this with Kennedy and he didn't react as you would have expected.'

It wasn't a question.

Tom nodded, shifting in his seat to get a better look at his friend.

'You say that like you're not surprised,' he said.

'The only thing that surprises me is your reaction.'

'And what's wrong with that? I mean, we're grown-ups. We know this sort of thing happens. But I thought that a man like Joe Kennedy, who spends his life wondering what the media will think, would be horrified at the prospect of families coming forward to complain about how they were treated by the guards. If we acknowledge their grievances now and are seen to be doing something, initiating some sort of internal inquiry – then at least we're ahead of the curve. That's how I thought he'd react. Cynical, but appropriate.'

Sean shook his head dismissively.

'You give him far too much credit – considering what you know, not to mention what you don't.'

'Say again?'

'Well, let's start with what you've established about Joe Kennedy's character to date. You're dead right about his press-savviness. But, of course, you're several logical steps ahead of him. Kennedy will handle the press effectively if the families come forward with horror stories about the guards. But in his mind, his job is to stop this ever becoming a news item, even if it means protecting guards who did wrong. You want him to pre-empt and prepare for the worst – which is why you would have made a better chief.'

Tom bristled, but knew he had no grounds to rebut his mentor.

'Kennedy doesn't think like you. His fear is that any action on his part could actually throw a spotlight on the issue. More importantly, there's his own background to consider. This is where you've made the fatal error. You were so happy, Tom, to see somebody, anybody but you, taking the job of chief superintendent that you didn't do your homework on who was getting it. If you had, you wouldn't have dreamt of going to him with these particular concerns.'

'What are you talking about?' Tom asked.

'Joe Kennedy's father, man. Christ, I've sweat patches under my arms. Here, let's take these drinks out the back. Would it kill you, Derek, to run a bit of cool air through this place?'

'Keeps your girly wine at a nice temperature, doesn't it?' The bartender had moved on to the crossword and didn't even look up as Sean reached over the counter and retrieved the bottle. He topped up his glass and offered Tom the same.

'Two words, six and seven letters, begin with R and B. Robin Hood's evil brother,' Derek called up from the page. 'Ah, I've got it. Robbin' Bastard.'

Sean strolled nonchalantly out through the back door of the pub, Tom in tow.

'I'm surprised you're not barred,' the inspector said, as they seated themselves at a table in the yard.

Sean peered at him quizzically.

'What in God's name are you talking about? I have a share in this pub.'

Tom's eyes widened. This afternoon was full of surprises.

'Well,' he rejoined. 'No clichés there. A guard owning a pub. You'll tell me next you own a rake of rental properties.'

Sean raised his glass and drank deep, silence his answer.

'Shit, Sean. Maybe I *should* have taken your job. Now, talk to me about Joe Kennedy's father. The suspense is killing me.'

'Got any cigars on you?'

The inspector reached for his jacket and then cursed. He'd left it in Willie's car.

'How can a man who visits Cuba and comes back sporting Fidel Castro's beard not have cigars on him?' Sean clicked his tongue.

'For crying out loud, will you ever just tell me what the *scéal* is on Kennedy?'

'Keep your shirt on. I can't believe you're not aware of it already. Joe's father was a detective.'

'I didn't know that.'

'I rest my case. And he wasn't just any detective. He was notorious. One of the Special Eight.'

Tom's eyes widened. The Special Eight were infamous – corrupt gardaí, the absolute antithesis of what it meant to be an officer these days.

A gang of eight detectives, the men were renowned for dodgy policing practices in the early seventies that led to numerous unsafe convictions. They'd acted pretty much with impunity for most of that decade, despite whispered rumours of beatings, threats and falsification of evidence. By the mid-nineties, however, a number of the convictions they had secured had been quashed and a tribunal of inquiry focusing on several of their cases was established.

The gang had operated more or less before Tom's time, but he'd always been aware of them as an unpleasant footnote in garda history.

He ran through their names in his head now.

'There was no Kennedy in the Special Eight,' he said.

'Joe's dad was Malachy Sutton. Kennedy is his mother's maiden name.'

Sean flicked a fruit fly from the side of his glass as Tom gaped at him.

'Holy crap!'

'Indeed.'

'He was the one who went after . . .'

'Susan Harte, yes. That's the one.'

Tom took a gulp of wine. How had he not known this?

The tragic case of Susan Harte was one of those that the tribunal into the Special Eight's activities was originally set up to probe. Harte had accused several men in her town of gang-raping her one night in 1976. The medical evidence in support of her claim had been overwhelming – one of the assailants had abused her with a beer bottle. The men's story was that Harte was an unstable woman who had consented to group intercourse and cited her affair with a local married man as proof of her loose morals.

But Susan was determined to see the men prosecuted. In a biography years later, she'd claimed that throughout the trauma that followed, not one senior guard had shown her compassion. She was warned that her sexual history would be printed in every newspaper if she pursued the case.

The Special Eight became involved when, a few weeks after the attack, one of Harte's rapists was beaten to a pulp with a baseball bat outside the garage he owned. He died within days. The tribunal established that the man had been fencing stolen cars for a criminal gang and was pulling a fast one with the profits. Because the man was related to a junior minister, Malachy Sutton was brought in to investigate, but chose to ignore the car fencing as a probable cause. He assumed that the recent rape allegations against the man were too much of a coincidence and concluded that Susan and her brother had beaten the man. This was despite her still recovering from the vicious attack she had suffered and her brother having an alibi.

The conviction was sealed when her brother confessed to a crime he hadn't committed. He insisted from the outset that he'd been tortured into making a false confession but he was tried and sentenced.

The tribunal would later vindicate him. Malachy Sutton came out of the investigation very badly.

'You can see why Kennedy doesn't use the father's name,' Sean said.

'It's amazing he's come so far,' Tom replied. 'Do many people know who he's related to?'

Sean shrugged.

'Top brass do. Nobody would be shouting it from the roof-tops, mind. Who wants to rake over the past? But you should always bear in mind, Tom – the Special Eight didn't operate in a vacuum. The seventies and eighties were a mad time, espe-cially with the war in the North at its height. The Garda Síochána was only fifty years old and finding its feet. Many believed the force had to be results-driven and that the end jus-tified the means. Garda attitudes towards the Special Eight generally ranged from active encouragement to tacit approval. Even those opposed to them didn't want to wash our dirty linen in public.

'I've spoken to you before about political policing – well, that was it on acid – and the people who oversaw it haven't all retired or died. Yes, these days the Special Eight is considered a stain on our record, but not by everybody. In any case, nobody is going to blame the son for the sins of the father. Joe Kennedy has worked very hard over the years to get where he is and he's gone out of his way to distance himself from his father's repu-tation. But blood ties run deep. He'll be extremely sensitive to the kind of accusations you're making. Not that he won't deal with them if the media gets hold of the story. Jesus, he'll be after those guards like the hounds of hell, just to make a point. Behind closed doors is another story, though. He never fell out with his father. Which would make you wonder.'

'Christ.' Tom took a sip of his drink. 'Kennedy didn't really say anything that I could pin down as supporting those guards' attitudes, but he certainly left me feeling like I was the problem, not them. And it infuriates me. How did you cope back then, Sean?'

'Behave. I'm only a decade older than you, man.'

'You know what I mean.'

Sean shrugged.

'I got my first promotion in the eighties. I remember the boss pulling me in to have a word about how things were done behind closed doors – after I'd officially been given the title of detective. "It's us and them, son," he said. "It's our job to nail the scumbags and sometimes you need to bend the rules. Just remember, go with your gut and if it's telling you he's guilty, he's guilty. The people are relying on us to get the job done. Show no weakness. No judge will worry about the odd black eye." It gave me a shock, I can tell you. I'm no soft-soaper, you know that, but I'd never gone beyond a bit of pushing and shoving with any suspect.'

'Did you see suspects being strong-armed?'

'Yes. I did.'

'What did you do?'

'The first time – I pulled the detective off the chap. He was being done for a house burglary. He'd taken a telly and some cash and my co-interrogator was ready to put him on life support. Nothing was said to me by upstairs, but the lads treated me differently after that. They'd offer me a coffee and spit in it, schoolboy stuff. It didn't stop me protesting when somebody was going overboard. So they stopped bringing me in for questioning. Tried to put me on desk work, that sort of thing.'

The inspector frowned. It was hard to imagine anybody bullying this hulk of a man.

'Hell, Sean. You were a regular *Serpico*. How did you deal with it?'

Sean exhaled heavily.

'June got me through it. I wanted to leave the force but she sat me down and gave me a good talking-to. "Why don't you stop waiting for somebody to do something about all this?" she said. "And be that somebody. You fix it. Make them change and bring some honour to your profession. Beat those idiots with sheer stamina, you great big oaf." She was right, of course. And I did. I kept at my job and became so good at it that they were forced to promote me and eventually I, and others, began to push the changes through.'

They both smiled at the thought of June's intervention. The inspector could imagine her saying those words, her tone sharp and soft all at once.

'Did you support Kennedy's appointment?' Tom asked the question that had been burning inside him since Sean had stepped down.

His friend scoffed. 'What do you take me for? You know I wanted you. When I accepted you weren't going for it, I recommended Natasha McCarthy, that cailín in charge of the sexual assault unit. She hadn't a hope, though. Too female and too black. They've already got Bronwyn Maher in the second highest top job. Sure, you couldn't go scaring the horses putting too many girls in charge.'

Tom rested his chin in his palm. The situation was a mess.

Sean had harassed him to the point of them almost falling out when he'd refused to go for the chief superintendent's job. But no wonder. He wanted to protect his legacy in the department and look at whom they'd replaced him with. The inspector had been dismissive of Joe Kennedy, thinking that the man was a lightweight. He had assumed that the worst he could expect from his new boss was inexperience. He hadn't considered that the incoming chief might be an impediment.

'Do you think he'll last?' he asked his former boss.

Sean swilled wine around his mouth and swallowed, looking thoughtful.

'No. No, I don't think so. He's a filler candidate. They're still waiting for you, Tom. Kennedy knows it and I think you do too. You just need to say the word and he'll be moved sideways – if you get in before he beds down. Joe is dying to be the architect of his own demise. He's too friendly with the media. His ego will be his downfall. Eventually he'll make a balls of something and then his buddies in the press will rehash the whole saga about his father. Top brass will shift him beforehand, if they get a chance. Will you give it to them?'

Tom studied the wooden table, mulling the possibilities. To stay in the job he was familiar and comfortable with, but have Kennedy or some other unknown quantity in charge, or to take on the responsibility of leadership? Ray was almost ready to move up to Detective Inspector and he'd be leading a great team. Laura, too, could be put in charge, young as she was. But Tom would miss being this close to investigations and he'd hate dealing with the media and the internal politics.

'I think Natasha would have made a great choice,' he said,

not looking up. 'And I'm up to my tonsils with this case. It's hard to think beyond that right now.'

'Hmm.'

The inspector didn't want to see the disappointment in Sean's eyes. And he didn't want to say that what he really wanted was Sean back in his old job and everything to return to the way it was.

'Right, so,' Sean said. 'The case. Fill me in and I'll tell you where you've been going wrong. Then I'd better get back. June keeps forgetting we're married and yet she hasn't lost the ability to smell booze on my breath and give me a talking to. Some things never change, huh?'

# CHAPTER 16

*Treasa, 2009*

Treasa wanted to die. Of that, she was certain.

She didn't know how long she'd been in the cellar, but it had been a while.

She did know that her family would be looking for her.

There'd be some who'd have written her off. 'Ah, that's Treasa for you. She's always on the rip. Probably gone off to Ibiza for two weeks.'

But her father would know something was wrong. Treasa rang him every day, no matter where she was or what she was doing. One time, she'd got on the wrong train out of Budapest and ended up travelling to Russia with nothing but her passport, a travellers cheque worth about €50 and a packet of ecstasy tablets stuffed in her bra. And she'd still managed to find a phone to ring him and tell him she was fine – though it had required giving some old lad in the last carriage a blowjob.

She had to ring her dad daily. He worried about her so much. Ever since . . . well, they didn't talk about that.

Eric would look for her too. Their relationship had been turbulent of late. It had started off as a bit of fun; she'd met him at a foam party in Lanzarote, for Christ's sake. But then he'd moved to Ireland to work in pharmaceuticals, of all the luck, in her hometown in Cork. She introduced him to a few nightclubs in the city, then they started to meet up regularly. He was fun, but as soon as it became apparent that he was looking to get serious, she'd felt the familiar panic. She couldn't go down that route. He was lovely, but she couldn't do it. Not again.

Treasa had a reputation to maintain. She was the mad party animal, unable to commit, looking to shag all around her. Her friends had got annoyed with her over Eric. He was marriage material – tall, dark, a great sense of humour and a fantastic job. They made a great match. Treasa was a beauty – even she knew that, but not in a cocky way. It was just something she had always been. Long blonde hair, big blue eyes and full red lips. She and Eric could have had stunning-looking children.

Her circle of friends were all in their thirties and biological clocks were ticking. What, exactly, was she waiting for, they asked her?

But they didn't understand.

Few people in her life these days knew about Kevin, her soul-mate. He'd died when they were both twenty-one. Just dropped dead on the GAA pitch while playing hurling. Sudden adult death syndrome, they called it.

Fewer still knew that he'd proposed to her the night before. Even though they were still so young and even though neither of them had ever been with anybody else.

'You'll get bored of me,' Treasa had laughed. 'You'll want to be off shagging all around you when you're up winning all-Ireland finals in Croke Park.'

'Never,' he'd said, serious, those big brown eyes she loved holding hers. 'How could I stop loving the most beautiful girl in the world? Who could hold a candle to you?'

And the next day he was gone. She'd stood beside his coffin in the church, her hand in her pocket fingering the silver claddagh ring he'd placed on her finger hours before he died.

So, no. Treasa couldn't settle with anybody else. And, yes, she partied – she had to do something to dull the pain.

His life had been cruelly taken from him. But she had wasted hers. She'd grown to hate herself. What would Kevin have thought of her? He was the first boy she'd ever even kissed, let alone anything else. Now, she couldn't count the number of men she'd slept with. Her life had spiralled and nothing she did numbed the pain any more.

This man, this animal that had taken her, he didn't know anything about her – how she really felt, the thoughts in her head, the dreams that haunted her. Even though he thought he did. He kept calling her a slut and a whore. Sometimes he beat her. Other times, he tried to be gentle. Giving her food. Telling her he loved her. It was all an act. He was a twisted, sick, evil bastard.

Why had she got into his car? Why hadn't she fought more when he drove her here? She'd left work feeling a little better than usual. She was off the following day and was going to pop to the shops to get some clothes for her next holiday, which wouldn't be far away.

And suddenly, all decisions were taken away from her.

The worst thing about being in the cellar was that it had given her time to think, to reflect.

Her kidnapper didn't realise that he wasn't the scariest thing in her world. No. That was what was in her head. She'd done everything to avoid spending too much time on her own for so many years. Now, she had nothing but time. And sober, to boot. She'd come to a conclusion.

She wanted him to kill her.

Something inside her had died when Kevin did. Perhaps she should have had that grief counselling that was offered. It was shock, they said. But it was more than that. Her heart had shattered into a million pieces. Nobody she'd loved had ever died – even both sets of grandparents had still been alive back then. The concept that anybody – especially somebody her age that she worshipped – could just drop dead, blew her mind. And it wasn't just that Kevin was gone. Her whole future had gone with him. The second time she'd tried to take her own life, they wanted her to talk to somebody, but she couldn't. She was afraid that what she had to say would sound so mad they'd stick her in a padded white room.

Yes, she loved her parents, her dad especially. But it was time for it all to stop. And this way, they wouldn't blame her. They wouldn't know that in the end, she was glad. She hadn't betrayed them by doing it herself. It had been done to her.

She wanted to get off this merry-go-round of pain.

Please, she thought. Please. Just make it stop.

# CHAPTER 17

'I think Fiona was seeing somebody, yes. I didn't know her too well. Only that she was one of the Hollands. Everybody knows the family. You'd see her about the place. Since they closed our shop, either myself or Bart make the effort to get to Luttrell village once a week.'

Wednesday found Tom and Michael sitting with Garda Paul Hackett in the large open-plan office in Trim garda station. He and Sergeant Bart Healy had manned a smaller station in the Hollands' village up to a few months before, until it became another casualty of cutbacks.

'Do you know the name of the man she was seeing?'

Garda Hackett shrugged apologetically.

'Bart said she had somebody on the go. She's a looker, Fiona. Not in a flashy, modern sort of way. There's something . . . ethereal about her. Fairy-like. You notice her. I'd say she had the blokes queuing up around the block.'

'Not you, though?' the inspector asked.

The uniformed guard shook his head fiercely, appalled at the suggestion. He pointed at his ring finger.

'I'm newly married, Inspector. Not to mention the girl is only nineteen. She's barely an adult. Despite everything.'

'Despite what?'

'The way she acted, by all accounts. Like she was a grown woman of the world already.'

They were waiting for Bart Healy, the man in charge of Fiona's missing person case. It was now four days since the discovery at Glendalough and eleven days since the Holland girl had gone missing.

They were making some headway. Most of those they wanted to talk to in Glendalough had been interviewed. They were compiling lists of sex offenders in key counties. And they were making their way through Steve Moore's old contacts to find out where Pauline O'Hara's former boyfriend had ended up after he left Waterford.

But the team was no closer to knowing what had happened to the five victims, or to discovering Fiona Holland's whereabouts.

The inspector woke up every morning with a knot in his stomach that felt like he'd done hundreds of sit-ups the night before. It didn't help that he was sleeping in an empty house with no distractions, now that Louise was down in Wicklow with the girls.

Today should see more progress, though. Laura was returning to West Cork to check out the former house of the taxi driver in the Mary Ellen case. In a surprise twist, when Tom had delegated the task to her, she'd requested that Ray, not Michael, accompany her on the trip.

'I've no problem with that,' he said. 'Do you mind me asking why, though?'

Laura went quiet for a moment.

'I don't want you to worry about this . . .' she started, and Tom began to worry. Was this the start of the Ray/Laura romance and was he being primed for future pair-up requests?

'It's Michael,' she said, proving him wrong. 'We sorted it out, but when we went down to West Cork we found ourselves a little at odds about the sergeant down there. The Doyle fella. I'm not saying Michael was in the wrong. If anything, I want Ray to come down so I can see if I'm jumping to conclusions too quickly. If Ray thinks Doyle is straight up, then Michael got it right and I was the one off-kilter.'

'But you think you got it right,' Tom said. 'Or you wouldn't have brought it up with me yesterday.'

'Well, yeah. But better to be sure. Mary Ellen isn't here to follow through on her allegations that Doyle tried to rape her, but if he really is a danger to women, we should be aware.'

The inspector had agreed. And so, Michael was accompanying him. Ray had been handed his golden ticket.

'Morning, folks. Sorry I couldn't get here quicker. I was up at the Hollands' when Paul rang.'

Bart Healy shook the two detectives' hands firmly. He was in full uniform, whereas everybody else in the station was down to shirtsleeves, including the visiting Dubliners. The day was overcast, but if anything the heat had become unbearably close. Oppressive. A good thunderstorm was required to break the spell and it felt like one was brewing.

'How are they holding up?' the inspector asked.

'As well as can be expected. I'm trying to talk Richard out of offering a reward. He wants to put up €20,000 for information. That sort of money – we'd spend the next six months dealing with crackpots.'

Tom nodded in agreement with Bart's assessment of the reward risk.

The sergeant sat down with them and rubbed his eyes. He had huge bags under each one, dark shadows on a pale face.

Beneath the tiredness, he was a handsome man – thick, curly brown hair, a broad smile on a kind face. Young-ish, perhaps in his late thirties.

'You're doing a good job up here, running the show,' the inspector said, reassuring him.

'Well, I'm glad to see you, to be honest. We've had so many resources cutbacks, it's impossible to run proper search parties for Fi. Her family and the locals are helping, but it's not good enough.'

'I hear it all the time. Let's hope the Hollands are right and she's just taken off. But let us assist you, just in case. Can you fill us in on what you know already? We're really desperate to get to the bottom of this boyfriend business. Her mother and brother both intimated there might be somebody dodgy in the background.'

Tom thought Bart stiffened when he mentioned Fiona's brother. He knew he was right when the other man began to speak.

'Yes, well, to be honest, Fi could have been going out with a choirboy and Fergus Holland, and her father too, to be fair, would have had a problem,' he said. 'The men in that family are extremely possessive of the women. Fergus acts more like a bodyguard than a brother. The dad puts Fi on a pedestal, but he's a bit less obvious about it.'

'How do you mean?' Tom probed. 'Is this something you've noticed yourself, or is it commonly known?'

Bart shook his head.

'It's no secret. That's why Fi kept everything from her family, I'd guess. There was trouble a few times, Fergus coming into pubs in the village and dragging her home. We got called in once or twice when he started fights with a couple of local lads, accusing them of screwing his sister – yep, those words and loud enough for everybody to hear, including poor Fi.

'He's always been a bit funny but he went off on one when she had the wee one last year. Got drunk one night in his local – I was there too, as it happens. You should have heard the filth coming out of his mouth about her. Disgusting. She was a young girl. Entitled to have a bit of fun. And to be honest, I think the more upset he got, the more she slept around. Just to prove a point.'

'Jesus,' Michael said. 'Sounds messed up.'

'I know. Richard doesn't need to go around swinging his fists. He's an important man – if you get me. You wouldn't want to be getting on the wrong side of him if you want a job in the county. They mollycoddled and suffocated that girl, the whole lot of them, and as payback, she told them nothing. Well, they're paying for it now.'

'It's hardly their fault she's gone missing,' Tom interjected.

Bart crossed his arms, his posture defensive.

'Sorry. I don't mean to sound flippant. Of course they don't deserve this. All I mean is that, you always knew . . . I don't know how to say this without it coming out wrong –'

'Try,' the inspector said.

'Well, if you'd known her, you'd understand. Something was always going to happen to Fi. You could just see it coming – like a car crash. She pushed her boundaries, was always looking to provoke a reaction, in any form. Everything at home was safe and cosy, but that girl liked danger. And she sought it out. Even when she came to regret it.'

'Regret what?' Tom asked, noting the sergeant kept slipping into the past tense for Fiona. He already had her dead and buried. The inspector hoped he wasn't speaking like that to her parents.

'You asked was she seeing somebody. She was. Keeping it to herself, as always, but one of her girlfriends confirmed it for me. He's a bad one. Older than her. Loves himself and the drink. By all accounts he could get a bit handy with Fiona. She never said it to her family or friends, but the odd bruise was noted and they told me she's been subdued these last couple of months. The thing is, from what I know of her, she'd think she'd be well able for somebody like him. But Fi is a slip of a girl and this fellow is a strapping lad with a nasty temper on him.'

'You know him, then?'

'Aye. She was seen leaving his house in the village the afternoon she went missing. I haven't mentioned his identity to the family yet. I'm afraid Fergus will be down there, stirring up havoc. But he was our main person of interest until all this serial killer business kicked off. Not necessarily that he'd murdered her – we just thought maybe she'd done a runner from him, or he'd promised her they'd go off together. I thought he might try to get money out of her folks or something.'

'I see. What's his name?'

'Stephen McCabe.'

The inspector and Michael exchanged a glance before Tom turned back to Bart.

'Stephen, you say? Not Steve? And he's older than her? What age is he?'

Bart rubbed his jaw.

'Thirty, I think. Maybe his mates call him Steve, I don't know.'

The inspector felt a frisson of excitement. Could this be Steve

Moore using a different surname? Moore would be about thirty-two now.

'Has he always lived in the village?' he asked.

'No. He's like most of us in this county, Inspector. Blow-ins from Dublin and elsewhere. The Hollands are native, but half the village is from beyond the borders. He moved to Luttrell a couple of years ago. He works in a restaurant here in Trim.'

'Interesting,' the inspector said. 'We might catch up with him here then and have a chat. If he was abusing her, sure at least we can give him a scare.'

Bart smiled grimly.

'I'd be in favour of that. Little toe-rag. She deserved better, Fi. Beautiful girl.'

'There's nothing else, is there?' Tom asked. 'Anybody who might have had it in for Fiona? We can't rule out the possibility that her case isn't related to the Glendalough discovery. We're checking the sex offenders' list to see if anybody has relocated here recently, but you'd have local knowledge of that, wouldn't you?'

Bart shook his head.

'I can't think of anybody who was gunning for the girl. She caused a lot of jealousy among females, I can tell you that. Young and old. And, as I said, the brother is a loose cannon. But I can't see anybody taking her. I really just thought, like most of the village, that she'd done a runner.'

Tom believed him. It was the recurring theme of this case.

'One more thing,' he said. 'Why didn't Fiona's file mention that she was a mother?'

Bart shrugged, a red dot in each cheek.

'I suppose it just slipped our minds. You'd never think of

Fiona as a mother. If you knew her, I mean. Her folks are raising the child.'

'Still,' Tom said. 'It's a fact. And the baby's father might come into play if she's not found.'

'I can't see him being found either, Inspector,' Bart replied. 'He's been on the missing list for quite some time.'

# CHAPTER 18

The drive from Dublin had been long. Very, very long.

Laura had agreed to them taking Ray's car for the trip, ostensibly so she could do some reading on the way down to West Cork. But she'd forgotten two things. One, she got carsick when she read for any length of time and two, with no driving to concentrate on, all she could think about was the man sitting next to her.

Ray was wearing large, pilot-style sunglasses and a fitted black v-neck T-shirt, tight at the arms where his muscles bulged. He looked fantastic these days, healthy and happy, with a glow that Laura hadn't seen in him for a while. She had a sinking feeling that he was seeing somebody. What else could put that smile on his face?

And here she was, the prize eejit, lusting after him again.

Why couldn't she help herself? She was a strong, smart woman, professional in every way – and she couldn't stop mooning after this bloody man who had no interest. Each time he reached down to the gearstick, she willed his fingers to brush against her bare leg, the skin visible below the cotton-pleated skirt that had ridden up over her knee. She was fixated on that hand – its strong grip, the little nicks and cuts on his fingers.

He had really masculine hands.

She sighed.

'Are you okay?' he asked. 'It's not too hot for you?'

'It's much too hot,' she murmured under her breath, lowering the passenger window. Yep. What she needed was a cold shower and a bloody good berating.

'Will we pull over and get some air?'

'No. We're nearly there. Just take this slip-road coming up now and we can avoid the traffic.'

Ray had hoped Laura would agree to a pit stop. He was trying to eke out their time together on this trip but she seemed determined to get down and back to Dublin in the shortest time possible. He had played out a scenario in his head where they had to stay the night in West Cork. He'd heard the area was a romantic hotspot and he reckoned if he just had some time to work on her, with that setting as a backdrop, he could thaw the wall of ice Laura had erected.

But it wouldn't come to pass if she had her way.

They arrived in the village a short time later and made their way directly to the garda station.

Sergeant Doyle was out searching for a dog that had been worrying sheep, so they spoke to his colleague.

'Oh, yeah, the taxi driver,' he said, when they asked about the man originally questioned in the Mary Ellen Lehane disappearance. 'Cormac Ryan. I came to the village after he'd left, but I know where he lived. Nobody has taken the cottage since, so they still refer to it as Cormac's. I can draw you a map.'

Laura looked over his shoulder as he sketched an outline.

'Who was the other guard here at the time?' she asked. 'Working with Sergeant Doyle, I mean?'

'That was old Jack,' the guard replied, his face set in concentration as he followed his outline with the pencil to make sure he'd got it right. 'I don't think he was so much working as part of the fixtures, if you know what I mean. One or two cops from the next town over would have come out to help if Ultan needed it, more from the city if it was required. Jack died in that chair you're sitting in.' He pointed to Ray, who jumped as if he had just been told he was sitting on old Jack's lap.

'Could you find out if anybody knows where this Cormac chap went?' Laura asked. 'Sergeant Doyle said something about relatives in England.'

'Aye. I can do that. I'll check with some of the locals here. They don't forget much; somebody's bound to have an old contact for him still – maybe he didn't change his number, wherever he went. Now, there you go.' He handed over the map. 'That should get you out there all right.'

'Won't we need keys?' Ray queried.

The guard and Laura exchanged a look.

'Dubliners,' the officer mocked, and Laura smiled.

'What was that about?' Ray asked, as they walked back to the car.

Laura stopped.

'Look around you,' she said.

He glanced left and right on the empty street and turned back to her, his face still puzzled.

'This village, Ray, is the hub of this area and we're in the throes of the tourist season. See many people? Well, this cottage he's just drawn us a map to is three miles further into the countryside and hasn't been lived in for four years. The neighbours will have a key, but chances are the door will be open and the odd tramp will have been using the place. If they haven't been able to sell it or rent it out, nobody is worried about its security.'

\*

They pulled into the neglected driveway of the abandoned cottage and parked up on a patch of tarmac dotted with weeds and potholes. Dirty net curtains still hung in the windows. The paintwork had peeled from the wooden frames and front door. Several of the windowpanes were broken, tiles had blown off the roof, and most of the front wall had been colonised by a hardy creeping ivy.

The cottage was crumbling. If it lay empty for much longer it would become uninhabitable. It was a shame. They were near the sea now and the surrounding landscape of hills and woods, leading down to a nearby, secluded sandy cove, was magnificent. With a little love and care, the house would be an idyllic spot to live.

'Honey, we're home,' Ray said, turning off the ignition. 'Reckon there's any chance of a glass of water in here? I'm parched.'

Laura shook her head. She could only envision brown sludge pouring out of the taps inside. The group scheme that supplied the area would have cut off the water long ago.

The pewter clouds that had been threatening for the last couple of hours drifted faster in the sky overhead, casting an added appearance of gloom on the deserted homestead. Laura shivered as she got out of the car. The air smelled metallic – of scorched earth and rain to come.

'You won't be long waiting for that drink,' she said, casting her eyes upwards.

He followed her gaze just as they heard a thunderous rumble, followed by the first flash of lightning in the distance.

It's like God is answering my prayers, Ray thought. It was going to pour down from the heavens, the roads would be flooded and they'd be forced to spend the night together in this lonely cottage, huddled together to stay warm. He'd have picked a nicer place, mind, but beggars couldn't be choosers.

'Let's get this over with,' Laura said, her words a cold shower on his daydreams. 'I don't want to be stuck here in that storm.'

She crossed to the front door and gave it a gentle push. It yielded immediately and Laura leaned in, announcing their presence. The deep silence of years of emptiness greeted her in return. She turned to tell Ray they were good to go in and jumped. He was already on her heel, mere inches away.

'Christ, Ray! Don't creep up on me like that. This old place is sinister enough.'

'Sinister? It's just a rundown cottage. You've an active imagination, don't you?'

He walked around her and into the house.

'Get behind me, I'll protect you.'

She scoffed and followed him in – all six foot of him – almost hoping they'd encounter a situation where he'd have to shield her from something.

They moved from derelict room to room, searching for evidence that the previous owner might have kept Mary Ellen prisoner there. Laura had no idea how thoroughly Ultan Doyle had gone over the place when the Lehanes had reported Mary Ellen missing. She'd have laid money on not very thoroughly at all.

They were in the rear sitting room when Ray found something that got both their hearts racing.

'What's that?' he asked, pointing at the wall.

Laura frowned.

'What can you see?'

'Look.' Ray crossed the room and ran his fingers over the decaying wallpaper.

Then Laura saw it. It was the imprint of a door, covered by the faded floral wallpaper.

'Jesus. Well spotted.' Excitement mixed with trepidation as she helped Ray pull a threadbare settee away from the wall.

Together, they ripped off the paper.

Behind it, they found the door, the handle removed.

'How will we open it?' Laura asked, her heart beating fast.

Ray pushed, but he knew it was futile. He could see from the hinges that the door opened into the room. He stood aside for Laura who dropped to her knees and peered through the keyhole.

'We need a hanger or something to get a grip in here and pull it open. That's if it's not locked.'

'Would a pocket knife do?'

She raised an eyebrow.

'I see you're familiar with breaking and entering, Detective.'

'One of my many talents.'

She let him do the job, inserting the knife into the lock, hoisting it up and tugging the door towards them. It came easily.

Behind the door was another obstacle, plywood this time, old and rotting. Somebody had gone to a lot of trouble to block off whatever was in the next room. Butterflies filled Laura's stomach as Ray poked at a disintegrating piece of the wood and made a hole.

'That's weird,' she said, peering through it. 'It looks like a small box.'

'Ah. Hang on. I've just thought of something.'

Ray left the room.

Laura peered through the hole and tried to summon the courage to put her hand in and feel around. There didn't seem to be anything in there, but she couldn't help but conjure up images of fist-sized spiders.

'Boo!'

She leapt back as light filled the space and Ray's face appeared.

'What the hell?' she yelped.

'I'm in the kitchen,' he said. 'You're looking into the back of a shelving unit. It's an internal door for the two rooms. The owners must have blocked it off so they could put cupboards on this wall.'

Laura smacked her forehead. They were idiots.

'Well, that was embarrassing,' Ray said, grinning in at her sheepishly.

She snorted. He really seemed to be enjoying himself.

There was nothing of personal value in the cottage to tell them about its previous occupant. Cormac Ryan hadn't left anything behind – no clothes, pictures or books, not even a newspaper. The old fireplace in the kitchen was covered in feathers and birdshit and the whole place reeked of mildew. A thick carpet covered the floor of every room, even the kitchen, in some places so damp it was like treading on a sponge. The sparse furniture was easily inspected and there was nothing in the rest of the desolate cupboards save the odd piece of broken crockery.

The rooms upstairs were the same. The only thing of any interest was a nest of mice hiding beneath the ancient divan bed.

Laura shrieked in terror as two of the poor creatures fled the scene and Ray dropped onto the bed, laughing.

'You're great value for money,' he said. 'It's like I've taken you to a haunted house. Come on, it's getting too dark to search. Let's get out of here before the Blair witch finds us. Or those giant rodents regroup and attack.'

Laura glared at him, her heart still racing. Her imagination was too vivid. She was well aware of that – in his company especially.

The first droplets of rain landed on the rickety windowpanes as they descended the stairs back to the ground floor.

'You're satisfied that taxi driver had no way of hiding Mary Ellen here?' Ray said, stopping in the hall. He wasn't jesting this time. He wanted Laura to know that, for all his banter, he was taking her concerns seriously.

She nodded.

'I can't see anything Ultan Doyle could have missed. I didn't spot any outhouses or sheds out the back. We could take a walk through the woods – but if there were any small buildings let with this cottage, Doyle would have known about them. No, I guess we have to take him at face value. The taxi man brought her home and he went back to the village. She must have gone missing after that, like Doyle says. I believe her family when they say they didn't see her, but maybe she was planning to leave and something happened on the way.'

Laura was disappointed and also a little relieved. It wasn't like she'd *wanted* to find some sort of macabre torture chamber. It was more that she'd hoped to prove Doyle wrong, show that the taxi driver might have taken Mary Ellen and it hadn't been fair to assume she'd done a flit.

Ray studied her face. He'd seen her enthusiasm and resolve ebb as they'd combed the house and found nothing. He hadn't even met this Doyle character and he was still on Laura's side.

It was then he had the light-bulb moment.

'I have a confession to make,' he said, just as she opened the front door.

'Excuse me?'

'My true blue Dublin blood is not as pure as I make it out to be. My granny on my mother's side is from Roscommon.'

'Roscommon? Jesus, Ray, you don't get more culchie than that.' She smiled, bemused. 'And why are you revealing this sordid secret?'

'We used to visit there when we were kids. I remember the cottage. A little like this one, as it happens. It had a big open fire in the kitchen that she used to light every evening, winter or summer. I remember sitting on the hearth as she rocked in her chair drinking Guinness – for the vitamins and the iron, of course. My job was to sweep up the fragments of logs and turf that had been spat out onto the stone floor. Laura, who puts carpet in a kitchen? Especially a country kitchen with an open fire?'

Laura blinked. 'Not anybody I've ever known.'

Ray led the way back into the kitchen. The light was fading fast and it had grown cooler. The storm, the culmination of weeks of unusually hot weather, had finally broken. Rain lashed against windows that had probably withstood much worse but still seemed on the verge of caving in.

The vacant building had suddenly become more ominous – the possibility of a hidden space beneath the floor of the once homely cottage unnerving both detectives.

Ray flicked the light switch in hope, but nothing happened.

'I can't believe we've been complaining about all that sunshine,' he said, dropping to his knees inside the door. He felt the edge of the carpet along the wall under the skirting.

'It's tacked, but loose,' he said. 'I should be able to . . .' He grunted as he pulled, eventually freeing the dog-eared fabric from the floor.

'Got it.'

They knelt on opposite sides of the carpet and began to roll.

As each inch of the original cold stone floor was revealed, Laura felt her nerves steady. How likely was it that a cellar lay under this solid mass? The taxi driver had only rented this accommodation. He was hardly ferrying in cement-breaking machinery and tunnelling into the ground.

And then, suddenly, it was there. A square wooden trap door, at their fingertips.

Laura released her grip like she'd been scalded and sat back on her heels.

'Christ!' Ray whispered.

They pushed the remaining carpet to the far wall and stood up.

'It's locked,' Laura said, pointing at the rusty contraption affixing the door to the floor.

Ray kicked hard at the lock. It broke on contact.

'Do you think that could be considered tampering with evidence?' Laura asked.

'Do you really want to wait for a locksmith? Anyway, I used my foot. No fingerprints. Now, is a trapdoor in the kitchen usual? Is it an original feature?'

'I haven't a clue.' She started to shake her head, but stopped suddenly. 'Hang on. We're in West Cork.'

Ray shrugged. That much was obvious.

'The Rebel County,' she explained. 'The War of Independence? I know you lot in Dublin think you were the only ones fighting in the 1920s, but Cork and Kerry were sort of holding it together for ye. Michael Collins grew up down the road.'

'Ah. A hidey-hole,' he said. 'For the guerilla fighters.'

'Exactly. A lot of the houses around here probably had secret cellars for stashing guns or hiding on-the-runs from the British army.'

'Or kidnapped women . . .' Ray said.

Laura felt her stomach lurch. She and Ray pulled on gloves and they knelt together, legs touching. He pulled open the door, cursing at its weight. It took all his strength to lift it.

The smell that rose to meet them was fetid – dank and musty air, undisturbed for years.

'I can't see anything,' Laura said, peering in. A cold tingle ran down her spine and she instinctively sat up and looked behind her to check nobody had crept in to push the two unsuspecting detectives into the open hole.

Ray withdrew his phone from his pocket and switched on its torch. She followed his lead and they shone the combined light into the space.

They saw steps, leading to an underground room. It was small, half the size of the kitchen it sat under. And it was empty, bar one item.

In the corner of the cellar was a bed frame.

# CHAPTER 19

'A picture of Steve Moore? God, I don't know.'

The sound of Barbara Gavan's children fighting in the background blasted down the phone line. The inspector waited while she thought about his request.

'Would you pair be quiet, I'm on the phone! I'd have to go through my old photo boxes, Inspector. Neither myself nor Pauline were on anything like Facebook back then, so I don't think there's anything online. I certainly don't have any pictures of him about the house. For obvious reasons.'

'I understand,' Tom said. 'Take a look for me and if you do find one, just pop into the garda station in Waterford City and they'll scan it into the system.'

Barbara promised she would.

'Any joy?' Michael asked.

'She's going to go through her old snaps, see if she has anything. Something may turn up from his old job yet – an ID picture on his file maybe, but this way will probably be quicker. Right, let's make a run for it.'

The rain was falling solidly, the streets of Trim almost deserted as ill-prepared, under-dressed shoppers and tourists dashed into cafés and stores in search of shelter.

Tom had struck lucky; he'd found a parking spot a few doors

up from the restaurant where Stephen McCabe, Fiona Holland's boyfriend, worked.

A waitress met them at the door and informed them that the restaurant wouldn't open for another hour.

'That's fine,' Michael said. 'We're looking for Stephen McCabe. Is he working today?'

She eyed the two men suspiciously.

'Why are you . . .?'

'Gardaí,' Michael cut her off.

Her features hardened.

'He's in the kitchen. Wait here, please.'

'No, we'll come with you,' Tom said.

The busy kitchen was in full preparation mode. Steam rose from pots and pans and heat blasted from the ovens.

'Stephen,' the girl called. A man chopping vegetables at one of the counters turned. He took in the visitors standing on either side of the waitress, dropped the knife and barrelled towards the door at the back of the kitchen.

Michael was too quick for him. The detective had raced competitively in his teens and now played Gaelic football three times a week. As he grabbed the fleeing man, McCabe swung at him, a nasty left hook that caught the side of Michael's head.

The inspector was upon him then, and with two against one, McCabe didn't stand a chance. He dropped his arms in defeat. Tom pulled them behind his back and slapped the cuffs on.

Michael felt the side of his head, his fingers skimming the graze that had been inflicted.

'You little dickhead,' he said, looking at the blood on his hand. 'We have you bang to rights now.'

Stephen turned his head and spat on the floor.

'Fucking pigs. What do you want with me?'

Tom spun the man around until he faced him.

'Where's Fiona Holland, Stevie boy?'

'How many fucking times? I never laid a finger on her. I can't even remember the last time I saw Fiona. She was just some young one I was shagging. A bit of fun.'

The inspector drummed his fingers on the edge of the table. They'd brought Stephen McCabe back to headquarters to interview him. Linda McCarn sat beside Tom, studying McCabe intently. She peered at him over glasses on the tip of her nose, tutting every so often. So far, though, she hadn't said a word and her silence was putting their suspect on edge.

They still had no photograph of Steve Moore to prove if the man in front of them was one and the same.

'So, you didn't see her on the day she went missing? Because there's a witness who saw her leaving your house that afternoon.'

'Who?'

'That doesn't matter.'

'Maybe she called by and I wasn't in.' He shrugged and examined his nails.

McCabe was good-looking. Sculpted cheekbones, big baby blues, wavy blond hair and olive skin. But he had a mean-looking mouth and a vicious tongue.

Linda broke her silence.

'She was a tad young for you, wasn't she – Fiona? Do you like them that age? Impressionable?'

McCabe chewed the inside of his cheek.

'What's it to you, Granny? Do you think I should be shagging oul' wans like you? Like a bit of rough, do you?'

Linda's features remained placid.

'Oh, darling. I wouldn't hire you to cut my grass, let alone tend to my bush.'

Tom's mouth fell open, but it was nothing compared to McCabe's reaction. He was so astonished at the retort that his eyes bulged out of their sockets.

The psychologist was at her best when she contrived to unnerve the other person in the room. Well, she'd certainly accomplished that with McCabe.

'Is that why you hit her?' Linda continued. 'Because she gave you lip? Don't you just hate it when women answer back? Sometimes you just have to slap that cheek out of them.'

McCabe shook his head, slowly. He was still recovering.

'I don't hit women.'

'Not even a little bit?'

'I said, I don't hit fucking women!'

'Enough!' Tom banged the table. McCabe jumped. His front was slipping. The inspector knew his sort. The bravest man in the world with somebody weak and vulnerable. He wasn't so hard when confronted by people who weren't afraid of him.

'We know you were hitting Fiona Holland. I only had to see you in action back in the restaurant to know your default setting is to lash out. Why did you run from us?'

'You're going to try to pin this serial-killer shit on me, aren't you? I read the papers. You think somebody has taken Fiona and that it's the same person who killed those other girls. But I didn't hurt her, or anybody. I never even met any of those women.'

'Really? What job did you do before you went to work in Trim? Where did you live?'

'Dublin. I worked in restaurants here, too.'

'Ever lived in Waterford?'

'Waterford?' McCabe's expression was one of bewilderment. 'I've never even been to Waterford.'

'So you didn't know Pauline O'Hara?' Tom leaned in, examining the other man's face closely for tells.

'I knew it. I fucking knew it. She's one of them dead ones, isn't she? What sort of sick bastard do you think I am? I've changed my mind, I want a solicitor.'

The inspector sat back.

Was McCabe telling the truth? It was hard to know. He was a scumbag, but, on the face of it, a relatively banal one. And yet, the man they were looking for had to be an exceptional liar to have gotten away with his crimes for so long.

'We'll sort out legal representation,' Tom said. 'But why don't you just talk to us, before we go down that route? You're going be charged for assaulting my colleague, but any cooperation you give us can be offered as a mitigating circumstance. Do you understand that? If you've done nothing to Fiona, it can only help your cause if you tell us what you know.'

McCabe glared down at his clenched fists, eyebrows furrowed. He was torn between wanting to seem tough and not wanting to get sent down for thumping a detective.

The pragmatic side won out.

'She was at my house that day,' he confessed, begrudgingly. 'We argued. I can't even remember what over. I was drinking and she was nagging me about something. I might have . . . pushed her. Then she left and I didn't see her again. Next thing I knew, she was missing. That's the truth.'

'Had she said anything to you beforehand? Had she concerns she was being followed, or anything like that?'

He shook his head.

'No. But she wouldn't tell me anyway. Fiona kept things to herself. She was seeing somebody else, as well as me. I knew that. I could smell him on her. She denied it, but I just knew.'

Tom sat up.

'Do you have any clue who it was?'

'Nope. But she was getting notions, so he must have been some big shot. I reckon he fathered her brat. I got the sense things had cooled between them after that, but now they were back on.'

'What do you mean, "notions"?'

'Getting brave, like. Thinking she could say whatever she liked to me. She would rile me up, just to see how I'd react. Like a fucking child looking for boundaries, then bawling when she discovered what they were. That's all she was. A little girl.'

'Who would know if she was seeing somebody else?' the inspector asked. 'Friends?'

'Fiona didn't have friends. She had people she hung around with sometimes. None of the girls trusted her with their boyfriends and all the lads wanted to do was shag her. And the family won't have a clue. She used to tell me about that brother of hers – how he'd look at her. Dirty little pervert, if you ask me – probably looking to get into his own sister's knickers. And the da thinks she's still ten – calls her princess and all that shit. There's something not right there.'

Tom was tiring of the man and his mouth. He wanted to finish up and check if that photo of Steve Moore had arrived.

'Tell me, Stephen,' he said. 'Did you ever give Fiona a bracelet like this, or see her wearing one?'

He held up the evidence bag, straightening it out to reveal the silver charm bracelet inside.

'Nope. Never gave her anything like that. The only thing I ever gave that little slut was a length of me—'

'Thank you,' Tom interjected. 'That's all I need for now.'

'No.' Linda shook her head. 'I can't see it. He's a little shit and he might just beat some poor girl to death one day by accident, but no. I can't see him as a serial killer.'

They'd retreated to the inspector's office, leaving McCabe with a free legal aid solicitor.

'We'll know if he's Steve Moore in a couple of minutes, anyhow,' Tom said. 'I've just got a text saying a photo has arrived from Waterford. What did you think of his description of Fiona's brother, Fergus?'

Linda cupped her mouth and considered.

'How old is Fergus?'

'Twenty-three.'

'And the first victim was six years ago. Fergus would have been seventeen – a bit young, but not beyond the realm of possibility. Maybe he has an unhealthy attachment to the sister and has been taking out his frustrations on other women.'

'Hmm.' Tom pursed his lips. 'But at that age, where would he have kept Pauline before he murdered her? How mobile would he have been?'

'There's that. And also, the theory would hold more weight if all the victims looked similar to his sister. You've five women of very differing appearance. Your serial killer has an issue with a type, not a look.'

'The father, maybe?' Tom suggested. 'He travels for work. His wife told us that. He's a strong man. Allegedly worshipped his daughter – maybe she's an unintentional victim. He snapped because he can't control her.'

'Hmm. Look into his background,' Linda said. 'A successful business, loving wife, grown-up family – it's not entirely ludicrous, but it would be one of the more unusual cases.'

The door to Tom's office opened and Michael appeared. The inspector knew from the look on his face that their theory about Stephen McCabe/Steve Moore had been proven incorrect.

'It's definitely not him. Here's the picture of Steve Moore.'

He placed a scanned photograph on an A4 sheet between Tom and the psychologist. The picture showed Pauline O'Hara's former partner at a party, one arm draped around somebody who'd been cut out of the picture. He had black hair and small dark eyes, too close together, but a winning smile – quite the baby-faced charmer. He wouldn't have passed for even a relative of Stephen McCabe.

'There's more,' Michael continued. 'The local guards in Waterford spoke to Moore's former employer and they say he took a job with another branch of their wholesale firm. In Galway.'

'So he's still in a job where he travels,' Tom said. 'Well, that's something. Just because Steve is not Stephen doesn't mean Steve is not the man we're looking for. Am I right, Linda?'

'Sounds like you're practicing tongue-twisters, but yes, that makes sense.'

'Nope,' Michael interrupted. 'I can categorically state that Steve Moore is no longer a person of interest.'

The inspector sat back in his chair.

'He's dead, isn't he?'

'Heart attack, three years ago. Rowing on the Shannon. He'd been taking steroids, apparently.'

'Right. Well, make sure that good news gets passed on to Pauline's sister. She could do with some this week.'

Michael left and Tom dropped his head into his hands.

'Back to square one,' he sighed.

'You've nothing at all from the bodies or the scene?' Linda asked. 'Nothing from that fat oaf who's meant to be helping?'

'If you mean Emmet McDonagh, he's assisting as much as he can, Linda. Honestly, will you two ever kiss and make up? It's such a tragedy the way you go on, when you have such a ton of history together.'

'What do you mean by that?' Linda's voice was clipped. Tom swallowed, realising he'd made an error. Louise had told him the circumstances behind Emmet and Linda's break-up, but it was meant to be top secret. The psychologist would know he was lying if he tried to wriggle out of this one.

'I know, okay?' he conceded. 'I know what happened between you two. You wanted to leave your husband to be with Emmet and it caused a rift in your family. He decided against leaving his wife and didn't tell you why and then you went around shouting the odds not knowing she'd cancer. It's a devastating story, but it's in the past. Surely it's time to forgive and forget?'

Linda glared at him.

'That's what you know, is it?' She stood up abruptly. Her gold bangles jingled on each arm as she threw her chiffon scarf over her shoulder. 'You don't know the half of it, darling.'

She strode out of the room, leaving Tom sitting there, puzzled.

There was clearly more to the story.

Unfortunately, he didn't have the headspace right now to be delving into Linda and Emmet's convoluted past. He'd two missed calls from Ray. Hopefully that meant something had turned up in Cork.

He was just about to dial his deputy's number when Michael burst back in, cheeks flushed and eyes wide.

'We've contact, boss. A letter. He has her. The killer has Fiona Holland.'

# CHAPTER 20

Ray and Laura hadn't yet searched the cellar. A crime scene unit was en route from Cork City, Emmet McDonagh having secured its speedy deployment.

In the meantime, Laura phoned Glendale village and summoned Sergeant Ultan Doyle.

'We can't rule out the possibility the cellar is just a coincidence,' she said to Ray, as they waited. 'The taxi driver might not have even known about it, let alone kidnapped Mary Ellen and held her there.'

'One step at a time,' Ray said. 'Let's see if our super sergeant found it when he searched the house.'

Doyle pulled up a few minutes later, car tyres sloshing on the wet approach to the cottage. They met him at the door.

'DS Brennan – good to see you again. I don't think I've met your partner, have I?'

The sergeant offered his hand to Ray.

'DS Ray Lennon,' he replied, shaking it. 'We'll show you what we found, then we can have a chat.'

At their request, Doyle had brought torches and bottles of water. By now, they needed the light for inside the cottage as well as for the cellar.

Ray shone the torch at the open trapdoor and the hole in the floor.

Doyle looked at the two of them, bewildered.

'Were you aware that this was here when you searched the building?' Laura asked.

The sergeant shook his head.

'No. But . . . what does it mean? Are you saying – are you actually implying that Cormac Ryan took Mary Ellen and kept her here? I told you already. We have about twenty witnesses who say he was back in the pub fifteen minutes after he dropped her home. It would have taken him half an hour to drive here and back – not including the time to get her into the cellar. Presumably, she'd have put up a fight.'

'What sort of car did he drive?' Ray asked.

'I can't remember. A saloon of some sort. A taxi driver's car. Probably a Toyota.'

'With a large boot?'

Doyle's eyes widened.

'You think he had her in the boot of the car the whole time? That he went back into that pub and sat there drinking orange juice and playing darts while she was locked in the car outside?' The sergeant shook his head in disbelief. 'No. That's incredible. I mean, what sort of psychopath could do that?'

'The sort who kidnaps and murders five women, then buries them in a scenic valley,' Laura said, her voice laden with scorn. 'Did he take any more taxi jobs that night, do you recall?'

Doyle flinched. His eyes flicked to the hole in the floor as he struggled to make sense of the new information.

'No. He didn't. He stayed in the pub for another hour. Then he went home. Alone.'

'It's interesting you recall that so clearly,' Ray observed. 'Was there something unusual about it?'

'Yes,' the sergeant said, his voice hushed now. 'He would have normally stayed until closing time and ferried some of the locals home. He said he fancied an early night.'

'I see. So, when you did come up here to search the house, how did he seem? Were you in this room much?'

Doyle cupped his jaw and nodded, worriedly.

'Yes. I sat at the table. It was in the middle of the room, just over that trapdoor. We talked for a while. He made tea. Jesus . . . he made tea and we sat here drinking it. This can't be right. If she'd been down in that cellar, surely I'd have heard her? She would have called out for help, wouldn't she?'

Ray shook his head.

'That trapdoor is several inches thick. If he'd tied her up and gagged her, you wouldn't have heard her through that and the carpet. And that's if she was conscious. He could have knocked her out, or given her something.'

The other man closed his eyes and groaned.

'Mary Ellen,' he whispered, shaking his head. 'I . . . I can't believe it. It can't be what you say—' Doyle stood up and rushed to the sink, where he relieved himself of the contents of his stomach.

Ray turned to Laura.

'Makes a nice change, huh?' he said.

'What?' she asked, distracted.

'It's usually me vomiting at a crime scene.'

The atmosphere in the incident room was tense. A copy of the letter that had been addressed to Tom was now projected onto the wall. The original was in the lab being analysed by Emmet's team.

'Okay so, first off, I've spoken to Ray and Laura,' the inspector said. His face was bathed in the projector light; the edge of one of the words appeared as though it was scribbled on his cheek.

'They're at the former home of the taxi driver who was questioned during the Mary Ellen Lehane disappearance in West Cork. They've discovered a cellar under the house, cleared of everything bar a bed frame. Now, we can't get too excited. Laura reckons the cellar is an old feature of the cottage – built to accommodate rebels during the War of Independence. It might be that this man, Cormac Ryan, has absolutely nothing to do with our case. A satellite forensics team in Cork is examining the scene, but they have their work cut out for them. Mary Ellen went missing four years ago.

'We're also working with the local guards down there to establish where Ryan went after he left West Cork. He claimed he was going to live with relatives in England, but our job is to establish if he ended up in any of our counties of interest.'

'Sir?' Bridget Duffy's hand shot up. 'Is the taxi-driver thing his method? We discussed before how all of the women just seemed to disappear – nobody was spotted being pulled into a car screaming or resisting. We talked about him posing as a boyfriend, but what if he didn't know them at all, or only knew them as a cab driver? It's the one car that a single woman will get into on her own with a man, without thinking anything of it. And, in a lot of these places, there'd probably only be one or two taxis in operation and the locals would know the drivers.'

The inspector nodded. 'That's a good theory, Bridget. If he was taxiing in their areas for any length of time he'd probably be told all sorts about everybody in the town. People talk to cabbies. He could have selected the women on the basis of the gossip about them.'

'Can we issue any alerts to the public while we're trying to find this Cormac Ryan?' Michael asked. 'I suppose we can't really issue a decree that women stop getting into taxis.'

'No,' Tom said. 'There's not much we can do until we track him down. Of course, we don't know if he was legally using a taxi plate or if that was even his real name. How many taxi licences are there in use in the State?'

Bridget keyed the query into Google on her phone, her snub nose scrunched up in concentration.

'About . . . twenty-five thousand,' she said. 'But a large concentration of that is in Dublin – ten thousand licences are registered in the capital. If you take what's left, you'd have to imagine at least one third of it, about five thousand, are registered in our counties of interest.'

'No, we'd have to work with national statistics,' Tom said. 'He could have got his licence in Dublin before moving down south. Twenty-five thousand. That's a phenomenal number. And, as I said, he could be driving somebody else's taxi or using an alias. But at least it gives us something to go on. We'll need to examine all the cases again and look for a taxi link.'

He turned to face the image projected on the wall.

'So – this communication. We've no way of knowing if it's from our man or a crank. We haven't had a calling card from him prior to this, so we've no handwriting to compare it with. And he doesn't say anything about the murders that would indicate he has knowledge beyond what the general public has been given.'

'He barely says anything at all,' Bridget said.

They all stared up at the sloping script.

Three sentences, twelve words in total. And it sent a shiver through the inspector each time he looked at it.

*I took Fiona like the others. You won't find her. Forget her.*

'There's some trouble outside.'

Ray had come to stand by Laura's side. She was waiting in the kitchen, concentrating on the light now emanating from the hole in the floor. The forensic scientists were working their magic.

'What is it?' she asked.

'Nora and Elizabeth Lehane have arrived. They want to speak to you and give Doyle an earful.'

'Shit. I'll go out to them.'

'Best if you do. Hey, before you go, should I book us in overnight back in the village? There must be a B&B or something up there. It's a tourist area, right?'

Laura couldn't help but shake her head. It was all she could do to stop herself from laughing hysterically. For so long she'd wanted to have this time alone with Ray, when she thought that she might have a chance with him. She couldn't decide if he really didn't know the effect he had on her or if he was a game player. Either way, she was getting tired of the whole silly thing.

'I'd rather go back up to Dublin,' she said, resolutely.

'Why? I mean, it's late in the day already. By the time we're finished up here . . . we'll be exhausted at the wheel. It's a four-and-a-half-hour drive.'

'I'll do it,' she said, 'if you're too tired.'

'It's not that. I . . .' he sighed. 'I thought the boss might want us to stay down here, in case something else needs to be checked. We can't do this drive every other day.'

'Oh,' she said, from behind a smile of ice. 'There was I thinking you just fancied getting me alone in a B&B.'

She spun on her heel, chestnut curls swinging, and exited the kitchen. Ray stood reeling in her wake. What the hell was that about?

'I knew you'd be back.'

Nora Lehane grasped Laura's hands in hers and squeezed.

'Aye. I said it to Elizabeth. "That girl cares." Was it that Cormac fella? Have you found something in there? Can I see?'

Mary Ellen's mother's eyes were wild, in keeping with the rest of her appearance. The rain dripped from her hair and face and she was shivering in a soaked cotton cardigan that provided little protection against the elements.

'Why are you standing out in the rain?' Laura exclaimed, appalled. 'Come into the hall!'

'I told them they couldn't come into the house,' Doyle barked from behind her. 'It's a crime scene.'

'You noticed that, did you?' Laura snapped. 'Better late than never, I suppose.' She guided Nora and her mother in the door and glared angrily at the sergeant as Elizabeth flashed him a triumphant look.

'Now. At least it's dry in here. Look, there's nothing for you to see. We're just searching the house to see if there's any possibility Mary Ellen was held here. But we've found no evidence of that yet.'

'You've found something, though,' Elizabeth said, in response to her mother's crestfallen face. 'We heard about the cars coming down from Cork City. Ye wouldn't have summoned them for no good reason.'

'I know the land around here,' Nora interjected, her eyes

fixed on Laura's. 'I know this area. All of the houses this way have hidey-holes built into them. The men who blew up the army barracks in Cork in 1920 were from this part of the world and their neighbours took them in when they were on the run. That's what you found, isn't it? A place he could have hidden her. I should have realised. I've thought about nothing else for the last four years. Lord, why didn't I think of that?'

Laura sighed.

'Nora. Elizabeth. I'm determined to find out what happened to Mary Ellen. The team I work with will turn over every stone. The experience you had with –' she looked around to make sure he wasn't eavesdropping '– Sergeant Doyle, it's not going to be repeated. As soon as we have anything concrete, we will let you know.'

'It wasn't just Doyle,' Elizabeth said.

'What?'

'Laura,' Ray had come through from the kitchen. 'Forensics want to talk to us.'

'Excuse me,' she said to the two women. 'Just give us a few minutes.'

Laura followed Ray back into the room he'd come from and looked expectantly at the forensics expert.

'Have you found something, then?' she asked.

'Yes and no.'

'What does that mean?'

'We've found absolutely nothing to indicate Mary Ellen or anybody else was ever held down in that cellar.'

The two detectives exchanged disappointed looks.

'But it's not all bad news,' the expert continued.

'How can there be good news following that?' Ray asked.

'Well, that's the point. We should have found something.

That cellar was built for a purpose – storage, hiding people, whatever. At some point in its past, a person or people were in that cellar. We should have picked up something – even historical. A hair, some blood, any indication of human DNA. But we didn't.'

'It's been scrubbed,' Laura said.

'Either that, or somebody built the thing while wearing full protective body gear and nobody has been in it since. You can come down if you like. Take a look. You won't be contaminating anything.'

Ray went down the ladder first.

The ground underfoot was solid, the stone walls bare.

Ray turned on the spot, even though he knew there was nothing to see, bar the solitary bed frame in the corner.

Laura walked over to the sole piece of furniture – the old brass bedframe, bolted to the floor.

'It was probably less hassle to leave the frame there.' The forensics expert confirmed what she was thinking. 'But I'm not sure why it was stuck to the floor like that to begin with.'

'He could put chains on the bolts,' Ray said, and Laura felt her stomach somersault.

She hunkered down and placed her hand on the slats, closing her eyes. Was this were Mary Ellen had lain? Staring at these walls, looking up at the trapdoor and praying it would open? Had it been pitch dark, or did he leave her a light? What had he done to her on this bed?

She was torn from her reverie by a sudden wail.

Nora Lehane was standing over the trapdoor staring down, her mouth hanging open in suspended terror. Behind her, they could hear Elizabeth roar at Doyle to leave her mother alone as he attempted to pull the older woman away.

'She was here,' Nora croaked, her face pale. 'My baby was here, the whole time.'

And then Doyle was joined by reinforcements and Mary Ellen's mother and sister were half pulled, half pushed out of the kitchen. Laura remained frozen to the spot, shivering in the cold stone prison.

She felt as though the ghost of the dead woman was standing beside her.

# CHAPTER 21

*Mary Ellen, 2008*

Something wasn't right.

Mary Ellen could sense the change in the atmosphere. It was coming. Something bad – if it could get any worse.

She estimated she'd been in the cellar for a week. She'd got the feeling he was going to keep her captive for a while, but now . . . now she wasn't sure.

When she had realised she was being kidnapped, Mary Ellen hadn't fought. She'd learned, bitterly, that resistance just caused more grief. Sometimes it was better to just give in.

Her docility seemed to confuse him. When she woke up in the cellar, her ankles and wrists were bound with chains and attached to the floor. Between that and the dark, she'd started to hyperventilate. She passed out again and this time, when she came to, he was standing over her.

'You will attempt to escape in the beginning,' he said, almost as if he wanted her to try. She cowered on the bed. 'But you won't be able to. I'm going to lock that trapdoor and it all depends on your behaviour how often I come down and what you get when I do. If you're good, and if you're quiet, eventually I'll take the chains off. I'll bring you food and drink. But you can't make a sound. No matter what you hear upstairs, you can't shout out. If you do, I'll beat you, do you understand? You'll be staying here with me. If you're good, no harm will come to you. Okay?'

He leaned down then and kissed her on the cheek, like she was his pet. She recoiled, bile rising in her throat. Even then, when she wanted to scream and spit at him, she said nothing. Whatever he expected from her, he wasn't getting it.

The people in her village thought they had Mary Ellen pegged. The downside of living in a small place. Everybody knew your business. If you drank one too many or kissed some man you shouldn't, it wasn't something you'd be allowed to forget. Other girls in other places got to wake up the next morning, cringe, maybe avoid a certain pub for a while, but then get on with their lives.

Not here. In Glendale, people made up their minds early and they stayed made up.

Mary Ellen had learned it was best to let them think whatever they wanted and try not to let it upset her. She knew she wasn't the slut they claimed she was, in spiteful whispers. She knew she wasn't an alcoholic, like her father had been. And her mam and sister knew those things, too. They were all that mattered to her, really.

Words couldn't hurt her.

But actions did.

It had been two years since the Moran brothers.

She'd gone back to the house with them – willingly. She admitted that, not thinking that was something she should feel guilty about. They'd bought cans and cheap plonk in the pub, the three of them. Everybody had seen. She'd gone to school with Ger, the younger brother. They all knew each other. What had she to fear?

Yes, she'd fancied Terence, the eldest. And yes, she'd probably thought something might happen between them. Maybe even that night.

But she hadn't realised what the brothers had planned. When she'd tried to fight them off, Terence held her down so Ger could rape her. They called her filthy names and spat at her the whole time. Then Terence had climbed on, taking over, while Ger poured his drink over her face and flicked cigarette ash on her body. All night, they'd taken turns. The following morning, she had fled, so sore she could barely move.

When she'd reported the rape, nobody had believed her. Even Elizabeth, who loved the bones of her, had made her feel like it was her fault.

'Why did you go back to their house?' she'd asked Mary Ellen, crying in despair. 'I'm not saying I don't believe you, but why did you do something so stupid? Why do you drink and put yourself in these situations? You need to be more careful.'

Mary Ellen had tried to stop putting herself in those situations. She still drank. By then it was less about living it up and more about forgetting. But she didn't leave herself as exposed any more. Except that one time, when she'd let Sergeant Doyle drive her home. She'd smelled the alcohol on his breath, but he was a guard and she hadn't thought too much of it. She hadn't been worried.

He'd pulled over at the crossroads and rammed his hand up her blouse, trying to stick his tongue down her throat and get her jeans off at the same time. He'd whispered in her ear that he knew she was up for it and he'd been waiting to get his hands on her. She kneed him in the balls and he smacked her in the head. Somehow, she had managed to get out of the car.

*She had done nothing wrong.* He was a guard. She should have been able to trust him. This time, when she told Elizabeth what had happened, they went down to the station together and threatened to report him to his superiors.

Doyle had denied it outright; then he angrily claimed that nobody would believe Mary Ellen anyway – sure, hadn't she accused half the village of trying to rape her? She'd asked him for the lift home, not the other way round. He'd changed tack then and tried to be kind. He was sorry if she'd got the wrong impression. She was furious at his deception, knowing that the look in his eyes was one of nervous guilt and shame, not remorse.

She'd known she had to get out of Glendale to shake off her past.

But she'd missed her chance.

One last drink, she'd told herself. One last night drowning my sorrows.

Then she'd got into the car.

How unlucky could one girl be?

The trapdoor was suddenly wrenched opened. Her kidnapper came down the stairs.

It was his face – she knew immediately what he had planned. His expression wasn't angry, or even gentle. He wasn't going to rage at her. He wasn't going to pretend to be nice.

He was resolute.

He stood in front of her.

'I thought you'd fight a bit more,' he said. He sounded disappointed. 'Look, I have to do this. I didn't want to, not so soon. But I have no choice.'

'Please,' she said, starting to shake violently. 'I won't tell anybody. I've learned my lesson. I'll never tell.'

But she knew it was pointless. He wouldn't give her the

chance to prove herself. He pinned her to the bed with his knees and placed his hands on her throat even as she kept meekly protesting. Then she started to shout. And fight. No. It wouldn't happen to her again. She couldn't let it.

Something bad was coming.

# CHAPTER 22

Tom stared at the bedroom ceiling, its white paint cast in a green-grey hue by the dull morning light and wet leaves dancing on the tree branches outside. He watched as a long-legged spider skilfully made its way towards the lightshade, stopping every so often to hang acrobatically from two or three legs.

It was still raining – the heat wave well and truly fractured. He listened to the welcome tap tap of the drops on the windowpane, the trickling sounds from the drainpipe, and felt relief. The high temperatures had made everything about this investigation feel feverish. The cool, calming rain would slow things down, give them time to think.

The spider was dangling precariously from a long silver thread now, his legs working overtime as he spun. Just as well Louise wasn't here to see the poisonous beast descending towards their bed. She'd have a heart attack.

He reached over to his mobile and dialled his wife's number. She answered with a breathless, 'Missing me, are you?'

'I want to say yes, but it sounds suspiciously like you're making love to another man. What are you doing? I thought you'd be in bed still.'

'I'm running on the beach.'

'At 7 a.m., in the rain?'

'We're staying with my parents, Tom. They go to bed at 9

every night. Maria is going out of her mind with boredom. Anyway it's only a drizzle. Maybe we should move to south Wicklow. Enjoy some of this clean living.'

'I'd miss all our nights clubbing and the easy access to hard drugs. How are your folks?'

'At Mass. They go every morning now. Hedging their bets with the big guy. Don't know why – they're in the full of their health. It will be a while before we inherit the mansion.'

Tom smiled, thinking of the tiny bungalow his in-laws owned.

'Have you spoken to Sean?' Louise panted.

'Yes, about work stuff. Why?'

'Ah, nothing really. It's just, I was talking to Mary yesterday. I rang the house and she answered. Sean and June were at the doctor's. She said her mother is deteriorating more rapidly than expected. They're sending her for tests.'

'For what? They know it's Alzheimer's.'

'They're concerned there might be something more at play. She might also have a growth on the brain. Shit! I have to stop, I can't breathe.'

She wheezed to a halt as Tom silently contemplated what she'd said. How much more bad luck could their old friends endure? Was that what June had meant when she'd said it was 'better this way'? Had she been having a lucid moment, referring to a possible tumour?

He sat up with a sudden jolt.

'Louise, are you running on your own on that beach?'

'What? Of course I'm on my own. I don't actually have a lover in Wicklow, Tom. The whole elderly parents thing isn't a ruse.'

'Where's your car?'

'In the car park. What's got into you?'

'Do me a favour. Keep talking to me and walk back to the car. I don't want you running this early on your own, okay?'

Louise said nothing for a moment.

'Okay. But Tom, if the papers are anything to go by, I'm not exactly his type.'

'I know.'

'This one is really bothering you, isn't it?'

He exhaled slowly.

'Of course it is. A serial killer has been operating under our noses all this time and we didn't clock it. Oh – also, tell Maria not to get into taxis.'

'Taxis? There's not much chance of that down here, love. There's only one taxi man in the whole village and, anyway, everybody knows him.'

'Yeah. That's usually how it is.'

'This letter is not giving us much.'

Tom was perched on the edge of Emmet McDonagh's desk, chewing on a sesame bagel smothered in cream cheese. His wife's absence had thrown up one positive – proper order at breakfast time had been restored.

'The paper is common, the ink from a regular biro,' the Tech chief continued. 'There's nothing to give us a clue to the environment in which the letter was written. One thing we did notice – the handwriting is forced – as in, whoever wrote it doesn't write like that naturally. He faked his script. You can see it in some of the characters, look.'

Emmet pointed to the 'v' in 'have' and 'n' in 'Fiona'.

'He inclined the pen to the left and tried to keep the letters long and fluid, but those two are inclined slightly right and more blocky. His normal penmanship is so ingrained, his hand betrayed him and slipped into it automatically.'

'Is that it?' Tom asked, disappointed.

'I have one more thing, though I'm not sure if it's of any use. The page came from a pad. It was a good few blank pages in, so the indentations are very light, but we picked up something that had been inscribed on the pages above it.'

Emmet pulled up an image on his computer.

Tom stared at the letters and numbers, trying to make sense of what he was looking at.

'I don't see anything logical here,' he said, squinting. 'S-pl. 500. F-er. What the hell does that mean?'

'Dunno. We've been playing brainteasers all morning. You can come up with a lot of words for those letters. Simple. Supple. Fucker. Simple supple fucker.'

'Thanks. Very helpful.'

Emmet shrugged.

'I'm not a miracle worker.'

'Boss?'

Ray stuck his head around Emmet's door.

'You look like shit,' Emmet said, jovially. 'Nice of you to let the rest of us mere mortals have a chance with the female of the species.'

'Even with leprosy, he'd have an edge on you,' Tom said, standing up. 'Let me know if you find anything else.'

Out in the hall, he took a good look at his deputy. Ray's eyes were heavy-lidded and ringed, his hair dishevelled.

'How early did you leave Cork this morning?' the inspector asked. 'I wasn't expecting you back up until later.'

'We came back last night, arrived about 3 a.m.,' Ray said. 'Laura didn't want to stay down there.'

'You crazy kids,' Tom said. 'You should have stayed in bed for a couple of hours. You're not much use to me struggling to keep your eyes open.'

'That was my plan but then Natasha McCarthy called. I was liaising with her on listed sex offenders. Did the sergeant handling Fiona Holland's disappearance mention a guy called Vincent Carney?'

The inspector shook his head.

'Not a word. Who is he?'

'He's on the offenders' list. A file full of misdemeanours involving women. He started off flashing and grabbing women's knickers off washing lines. Graduated to groping and then attempted rape. More to the point, he lives a mile away from Fiona Holland and she made a complaint against him last year. She dropped the charge, though.'

'You're shitting me.'

Ray shook his head.

'Let's go out there, so,' Tom said. 'We'll take my car. I'm not letting you behind a wheel. You can snooze on the way.'

'Fair enough. Can I suggest we go via the Hollands'? Apparently Fergus Holland thumped the head off this Carney fella in the not-too-distant past.'

'Yep. But first, we're popping in to see Sergeant Bart Healy to ask him why he didn't give us the heads-up on the local sex perv.'

'To be honest, now, it wouldn't have occurred to me.'

Healy's tone was relaxed, but Tom could see he was on the defensive. They'd caught up with the sergeant in the village near the Hollands' house, after a fruitless trip to Trim garda station.

'He's a bit of a simpleton, Vincent. I checked him out when I moved to the area, ticked all the boxes in that regard. There's no real harm in him.'

'No real harm?' Ray parroted. 'The man was prosecuted for attempted rape!'

The sergeant flushed.

'When you meet him, you'll see what I mean. He's not all there. That attempted rape charge – he wouldn't have understood that what he was doing was wrong. There'd have been no real intent. That's all I'm getting at.'

The inspector observed Healy coolly.

'Nevertheless, you should have told us he lives in the vicinity. It wouldn't be the first time a known sex offender had gone further than his priors.'

'Look, I know that. But, come on, he's not a serial killer. Vincent Carney has the IQ of a child. He's not traipsing around the country luring women to their deaths. If Vincent was holding a woman in his house against her will, he wouldn't have the good sense not to broadcast it.'

'Firstly, as you must be aware, Fiona's case might not be connected to the serial killer,' Tom spelled out. 'This Carney chap could have tried something on with her and got a bit carried away. He had a go before, so why not again? Secondly, has it ever occurred to you that the simpleton thing might be an act?'

The sergeant's face reflected how incredible he considered the latter suggestion, but Tom could see a hint of something in his eyes – doubt had crept in.

'Anyhow, we'll be heading to see him later,' he said.

'Why don't I come along?'

Tom shook his head.

'No, thank you. I think it's better if he realises how serious this is and two strangers are more likely to make that point.'

They left the village. A black plume of smoke billowed in Healy's direction as he stood in the soft rain, observing their departure.

'Something's not right there,' Ray said.

'With Healy?'

'Yeah. And with your car.'

'I keep telling you. It's diesel engines.'

Ray snorted and closed his eyes. He was still playing catch-up with sleep.

After a quick stop at the Holland home, Tom and Ray were back on the road to the family's landscaping business. Fergus was there, according to his mother, keeping everything going while she and her husband concentrated on finding Fiona.

They'd heard of Vincent Carney but claimed to have no knowledge of his supposed attack on Fiona the previous year.

'Do you think it's him?' Richard Holland asked, the veins throbbing in his thick neck as he tried to stay calm. 'Christ, wasn't he done for some kind of sex attack before? I should have thought of him, but . . . the police kept telling us Fiona had probably just run away. I didn't want to think . . . well, not until this serial killer business kicked up.'

'We don't know if he's involved,' Tom said, truthfully. 'We just want to speak to him. You're sure Fiona never mentioned anything? She made a report to the police.'

'Quite sure,' her father replied. 'I'd have killed him if I'd thought he'd laid a hand on my daughter. You'd better warn him to steer clear of me, Inspector. And why the hell has that man been allowed to remain in our village? Why isn't he locked up somewhere he can't get at women?'

'Mr Holland, as I said – he may not have had anything to do

with this. I know it's hard, but please don't go getting yourself riled up.'

The last thing they needed was a witch-hunt against Carney.

'Look, before we go, I wanted to ask you both – have you lived in this area all your lives?'

Richard and Caroline looked at each other.

'Yes,' Caroline answered. 'Why?'

'You've never worked abroad for any period or in another county? You especially, Richard?'

Fiona's father shook his head, confused.

'No. I travel around the country for landscaping contracts, but I rarely stay more than a couple of days in any spot.'

'So your parents were from here, too? You've no family home in any other part of Ireland.'

'Mine are from Navan, but Caroline's moved to Luttrell from Dublin. Why is any of this relevant, Inspector?'

Tom shrugged.

'I just wondered about your own backgrounds,' he said. 'Whether somebody from your past might have had cause to harm your daughter.'

'But if it's this serial killer who's taken her, it couldn't have been somebody in our lives,' Caroline said, staring at him suspiciously.

The inspector just gave a noncommittal grunt.

'We've been wondering,' Richard said, 'if we can give another press conference. Plead for him to bring her back. We want to help. We're going mad here, waiting.'

'Let me think about it,' Tom said.

They found Fergus on the shop floor of the Hollands' huge garden centre. The family appeared to have a roaring trade in supplies for DIY gardeners, if the bustling centre was anything to go by.

'We need to talk to you,' Tom said. Fergus was moving heavy ceramic plant pots, aided by another man. He placed his load on the floor near Tom's feet and stood up straight, his face red from exertion, dark eyes intense and angry.

'Find my sister yet?'

'No.'

'Then what do you want with me?'

'We want to ask you about Vincent Carney.'

Fergus looked like he was going to spit on the ground. Instead he pulled off his gloves and handed them to his assistant.

'Finish these off, then bring in those bags of fertiliser, Charlie.'

'There are five hundred bags!'

'Then get one of the lads to help. Christ! Do I have to do everything?'

The other man nodded and tried to keep his expression neutral. He looked to be in his late thirties and the inspector could tell he was bristling at having to take orders from the boss's charming son.

'We can do this in the office,' Fergus barked over his shoulder at the detectives as he strode ahead.

Tom and Ray dutifully followed. Once inside, the inspector shut the door and peered out through the window blinds. He watched as the employees on the shop floor cast surreptitious glances at the office and whispered amongst themselves.

'It can't be easy,' he said, turning to face Fergus. None of them sat; instead, they hovered around a table strewn with various files, a phone and a desktop computer.

'What?' Fergus muttered.

'Having to deal with that lot when you'd rather be out looking for your sister. I'm sure they're well-meaning, but it's just a sideshow for them, isn't it?'

Tom was trying to be sympathetic. Fiona's brother was prickly, but at the heart of it he was a young man trying to hold his family business together and deal with his baby sister vanishing off the face of the earth.

Fergus's eyes flicked to the window behind Tom. His fierceness wavered. The inspector could see a slight softening in the boyish face hidden behind the beard.

'Nosy bastards,' he said, by way of response. 'Look at them. Little worker ants. They're trying to come to terms with me being the boss, that's their main problem. Dad just comes in to oversee the orders – I'm in charge of everything else at the moment. I'm not as soft as the old man. I don't give a shit if they need the afternoon off for a doctor's appointment or to collect their kids. They're paid to work.'

Tom sighed.

'Alright, let's talk. What happened with Vincent Carney?'

Fergus dropped onto the leather chair behind the desk. He was roughly the same size as his father and yet the chair swamped him.

'He tried to feel Fi up. He scared her. Well, he must have. She told me about it and she didn't tell me nothin'. It's not right, you know?'

'What isn't?'

'A pervert like that, allowed to live among normal people.'

'She reported it, but you still went after him.'

'Only because nothing happened.' Fergus glowered. 'She told her buddy – Sergeant Healy. He made the right noises but all he did was go out and have a little chat with Vincent. He claimed the dirty sod didn't know what he was doing. Then Fiona dropped it altogether. So, I thumped Carney. I only did what anybody would've done.'

'Did he go near Fiona again?' Tom asked. 'Or any of the other girls in the village?'

Fergus shook his head.

'No. It seemed like he'd learned his lesson. I didn't hear about him harassing anybody in the village after, anyway. Why are you raking all this up? Do you think he has something to do with her going missing? Shit – he's not your serial killer, is he?'

Tom shook his head. They were poking at a wasp's nest here. Now they'd introduced Carney into the equation, keeping Richard and Fergus Holland away from the man was going to pose a challenge.

'We're just going to talk to him,' the inspector said. 'Rule him off our list. How come your parents didn't know about any of this?'

'Why do you think? Fi didn't tell them anything about her life outside the house. She wouldn't have told them about the baby if she wasn't growing a great big massive belly on her. Fi was one thing for Mammy and Daddy and another thing out in the big, bad world.'

'But you were trying to protect her,' Tom remarked.

'Didn't succeed, did I? He has her, doesn't he? The serial killer. She's probably dead now. We may as well just accept it. Fiona's . . .'

Fergus' voice broke. Tom's heart went out to him.

'Fiona's gone. My sister is dead.'

# CHAPTER 23

Fergus walked Tom and Ray back out to their car.

'By the way, your lot were on looking for a list of all our employees,' he said. 'I'll email it. What do you want it for?'

'We want to gather the names of all those who know Fiona closely or would have had reason to interact with her,' Tom answered.

'None of them up here know her. She never did anything for the business.'

'Still. She's the boss' daughter.'

'S'pose. Here, I'll write you out directions for Carney's place. It's impossible to find if you don't know what road to take.'

Fergus scratched some notes on the back of a leaflet picked up at the door of the garden centre. Tom accepted the paper gratefully and offered his hand. The young man looked at it like it was a strange object, then shook it, his grip firm.

He stood by the truckload of fertiliser bags outside, watching them as they got into the car.

'He's an oddball, that one,' Ray said. 'Are we going or what? Fergus still has his beady little eyes on us.'

Tom cursed. He'd already turned the key in the ignition twice and got nothing. He was almost embarrassed to tell his deputy.

'You're having a laugh,' Ray said, figuring it out. Fergus

began to walk towards them, the still-falling rain not bothering him in the slightest.

'Did you leave the radio on when we got out or something?' his deputy asked.

The young Holland man knocked on Tom's window. The inspector opened the door, unable to lower the electric pane.

'Not starting?'

'Not a gig.'

'Pop her open. I'll get some jumper leads.'

They spent the next ten minutes trying to bring the Citroën to life without any success.

'If it's not your battery, it might be the starter cable,' Fergus said. 'You in the AA?'

Tom nodded. He had them on speed-dial.

He went through the rigmarole with the lovely Lisa, who remembered him from last time. When he hung up, his face was as dark as the overhead clouds.

'She's sending somebody out, but it could be an hour,' he said.

Ray swore at the open heavens.

'I'll drive you.' This was Fergus.

The inspector frowned.

'I don't think that's a good idea, son. Not with your history with Carney.'

Fergus shrugged, as though it had been a casual offer, but the inspector knew he was peeved.

'Fine. Just trying to be helpful. I'll get one of the lads to run you up. When you get back, your car should be fixed. Charlie!'

He roared at the man still unloading the bags of fertiliser. He was a little distance away but the inspector could see the man tense and mouth something unpleasant.

'Yes, Fergus?' he answered, wearily, as he crossed the car park.

'Give these two a lift, will you? They're going up to Carney's.'

Charlie nodded, seemingly relieved to be escaping the garden centre.

'My work jeep is over here.'

He led Tom and Ray to a black vehicle parked amongst several others. 'Don't mind the mess. I had to do a delivery this morning, haven't had a chance to clean it up. Charlie Lane.'

He extended his hand and the inspector and Ray took turns to shake it. 'Don't worry about that,' Tom reassured him. 'We're just glad of the lift. Sorry to be putting you out.'

Charlie unlocked the jeep and they climbed in.

'Jesus, you're not putting me out at all. I'm thrilled to be driving ye up. Get a break from Little Lord Fauntleroy there. He's always been a shit, but it's gone right to his head now his father has left him in charge. You'd think, wouldn't you, that he'd be a bit more concerned about his sister? I wouldn't be able to eat, let alone put in a working day. All the lads are saying it.'

'You know where this chap lives, do you?' Tom asked.

'Sure, everybody around here knows where Vincent lives, Inspector. I'm going to take us the scenic route, though. There's a quicker road to Carney's but all it needs is a centimetre of rain and the thing floods.'

'You're from the area, are you?'

'Born and raised. Had to emigrate to Britain for a while to get work. I came back here when the Hollands were advertising jobs in the area. I was looking for a way to come home. You miss the place, you know. I'm living in the house my grandfather grew up in. It's the way it should be.'

'I'm a home bird myself,' the inspector said. They were

driving down a narrow road under a fairytale canopy of inter-twining trees. Every Irish generation had been cursed by emigration and Tom knew that the country became greener and more beautiful the further away her children were forced to move. His family had been very lucky in that regard. So far.

'When you say everybody knows where Vincent lives, I assume you mean he has a reputation.'

The inspector glanced at their driver. He had sideburns, giv-ing him an Elvis-like profile, especially with his lip as it was now, raised at the corner in disdain.

'Yep. That's putting it mildly.'

'But he's harmless, surely?' Tom decided to try Sergeant Healy's tack.

Charlie threw him a sharp glance.

'Who told you that?'

'Just heard it on the grapevine.'

'You heard wrong. He might be a bit touched, God love him, but he's not a gentle soul. Vincent is a dirty little bastard. Women aren't safe around him. He's barred from every pub in town for harassing female customers. The man is a menace. I wouldn't want any girl of mine left alone with him.'

The inspector looked over his shoulder and met Ray's eye. Their driver had no axe to grind with Vincent Carney. He was just an ordinary local man and what he was telling them was a far cry from Bart Healy's account. Why had the good sergeant spun a different line?

'There are rumours,' Charlie continued, 'going about the village.'

'Concerning?'

'Carney and Fiona Holland. Apparently he gave her some grief last year. And now she's gone missing and all . . .'

'Has he always lived around here?' Tom asked, neatly side-stepping the loaded statement. Their driver was fishing for gossip, but he wouldn't get it from them.

'He's from here, but he comes and goes.'

'Does he work?'

'Not that I know of. Not regular work, in any case. He might have something on the side, cash in hand, that sort of thing.'

They drove on for another few minutes, the inspector mulling over what sort of casual work Carney could be doing that would lend itself to travelling. Taxi driving was a clear contender.

'This is his place,' Charlie said, turning the jeep down a narrow, pot-holed lane, the untended hedging on either side scraping the sides of the vehicle.

He came to a halt outside a grey pebble-dashed, farm-style bungalow. The property had been built onto, but in a higgledy-piggledy way; there was no real strategy to its various offshoot rooms and the sheds surrounding it. They were ugly, functional buildings, with dirty windows and doors and a general air of neglect.

'Does he live here alone?' Tom asked.

'Yep. Parents left it to him. They died about ten years ago, I'm told. There was speculation about that, too.'

'What sort?' Tom asked.

'They'd built up debts against the farm. It's gone now – Vincent sold it off, but mainly just to pay what was owed. He made a few bob, though, and kept the house and a bit of land behind it. Anyhow, his folks had a bad end. They got into a car in the garage, shut all the doors and turned the engine on.'

'They killed themselves?'

'Apparently. People thought it was convenient that Vincent

wasn't home that night. Otherwise, he would have noticed, surely? Your parents going off into a locked garage, then the sound of an engine running. I'll hang on for you out here, if you don't mind. I can't imagine you want me doing your interview with you, and this place gives me the creeps.'

It was starting to give Tom the creeps, too.

He and Ray jumped out, straight into the sodden mud that served as the man's driveway.

They crossed to the front of the house, ducking under the small porch to get out of the rain. Ray rapped hard on the off-white aluminium door. They waited a minute, then knocked again.

Charlie lowered the window.

'He's in,' he called over. 'I can see his van parked at the side.'

Tom waved an acknowledgement.

'Let's head around the back,' he said to Ray. 'He won't be able to ignore us if we're peering through a window at him.'

'I hope he doesn't have dogs,' Ray said, nervously. He'd been attacked by a dog as a boy and had never recovered his nerve. It was ridiculous, he knew – a grown man over 6 foot tall, and even a yapping terrier could send him into a panic.

They'd just rounded the side of the house when a deafening bang sounded to their right. Stone splintered from the wall of a nearby shed and debris flew in all directions.

'What the . . .?' Ray started. He didn't get to finish. The inspector, reacting swiftly, pulled him to the ground as another explosion erupted against the side of the house.

Tom covered his head as the fragmenting plaster and stone grazed his hands.

'Back!' he roared at Ray and pulled him to his feet. Both men ran towards the front of the house, where Charlie was revving the engine. To his credit, he hadn't sped off when the shots were fired.

They jumped in and their driver put his foot to the floor and tried to reverse at speed out of the drive. The wheels slithered on the wet mud, slowing the car enough to give them time to see Vincent Carney stroll nonchalantly around the side of the house, his shotgun pointed at the windscreen.

'He's going to shoot at us,' Ray yelled and all three men ducked. Mud from beside the car sprayed in all directions as the shot missed its target. The wheels finally found solid ground and the car jolted into action. Charlie kept his foot on the accelerator as they sped backwards a hundred yards. He sat up, pushed the gearstick into first and turned the car, just as another shot rang out, again wide of its target.

'Make for the main road,' Tom ordered. He pulled out his phone and dialled dispatch. 'Detective Inspector Tom Reynolds of the NBCI. Immediate assistance needed. Shots fired at officers and a civilian. Where the hell are we? Charlie, give them directions.' The inspector put the phone on speaker as Charlie shakily issued their exact location.

'We need the Emergency Response Unit,' Tom ordered, when they had the coordinates. 'Suspect is armed with a shotgun.'

They'd arrived back out on the main road. Charlie crossed it, spun the car through one hundred and eighty degrees so it faced the lane, and slammed on the brakes. They sat there, all three of them watching the road they'd just come down, breathing heavily.

'Is there another way out of the property?' the inspector asked, his heart racing.

Their driver shook his head, too shocked to speak. He'd had enough adrenalin pumping through his veins to get them out of there, but now they were clear of immediate danger, he was almost paralysed with fear. The inspector gripped his shoulder.

'You're safe, man. We'll see him coming.'

It took a moment for Charlie to find his voice.

'Shit. I can't . . . Who knew he had it in him? He could make a run for it on foot, over the fields at the back. But there's nothing that way for miles.'

Tom turned to Ray.

'Are you armed?'

His deputy nodded.

'You?'

'Yep. Not sure what use a Walther P99c will be against what he has, though.' The inspector turned back to Charlie. 'We have to watch for him, in case he tries to leave. Is that okay? We'll need your vehicle, to give chase if he does. Is there a nearby house you could go to?'

'I . . . I live n-near here,' Charlie stammered, as red blotches broke out on his face. He shook his head. 'Sorry, I wasn't expecting that. Can you handle the jeep?'

'We'll be grand. Try to stay off the road and if you hear any vehicles speeding towards you, take cover, okay? We'll get the car back to you.'

'Don't worry about it,' the other man said. He shook Tom's hand. 'Good luck.'

With that, he jumped out of the car and broke into a sprint.

'Jesus, who knew Usain Bolt was driving us?' Ray said. He climbed into the front and familiarised himself with the jeep's controls. 'Not being funny, Tom, but I've never been so thankful for your dodgy car. If that chap hadn't been with us and kept this car running we'd never have got out of there alive.'

Tom kept his eyes focused straight ahead. His hands were

covered in cuts and grazes, the only damage sustained in the attack.

'Didn't you find anything odd about what just happened, Ray?'

'What do you mean?'

'Well, he's either a terrible shot or he was just firing to scare us. He missed four times.'

His deputy snorted. The shots had been close enough for him.

'Tom, if he doesn't come barrelling down this lane and we resolve this without either of us copping it – I'm asking Laura out on a proper date.'

'Your life flashing before you, is it?' the inspector said, but he was only half-joking. He'd have been happy himself to be home with Louise right now.

They heard the first siren after twenty minutes, with no sign of anyone or anything emerging from the Carney property. The cars started to arrive – the Emergency Response Unit and the regional support teams. Joe Kennedy had already rung Tom in full support mode. The inspector was short with him, his memory long. He knew how much Kennedy would enjoy all this excitement and it left a bitter taste in his mouth. He'd turn up when the situation had been brought to a conclusion and none of the viewers of the Six One news that night would know that the chief superintendent had been cosy and safe in his office when Tom and Ray and some innocent bystander were being shot at.

The inspector was engaged in conversation with the head of the ERU, Jim Knowles, when Sergeant Healy turned up.

'Harmless, you said,' Ray snapped, as the man approached.

Healy held his hands out in a conciliatory manner, his face wan and worried.

'I'm sorry. I truly am. I'd no idea he was capable of this. Can I help at all?' he addressed this to the ERU chief. 'I know him.'

'Is he likely to talk to you? We'd prefer a family member if possible.'

'He has no family left.' Healy shook his head.

Knowles looked to Tom.

The inspector shrugged.

'We can't assist. Last time I went in there, he tried to shoot me. Sergeant Healy might be your best chance.'

'Are you confident to approach the house?' the ERU chief asked. 'We can get you kitted out and there'll be full support from all sides.'

Healy nodded, clearly anxious to provide aid.

The rain had stopped and Tom and Ray sat resting against the bonnet of the jeep. They had the frustrating job now of waiting. There was nothing else they could do.

'Do you think it's him?' Ray asked.

'I hope it is,' Tom said. 'It's the only reason I can think of for his reacting like that. And I hope he hasn't done a runner.'

His phone rang. It was Louise.

'I'm safe,' he said immediately upon answering. He'd texted her to tell her where he was so she wouldn't be alarmed when she heard the news.

'Are you still there?'

'Outside. The ERU have gone in.'

'Can't you leave?' she asked. 'Why are you hanging around?'

'It's my job, pet. The lads will get it sorted.'

'Tom Reynolds, you are to come home safe tonight. Do you hear me? I'm packing the car and we're on our way back to Dublin.'

'We'll be fine,' he answered. 'I love you.'

'I love you too.'

Ray looked at his own phone, a shit-eating grin spreading across his face.

'What has you so happy?' the inspector asked.

'I sent Laura a text. I've three missed calls and a message asking if I'm okay. You've fallen off the map, you don't even get a look-in. Who knew getting shot at could generate such good luck?'

'Ring her back, you silly bugger.'

He watched as Ray slinked off, phone to his ear, beaming.

Jim Knowles signalled and the inspector walked over to the ERU command post, set up in the back of one of their vans. The communications radio was issuing static as the back-up officers waited for information from the scene.

It crackled as it came to life.

'Sergeant Bart Healy is in situ and approaching. He's calling out to house . . . he's announced himself.'

There was silence, each of those present holding their breaths and all praying they wouldn't hear gunfire. The inspector was unsure about Healy, but he didn't want the man to come to any harm. Especially considering the bravery he was displaying.

'Somebody is shouting back. Yes – suspect is in the house. He's engaging with officer.'

Silence again.

'Hold steady.'

Silence.

'Officer is speaking. Suspect is quiet.'

Static.

'Okay, lads. Keep alert. Officer has asked suspect to emerge. Suspect has confirmed he is coming to the front door.'

Tom could feel his heart thumping.

'Door opening . . . suspect in frame. He's empty-handed. I repeat, empty-handed. All eyes stay trained.'

Static.

'Suspect allowing officer to approach person. He's . . . turning around . . . has offered wrists. And he's cuffed. Stand down, lads. Good job.'

Knowles gripped the inspector's shoulder.

'Thank God, hey?'

Tom nodded, feeling bewildered.

What the hell had just happened? Just over an hour had passed since Carney had pulled his stunt. Then Healy turns up and the man walks out of the house and offers himself up for arrest in minutes? Tom had thought they were on course for a siege of some sort.

This wasn't right. Something was very off about the whole scenario.

# CHAPTER 24

Tom and Ray stayed behind at the scene with a team of uniforms as Vincent Carney was taken to headquarters. Laura and Michael would conduct an initial interview to see if he was willing to talk, while his house and land were searched.

The inspector felt his pulse quicken as they walked towards the house – both from the lingering memory of being shot at and the possibility that they might find Fiona Holland there.

'There are a lot of outhouses,' Ray said. 'Plenty of places to hide somebody.'

Tom murmured agreement. He prayed they'd find Fiona alive. She'd disappeared less than two weeks ago and they'd speculated about the possibility of the killer keeping his victims alive for a period of months. But everything felt wrong about this situation. Why had Carney given himself up? What had he done in the intervening period between shooting at them and Healy's arrival?

Hopefully, he hadn't been tidying up loose ends.

They split up to conduct the search. Tom and Ray took the main house. They ripped up all the downstairs carpets, but found nothing. The only space inside the house to hide somebody was the attic, and that was empty bar old cardboard boxes and bin bags stuffed with clothes.

The house was clean and tidy inside, if old-fashioned. The curtains, flooring and furnishings all dated to the seventies.

They found a stash of pornography in what appeared to be Carney's bedroom.

'It's pretty normal stuff,' Ray said, flicking through the magazine he was holding. 'He's a boobs man. Nothing hardcore.'

The inspector walked to the next room. The prospect of finding Fiona here was diminishing with each passing moment. He opened the second bedroom door and froze.

A cold chill crept down his back as he took in the sight before him.

'How long ago did Charlie Lane say Carney's folks had died?' he called out to Ray.

'Ten years.' His deputy appeared behind him.

Tom walked into the room to give him a better view.

'Jesus Christ,' Ray whispered. 'Looks like we've stumbled into the Bates Motel.'

To the unsuspecting visitor, the room would have seemed perfectly normal.

Only those who knew how long Carney's parents were dead would find it disturbing.

The large divan was covered with a floral bedspread. Blush-pink curtains were open at the window; a deep-pile beige rug sat atop a rose-coloured carpet. A dressing table was covered with various perfume bottles, make-up and ladies' accessories. Beside that stood an old trouser press, a pair of grey slacks draped over its wooden top.

Two outfits had been laid out on the bed. A billowy teal dress, beside a set of off-white older woman's pants and a bra; and a gentleman's dark suit, over a pale blue dress shirt.

'This is messed up,' Ray said. He walked into the en suite. 'He has the toothbrushes laid out beside the toothpaste. It's all ready to go. There are glasses of water on the bedside lockers. What was he at? Are you thinking what I'm thinking?'

'What?'

'Did he bring the women here and make them play at being Mammy and Daddy?'

'We need to talk to Linda,' Tom said. 'Either he really misses his folks, or your theory is correct.'

They went downstairs and checked with Ian Kelly to establish what was happening in the search of the rest of the property.

Nothing had been found in any of the buildings outside.

'We'll leave you in charge of the grounds search,' the inspector told Ian. 'We need to get back to HQ and have a chat with the suspect. I'll take that chap's jeep back up to the garden centre and collect my car.'

'Anything upstairs?' Ian asked.

Tom and Ray exchanged a glance.

'Best you take a look yourself,' Ray said. 'Just so you know, if you find any mummified remains of an elderly man and woman about the place – that'll be Carney's folks.'

'He's refusing to talk to us.' Michael greeted them with the bad news when they landed back in headquarters. 'If you ask me, he doesn't seem right in the head. Did you find anything out at the house?'

'Not what we were expecting,' Tom replied.

The inspector had taken pictures on his phone inside the sinister bedroom and sent them through to Linda McCarn, then rang her as they drove to explain their context.

'Is that the behaviour of a serial killer?' Tom asked.

'It could be,' she said. 'You'd be surprised, though, at the many strange ways people deal with grief. If the man's parents committed suicide, the shock of that could have led to a reaction that strikes you or me as odd. But he's not alone. There are so many people who, when loved ones die, won't throw out their clothes and belongings and yes, sometimes they even keep their rooms exactly as they were before they died. Leaving out the clothes is peculiar but again, it might just be a symptom of a mind greatly disturbed by sudden loss. It seems strange to you because of the context in which you were searching his house but he could just be in denial.

'Of course, serial killers are extremely sick individuals. If it is Carney, who knows what games he plays with his victims? We don't know why he keeps the women so long – it might be that he's making them take on the role of his mother.'

'Ray said it reminded him of – what's it called, Ray? *Psycho*, that was it. Norman Bates.'

'Darling, you do know that's a film, right?' Linda snorted. 'Sorry, I'm being facetious. Many movies about serial killers are based on real-life killers. Look, I'm due to give a lecture now, but I'll rush it and get to headquarters straight after. I'll brief you on what to ask and watch in on your interview with Carney. See if he gives anything away.'

But according to Michael, Vincent wouldn't be giving them anything.

'Where's Laura?' Ray asked.

'She's on a call,' said Michael. 'Said she had to follow up on something from Cork.'

Ray had been hoping to see her. During their quick call earlier he'd heard real concern in her voice (she'd even got round to asking after Tom). He'd mentioned that he wanted to talk to her later. He was determined to lay all his cards on the table, as soon as he got the opportunity – and before his nerve left him.

'Has Carney asked for a solicitor?' Tom queried.

'Not yet.'

'Have one on standby, just in case. I don't want to be accused of not doing this by the book.'

They made their way to the interview room, grabbing coffees en route. Neither man had eaten since that morning and Ray, despite and perhaps because of the burst of energy during the afternoon, was flagging from his lack of sleep the previous night.

'We'll speak to him, then you head home,' Tom told his deputy.

Ray nodded and gulped the coffee in the hope that it would perk him up.

Carney's hands were cuffed. He'd placed them on the table and rested his head down between his arms onto its cool surface.

The inspector placed the third coffee he'd picked up in front of the suspect.

'Sorry. Wasn't sure what you drank, so I just got you what I was having. Hope you like milk in it.'

He stared at the top of the man's head, the mousy brown hair greasy and matted to his skull. Tom had yet to get a proper look at Carney. It was hard to register somebody's facial features when they were pointing a shotgun at you.

The man looked up, his pale blue eyes expressionless. He had small, almost feminine features – plump red lips, eyelashes so dark they appeared as though he was wearing mascara, soft, fleshy white cheeks.

He looked like he wouldn't hurt a fly.

'Told the girl,' he croaked. 'The pretty one, with the curly hair. I'll only speak to Bart. Get me Bart.'

Ray flinched at Carney's mention of Laura. He didn't want this attempted rapist thinking of her as pretty.

'Bart isn't coming,' Tom said. 'Why don't you talk to us, Vincent?'

'Nope.'

The man put his head on the table again.

'You're aware that you can have a legal representative present for this interview, aren't you?' Tom confirmed.

Nothing.

The inspector lowered his voice and spoke again, very gently.

'You're in a lot of trouble, Vincent. You shot at members of An Garda Síochána. That's a really serious offence. Don't make this any worse for yourself. Why did you fire the gun at us?'

The other man remained silent.

'We found your mother and father's room,' Tom said. 'You've kept it lovely for them, Vincent. I imagine they'd be very proud of you.'

The man stirred. He lifted his head a few inches from the table and peered at Tom from under wet lashes. He was crying.

'You think I'm a retard, don't you?'

The inspector shook his head.

Any engagement was good. Just get him talking.

'Why would I think that?'

'They all do. Up in the village. They think I'm slow. Especially the . . .'

'Who, Vincent?'

He'd clamped his lips shut again. Carney's words were slow, his speech deliberate. The man did come across as having some sort of intellectual incapacity, but it could all be an act.

Tom took a deep breath. His parents. That was the key.

'Your folks didn't think you were slow.'

Vincent shook his head.

'Nope. They loved me.'

'And you loved them. Is that why you keep their room so nice? Do you think they'll come back?'

The other man's face was scornful.

'Can't come back. They're dead. 'm not stupid.'

'I know. It's just, sometimes, when we lose somebody, it can be very hard to let them go. To accept that they're not going to return. Especially when they die unexpectedly. Your parents died suddenly, didn't they?'

''Twas an accident. They didn't mean to. Mammy and Daddy wouldn't have wanted to leave me. I just like to keep their stuff nice. So they'll know. Up in heaven, like. I'm a good man.'

Tears welled in Carney's eyes again and he tried to wipe them, awkwardly, because his wrists were bound.

'Ray, take those cuffs off,' Tom said.

His deputy circled the table and removed the restraints.

Carney kept his eyes on Tom. When the cuffs were off, he rubbed his wrists and reached out for the drink. He raised it to his lips, then screwed up his face with distaste.

'Bitter,' he said, spitting the liquid back into the cup.

'Sorry,' Tom said. 'Our canteen isn't the best. Will I send for some sugar?'

'Never had coffee before. Mammy didn't like me to have it. Tea with two sugars and a hot cocoa at night.'

'I see.'

Ray stood again and opened the interview-room door.

'Can we get a tea with two sugars, please?' he asked the guard outside.

'There, we'll get you sorted,' Tom said.

The other man blinked. He bowed his head, a sign of gratitude.

'Sorry I shot at you. I was scared. I wouldn't have hurt you.'

'You didn't just miss, then?' the inspector probed. 'You knew what you were doing?'

Carney snorted.

'Never miss.'

That solved one puzzle.

'Vincent, you've been questioned by the guards before, haven't you? You were even convicted for assaulting a girl.'

Carney shrugged.

'I didn't mean to do nothing bad. I'm a good-looking man. Mammy always told me. I have a house. 'm not stuck for money. I can get married. I was telling the girl that. I did nothing wrong. I just wanted to have sex. But she got upset.'

'When you said the people in the village made fun of you – who in particular upset you?'

A pause.

'All the girls. Mammy said I'd be a heartbreaker when I grew up. But I'm not. They laugh. When I try to buy them a drink or kiss them, they laugh and push me away. Call me names. "Fucking retard". "Stupid 'capper".'

'Did Fiona Holland call you names?'

Vincent stared down at the table.

'She had pretty hair. I touched it. I wanted to hold her. But I made a mistake.'

'What was that, now?'

'I called her Fi.'

'What was wrong with that?' The inspector leaned forward in his seat, barely able to breathe. He didn't know if this was a confession to the incident last year, or something more recent. 'What did she do when you touched her?'

'She spat at me. "Only my fucking family call me Fi, you fucking loser. Get off me." Pushed me away.'

'And what did you do, then?'

'Nothing.'

'Nothing? You didn't push her back? It sounds like she was very mean to you, Vincent. Didn't you want to hurt her, like she'd hurt you?'

Carney shook his head adamantly.

'Didn't want to hurt her. I'd never hurt a girl. Mammy said real men don't hit girls. I wouldn't have hurt Fiona. You think I killed her, don't you? *He* said. I'm not talking to you. Want Bart.'

'Is Bart your friend?'

'He's my pal. Gives me beer and magazines. I'll talk to Bart. Only him.'

Tom tried a few more tacks but realised after a few minutes that they were getting nowhere.

They left Carney and made their way to the incident room.

Linda and Laura were waiting for them.

The inspector turned to Ray.

'Go home,' he said. 'I'll finish up. You're exhausted. We can resume with Carney in the morning, maybe get Healy in and see if he'll tell him something he won't tell us.'

Ray met Laura's eye. He really wanted to talk to her, but didn't see how he could with everybody still around. Deflated, he turned on his heel.

He'd made it a few steps down the hall when he heard his name being called. Laura had stepped out of the room and was walking towards him.

'Hi,' he said, walking back to her. She'd plaited her unruly curls and was fiddling with the hair poking out at the end of the bobbin. It made her look younger, and nervous. Ray's heart beat faster.

'Good to see you made it out of the O.K. Corral,' she said. 'You had us all worried there for a bit.'

He smiled, shyly.

'Tom is sending me home.'

'I heard him. Sorry I made you drive back up from Cork last night. It wasn't fair. I got a kip in the car, but you must be wrecked.'

'Ah, I'm okay. Can we, eh, catch up tomorrow?'

'Sure.' Laura sounded uncertain. What did he mean by catch up? On the day's events, or something else? He'd said he wanted to talk to her earlier. She'd thought he meant something serious.

He, in turn, studied her face, watching as her expression transformed from hope to confusion to disappointment.

It was like somebody had opened the curtains and let light stream into the room. Ray felt like smacking himself on the head.

Jesus, he'd been an idiot. Tom was right. All this time, Laura hadn't gone off him. She'd just been waiting.

'I'd really like it if we could . . .'

'Laura! Where are you?' the inspector yelled from inside the meeting room.

She shrugged at Ray and made to go back in the door, but he grabbed her arm.

'Wait. He can wait. I'd like it . . . will you . . . shit! Come for a drink with me when all this calms down. Just us. Alone. I mean, I'd like to spend some time with you. If that's okay with you.'

At last. He'd put it out there. Clumsily, but he'd said it.

Laura's face flushed, the corners of her lips tugging upwards.

'I'd like that,' she said. She turned and headed back into the incident room.

Ray felt his heart soar. He made his way down the corridor, a bounce in his step.

'Over here, Laura,' Tom said and beckoned her into the far corner. She perched on the desk beside him and Linda, feeling almost giddy at what had just happened and trying not to give anything away.

'Well, Linda, what did you think?'

'He's a disturbed man, that's not in doubt,' the psychologist replied. 'It may be an act, but he really does appear to have an intellectual disability of some sort. You'll need to requisition his medical records to establish it for certain – though it might not be as clear cut as that.'

'Meaning?'

'A mild mental condition could have gone unnoticed. He's what? Mid-thirties? The state wasn't as good at spotting this stuff back in the eighties, when he was a child and should have been diagnosed. He may have been pegged as a bit slow, a tad peculiar.'

'I don't think he's faking it,' Tom said. 'That doesn't mean he's not our man, but my instincts are telling me he's not capable of what this killer has done. I can't see him being organised enough.'

'If he's faking it, he absolutely is your man, because that was a compelling performance. He has me convinced, initially in any case. But I'll sit down with him myself and study him for a bit. It's very difficult to maintain an act for any length of time under close supervision.'

The inspector stroked his beard.

'We'll get the ball rolling on his medical records tomorrow. It's late now and I can't think any more without some dinner. Laura, what were you following up on in Cork?'

'Something Elizabeth Lehane said, but I won't know anything definite until the morning. I have somebody down there checking it out for me.'

'Let's call it a day, then. They found nothing in the search of Carney's property after we left, so if he did take Fiona, he brought her somewhere else. Maybe his pal Healy knows where. We'll find out tomorrow.'

# CHAPTER 25

Tom texted his wife to tell her he was on his way home and would pick up dinner. A message came back ordering Singapore noodles, hoisin duck, prawn toast and spicy chicken wings for her and Maria. He wasn't getting any special treatment after the trauma of the shooting, that was for sure.

'Dad, you scared the living daylights out of us,' Maria said, meeting him at the door. She had Cáit on her hip, the tot ready for bed in a soft pink babygro, freshly washed and smelling wonderful.

'Gan-gan,' she greeted Tom, with outstretched pudgy arms. He took her and planted a big wet kiss on her cheek, squeezing her a little tighter than usual.

'I missed you! How's Granddad's little monkey?'

'Teeties?'

'What does she want?' he asked, handing her back to Maria.

'Ignore her. Great Granny and Granddad kept giving her jellies in Wicklow. She's asking you for sweets.'

Maria brought the baby upstairs as Tom made his way into the kitchen.

Louise had set out plates and cutlery and was uncorking a bottle of 2008 Alabaster Tempranillo that they'd received as a present for their most recent wedding anniversary.

'You're breaking out the good stuff,' Tom observed, putting the bag of food down.

His wife crossed the room and wrapped her arms around him in a bear hug.

'Hey,' he said, holding her tightly. 'I'm fine. Really.'

'Tom Reynolds, you got shot at four times and I just saw the state of your hands.' She pulled back and took them in hers, kissing the knuckles where they'd been cut and grazed by the exploding wall fragments.

'You put the heart across me, love. Did you even read that text you sent me?'

'What do you mean?'

'What do I . . . "Man shooting at Ray and me, still at scene, but alright." That's what I mean, you bloody idiot.' She dropped his hands and pushed him in the chest.

He couldn't help laughing.

'Sorry,' he said, seeing the injured look on her face. 'It does sound funny when you say it back. I wasn't thinking, I just wanted to forewarn you.'

She tutted, but let him hug her again.

'If I'd known we were opening a € 140 bottle of wine I'd have picked up something fancier than Chinese,' Tom said, as he removed the foil trays from the brown-paper carrier bag.

He stopped complaining after the first sip of the alcohol. It would make anything taste good and seemed to work particularly well with his roast pork kung po. Who knew?

Later, when his wife and daughter had gone to bed, Tom sat in the back garden and smoked one of his remaining Cuban cigars while he admired the twinkling stars overhead. The rain had cleared, leaving a still sky and pleasant night.

His brain hadn't switched off yet. The events of the day had jarred with him – he knew there was something he wasn't seeing properly. He'd never sleep at this rate, so he had no option but to stay up until he figured out what it was that was bugging him.

Bart Healy hadn't always worked in the Meath area, yet he and Vincent Carney had struck up a rapport – so much so that the man was happy to give himself up as soon as Healy asked him to. But there was something else Carney had said, something about Fiona. What was it?

Tom closed his eyes, inhaling the rich cigar smoke and heady smell of the night-blooming jasmine growing in pots beside the French doors behind him.

As was always the way, as soon as he started to relax, it came to him.

A rushing noise filled his ears, the sound of his own blood flooding to his head.

*Only my family call me Fi.*

That's what Carney claimed Fiona had said to him.

But somebody outside her family had called her Fi, and it wasn't Stephen McCabe, her on/off boyfriend.

It had been Bart Healy.

The following morning, Tom summoned his team to his office.

'Why are we meeting here?' Michael asked, the last to arrive.

'I don't want the uniforms downstairs to hear this,' Tom said. 'Not until I've discussed it with you five.' His real fear was that somebody in the wider team would report the latest development back to Chief Kennedy before the inspector had all his ducks in a row. After the lecture about undermining colleagues, Tom didn't think his boss would respond too well to what the inspector planned next.

'I have something big to report from Cork,' Laura blurted out. She wrung her hands together, anxiety writ large on her face.

'We'll get to it in a moment,' Tom said, then proceeded to fill them in on his theory. Out of the corner of his eye, he noticed Laura getting more antsy as he spoke.

'Okay, I'm just playing Devil's advocate here, but isn't it a bit of a jump to think that Healy could be the other man Fiona was having a relationship with, and perhaps our killer, just because he calls her Fi and not Fiona?' Ray asked.

'On that alone, yes, it's a flying leap,' Tom said. 'But it got me thinking. Healy seems to know a lot about Fiona and said he'd got the information from friends – but what have people close to Fiona being telling us for the last few days? That the girl didn't have any real friends. That Fiona kept stuff to herself. None of her family knew about Stephen McCabe, but Healy did. We haven't found one proper "friend" to interview yet who could tell us she was seeing somebody. In addition, she went to Healy when Carney attacked her. From everything we've heard about Fiona, she doesn't strike me as somebody who'd go running to the guards too often.'

'Sir, I really need to tell you about the Cork thing,' Laura said, fidgeting. 'It's more relevant than ever now.'

'Sorry, Laura. Go for it.'

'Well, when we made the discovery in the taxi driver's house, the Lehanes arrived. They were in a state and Sergeant Doyle was being a shit to them. I told them that what they'd experienced with him in the past, that dismissive attitude, wouldn't be repeated, at least not by us. Elizabeth said something like, "It wasn't just Doyle", but I got called away before I could establish what she meant.

'I spoke to them yesterday and she explained. You see, four years ago, the other guard in the village was this old-timer who should have been retired. When Doyle needed back-up, he'd call in guards from surrounding villages or Cork City. When he was conducting the search for Mary Ellen, he called in some help and Elizabeth said they were just as useless. She said one of them kept asking about Mary Ellen's sex life – and was just generally inappropriate. She couldn't remember his name, so I had to get a pal down in Cork to check it out for me.'

'Are you seriously going to tell us it was Bart Healy?' Michael said, agog.

Laura nodded.

'It's our smoking gun. He took up the sergeant's job in Luttrell village where Fiona lived three and a half years ago. Before that, he was based in Cork City. And do you know where he's from originally?'

The group collectively shook their heads.

'Waterford.'

'Shit.' Ray let out a low whistle.

'That's excellent detective work, Laura,' the inspector said. 'Really excellent. So we have him residing and then working in three of the counties where the victims lived. And possibly engaged in a relationship with Fiona Holland. There's one other thing that might be relevant – one of your theories, Bridget.'

Bridget stopping playing with her dark ponytail as the focus fell on her, her facial features scrunched up in confusion.

'My theories?'

'Yes. The one about the type of car a woman on her own would get into without being scared. Taxis, yes. But a garda car – absolutely.'

'Of course! I hadn't even considered that.'

'The attempt in April, though,' Ray said. 'We couldn't get a clear description of the car involved in the alleged abduction, but she's the daughter of a guard. She'd have recognized a garda car.'

Tom nodded.

'I agree, but she wasn't actually abducted so we can't let the details of that incident dictate how we approach the rest of the evidence. Let's get Healy in and have a chat, that's all I'm saying. Meanwhile, we continue to look into this Cormac Ryan fellow. Laura, I'm leaving you in charge of that. And did you get the list of people who work for the Hollands? Fergus said he'd send it through.'

'Yep. Forty employees.'

'Michael, give her a hand with that list. Brian and Bridget, when we're interviewing Healy, you have a discreet look at his background. Find out the number of his assigned vehicle and check if it's been spotted out of its district, that sort of thing.'

Tom noted that not one of his team had been horrified or incredulous at the prospect of one of their own being involved in the Glendalough killings. They'd all been involved in the Kilcross case eighteen months ago. After that, there was nothing that could surprise his detectives.

'Do you think there could be more than one killer?' Ray asked. 'Could Healy have been keeping Mary Ellen at the taxi driver's house in West Cork? Is he working with Carney now?'

Tom shrugged.

'From what Linda has told us, serial killers tend to work alone for the most part, with notable exceptions. And when they do, they're usually in a relationship. Fred and Rose West, for example. As Linda said – without a familial connection, one of the killers might have deviated from the rules at this stage.'

As his team left to pursue the various jobs, Tom mulled on his next move. He was bringing in Bart Healy and he knew Joe Kennedy was not going to like it.

The inspector made an executive decision. He wouldn't even mention it to Kennedy until after they'd conducted the interview. They'd arrested somebody from Healy's patch who was claiming he'd only speak to the sergeant. So, for all Kennedy knew, that's why they were summoning Healy to headquarters.

He'd deal with the fallout in the aftermath.

'Is he there? I'll be back in five.'

The inspector ended the call with Ray and put his phone back in his pocket.

He had walked over to the Phoenix Park's tearoom, in need of fresh air. The summer sun had returned, this time with more bearable temperatures – a world away from the intense heat of the last couple of weeks.

It was a perfectly peaceful day and yet, inside, Tom was in turmoil.

If Fiona Holland had actually been taken, the hope of finding her alive was fading. She was missing a full two weeks now. What condition would she be in? Was her jailer feeding her? Abusing her?

He was tormented by those questions, but Tom knew he wouldn't let fear overwhelm him. It would impede his ability to do his job. Nevertheless, it was there, tapping away at the edge of his thoughts. Keeping him sharp.

He deposited his empty water bottle and Mars bar wrapper in the bin and hurried back towards headquarters. He passed families queuing for Dublin Zoo, also based in the Phoenix

Park, the kids yelling excitedly and parents chatting animatedly. They were a world removed from his professional life and he was glad of it.

'I put Healy in your office,' Ray said, meeting him in reception. 'So he wouldn't suspect anything.'

'Good stuff. Where's Carney?'

'Custody suite.'

'Okay. Let's throw some mud at Sergeant Healy and see what sticks.'

The Meath sergeant stood when the two men entered the office. He was in full uniform again and greeted Tom apologetically.

'Inspector, how's it going? I've been going over and over what happened with Vincent yesterday. I can't apologise enough. Do you need me to talk to him, is that why you asked me to come up? I've barely slept thinking about it all. I mean, if he's capable of shooting at you, he's already capable of more than I imagined. Is he the killer, do you think?'

Tom took his seat.

'I do want to have a chat with you about Carney,' he said. 'We've already established that you know him well enough. He also mentioned yesterday that you drop stuff out to the house for him. Magazines, that kind of thing. Do you often spend time with him?'

Healy's cheeks flushed.

'I'm just keeping an eye on him. I give him the odd dirty mag – it keeps him occupied at the house, stops him wandering into the village looking for the real thing.'

'That's fairly innovative of you,' Tom said, his eyebrows raised.

'Yeah, well.'

The sergeant shifted uncomfortably in his seat.

'Why do you feel so sorry for Vincent?' Tom persisted. 'He's a registered sex offender.'

'He's also a person,' Healy snapped.

Tom leaned back, surprised.

The sergeant caught himself. He shrugged, contrite.

'I apologise,' he said. 'Maybe I should explain.'

'I think you should,' Ray barked.

Healy flashed him a defiant glare.

'A little bit of empathy can go a long way, Detective. My younger brother is similar to Carney. He was deprived of oxygen during birth – the umbilical cord twisted around his neck. He has a good life, but other people don't make it easy for him. They make assumptions. Donal is very affectionate. He'll come right up to you, even if you're a stranger, and try to kiss you. And because at first glance he looks normal enough, people react badly. Women especially. Obviously. I don't blame them – Donal's a big lad. You have to look closely to see the innocence in his eyes. That's all it is, he just wants to be loved.'

The inspector rested his elbows on the desk.

'I understand,' he said. 'And I guess I can see why you'd instinctively feel sorry for Vincent. But your brother sounds like a gentle soul. Vincent isn't gentle.'

'No. As I said, I misjudged him.'

'Hmm.'

Tom pulled a piece of paper from his file.

'We had a chat with him yesterday. He said a couple of things that bothered me. For example, he mentioned that only people in Fiona Holland's family call her Fi. And yet, that's what you call her.'

Healy's eye twitched and he started to pick at the stitching on the seam of his trousers.

'I've been around her family a lot these last couple of weeks. I must have picked up on it. Why is it relevant?'

'Bart, I'm going to be straight with you. Stephen McCabe told us Fiona was seeing somebody as well as him. He reckons this guy is some kind of big shot. Were you sleeping with Fiona?'

The other man swallowed, then licked his dry lips.

'Seriously? Is this why you called me up? That's ludicrous.'

'Do you deny it?'

Healy shook his head.

'I'm not even going to dignify it with an answer. What kind of stunt are you pulling here? I'm heading up the investigation into this girl's disappearance and you want to start throwing wild innuendo and accusations around on the basis of what some scumbag and the village idiot said?'

'The village idiot?' Tom repeated calmly, studying Healy. 'He was a human being a minute ago.'

Healy stood up abruptly.

'I'm not sitting here and listening to this shit.'

'You're either sitting here and listening to this shit or I'm arresting you.'

The other man laughed in disbelief, then his face grew sombre.

'Arresting me for what? On suspicion of having had sex with Fiona Holland, something that couldn't be proved even if it were true?'

'Vincent Carney knew we were coming,' Tom said, quietly, and Healy's jaw dropped. 'Somebody told him. He said, and I quote: "You think I killed her, don't you? *He* said. I'm not talking to you. Want Bart." Now, Bart. Who was he referring to when he used the words "He said"? Did you tell him we thought he was a murder suspect when you told him to come out of the house and offer himself up for arrest? Or did you mention that when you rang to alert him that we were on the way?'

Healy collapsed back into the chair.

'I didn't ring him to say you were on the way.'

'Really? He was just roaming around the farm with a shotgun looking for Dublin detectives to take potshots at, was he? Will I tell you what I think?'

Healy stared at the inspector coolly.

'I think you rang Carney to warn him, knowing he'd get riled up and do something stupid. There's no way you've got to know him that well and not realised the man is volatile. Maybe he knows you well, too. Maybe he knew about your little thing with Fiona. I can imagine her telling him she was going to inform her boyfriend Bart if he tried to touch her again. And that would have scared him. And you, because now somebody knew you were shagging a girl half your age and barely legal. So you went out to see Vincent and told him there'd be no charges pressed because you're his buddy. And you've been keeping him sweet ever since.'

Tom paused and watched as the various emotions flashed over Healy's face, while he tried and failed to disguise them – dismay, panic, shock. What, if any of it, was genuine?

'You know what else? Maybe you told Vincent little fairy stories. Tales about when you worked in Cork and got to know Mary Ellen Lehane – what a dirty little slut she was. Isn't that what you were implying when you kept asking her family about her sex life back then? And Vincent lapped it up, but now he knows too much about you. And if he shoots at two detectives, maybe we'll fire at him in self-defence, or the ERU will gun him down . . .'

'Woah, woah, woah.' Healy had turned puce. 'What the hell are you saying? You think I'm . . .? Jesus Christ, have you lost your mind?'

'You didn't even mention that you'd been involved in Mary Ellen's case.'

'Because I wasn't! I mean, I was, but not in the way you mean. I was asked to go over to Glendale and help with a bloody search party. I talked to the family once or twice. I was based in Cork City, for crying out loud, I could have been asked to help out with the other missing girl, Treasa, as well. But I wasn't.'

'It's not looking good, Bart,' Ray said, tipping his chair back onto two legs with his heels. 'You're from Waterford too, aren't you?'

'I left Waterford when I was eighteen, for crying out loud!'

'Still, you know the county and that's where Pauline O'Hara and Una Dolan went missing. You can't really believe we won't be able to prove you had a thing with Fiona? Somebody is going to talk. Vincent, most likely. Maybe Fiona told others, too. If you lie to us now, it's all going to be used against you when you're charged.'

Healy sucked air into his cheeks, shaking his head.

'Look, this is mad. Absolutely bloody crazy. Fine, I'll admit it. I had a fling with Fiona. She threw herself at me. I'm only human, for crying out loud. But it wasn't serious and I wasn't breaking any laws. She's an adult, whatever the age gap. I was fond of her but I knew the whole thing was a little embarrassing. That's why I never mentioned it. And yes, Vincent knew about it. She told him, used me to threaten him, even though I'd asked her to keep it to herself. I understood why – he'd given her a fright.

'But as for the rest of it, you're way off. I'm as much in the dark about where Fiona's gone as you are and I had nothing to do with those other girls. I never met Mary Ellen Lehane nor knew of her until I was sent down to Glendale that week. And I did not ring Vincent to say you were going up to his farm. I swear it. You can check my phone records.'

Tom crossed his arms and studied the other man. Where did the truth start and end?

'This fling you had with Fiona. It didn't happen to result in a little package last year, did it? Her son, Cían?'

The colour drained from Healy's face.

'She's nineteen now, isn't she, Ray?' Tom turned to his deputy. 'So that would make her eighteen when Cían was born and either just turned eighteen when he was conceived – or maybe seventeen?'

Ray nodded.

'That's right, boss.'

They looked back to Healy, who appeared to have shrunk into his chair.

He was up shit creek without a paddle now.

# CHAPTER 26

'This can't be happening.' Joe Kennedy's voice was muffled, his head buried in his hands, spectacles removed and placed on the desk.

Tom had brought Ray into the chief's office with him. He wanted to see how Kennedy performed with an audience. In front of a witness, would he make the same subtle threats about Tom undermining garda colleagues?

Kennedy picked up a stress ball and squeezed it, his knuckles white with the tension.

Ray gave Tom a look that said *He's gonna blow*.

But when Kennedy released the ball, he just sighed. He picked up his glasses and chewed on one of the arms.

'You don't actually have anything to charge him with. He hasn't admitted to being the father of Fiona's child and even then, it's just an embarrassment. The rest is speculation.'

'You're correct. We've nothing concrete as of yet.'

'Who else knows you brought him in?'

'Just my immediate team. There's been no briefing in the incident room. People know he's in the building but they assume it's to help with interviewing Vincent Carney.'

'And where's Carney?'

'He was in the custody suite, but he's being charged in the

district court now for possession of a weapon with intent to cause grievous bodily harm,' Ray answered.

'Okay. Then, we can keep Healy on site a bit longer without anybody suspecting anything. You have a very limited time span to establish some concrete evidence, Inspector, or it'll be a grovelling apology for Healy. Is that clear?'

'Of course,' Tom said. 'That was my plan anyway.'

'I'm sure it was. One more thing – the next time you plan to bring another member of the force in for questioning, run it by me first. You left me ridiculously exposed today. Imagine if the press had got wind of this and I hadn't been aware that Healy was here? Do you want the head of the NCBI to look that stupid? Would you have put Sean McGuinness in that position?'

The inspector clenched his jaw. He wouldn't have dreamt of bringing Healy in without consulting with Sean, but then it hadn't been Sean who'd been lecturing him the other day about the force being whiter than white.

'I apologise, Chief,' he said. 'To be honest, I think Sean's gut reaction in this situation would be to string Bart Healy up by the bollocks. Because even if he has nothing to do with the Glendalough women, Healy is a senior officer who's been caught screwing a teenager.'

Kennedy tilted his head back and observed Tom steadily.

'I'm well aware of that, Inspector. We can deal with that in due course. But having sex with Fiona Holland is a little less serious than kidnapping and murdering five women, so let's keep focused on ensuring a member of An Garda Síochána is not wrongfully accused of that, shall we?'

'I can't put my finger on why, but I find it really hard to like our new chief,' Ray said, as they walked back downstairs.

'It doesn't matter whether we do or don't like him – he's the boss,' Tom replied, even though it pained him. 'You heard him. We need to get something solid on Healy. And unless we catch him leaning over a shallow grave with a dead body in his arms, I don't think we'll be allowed a second go at him.'

'Can we get a warrant to search his house?'

'Like that's going to happen. We'll have to lean on Carney again, see if he knows something. When will he be back?'

'Not for a few hours. I spoke to the uniforms who brought him to court; there's a backlog of cases up there.'

'Let's have a chat with that chap Doyle down in West Cork,' Tom suggested. 'Maybe he remembers something about Healy that could help. We'll get the others to look up his phone records for yesterday. And we'll go over the Pauline O'Hara details again. Waterford is where it all started and it's Healy's hometown. Maybe we can pin something down there.'

# CHAPTER 27

*Pauline, 2008*

Even when her kidnapper's hands were wrapped around her throat, she hadn't thought she was going to die.

It was painful, yes. Distressing.

But violence was something Pauline was used to.

Steve had liked to hold her neck sometimes when they had sex. He used to claim, back when he felt the need to explain himself, that it turned him on and that he thought it turned her on too. Neither of them wanted to admit what it actually was. He was raping her. Nearly strangling her was part of the fun – her powerless beneath him, crying and gasping for breath.

But Steve hadn't wanted to kill her. He never took it that far. What would be the point when she so willingly let him beat her, the thing he got his real kicks from?

So when her kidnapper sat on her stomach and pinned her to the bed, then started to choke her, Pauline thought he'd stop. Maybe when she'd passed out, or perhaps just before. The trick was to struggle and, to be honest, it came naturally. If he was like Steve, he'd enjoy that.

She had been surprised at the sudden attack, even if she had provoked him by screaming and yelling. At the start, when he brought her to the house, he'd been kind. She had still been terrified, but his consideration had unnerved her. He claimed he just wanted her to stay with him for a while. He talked non-sense about them having a life together. She didn't even know him, for God's sake!

He kept the door to the bedroom he'd put her in locked, but it was a comfortable room, and he brought her food and drink and let her go to the toilet. She kept waiting for him to try to have sex with her, but he didn't. A couple of times, when she'd tried to escape, he had hit her. As soon as he saw she was hurt, he had started crying.

That, she was all too familiar with. The lashing out, then the apologies.

A tiny voice inside told her that what was happening with this man was different. She'd loved Steve and wanted to help him. In the beginning, at least.

Her sister Barbara had thought she was nuts. But Barbara was young. She didn't understand that in real life, relation-ships are never perfect. Pauline worked in a doctor's surgery. She'd seen plenty of women come in wearing sunglasses on a cloudy day to cover the black eyes. They were usually there to get a prescription for valium – not have their injuries seen to. She wasn't alone. In real life, men hit women. There were only six years between Pauline and her younger sister, but they were a lifetime apart in worldly experience. Pauline had seen their father hit their mam. Barbara hadn't, or at least had no recol-lection of it. She would lecture Pauline on women's rights, about 'domestic violence' and 'suffering in silence' being a thing of the past – as though every man bar Steve was a saint.

And it was easy for her sister to ignore the nice side of Steve, something Pauline couldn't do. Yes, there were bad times, but there were also moments of pure joy – when they were happy, and he was tender and loving and she was the centre of his universe. Sometimes, she thought she could take the worse bits, just to keep hold of that.

Pauline wasn't a complete idiot. As time went on, it was obvious Steve was getting more vicious and that the only change she would ever see in him was for the worse. She knew then that she'd have to leave him eventually. She couldn't help him.

But this man, her kidnapper, was a complete stranger. She didn't know where to begin to make him feel better. And it wasn't her responsibility to do so.

She hated him for taking her, especially when she'd been just on the cusp of freedom from this sort of life. Who needed men anyway? Barbara would have had the baby by now and Pauline's time would be taken up helping her care for him. It didn't matter how nice this bloody bedroom was or that her kidnapper was less violent than Steve – it was still a cell and he was still a man who was abusing her.

There must be a sign on my forehead, Pauline thought, her mind retreating into itself even as her lungs fought for air and her body for life. I must have 'victim' tattooed on my head. That's how they find me, these monsters. Barbara was right. I have to toughen up. Maybe women shouldn't suffer in silence.

So she'd stared into her attacker's eyes as he throttled her, knowing she was going to pass out but telling herself that when she woke, she'd be a stronger woman. She wouldn't let a man do this to her again.

She wouldn't be a victim any more.

# CHAPTER 28

'Anything from your lot?'

Michael placed a glass of water and a bag of sour jellies on Laura's desk. They were working on the list of Holland employees and had taken twenty names each, delegating the basic background checks to the uniforms so they could concentrate on deeper research if anything came up.

Laura shook her head and took one of the fizzy worms, her face contorting as she sucked the bittersweet sugar coating. Her eyes were tired from staring at the computer screen. She'd gone through name after name and nothing had jumped out at her.

'Zilch,' she said. 'This week, all that bloody travel, it's catching up on me. I can't concentrate on anything today.'

It was late afternoon and she wanted to pack it all in and go home. Scratch that. She wanted to go for that drink with Ray. They'd barely exchanged two words all day and while she knew it was because they were busy, she was starting to wonder if yesterday had actually happened. The whole exchange had been eerily similar to the daydreams she used to have.

Michael gave her a comradely pat on the shoulder and wandered off to answer the phone ringing on his desk.

Laura looked at her screen again, speed-reading down the Excel sheet. The names had been formatted with ages; addresses for when they'd applied for the job and their current abodes; length of service in the Hollands' business; job description; and anything of note in the person's background. She'd bet there was plenty on here the Hollands weren't aware of. Her eyes flicked to the name of a girl who'd been sacked for stealing from a former employer. There was no way she'd included that in her CV. Another man had faced an accusation of rape of a minor. That one had given Laura pause for thought. But when she'd dug deeper, it turned out he'd been seventeen at the time and the person he was accused of raping had been his fifteen-year-old girlfriend. Her parents had pursued the prosecution, but the charges had ultimately been dropped.

Fergus Holland was listed as an employee, his job title simply 'landscape and delivery'.

Laura looked away from the screen.

She glanced around the room at her colleagues, all beavering away at various tasks. The guard across from her was on the phone again to the liaison officer in Scotland Yard. They were still trying to establish if any suspected or known killers in Britain might have fled to Ireland in the last decade and slipped through the police communications net.

The officer behind Laura was on the phone to Natasha McCarthy's unit, trying to get an expanded list of registered sex offenders – historical cases that might not have been included in the current files.

The volume of information they were wading through was incredible, but it was getting them nowhere.

Laura closed her eyes and an image flashed before them.

There *had* been something on her screen that stood out.

She looked back to where her mouse arrow had paused on Fergus' name, trying to see what it was she'd spotted.

There. It was probably nothing, she thought, scanning the details. But then, they didn't have much to go on.

She looked up to say it to Michael, but he was gone.

'Did anybody see where DS Geoghegan went?' she called out.

'He said he was getting some air,' the officer behind her said, hand covering the phone receiver.

Laura jogged down the stairs and through reception. Outside, she cast her eyes left and right to see if she could spot Michael. When she couldn't, she tried his mobile.

'Where are you?' she asked.

'Shit, has something happened?'

He sounded worried.

'No, nothing like that. I just want to go check something out.'

'Thank God for that. Sorry, I should have said. Anne needed to pop out for an appointment and the babysitter cancelled. I've nipped home. Can it wait a half hour and I'll leave Matthew off in my mother's?'

'Don't do that,' Laura said. 'You're fine. It's probably nothing. I'll catch you later.'

She hung up. Michael lived in nearby Chapelizod, on the other side of the Park. He probably thought he could be over and back before anybody even noticed he was missing, given how busy they all were. Well, she wasn't going to dob him in for skiving. If Ray had turned up offering her a late lunch, she'd have been out the door in seconds.

She'd follow up the query on her own. Her other colleagues were busy and Laura didn't want to drag one of them away on what she was pretty certain would end up being another wild goose-chase. She just needed to finish the day doing something concrete. She'd spent most of it thinking about Ray, entirely distracted.

Laura had driven a good distance when the man himself rang. She hit the answer button on the hands-free set.

'Hey, where are you?' he asked.

'Driving. Do you need me?'

'No. Well, yeah. I just called down to see you and you weren't there. It was only to tell you I'm tied up this evening, but I was wondering if I could drop you home tonight?'

Laura felt a rather pleasant sensation in her stomach.

'That's thoughtful of you,' she said, smiling. 'But I do have my own car.'

'Of course you do.'

Neither of them spoke for a moment, both suddenly shy.

'Can I . . .'

'Could we . . .'

They were talking over one another. Laura laughed.

'Can I still get you some dinner, later?' Ray said, seizing the initiative. 'Just take-out to the station, I mean. We have to talk to Carney again, so I can't leave.'

'I'd love that,' Laura said.

'Brilliant. I mean, thanks – I'll see you later.'

'See you later.' She ended the call. She hadn't imagined it, so. He was interested. Though with the way things had gone over the last couple of years, she didn't think she'd truly believe it until she was waking up with him in the bed beside her.

Laura caught sight of her reflection in the rearview mirror, her cheeks flushed.

'You're a lustful disgrace,' she told herself, still smiling and blissfully happy.

She found the house without much trouble. She wasn't familiar with Meath, but the Hollands' business was well signposted and she knew from Google maps that the house was situated not too far from there.

Laura pulled into a gravel drive that ran alongside a perfectly landscaped garden. It was a big house, expensive-looking. And isolated. Nobody around to hear you scream, she mused, then chastised herself for being silly.

She got out of the car, admiring her surroundings. Not bad, for somebody who was essentially a gardener.

Nobody answered her knock at the front door. She tried again, then decided to walk around the building. Maybe the residents of the house were out back and couldn't hear her.

If Laura was honest with herself, she was a wee bit concerned. If her theory was correct, as outlandish as that seemed, could this actually be their man? It was so ridiculously inconceivable that the case could be solved with some guesswork and a stroke of luck. But if she was right . . . maybe she shouldn't have come out on her own.

Laura shook her head. She was being daft. It was broad daylight. The sun shone in the sky, birds sang in the trees. In all likelihood, there was nothing of interest here and once she'd had this chat, she could go back to the station and get that dinner with Ray. If this man had answered his bloody phone, she wouldn't have had to drive out here at all.

And when the doubts crept in again, Laura reminded herself that she'd left him a voice message. He knew she was a detective. Their serial killer was selective and had a particular methodology. Even if her madcap notion was correct, Laura wouldn't find anything out on this trip. But at least she could say her day had been productive.

She walked along the side of the house, peering in windows as she went. Everything looked normal inside, cosy and welcoming. She could imagine living here. At the very last window, she thought she saw something inside the house. She cupped her hands to the glass and peered in. She hoped she wouldn't cause too much alarm if anyone inside caught her gazing through the glass.

She didn't hear him approach until it was too late.

The blow, when it landed, was completely unexpected. Just a blinding pain, then darkness as Laura collapsed to the ground.

She was still clutching her mobile phone, set up as a caution with Ray's number on the screen so she could dial fast if anything happened. She'd known he would answer straight away. Even as she'd told herself that nothing untoward was going to happen, she'd been prepared in case it did.

The phone crashed to the ground, its screen shattering.

# CHAPTER 29

They'd made no progress with Carney. He wouldn't even confirm that he'd had knowledge of Bart Healy and Fiona Holland's relationship.

'Vincent,' Tom said, almost pleading. 'I know Bart is your friend. I know you are loyal to him. I don't want to hurt Bart. But I need to find out if he knows where Fiona has gone. You said, didn't you, that your mother told you it was wrong to hurt girls?'

Carney picked at the skin around his thumb.

'Yeah. Not right. No gentleman would hurt a lady.'

'Somebody might have hurt Fiona, Vincent. We're worried she might have been taken somewhere and held against her will. Alone, frightened, maybe in pain. She will want to come home. Do you know she has a little baby? His name is Cían. He needs his mammy. Fiona is a lady. It's wrong, isn't it, if somebody has hurt her?'

Carney shook his head.

'Nope.'

'Nope what?'

'Fiona is not a lady. She uses bad language. She says fuck. All the time. Ladies don't swear.'

Tom sucked in his cheeks.

'What do you mean, "All the time"? Have you heard her use the word lately?'

'Haven't seen her lately. I don't go near Fiona.'

'And Bart, he never told you about any of his other girl-friends? Did he ever mention Mary Ellen? Or Treasa? Pauline?'

Carney put his thumb in his mouth and sucked it, shaking his head.

The inspector sat back. This was torture.

'Fine,' he said. 'Vincent, you understand bail was denied to you today? You're going to be remanded in custody until your trial. We can try to get that sped up for you, if you can tell us anything, anything at all that will help us find Fiona.'

The other man stared at Tom. The inspector could see him retreating into himself, his expression vacant.

'Interview terminated at 8 p.m.'

Tom and Ray left the room.

'What now?' Ray asked.

The inspector could see he was itching to be somewhere.

'I don't know,' he answered, truthfully. 'We've nothing to go at Healy with. There's zero coming up in his work history bar that connection to the Mary Ellen case. He never worked in Kerry and his car hasn't ever been spotted outside his jurisdiction. His record is exemplary. Ultan Doyle remembers nothing unusual about him and says he hadn't been in Glendale before the missing persons case. And Carney is about as much use as a chocolate teapot. Linda spent some time with him this morning and she's saying that in her professional opinion, he has a very low IQ and wouldn't be capable of committing the crimes we're investigating. We're stuck, Ray.'

Tom felt his shoulders sag.

'What did Carney's medical records say?' his deputy asked.

'We haven't got them yet. Linda spoke to a psychiatrist who dealt with him at the time of his parents' death. She got her off the record, so none of this can be repeated. The doctor said Carney was traumatised by their deaths. She felt he was blaming himself because he was "slow" and got into trouble a few times, even though the whole concept of debt and his parents' problems were explained at length to him. A solicitor helped him with the sale of the farm afterwards and some money was left in a small trust for him from his parents' insurance, so they didn't leave him without.'

'Hmm, interesting,' Ray remarked.

'Why "interesting"? Did you get hold of the file on his attempted rape prosecution, by the way?'

'I did, actually. And that's what has me curious. I was hoping Linda would come back and say he was faking everything.'

'Why's that?'

'Well, the way he described that rape attempt yesterday, it all sounded fairly innocent on his part. But the details of that assault complaint were far more sinister than he tells it. Carney followed the girl into her house, dropped his trousers and grabbed her. He forced her onto the ground and tried to get her jeans down, holding her by the neck while he did it. She'd taken some self-defence course and managed to knee him in the balls. That's when he backed off.'

'Not pleasant, but where are you getting sinister from?' Tom asked.

'After she got him off her – he didn't leave. He locked the front door and said she was staying there with him until she agreed to have sex with him. It was only when her housemate came back with her boyfriend that he did a runner. The girl was terrified. He kept her locked up for two hours.'

'That is interesting,' the inspector mused. 'So, he has form for holding women captive. But it sounds like it was all a bit slipshod, Ray. Our victims were spirited away and kept alive, possibly for months, not locked up in their own homes for a couple of hours. And, also, according to Moya's evidence, it doesn't look like the victims were raped. Which you'd have to imagine would be Carney's motive for taking anybody.'

Ray shrugged. Was it possible that Carney was pulling the wool over everybody's eyes?

'Unless he drugged the Glendalough victims to rape them,' he said. 'I don't know. I'm too tired to think.'

'Look, head home,' Tom said. 'I'm going to tidy up a few loose ends and plan tomorrow.'

'You sure?'

'Absolutely. I'm leaving myself shortly.'

Ray practically skipped off. Tom watched him go. At least somebody was full of the joys. He felt like he'd the weight of the world on his shoulders – not least because Joe Kennedy was going to be absolutely thrilled that they'd nothing on Healy.

It was disgusting; the chief would prefer a serial killer was still at large than have the suspect be a member of the police force.

Ray opened the incident room door and ducked his head in. There was no sign of Laura. He crossed to her desk – she'd left nothing there, no indication she was off in the toilet and would be back soon. Her computer was in sleep mode and her bag and cardigan were gone.

'Hey,' he called to Brian Cullinane. 'Have you seen Laura this evening?'

Brian shook his head.

'Not since this morning.'

'Oh. Never mind. I'll ring her.'

Ray dialled her number. He was hoping she'd also finished for the day and would say yes to a proper dinner, as opposed to a quick takeaway.

That was odd. Her phone was switched off. He tried a couple more times, then dialled Michael.

'Ray, what's the story?'

'You were working with Laura today, weren't you?' Ray asked.

'Yeah. Earlier.'

'Do you know when she finished up?'

'No. I was out for a while and she was gone when I got back.'

'I see. Okay, then.'

'Is everything alright?'

'Yeah. We were just going to . . . It doesn't matter. She must have changed her mind.'

He ended the call and placed his hand on the back of Laura's chair, removing a long curly hair from the fabric.

She'd sounded up for dinner, but maybe she had got sick of waiting. He didn't want to turn up at her apartment unannounced. She shared with Bridget Duffy and she mightn't be happy to have another team member knowing her business.

He'd try her phone again later.

Ray left the incident room, excitement turning to despondency with each step.

# CHAPTER 30

*Laura*

Laura was cold and stiff. And sore. She felt really sore. What had she been doing last night?

She lay there trying to summon the memories, but the pain in her head was too bad. She tried to recall what she'd drunk. Bridget must have ordered shots.

Actually, had she been drinking?

Laura opened her eyes, but it was like she hadn't. It was so dark. It must still be the middle of the night. Or she was dreaming.

But would she be in this much agony if she was still asleep?

She tried to sit up and it was then it came to her.

He'd caught her, completely unawares. At just the last second she'd seen his reflection in the window, his arm raised, hands clasped around some sort of long object. Before she could react, he'd hit her.

A cry spilled from her mouth and she put up her hand to stifle it, causing another groan. Even the slightest movement hurt.

She sat there in the dark trying to make her eyes adjust. Where the hell was she? She couldn't see anything, not even a sliver of light. Tentatively, she reached her hand up to the back of her head and felt wet, matted hair. The wound was too tender to touch and Laura knew it needed medical attention.

Her eyes filled with tears; her breathing quickened into short, panicky gasps. She placed a hand on her chest. She had to calm down, hold it together. Her phone. Where was her phone? She'd had it in the car – had she taken it with her? Yes, it had been in her hand. She remembered it there, its warm, comfortable familiarity. But where was it now? She felt around the floor, hoping it would be there, knowing it wouldn't.

Laura turned onto her knees, ignoring the pleas of her limbs to stay still. She started to crawl around, trying to get her bearings. It was a large space, with boxes and tins dotting the floor. Then she felt a stair and another stair. Her heart sank and the tears began to flow down her cheeks.

She was in a cellar. His cellar.

Terror welled in her. She felt like she couldn't breathe, like she wasn't in her own body.

And what was that?

Was that somebody else breathing, or the sound of her own wheezing?

Laura felt the blood in her veins turn to ice. Then she opened her mouth and a tiny voice, a voice she didn't even know she had, came out.

'Is somebody there? Fiona – is that you?'

# CHAPTER 31

The atmosphere in the incident room the next morning was lethargic.

Yesterday, the tiredness caused by all the long shifts had been temporarily forgotten. Carney's arrest had raised everybody's hopes. The end was in sight.

Now, with him revealing nothing and it looking increasingly less likely that he was the killer, heads were down. And most of those in the room didn't even know about the Bart Healy affair, which had sprung up and just as suddenly fizzled to nothing.

The inspector gave the team a quick update on the various strands of the investigation, then crossed over to the area of the room his detectives had colonised.

'Where's Laura?' he asked Michael. 'All we're missing is her briefing on the rest of the Holland employees. Tell me she's found something and is chasing it. I need some good news.'

Michael shrugged.

'She hasn't come in.'

Tom frowned. That was strange. Laura was the most conscientious member of his team. She was usually the first one in each morning and the last one out at night.

'Is she following up on something?' he asked. 'Did she ring anybody?'

The team members shook their heads. Ray and Bridget both looked uneasy.

'I tried to ring her earlier,' Brian said. 'Her phone was off.'

'She was supposed to have dinner with me last night,' Ray said, blushing. 'But she'd already gone home when I went looking for her.'

'Hold on,' Bridget interjected. 'She told me yesterday she was staying late and grabbing dinner with you in here. She was . . . she was looking forward to it. She never came home. I thought she got stuck here or that you two had . . .' She froze, flashing their boss a quick glance as Ray turned bright red.

'What time did she leave, Michael?' Tom asked, ignoring the sideshow.

The detective chewed his lip, his face pale and worried.

'I don't know. I left early in the day to deal with a personal matter and by the time I got back she was already gone. I'd spoken to her on the phone and she said she was going to check on something. When she didn't come back, I assumed she'd gone home.'

'She was driving somewhere when I rang her,' Ray said.

The team stood looking at each other, all of their thoughts landing in the same place.

'Okay, well, let's not overreact,' Tom said, trying to subdue the panic he could feel building. It was so unlike Laura to go AWOL. He wouldn't have said it aloud, but with any other member of the team, he'd have taken it for granted that they'd slept in or were about to ring in sick. 'Somebody call her again.'

Bridget tried.

'Her phone is still off. I can't even leave a message. It's just the network saying "Not in service". '

The inspector felt the knot tighten.

'Ray, you ring her family and see if they've heard from her. Bridget, try her friends and check back in your apartment. I'm sure it's nothing, but it's out of character for Laura to miss a team meeting and not phone and I'd prefer we got to the bottom of it – otherwise we'll spend the day worrying. Did she mention at all where she was driving to yesterday or what she was pursuing?'

Michael and Ray both shook their heads.

'And it was just the Holland staff she was working on, wasn't it? Or had she gone back to try to pin down where Cormac Ryan went when he left West Cork?'

'She didn't get as far as Ryan,' Michael said. 'We were going through the Holland employees all day. She hadn't spoken to anybody about the taxi driver.'

'Okay. Go. Make the calls. I'm going to ring around a few stations and see if she's called in anywhere.'

The inspector took the stairs two at a time up to his office, feeling like his heart was in his mouth. It could all amount to nothing. Laura could saunter into the office any minute, with a perfectly rational explanation as to where she'd been all night. For all they knew, a family member had been taken ill or had had an accident. She might have been in an accident herself. He didn't want that to be the case, but he did need to know there was a reason for her absence.

His imagination was running ahead of him. Could Laura have stumbled on something related to the case that had put her in danger?

As soon as Tom thought it, he dismissed it. She wouldn't have put herself in peril. Laura was an experienced officer.

And yet . . . she was in her early thirties, single and pretty – a little too close to the serial killer's type for comfort.

Tom had this cold feeling in his gut that something wasn't right. Laura was the sort who'd send a text even if she had two broken legs, just so nobody would worry where she was. If she had been in an accident and was incapacitated, surely her family would have been contacted by now? And if that had happened, they'd have got in touch with her job.

Tom went through the numbers of colleagues in other stations on his phone, dialling each of them on the landline in case one of the team tried to ring or text his mobile.

After thirty minutes, Michael and Ray arrived in his office.

'Nobody has heard from her,' Ray said, unable to keep the alarm from his voice. 'Not her family, not her friends. Nobody. Bridget's at the apartment and says Laura hasn't been back there. Her phone is still out of service. Brian is ringing the hospitals. Tom — '

His deputy's voice broke and the inspector felt his chest constrict.

He took a deep breath.

'Okay. Let me think.'

'Something has happened to her,' Ray groaned. 'I know it. She was excited about dinner yesterday. She wouldn't have just gone off like that without saying something. This is Laura. You know what she's like.'

'This is all my fault,' Michael whispered. 'If I hadn't left yesterday . . .'

The inspector shook his head.

'Michael, stop. Let's establish where she is before we start panicking. And remember, Laura is a grown woman and a great detective. She's not exactly known for making rash decisions.'

Neither Michael nor Ray replied – Michael, because he was consumed with guilt and Ray because he was thinking Laura might not have been herself yesterday. She might have been distracted, just like he had, thinking about their date. What if that distraction had led her to make a snap decision that had put her in danger?

'Okay,' Tom said, his mind made up. 'We're going to work with what we know. We're assuming that Laura discovered something to do with the case and went to check it out. Let's trace her movements, starting with the last thing she was doing in the office yesterday. You two get on that. I'm going up to speak to the chief.'

Tom paused on a small landing in the stairwell.

He took out his phone and dialled Sean's number. He felt bad – he knew Sean was under pressure, but he also knew that in these circumstances, his former boss would want to know what was happening. He liked Laura and rated her highly.

And Tom needed some moral support.

The phone rang umpteen times but wasn't answered.

'Come on,' the inspector urged, but it kept ringing.

'Damn it.' He shoved his mobile back in his pocket and banged the wall in frustration. He'd try again later.

Kennedy beckoned Tom into his office with a wave of the hand and signalled for him to sit as he concluded his phone conversation.

'Yes. I'll see to that personally. Of course, Bronwyn. Thank you.'

The chief placed the phone on its cradle.

'Bronwyn Maher,' he informed Tom, referring to the assistant commissioner. 'She wants me to remind you that there's a protocol for interviewing another member of the force, and it involves a member of the police union being present.'

'For a formal interview,' Tom replied. 'We didn't conduct a

formal interview with Bart Healy. It was all very relaxed so we didn't have to initiate proceedings that would be recorded. I would have thought that was preferable.'

He could see that his explanation left Kennedy stumped. And how had Maher discovered that Healy had been in for questioning? The chief would have had to ring and tell her – no doubt to drop Tom in it.

'Yes, well, it turns out it was a waste of everybody's time, wasn't it?' Kennedy retorted, pushing his glasses up his nose, his upper lip curled in distaste.

'Chief, if I'd had doubts about Healy and hadn't interviewed him, wouldn't that have been worse?'

'I think we need to put the whole Healy thing to rest now, Inspector. It's caused you enough embarrassment.'

Tom bit his tongue. It wasn't the time to have it out with his superior, but he could feel that argument brewing. It would happen before this case was over, he was sure of it.

'I have a problem I need to make you aware of,' he said. 'A member of my team has gone missing. Laura Brennan.'

Kennedy shifted into business mode.

'Gone missing? Since when?'

'We believe that at some stage yesterday she went to check on something related to the case. Alone. She didn't return home last night and didn't come in this morning. Her mobile is off and nobody has seen her, including her family and friends.'

Kennedy frowned.

'So, she's not even been absent for twenty-four hours? Tom, I can see from your face that you're concerned, but I can't understand the reason for it. Maybe she's off with a boyfriend? And how do you know she's not at home now? She could be sleeping off a hangover.'

The inspector gritted his teeth.

'She lives with another detective on the team,' he said. 'And she doesn't have a boyfriend.'

'As far as you know,' Kennedy smiled, trying to look fatherly. 'Look, don't let a silly girl distract you from the investigation at hand. DS Brennan will turn up, and when she does, give her a slap on the wrist for causing you concern. Your sole focus needs to be on finding Fiona Holland, not worrying about an errant detective.'

The inspector stared at his boss in disbelief. He could have pointed out that Laura was not the 'silly' sort. He could have said that she would never deliberately cause her colleagues any worry. He even could have asked why Kennedy had been so concerned about Bart Healy being brought in for questioning but didn't seem bothered when a young female detective vanished off the face of the earth – especially when they were in the middle of a hunt for a serial killer who targeted young women. But Tom didn't say any of those things because he knew his concerns would fall on deaf ears.

Kennedy wasn't on his side. He was steadily and subtly undermining the inspector. He knew Tom's credentials and knew that he wouldn't have called into the chief's office unless it was serious. But instead of treating it as such, Kennedy had dismissed him.

Even though the inspector felt red-hot anger building inside him, he refused to rise to it. He'd more important matters at hand.

'Fair enough,' was all he actually said, then left the office.

Tom bounded down the steps to the incident room, threw open the door and strode up to the front.

'Listen up!' he called out over the usual daily clamour. 'Folks, put down whatever you're doing. This is important.' Guards hurriedly ended phone calls and raised their eyes from their laptops. His own team hovered nervously and expectantly by their desks.

Tom waited until there was absolute silence.

'One of our own appears to have gone missing. DS Laura Brennan.' He paused to let it sink in. 'Now. This may yet turn out to be something trivial, but we all know Laura and we know how seriously she takes her job. So as of right now, I'm making determining her whereabouts a priority. We believe she uncovered what may have been vital information pertaining to this case and was pursuing it – so her disappearance may be related. I don't have to spell out for you what that means. DS Michael Geoghegan will be coordinating our efforts. DS Lennon and I will try to establish what exactly Laura had stumbled on.'

Every head in the room nodded. Laura was a popular and well-regarded workmate. Not a man or woman there would rest until she was found. They didn't need to be convinced.

The inspector joined Ray at Laura's desk. He'd retrieved the last file she'd been viewing, the list of Holland employees, and displayed it on the screen.

'So, did she glean something from this list, or did somebody mention something to her in passing that jogged her memory?' Tom said, staring at the names.

Ray shrugged heavily. 'I rang downstairs. No calls were put through to her on her landline yesterday. She may have taken a call about something significant on her mobile. Nobody in here spoke to her about anything other than this list before she left, and that was just regarding background checks. The same information that's on this screen.'

Tom pulled over an extra chair and they began to study the names.

They paused at the employee who'd been accused of rape, a name she'd highlighted in bold. It took thirty minutes for them to establish what Laura had yesterday – that the accusation had been for statutory rape and the charges were dropped. Laura hadn't had a chance to write up her notes on what she'd found. They discussed for a few minutes whether she'd gone out to see the man anyway.

'But even if she had – that man is hardly a danger,' Tom concluded. 'We'll send a car out, but no. I think it was something else.'

He rubbed his eyes and leaned back from the desk.

'I'm just going to try Sean again,' he said. 'He'll want to know about this.'

Once more the phone rang out. Christ, where was the man? He tried Louise.

'Hi, love,' she answered.

'Louise, Laura has gone missing.'

'Laura? Your Laura? What do you mean?'

Tom gave her the highlights.

'I'm trying to get hold of Sean,' he said. 'I need his help and he'd want to know. He's not answering his phone so I guess he's tied up with June. Could you do me a huge favour?'

'I'll go straight over and send him in. Keep me posted, Tom.'

'I will. Thanks, pet.'

He hung up and stared at the names again.

'That's interesting,' Ray said, noticing something. 'Here, get Willie on the phone, will you?'

Tom dialled and put Willie on loudspeaker when he answered.

'Willie, Laura's gone missing. Ray's here with me, he wants to check something with you.'

'Jesus. Sure. Shoot.'

'Willie, I know the Holland house has some mad name and is just outside Luttrell village, but what is their actual address? It's something Row, isn't it?'

'Trilby Row. Riverdale is the name of the house.'

'That's it. Thanks.'

'I'll be right up,' Willie replied. 'I'm just parking.'

'Look at this,' Ray said. 'Fergus Holland is named as a delivery driver and his address is actually a house in Luttrell Village. He doesn't live with his folks.'

Tom was staring at the screen. Something had jumped out at him, too.

'He has somewhere to take the women,' Ray said, his eyes wide. 'Maybe that's what Laura saw.'

'Go and check it out,' the inspector answered. 'I'll wait for Willie.'

'Why – what are you going to do?'

'I'm just going to make a couple of calls and I'll be right behind you. Take Bridget.'

Ray didn't hang around to ask any more.

Tom picked up the phone and dialled a number, still looking at the computer.

'Sergeant Doyle.' The man answered abruptly.

'Sergeant. It's Detective Inspector Tom Reynolds here in Dublin. I'm wondering if you can give me some more assistance?'

'Inspector. Good to talk to you again. I hope the information on Sergeant Healy was of help. What can I do for you now?'

'Did one of my detectives ring you yesterday? You've already met her – Laura Brennan?'

'No, I can't say she did. I've no missed calls. Unless she rang the station and didn't leave a message.'

'I see. I'd asked her to follow up with you on Cormac Ryan. Have you had any joy tracing him?'

'Actually, we haven't. Backwards or forwards.'

'You've lost me,' Tom said, confused.

'Not only can we not establish where he went when he left here, Inspector, but we can't unearth his past either. I've put a lot of effort into this over the last few days. It's been playing on my conscience, the thought that he could have taken Mary Ellen and had her in that house while I was there. We didn't always see eye to eye but I wouldn't have wanted to see her harmed. Nobody deserves that.'

'No,' the inspector said, wishing he'd hurry up.

'Anyhow, Cormac Ryan said he moved to the area to get away from a stressful job. He told the locals that he'd worked for the Bank of Ireland. This was in 2008, in the middle of the financial meltdown. It was a credible story. But the bank has no record of a Cormac Ryan working for them at that time. They've a man with that name now – but he's a completely different guy, in his early twenties. So I went down the taxi route. There, I was able to trace him back a couple of years. Well, from the point he got his licence, anyway.'

'When was that?' Tom asked. He'd set his team the task of tracking down Cormac Ryan's taxi number but with all the Carney and Healy palaver, they hadn't got around to it.

'Two thousand five. Registered in Waterford. So that was actually his job even before he moved to the area. Anyhow, that's where it gets sticky. I can't find anything on him prior to 2005. It's like Cormac Ryan didn't exist. Then, when he leaves here, he disappears off the map. Two thousand eight is too far back to check for passenger logs on ferries or planes, but maybe he did go to Britain.'

Tom thanked Doyle and put the phone down. On the page in front of him, he'd written '2005, Waterford'.

Willie Callaghan had arrived and was standing in the doorway scanning the incident room and looking for the inspector.

'Willie!' he called and his driver approached, sitting in the chair Ray had recently vacated.

'What do you need when applying to be a taxi driver?' Tom asked.

Willie stroked his moustache.

'When you're applying to sit the SPSV test, that's the one to get a taxi licence, you need to give them your contact details, a credit card, your public service number and your driving licence.'

'Got any pals down in the test centre in Waterford?'

Willie had pals everywhere.

He pulled his phone out of his pocket.

'Who are we looking up?'

'Cormac Ryan. Got his licence in 2005.'

Willie dialled and Tom listened as he made small talk with his contact.

'Hey, Richie, you know that fifty you owe me? Get up the yard, you remember it well – yeah, I said your man would go down in the fifth round and you said he'd win on points. That's the one, you cheeky bastard. Well, I'm willing to let it slide but I need you to look up somebody for me. It's urgent. Yeah. Cormac Ryan. Two thousand five. Good man. You can ring me back on this number.'

Willie put his phone down, the smile he'd forced dying on his lips.

'He needs a few minutes.'

The inspector waited impatiently, casting his eyes around the room. His colleagues all wore worried looks, their heads bent over their desks, fingers clacking on keyboards and nearly every phone on the go.

The door opened again and Linda McCarn strode in, took one look around and made a beeline for Tom.

'I'm here to help.'

The inspector felt momentarily panicked. If word had started to get out that he'd directed the team to look for Laura, Kennedy would hear of it and come stomping down to the incident room to set the inspector's priorities straight. Tom was ready for him, but he'd rather not have to deal with that right now.

'I caught your deputy on the way out,' Linda said.

'Ah,' Tom breathed a sigh of relief.

'You're worried he's taken her, aren't you? Ray looks like he's dying inside.'

Tom nodded.

'It would be a departure from his routine,' Linda tried to reassure him.

'Fiona Holland would have been a break in the routine,' he replied. 'You said that snatching her in July could show that he's escalating.'

The psychologist placed her hand on his shoulder, well aware of her own words and wishing and praying that she'd been wrong.

'I'm starting to wonder,' Tom said, 'if Fiona Holland was taken by this guy at all. Maybe he was just waiting out the year or he has somebody we don't know about.'

Willie's phone sprang to life on the desk, causing all three to jump. He'd recorded his grandchildren laughing while he tickled them, so the ringtone was one of manic giggles.

'Sorry,' he said, answering it quickly.

'Richie. What? Yes, that's excellent. Okay . . . I see. That is interesting. Email it up to me, will you? Good man. No, don't worry, it's for DI Tom Reynolds, head of the murder squad. You won't get into trouble and if we need to, we'll sort out a warrant. Yeah, maybe I will take your offer up. I wouldn't be the first copper to moonlight with a bit of taxi driving.'

Willie hung up and turned to the computer.

'How do you work this thing?' he said, unfamiliar with Macs.

Tom pulled up Safari for him and showed him where to type in his email account. Willie entered his Yahoo! ID. They waited for another moment until a new email suddenly appeared in his inbox, file attached.

'So, Richie spotted an anomaly,' Willie explained, as they waited for the document to download. 'The licence application was for a part-time plate. This Cormac Ryan fella had another job. But that wasn't all. It turns out he had a different name too. His public service number was in one name and his ID in another.'

'Then how on earth did he get the licence?' Tom asked.

'It was legit. He had a double-barrelled surname and two first names. For ease, he must have started using just his first and last name and that was on his ID. I'd say he was from some posh family, with that many names.'

Willie found the document in the download file and opened it.

Tom ran his eyes over the details, stopping at the most important part.

Cormac Ryan's full name.

The blood drained from his face.

'Are you okay?' Linda asked, alarmed.

Tom shook his head.

He'd never been less okay.

It had all been an act, and they'd been taken in.

They'd let him walk away and go back to Fiona.

And now he probably had Laura too.

# CHAPTER 32

For the second time, Laura found herself waking in the cellar. This time it came to her far quicker where she was and why she was there. She lay still for a few seconds and had a stern conversation with herself. She'd got herself into such a state that she'd caused herself to faint. It couldn't happen again. She needed her wits about her.

She sat up. If there was somebody in the cellar with her, they were being very quiet. She was sure she'd heard somebody breathing, but Laura was so scared it was utterly conceivable that she'd imagined it.

Just in case, though, she felt around the ground until she felt the steps again. She crawled up them. If somebody came at her and they weren't friendly, she would have height as an advantage.

She felt something unfamiliar in her trousers as she sat down and reached inside her pocket. It was the bag of sugared jellies that Michael had left on her desk. She must have picked them up when she was leaving the office. Laura placed one in her mouth, nearly crying with relief at its sweet familiarity. She wasn't going to starve. Not for a while, at any rate.

They'd be looking for her. She didn't know how long it had been, but she knew her absence would set alarm bells ringing.

Laura had taken two sick days in her entire career and both times she had rang in to make her excuses. If she'd been unconscious so long that a whole night had passed, Bridget would know she hadn't come home. And Ray had been expecting to see her at dinner.

Laura pulled her flimsy summer cardigan tight around her body. She was freezing cold. The shock and the head wound weren't helping her body temperature, though at least the sugar was dealing somewhat with the former.

They'll find you, she reassured herself.

But her inner fears wouldn't stay silent.

How can they find you, when they don't even know where to look? Who would make the leap that you did? She hadn't even taken it seriously herself – that's why she'd come out to the house so casually, on her own, fearful of nothing. Even when the little niggling doubt that she might have acted in haste crept in – she hadn't entertained it the way she should have. She hadn't even had her sidearm primed. Laura's hand moved to her hip, as it had the first time she'd woken. Of course it was gone. He wasn't stupid.

Despair was tightening its grip. She hugged her knees to her chest and started rocking backward and forward, as much to stay warm as to provide comfort.

She heard a noise. Footsteps moving quickly overhead. She'd positioned herself on the stairs in case there was somebody in the cellar with her, but she'd forgotten that the real horror was above her.

The trapdoor was flung open and a blinding light filled her eyes. She'd barely time to react and descend more than one or two steps before he grabbed her under her arms and hoisted her up into the room overhead.

'You're coming with me,' he growled, while Laura kicked and screamed.

He was far too strong for her. Even as she was fighting for her life the thought crossed her mind that it wouldn't have been any bother to him to carry his victims through Glendalough and down to his burial site.

'Please,' she cried, the image of the five graves filling her head. She didn't want to die. 'Please, no!'

The man behind her clamped his hand over her mouth and brought his lips close to her ear. She could smell saltiness on his breath, a musky scent on his body – the smell of the outdoors.

'I don't want to do this,' he whispered, as gently as a lover. 'I tried to stop. You were meant to stop me. I dug the last one up so you'd find them. My sleeping beauties.'

He kissed the back of Laura's neck and she recoiled, her stomach churning.

'Your hair,' he said, inhaling the back of her head as she strained to free herself. 'So soft. Just like hers.'

He removed his hand from Laura's mouth and wrapped a lock of her hair around it, caressing the back of her neck. She froze, every part of her body paralysed with fear. Was he going to rape her?

And then he yanked her hair back so hard she felt the roots rip from her head.

'Fucking whore!' he yelled and, lifting Laura up by the waist, he carried her out of the house.

She didn't start fighting again until he opened the boot of the car and flung her in. Then she lashed out, trying to keep her limbs extended so he couldn't close the boot. He leaned in and grabbed her by the throat.

'Stop fucking squirming or I'll strangle you right now, bitch.'

Laura dropped her hands and legs, terrified. She couldn't win in this scenario. She wouldn't survive if she tried to fight him in the car. She had to do what he said.

He slammed the boot shut and she was in the dark again.

# CHAPTER 33

Willie drove as Tom spoke to a contact on the phone. She was a social worker and had gone over and above to give the inspector a dig out. He'd recently helped her deal with a toe-rag of a father who'd been sent down for battering his wife to death thirteen years previously, while their one-year-old son watched. Out of jail for 'good behaviour', he'd started harassing the now-teenage child's foster parents, looking for access. The social worker knew he was on hard drugs. Tom, who'd handled the initial murder inquiry, intervened with a particularly hard-hitting report to the man's probation officer and the father's early release had been revoked.

The social worker felt she owed Tom one.

'It's a tragic case, I can see why your suspect altered his name,' she said, as the inspector listened. 'The extended family were extremely wealthy at one stage, but they lost it all. Still had a large house and a bit of land, though. His mother lived at home with her father, the boy's grandfather, but she was troubled. Alcohol problems. She had a record for soliciting, on top of a litany of petty crimes. Anyhow, she got pregnant and tried to clean up, apparently. There's no dad on the birth cert. And he wasn't her only child – she'd another son, a few years later. He had some sort of birth defect and died young. That must have knocked her off the wagon. Especially as they believed it was something she did in pregnancy that caused the defect, either drinking or drug-taking, I imagine. When the eldest boy was ten, she walked out. Abandoned her son to his grandfather.

'It seems the grandfather was quick with his fists, despite the well-to-do background and nice house. And he lost it completely when his daughter left. He was paranoid. Thought people were talking about him and blamed the boy for the damage to the family's reputation – what little was left of it. He stopped sending his grandson to school but eventually social services called to the house. The grandfather knocked out two of them and was arrested. A female social worker found his grandson, near beaten to death and half-starved. He'd been kept in the cellar for weeks at that stage. Horrific.'

Tom thanked her and ended the call. They were fast-tracking the warrant, but the inspector had no intention of waiting for it. If he was wrong, and he knew he wasn't, he'd deal with the consequences later. He looked at his phone. Still no word from Sean McGuinness.

He turned to Linda in the back of the car. She'd insisted on coming.

'It's him, then?' she asked.

'Looks like it.'

'How did Laura figure it out?'

Tom shrugged.

'It must have caught her eye like mine. He's a gardener, so he knows everything about plants – which we'd surmised early on. His job is described as landscaper and deliveries, so he was used to driving about the country. People expected him to be gone for periods of time and he took advantage of that. When he left Meath, he must have taken his taxi plate. That's how he got his victims in the car. He was living in Cork for that short period, but it must have scared him when he fell under suspicion after the Mary Ellen affair. He told the Cork ones he was moving to England. That wasn't a total lie. He did go to Britain for a while, before coming home. That's what Laura saw. His address when he applied for the job was a British one. Actually . . .'

'What?' Willie asked.

'Something else just fell into place for me. I need to check it out.'

Tom dialled through to the detention centre where Vincent Carney was being held on remand. He got hold of the desk sergeant and told him what he needed. Within minutes, Carney was on the line.

'Vincent, I have something very important to ask you. If you help me, I'll make sure you're taken care of as much as possible by my colleagues, do you understand?'

There was a mumble of assent down the phone.

'When we drove up to your house that day and you shot at us, somebody told you we were coming,' Tom said. 'He told you we suspected you of murdering those girls that were found, didn't he? He's a bad man, Vincent. He shouldn't have said that to you. That's why you lost your temper. Who told you we were on the way?'

There was silence for a couple of moments. Then Vincent spoke.

'Cormac rang from the Hollands' garden centre. He said you told Fergus that you were coming to see me and you knew I'd killed Fiona. But I didn't. Do you believe me now?'

'I believe you,' Tom said, his countenance grim. 'Have you known Cormac a long time, Vincent?'

'Sort of. He went away for a little while. He was Cormac but when he came back he wanted to be called his other name, the name his mother used to call him. I still think of him as Cormac – that's what he was in school. He wasn't happy here, when he was little. But he's happy now. That big fancy house he's got. Seven bedrooms it has!'

'Thank you, Vincent,' Tom said, before hanging up. He looked at the name written on the sheet of paper he'd printed out back in the office.

Cormac Charles Lane-Ryan.

# CHAPTER 34

*Charlie, 1984*

It was so dark. So very, very dark. Not the sort of blackness you get used to, either. To move, Charlie had to feel around the walls with his hands. He'd become familiar with all the objects on the floor and the shape and size of the cellar. The paint tins he sat on, the length of pipe he held onto when he was relieving himself.

The pain from the last beating had subsided, but the little boy imagined it was just a temporary relief. He'd tried to hit his grandfather back during that attack, but the older man barely registered the blow. It was like the flapping of tiny wings against a larger predator.

As each day passed, Charlie wondered if anyone would come for him. Did anybody even know he was there?

Cold and hunger had been replaced with despair and abandonment.

More than anything, he wanted his mother.

On one of the nights, Charlie had no idea which one or how long ago, his grandfather had opened the cellar door and thrown down some dinner scraps.

The little boy had discovered a tap at the edge of the cellar, so he'd had water to drink, but that hadn't been enough to stem the hunger pangs that gnawed at his swollen belly.

He was so grateful for the food that he swooped on it without thinking, stuffing soggy potatoes into his mouth. He had swallowed so fast, he'd almost vomited, his stomach contracting and trying to repel the now foreign feeling of sustenance.

It took a few minutes before Charlie realised that his grandfather was still standing at the open hatch, looking down at him.

'Animal!' he spat, when the little boy looked up. He dropped his trousers and urinated down the cellar steps, the sharp, overpowering stench filling the small space, worse than the collection of waste already in the corner of the room. Drops splashed at Charlie and onto the food, even as he jumped out of the way. He caught his grandfather's satisfied glance before he dropped the door shut with a bang.

The young boy's eyes filled with tears. He'd mistaken the scraps for a sign of kindness – a message that he hadn't been forgotten.

As he ate food covered in piss, he knew he preferred the beatings to the torture he was being subjected to. He would rather the feeling of fists landing on his face because that was real and something he understood. This treatment, this captivity and . . . hate. His young mind couldn't comprehend it.

It was sending him mad.

For four weeks, Charlie lived in the black cellar, surviving on the odd scrap of food and the tap water. He didn't know how long he was there. Days faded into nights, nights faded into weeks. All he knew was that he'd been made to disappear. The little boy who shouldn't have been born in the first place.

He was alone. Even his little brother was gone – and that had been her fault too. She'd taken drugs when the baby was in her tummy and he'd come out too small. There was something wrong with him. And still, Charlie had loved him.

His mother had been a slut. That's what his grandfather roared over and over, the words cutting into Charlie's skin, tattooing themselves in his thoughts. Her behaviour was his shame to carry. As time passed in the cellar, he began to believe it. He was only ten when she'd abandoned him that spring, days before Easter when the only worry he should have had was how many chocolate eggs he would get. She'd left him at the mercy of the evil man upstairs. So how come he still longed for her? For her gentleness and warmth. She could be silly at times, especially when she drank, but she never hit him. She used to cuddle him and tell him he was her little prince. Her Charlie.

Then, one day, after he'd been in the cellar for a long time, he heard yelling. Not his grandfather's voice. It sounded like a stranger.

Charlie climbed up the stairs to the trapdoor. Survival instinct, something he didn't even know he had left, kicked in. At the top, he summoned everything he could and screamed, bashing at the door with his little fists.

Realising the clamour probably wasn't enough, he scrambled back down the steps and found one of the empty paint tins. Despite his weakness, despite the pain in his limbs and near starvation, he raised the tin over his head and started to hit the trapdoor with it. Bang, bang, bang. He gave his arms a rest and listened. The noise overhead had stopped.

Charlie panicked and began to bang again, roaring at the top of his lungs. He was so lost in what he was doing that when the trapdoor was flung open, he barely noticed. Suddenly he was blinded by light. He dropped the tin and looked up, shielding his eyes from the stinging beam.

A woman was standing there, staring down at him – a skinny

little boy, covered in his own filth, eyes wide with fear. She was wearing a plain grey jacket and skirt, the clothes of a professional woman. Her eyes were wide with shock; her nose wrinkled at the smell that had spilled out the door.

To Charlie, she was beautiful. The prettiest princess he had ever seen. Like the ones from the story his mother used to read.

Maybe this wasn't real at all. Maybe he was no longer alive and this was heaven. She was an angel.

'Charlie?' she said, her voice filled with horror. 'Are you Charlie?'

He nodded mutely. His eyes were dry, but inside, he was crying.

'Oh, my sweet Lord,' she said. 'Oh, you poor little boy. You're okay. You're alright now. He's gone. Your granddad is gone.'

# CHAPTER 35

'Open up!' Ray yelled, and banged again on the door of Fergus Holland's house. The building was on the main street of the village, its door just off the pavement. No garden, no privacy. People came out of their homes on either side to see what was going on. They were in for a treat. Ray was going to break the door down with his fists if it wasn't answered soon.

'There's the boss,' Bridget said, pointing at the car pulling up beside them.

'Follow us,' the inspector called, leaning across Willie. 'It's not Fergus. It's Charlie Lane.'

'Who?' Ray was too angry to think straight. 'Who the hell is Charlie . . . wait, is he the one who drove us up to Carney's that day?'

'Yes!'

Ray's jaw dropped. He and Bridget ran back to their car and jumped in.

'Do you know where he lives?' Bridget asked.

'I haven't the foggiest. I barely remember what the man looks like.'

'Well, don't bloody lose them, then. They're nearly out of the village already.'

But Willie had slowed down and Ray managed to catch up.

They drove at speed. Willie turned off the main road and a

few minutes later they were on a narrower route that Ray recognised as the one they'd taken to Carney's house.

'He said he lived near here,' he said, recalling the man's words before they'd sent him on his way that day.

They drove on for another half mile, before turning in through a set of open gates. They were in the driveway of a large, white-walled house, the gardens around it beautifully maintained.

Ray was still struggling to make the link as to how it could be Charlie Lane, and how Laura, who'd never met him, had figured it out, even as the tires skidded to a halt on the gravel.

He jumped from the car at the same time as Willie, Tom and Linda McCarn emerged from the vehicle in front.

'No, you don't,' the inspector said to Linda. 'Go close those gates and get in the car, driver's side. If he comes out of that house running, feel free to give him a little tap with the bonnet. Ray and Bridget, you take the back, we'll go in the front.'

The two detectives jogged around the side of the house, just as they heard the sound of the wooden front door splintering. Ray hoped Tom was right, or there was going to be trouble over that unorthodox entry. Just as that thought was running through his head, he saw broken glass glittering in the late afternoon sun, an incongruous mess on the otherwise pristine stone path.

'Ray!' Bridget grabbed his arm, and they both froze. They approached the debris with caution. Ray took a glove from his pocket and bent down to pick up the smashed smart phone. He saw the white line of Tipp-Ex painted on the back and felt his knees go weak.

'That's hers,' Bridget said, her voice faint. 'She put the Tipp-ex on it because we've the same phone and keep mixing them up at home.'

Ray stood, feeling like he was going to vomit. This couldn't be happening. He clutched the windowsill and pulled himself to a standing position.

'Oh, my God.' Bridget clasped a hand over her mouth and Ray followed her gaze. The white windowsill and wall was sprayed with blood. They hadn't seen it immediately because of the glare of the sun.

Feeling like his heart was beating out of his chest, Ray broke into a run, racing around to the back of the house. He found the rear entrance and was about to throw himself at the door when it opened.

Willie was standing there, his face white as a sheet.

'What is it?' Ray cried, his voice hoarse. He pushed past Willie. They were standing in a sitting room, a large fireplace to one side, a three-piece leather suite and coffee table gracing the polished floorboards. A rug had been pulled up in the middle of the room and the trapdoor beneath flung open.

Tom's head popped up.

'She's not down here,' he said. 'The room was like this when we came through.'

Ray crossed the room and the inspector descended the steps to allow his deputy entry. They used the torches on their phones to search the floor, just as Ray and Laura had in West Cork.

This cellar wasn't empty, though. It was full of all the things that you'd expect to find in such a space. Tins of paint. Cardboard boxes of old crockery. Small pots of seedlings.

And in the corner, a bed.

'That's blood,' Tom said, pointing to the congealed stain on an area of the floor that wasn't cluttered with the detritus of Charlie Lane's life. Ray leaned back against the steps, feeling overwhelmed. He put his hand on the wood and felt something small and round. He picked it up and shone his light at it. It was a button, like one you'd find on a cardigan.

'She was here,' he said, clasping the small object in his palm. 'We found her phone outside.'

'But where the hell is she now?' said Tom. 'We need to check the house and see if he has any other hiding places. Fiona Holland could be here too.'

# CHAPTER 36

'The burial site at Glendalough is in lockdown,' Tom told Ray and Linda. 'He'd be mad to bring her up there.'

The inspector had just ended a terse phone call with Joe Kennedy. The entire police force was on red alert, but Tom was still angry at Kennedy for not taking Laura's disappearance seriously in the first place.

'We'll find her,' he assured Tom, and even though the inspector disliked the man, the words had held some comfort. And at least he'd made the effort. The inspector had heard nothing from Sean, or from his own wife, for that matter, for most of the day. He'd eventually sent her a text asking what was going on and she'd sent a short reply just saying Sean couldn't make it and she'd speak to him later, then asked if he'd found Laura. He typed 'No'. He wasn't as annoyed as the one word reply probably came across. He knew how tough it was for Sean at the moment. But he was upset that his old boss couldn't even lift the phone and offer a few words of reassuring guidance.

They'd torn Charlie Lane's house asunder, searching for any clues as to where he might have taken Laura. They'd found nothing, including very little that would give them any insight into the man's personality. There were few family photographs, just a couple that they'd found in a small album on a bookshelf upstairs. Even that had most of the pictures removed. Those that remained showed a young woman and two boys – Charlie, his toddler brother and his mother, the inspector presumed. On closer examination, he realised the woman in the picture bore a resemblance to Pauline O'Hara. It was in the eyes and the mouth. Was that why Lane had started? Because he'd seen a woman who looked like the mother who'd abandoned him? Had it been that simple?

The man had erased all traces of his grandfather. It was amazing he'd come back to this house at all. The only other item of interest had been a copy of an old fairy tale. *Sleeping Beauty*. Tom had flicked to the title page, where an inscription read:

*To my little prince, Charlie, from your mama.*

'He must have another house somewhere,' Ray said, stomping around the kitchen, where they'd set up base. 'Where's Fiona Holland? There's nothing to say she was here.'

Maybe she's already dead, Tom thought, but didn't say aloud. He didn't have to. Ray had already considered it. He just couldn't iterate the words for fear of what that could mean for Laura. If Lane had a second house – then that's where Laura could be now.

The forensics squad was hard at work in the cellar. Emmet had indicated that there were historical traces of blood and human DNA, as well as the more recent blood on the floor and outside the house. They would be gathering evidence all night.

Linda McCarn sat at the table, her head in her hands.

'So all avenues of approach to Glendalough have been blocked off,' she said.

Tom nodded.

'From the main road to the valley. It's part of the Wicklow

Mountains National Park, though, and that's spread over twenty thousand hectares. We have the main trail and the woodland between the lakes guarded, the two car parks, and there are patrol cars doing circuits of all the roads at the far end of Glendalough, the ones that could provide access points to the more difficult terrain at the rear of the valley. There's a helicopter in the air, too.'

Linda rubbed her temples, her lips pursed.

'It means something to him – that area. And it's part of his ritual.'

She glanced at the book of fairy tales that the inspector had brought down from upstairs.

'In the end, he hated his mother for abandoning him. That's why he's been taking the women, but not killing them immediately. He holds them captive so he's no longer alone, but also so they can experience what he went through. Ultimately, he knows they're not his mother and, once he acknowledges that, he allows his rage to take over and murders them. He kept this book and photos of his mother, while there's nothing of his grandfather. His feelings for her are far more complex than those he had for the old man. He loved and reviled her. When she was here, when she was mothering him and protecting him from his grandfather, she must have shown him kindness. This book – she's the princess in it and he's the prince. I think that's why he gives his victims the bracelets. Out of love. They're all his princesses.'

'If it's about his mother, does that mean he is or isn't sexually assaulting them?' Ray asked.

Linda frowned.

'I would guess no. This isn't about sex for him. It's about owning the women. But I can't be certain. Rape is not about sexual satisfaction, after all. It's about power. He could be using it to exert his control over them. Oh, darling, I'm sure that's not . . .'

Ray had paled.

'Linda, why does Glendalough mean so much to him?' Tom asked, wanting to move the conversation on. 'Could his mother have brought him there?'

Linda glanced at Ray again, thrown for a moment. She took a deep breath and gathered herself.

'I suppose so. Yes, that could be it. It may have been a special place for them, somewhere they shared a happy memory. Like so many Irish children. He was a child in the eighties and the Catholic Church was dominant then. Perhaps the combination of his mother bringing him there and the religious aspect, which you speculated about earlier in the case, gave him a particular affinity for the place. Once he buried his first victim there, the subsequent burials were a natural progression. He would have become fixated on keeping all the women in the same place.'

'Didn't you mention something about the round tower in the monastic settlement, too?' Tom said, squinting as he recalled. 'How it had fairy-tale connotations?'

'Yes . . .' Linda suspected where he was going. 'But if Glendalough is blocked off, surely it's all irrelevant now?'

'The security has only been in place for the last couple of hours.'

'So he could have got to it beforehand? That tower is only accessible by ladder, Tom. The door to it is twelve feet off the ground.'

'I know. But we'll get the lads out there to check it out.'

The inspector rang through his orders to the central

command unit, explaining the team would need a ladder and why it was necessary. He sat down at the table and grabbed one of the open laptops. It came to life with the briefest touch and he typed 'Glendalough' into Google maps, bringing up the satellite image.

He stared at the topography on the screen, then signalled to Willie, who was smoking a cigarette outside the back door.

'Where are we going?' his driver asked.

'Linda, he's no longer thinking rationally, is he? You don't kidnap a police detective. And he must have realised who she was as soon as he knocked her out and checked her ID.'

'I would say he hasn't been thinking rationally for a long time, but yes, he's spiralling. This is totally out of control for him.'

'That's what I thought. We're assuming he won't do anything to put himself at risk of capture. But if he's lost it, protecting himself is no longer his sole focus. He needs to follow through with what he usually does, his routine of killing and burying. As you say, he's fixated on that area. We can't find another house belonging to Lane. This is where he kept the more recent women. Laura's not here, which means he's decided to kill her already. If he can't get to his usual burial site, he'll try to bring her as near as possible, despite the danger.'

'Is Laura already dead?' Ray choked.

'I don't know,' Tom said, shaking his head, a shiver running down his back. 'But if she's not, she will be soon. We need to find her, quickly.'

'Where do we start?'

The inspector planted his hands on the table and closed his eyes. He was about to make a decision that could pay off or end in complete disaster. But he had no choice. They had to search somewhere.

'There are several lakes in the national park,' he said. 'Willie, I need your expertise. Tell me what I'm looking at here.'

Willie leaned over his shoulder, pointing at sections of the screen.

'That's the Glendalough valley at the far end,' he said. 'But approaching from the Dublin side, you have that small lake at Tinnehinch and then Lough Dan near Crone.'

'Lough Dan is the largest one and it's nearest to Glendalough,' Tom remarked.

'That's right.'

'Then that's where we're going. Laura said it herself – how peaceful it was by the lake. He could have chosen anywhere in Glendalough, but he chose near the water. He'll have been waiting for dark and it's nearly pitch black outside now. We need to get a move on.'

# CHAPTER 37

The drive from Luttrell village to Crone in Wicklow normally took an hour and a half. They did it in an hour and ten minutes and it still felt like the longest seventy minutes of any of their lives.

'What makes you think he'd wait for nightfall?' Ray asked, willing the car to go faster. 'It's so remote out here – couldn't he just have come straight out? And what would he have been doing all that time?'

'Just driving around, I imagine,' Tom said. 'Or maybe he's parked up somewhere. It's remote, Ray, but it's the middle of the school summer holidays and this whole area is frequented by tourists and locals, even the lesser-known lakes. He will have had to bide his time.'

The inspector prayed he was right. Lane deciding to kill Laura at the lake and waiting for dark gave them a slim chance of finding her alive.

The police radio crackled just as they exited the M50 and merged onto the N11: 'This is dispatch. Patrol unit eleven have just clocked a car driving on the Wicklow Way access road towards Lough Dan woods, coming from the Oldbridge direction. It's a dark saloon, matching the description of the suspect's vehicle.'

Tom picked up the radio.

'Unit eleven, keep it in sight. If it stops, wait close by. Signal us as we approach.

'How far?' he asked Willie.

The other man grimaced.

'Fifteen minutes.'

They sped down the N11, coming off at the village of Roundwood.

It was a clear night; a full moon lit the sky overhead. The houses began to thin out as they drove deeper into the country-side. They were at the foot of the Wicklow Mountains and could feel the ascent. The minutes passed, and soon they saw the woods in the distance, a thicket of trees amongst the vast farm-lands that surrounded them.

'Nearly there,' Tom said to Ray.

His deputy nodded, not trusting himself to speak.

As they drew closer, a patrol car flashed its lights at them from a side road.

Willie slowed and Tom lowered his window as one of its occupants jumped out and approached.

'Did the car come up here?'

'Yes. It's his vehicle. It's parked up ahead now. We checked; it's empty.'

'Okay. You know the terrain about here?'

'Yep. The car park is at the foot of the main walking trail. There's a bit of a climb through the woods, nothing strenuous, then the path dips and leads to the lake. The woods converge to a narrower point at the lake's shore.'

'Is it thick woodland? Any clearings?'

'It's not too dense. There are plenty of glades and the lake's periphery is fairly open.'

'Okay, thanks. Follow us.'

Tom signalled to Willie to drive on until they reached the car park.

They pulled up across from the lone vehicle, a Toyota Avensis. Lane's taxi-plate licence was registered to the make and model of the car they were looking at now.

'That's the right reg.' Willie said.

Tom and Ray directed their torches and weapons at the vehicle, advancing towards it cautiously.

It was empty.

The sound of another car attracted their attention. Michael and Bridget had arrived. The inspector had left Brian in charge of a team at Lane's house as a precautionary measure.

'What's the plan?' Michael said, as he jumped from the car.

'We have to assume he's in these woods,' Tom said. 'Unless he's playing games with us. There are reinforcements coming but we need to go in now and start a search. We don't know what sort of weapons he has, if any, but let's keep ours primed. We'll split up to help speed things up. Bar you two,' he nodded at the uniformed guards. 'You're not armed, so stay together and radio through if you spot anything. Do not approach him.'

The two officers nodded.

'I'm coming,' Willie said.

'Go with the uniforms,' Tom sighed. There was little point in telling his driver to stay in the car. Willie was a trained guard. He wouldn't be sitting this one out.

'Are you alright?' the inspector asked Ray, as they pulled on their Kevlar vests.

Ray nodded.

'I'd finally asked her out,' he said, his face grim. 'She said yes, Tom. Ten months it's taken me, since I messed it up the first time. And every day, every night since then, I've thought about her. Watching her as she worked, noticing all the things I'd never noticed before. Like how bloody beautiful she is.' Ray rubbed roughly at his eyes. 'Sorry, you don't want to be listening to this shit. I sound like an idiot. I sound like a bloody stalker.'

Tom strapped the sides of his vest together.

'We'll find her, Ray.'

His deputy nodded, unable to meet the inspector's eyes.

They separated off the main trail in five different directions. Their radios were set on the lowest volume so they could communicate without alerting the suspect to their presence.

Tom could hear his heart thumping in his chest as he made his way across the fern-strewn ground. The officers at the scene had been correct – the woods were visitor-friendly, plenty of trails between the trees, which also meant the moon's light broke through and made the job of walking easier.

He walked at a brisk pace, casting his eyes left and right. There was a mile and a half of woodland between him and the lake, but Lane could be anywhere. The inspector summoned up the image of the man. He'd been average height. Fit – they'd noticed that when he ran from the car. When they met him first, he'd been moving heavy pots around the garden centre with Fergus and then progressed to taking the bags of fertiliser off the delivery truck. He'd dark hair and sideburns. That was pretty much all Tom could recall and that was the scary thing.

The man had kidnapped and murdered five, probably six, maybe seven women, and he really wasn't very remarkable at all.

Tom had traversed at least three-quarters of a mile. The quiet static on his radio told him nobody else had spotted anything.

Please God, let this be the place, he prayed. If Lane was

carrying or dragging Laura, he couldn't have moved much faster than the detectives. But he had twenty minutes on them. The local guard had told them that the woods narrowed as they approached the lake, so Tom would start seeing his officers through the trees on either side shortly.

Where was Lane?

If they'd – if *he* – had got this wrong, they would have to start from scratch, and time was running out for Laura.

Tom began to jog, his lungs burning from the now unfamiliar exercise. He hadn't run in a long time and sadly, his legs had lost their muscle memory. His wife was right. He was out of shape.

Let us find her, he pleaded with the gods. Let us find her safe and I'll go running every damn morning.

The twigs and leaves crunched underfoot as he trotted along, making a little noise but not enough to raise concern. His breathing was louder than anything else.

His radio came to life and he froze, then lifted it to his ear.

'He's here. I see a light ahead.'

It was Michael.

'Where are you?' Tom heard Ray hiss back.

He stood and turned in a circle. They were a half-mile away from the lake. Which direction had Michael set off in? The inspector had gone left from the main path. He closed his eyes and thought back. Right. Michael had gone right.

Tom turned on his heel and veered diagonally in that direction, assuming Michael would be ahead of him. The younger man was fitter and would be moving faster.

'The trees are clearing,' Michael whispered into the radio. 'I'm near the lake. His light has stopped flickering. I need to go to radio silence – I'm approaching.'

Tom picked up the pace. Ray had taken the same direction as Michael at the opening to the woods, so he had to be close. If they could come at Lane in a pincer movement, they would have him.

A single shot rang out, bringing Tom to an abrupt halt. The woods were filled with a deafening silence in its aftermath.

'Who's shot?' he whispered frantically into his radio.

'I'm fine,' Bridget hissed back.

'We're all okay,' Willie added.

Michael had turned his radio off. Tom waited to hear something from Ray, but there was nothing.

His heart pounding, he started to run again, ignoring the ache in his knees and the fire in his chest. He crossed the main trail and plunged into more woodland.

He could hear something between the trees ahead. Tom slowed down and concentrated on controlling his breathing. He trod more softly on the path as he neared the place he thought the sound had come from.

As he emerged from behind a large pine tree, he saw a figure huddled over a person lying on the ground.

He could hear a man's voice. It was Ray. Tom lowered his weapon and jogged over.

Michael was down. He clutched his arm.

'I don't think he actually saw me,' he winced, as Tom knelt beside him. 'I think he must have heard something and got spooked and fired into the woods. I tried not to make any sound when the bullet hit. Go, I'm fine. It's only my arm – probably just a flesh wound.'

Ray was itching to carry on, but reluctant to leave his colleague. Michael's face was white from the pain and his breathing was ragged.

'We need to tie something around the arm,' Tom said. 'Ray, give me your sweater.'

The detective pulled off his vest to remove the dark top.

'You go,' the inspector told him, taking the clothing. 'I have this. I'll be right behind you. Ray, don't do anything stupid. He's nervous and clearly trigger-happy. Stay hidden in the trees until you've a clear shot or I catch up with you.'

The inspector wanted to find Laura, but Michael was also a member of his team and he was wounded. He had a duty of care to ensure the man didn't bleed out on the ground, alone.

Ray nodded distractedly and stood up to go.

'Ray.' Tom grabbed his arm. 'I'm serious. If we find Laura and you get shot in the process . . . she'll kill me.'

'I won't do anything stupid,' his deputy said, before taking off at speed.

Tom tied the sweater around Michael's arm.

'You really are going through the mill in this investigation, aren't you, son?' he said, tightening the tourniquet. 'First Fiona Holland's fella thumping you and now this.'

'I want a medal for bravery.'

Moments later, Bridget arrived.

'Stay with him,' the inspector instructed. 'Keep him warm. I've radioed for an ambulance.'

Bridget nodded, her face shocked and drawn. She loved Laura like a sister and was very fond of Michael. It was all too much. She sat down and cradled Michael's head on her lap.

'Ooo-er,' Michael wheezed, his voice weak. 'Don't tell the wife.'

'Shut up, you idiot, or I'll poke my finger into that bullet wound.'

Tom left them, picking up the pace so he could catch Ray.

He'd gone a couple of hundred metres before he slowed down. The ground had evened off and now it was descending. The inspector could see light between the trees below. Further on, he could see the still surface of the lake, the water glistening in the moonlight.

A low whistle to his right notified him of Ray's presence.

'He's down there,' his deputy whispered.

Together, they moved silently through the trees, placing their feet carefully and slowly so as not to alert Lane.

The man they'd been hunting was just beyond the tree line, making his way to the lakeshore. He wore denims and a black sweater; the back of his hair was neatly cut; a normal-looking man if ever there was one.

He was striding calmly towards the lake, dragging a body.

Laura was still dressed in the cut-off trousers, white vest and cardigan she'd worn to work yesterday.

Tom felt his chest constrict at the sight of her limp figure.

She was already gone.

Beside him, Ray made a choking sound that sounded like a sob.

Tom was about to say something when he saw movement in the corner of his eye.

It was Laura. She'd kicked out one of her legs.

She was alive, and still trying to fight her captor as he ploughed onwards.

The arm wrapped around Laura's neck also held a torch. In his free hand, Lane had his gun. He didn't have anything to dig with, Tom realised. No shovel. He had no intention of strangling and burying her, like he had with his other victims.

'Shit,' he hissed at Ray. Laura slumped again and then tried to pull Lane's arm away from her neck, kicking again at the ground in a futile effort to slow the relentless march. 'He plans to drown her.'

They sped down the last hundred metres until they were at the last line of trees before the open ground.

'There's no shot,' Ray whispered urgently, his voice just an octave below hysterical.

'He's dropped something,' Tom replied, squinting desperately. 'It's the torch, is it? I can't see its light any more.' He pointed at the ground ahead where a redundant object lay on the ground. Lane was facing away from them, striding forward as he pulled Laura behind him. 'Does he still have his gun? Can we get a shot at him while he's moving? Ray! Ray!'

His deputy had dived out of the trees and was bounding towards the lake.

The inspector took off after him, cursing.

'Let her go!' Ray roared, causing Lane to freeze on the spot. He turned as the detective rushed closer, slowly raising the gun in his left hand to the side of Laura's head.

Ray froze just as Tom arrived beside him. Both detectives pointed their weapons.

Now they had a proper stand-off.

'You found me,' Lane said and almost sounded relieved. His voice was soft, not threatening. 'I was beginning to think you never would.'

'We did,' the inspector said.

Laura was gagged, her eyes wide with anguish and terror. Tom couldn't see any obvious injuries, but they knew Lane had hit her somewhere, probably the back of the head, to knock her out. Her body slouched over, exhausted from the struggle. The inspector could feel the anger radiating from Ray and willed him to keep it together.

'This can't end well for any of us with everybody waving their weapons,' Tom said. 'It's all over now, Charlie. Time to let her go.'

'I don't want it to end well for me,' Lane snapped, his voice suddenly furious. 'Haven't you figured that out yet? I'm sick. I want it all to be over.'

'Then let her go,' Tom said. 'We can end this.'

'No. If I don't have her, you'll just arrest me. And I'll have to live with what I've done for the rest of my life. I don't want to be this monster. I never wanted to be like this. I want you to shoot me.'

'I can't do that while you're holding my detective,' Tom almost shouted.

'Then I'll shoot her.'

'No!'

Both Tom and Ray yelled as Lane cocked his weapon. Laura's eyes filled with dread.

'If you hurt her, I won't kill you,' Tom growled. 'I'll shoot you so you're incapacitated and then I'll arrest you. I swear, if you harm another hair on that girl's head, I will make it my business to ensure your life is hell.'

'I'm already in hell,' Lane roared.

The inspector cast a sideways glance at his deputy. He seemed to be having some sort of silent exchange with Laura. If they could just get her to duck or move in some way, the detective might have a shot. He needed to keep Lane talking, keep him distracted.

'Don't you want to know how we figured out it was you?' Tom asked, his brain racing. 'You rang Carney, didn't you, when we went in to Fergus' office that day? You wanted us to think it was him and you knew he'd react violently. If you'd wanted to die so badly, why did you get us out of there that day when he started shooting?'

'I don't know! I didn't know I'd be driving you up there. I panicked. I'm a . . . I'm a coward. I've tried to end my own life but I can't. You need to . . . you . . . Just shoot me, for fuck's sake!'

Ray stared at Laura. He couldn't breathe, couldn't think while witnessing her terror. A feeling of helplessness had enveloped him.

He shook his head. He couldn't give into despair.

He steadied his nerve and his resolve.

Ray blinked and met her eye again, slowly nodding his head.

He looked at Tom, who was doing his best to keep Lane distracted.

Laura watched her two colleagues. She knew what they needed from her, but she was so tired and Lane was so strong. They had no idea how strong he was. She closed her eyes and tried to calm down.

I'm panicking, she told herself. I was caught off guard from the start and I haven't been thinking straight since.

There's always a way out.

What have I learned over the years that I could use?

She tried to recall every self-defence lesson she'd ever had.

Slowly, hesitantly, it came to her.

She had to stop fighting Lane and disable him. She still had her shoes on, and they had small block heels. The man holding her wore trainers, not boots. She'd noticed them when he'd carried her to the car boot.

Now – while his attention was directed at Tom – this was her best chance.

Laura opened her eyes and looked straight at Ray.

She finally nodded back with the faintest movement of her head.

One. Two. Three, he mouthed.

She summoned every ounce of energy she had left and, all at once, stamped hard on Lane's foot, forced the pointy tip of her elbow into his ribs and bent back the fingers of the hand gripping her shoulder. Three small but painful manoeuvres designed to unhand any attacker.

Lane cried out in shock at the triple-pronged approach and loosened his grip just enough for Laura to slide down his body and lean to the side.

The sound of a shot filled the air as Ray swiftly aimed and fired.

The bullet landed on target, hitting Lane in the upper body and sending him stumbling backwards. His weapon flew from his splayed fingers.

Laura stood upright and ran to the gun. She threw herself on the ground and grabbed it, then pointed it at her assailant.

There was no need. Lane was down.

Tom ran at him as several more guards emerged from the trees behind them.

Laura collapsed backwards into a sitting position just as Ray arrived and skidded to his knees in front of her. He pulled the gag from her mouth and she sobbed, gulping in great gasps of air.

'About bloody time you lot showed up,' she cried, as tears spilled down her cheeks.

He cupped her face, his palms on the curls stuck to her cheeks. Leaning forward, he rested his forehead on hers.

'I've been meaning to tell you something and I don't think it can wait any longer. I think I'm in love with you.'

She cried again, from relief or happiness she wasn't sure,

and he pulled her close, every fibre of his body thanking God that she was safe.

Behind them, the inspector leaned over Charlie Lane. The serial killer gazed up at Tom, his expression like that of a lost little boy.

He wasn't an ugly man. He could even be described as quite pleasant-looking.

But as he'd said himself – he was a monster.

'Where's Fiona Holland?' Tom said, his voice low and dangerous.

A puzzled look crossed Lane's face, replaced with a knowing one.

Then he passed out.

# CHAPTER 38

All the lights were still on in Tom's house when Willie dropped him off in the early hours of the morning. He hadn't been in touch with Louise all night, though he'd presumed somebody at headquarters had told her what was happening. She was probably worried sick.

Charlie Lane had been taken to hospital under armed guard. If he was deemed fit enough, they'd interview him in the morning and try to establish Fiona Holland's whereabouts. They were still going through his bank details and the property register to establish if he owned another house or had a rental somewhere.

A team had been deployed to search the woods at Lough Dan, in case he'd already murdered and buried the girl.

But it was looking for a needle in a haystack. They'd need him to talk in order to find her.

Tom kicked off his shoes inside the front door and threw his suit jacket onto the end of the banisters. He was fit to collapse.

He went to the kitchen first, where Louise usually waited up for him when he was late.

She wasn't there. He poured himself a glass of water and stood at the sink drinking it.

A few seconds later, he heard Louise call his name.

Tom put the drink down and walked into the hall. His wife was standing in the door frame of the sitting room. Her eyes were red, her cheeks puffy. She'd been crying.

'Oh, Jesus, Louise. I'm so sorry. I should have rang to tell you we were all okay. It was just crazy. Were you worried?'

She nodded.

'Can you come in here for a moment?' she said, her voice hoarse.

The inspector frowned. Something was wrong.

He followed his wife into the sitting room.

Sean McGuinness sat on the edge of the couch, his big hands cupped around a mug of coffee.

'Sean!' Tom exclaimed. 'I've been looking for you all day. Did you hear what . . .'

He trailed off. The man in front of him looked like Sean, but Tom had never seen anybody's features change so much in the space of a few days.

His old friend was . . . haunted. There was no other word for it.

Tom found himself sitting on the chair beside him. He didn't think his legs could support him for what was coming.

'What's happened?' he asked, an audible tremor in his voice.

Sean put down the cup.

'I couldn't call you,' he said. His voice was raspy. It sounded like it was coming from under water. 'It's not that I didn't want to. I just couldn't. Not with this case you're dealing with. And I couldn't answer your calls, because if I'd told you, you would have dropped everything. Then Louise came over and told me what had happened with Laura. I'm glad she's safe. I'm sorry I couldn't help.'

The inspector shook his head.

He felt like whatever was coming, once said, would leave the world changed utterly.

'June went missing last night,' Sean continued. 'I woke up and she wasn't in the bed with me. I went downstairs and found the front door open and the car gone. She'd left a note. It said she was going shopping. She didn't come back.'

'Christ,' Tom said. His hand rose to his mouth. Whatever he'd been expecting, it wasn't this. All day they'd been looking for Laura and that whole time . . . Poor Sean.

'June is missing? Jesus. Right, let me splash water on my face and I'll come with you. Who's looking for her? Your kids . . . but you must have told our lot as well surely?'

Sean shook his head.

'Then come on, we'll get it sorted. We'll find her, Sean.'

Tom stood up, his tiredness vanquished. Adrenalin pulsed through his body once more.

'Tom,' Louise said. She grabbed his hand. Her voice shook. 'They found her.'

The inspector stared at his wife and looked back to Sean.

'I don't understand.'

'They think she might have had an aneurism.' The words sounded like they were coming from somewhere else. Not from Sean's mouth. 'She'd been going the right way for the super-market. Residual memory. The same memory that enabled her to drive the car. She drove straight into a tree. She died instantly.'

His voice cracked.

Tom sank back onto the chair, a ball of pain threatening to explode in his chest. He dropped his head into his hands.

June. Beautiful June. Their beloved friend for decades. The woman who'd taught the smallest of children until her retirement and who had been loved by every pupil she'd ever had. The woman who never forgot a birthday or an anniversary, who had a kind word for everybody she met and a no-nonsense approach to life. A woman who had kept her wit and humour even after she'd received a debilitating and devastating diagnosis.

Tom pictured her the last time they'd all been together, her hair tucked under in the neat little bob she always wore, the stylish cut silk blouse and the simple but elegant string of pearls.

And what had he said to her at Sean's the other day?

I'll see you soon. We miss you.

The inspector lifted his head from hands now wet with tears.

'Sean, I'm so sorry,' he tried to say, but his voice broke.

Instead, he sat there, with his arm around his old friend, shell-shocked and unable to offer any words of comfort.

Louise stood in the middle of the room, her hands clasped against her chest. She looked down at the pair of them, two of the strongest men she'd ever known, their shoulders huddled in grief.

Her heart felt like it was breaking.

# CHAPTER 39

The doctors were just trying to do their job.

Charlie Lane had sustained significant blood loss and was barely out of intensive care.

He couldn't be put under the sort of pressure an interview would bring.

And the inspector really didn't give a shit.

He didn't want to be here at all. But what choice did he have? They'd no idea where Fiona Holland was. Unless she was already dead, she was locked up somewhere and now they were in a race against time to ensure she didn't starve to death.

'It's like this,' he snapped, and planted two hands on the hospital administrator's desk. 'We either interview Charlie Lane today, or I am going to have you charged as an accessory in a crime.'

'What are you talking about?'

The man sitting across from Tom laughed nervously. He was used to dealing with members of the emergency services, including the guards, and knew they could get hysterical at times. Everything was always of the utmost importance and urgency, regardless of how ill a patient was. And normally, he, the man in charge of that access, could handle these hyperactive officers. But the man who stood in front of him now looked nearly psychotic. His eyes were ringed with dark circles, his cheeks purple beneath the salt-and-pepper beard, veins throbbing at the side of his forehead. He'd heard of Tom Reynolds, but usually in the most respectful of terms. If people only knew!

'The man lying in the bed upstairs kidnapped and murdered five women. He tried to kill one of my detectives. And somewhere, there is a nineteen-year-old girl waiting to be found. For all we know, she is lying in a dingy cellar, freezing and starving to death. Charlie Lane is the only person on this planet who knows her whereabouts. So, yes, if you don't allow me to interview him and we don't find that girl, or we find her too late, I will have you charged.'

The man at the desk was beginning to accept that there were some battles not worth winning.

'I will speak to his doctors and see if he can be made comfortable enough for questioning.' The administrator conceded defeat. 'You won't have long with him. There is absolutely nothing I can do about that and you can arrest me for it if you want.'

'Fine,' Tom said, his voice a little kinder. 'I'll be up with the detective who was admitted last night. Find me there. Quickly, please.'

The man nodded and picked up his phone to indicate to the inspector that he was getting right on it.

'When did you know?' she asked.

'About Lane?'

Laura blushed, the colour vivid against her pale skin. She was sitting on the edge of the bed in a hospital gown, her legs dangling over the side. The back of her head was partially covered by a large bandage. She wanted to get out of there, but Ray was trying to talk her into staying. And if he wouldn't let her leave, then they could finally have the conversation they needed to have. Laura was still woozy from the meds they'd given her and was feeling slightly braver than usual.

'I don't mean Lane. What you said to me last night. Where did that come from?'

It was Ray's turn to flush red.

He smiled shyly.

'Last year. Around autumn. We'd spent time together during the summer when I was helping your mam look for her sister's grave, remember? And then you sort of disappeared, because you were off seeing Eoin Coyle. When I asked you out for dinner to the Japanese place that time, I really wanted to tell you then, but you left early.'

'I remember that night. You started talking about your feelings for another woman!'

'I know.' Ray shook his head. 'I was an idiot. But I did try to tell you that, afterwards. Then you dumped Eoin and I thought I had a chance. But you didn't seem interested any more.'

Laura tried to find the words to explain how she hadn't had a clue what he was thinking. Now she wanted to know everything to make up for the lost time – what she'd done to make him suddenly notice her; what she'd been wearing; what she'd said. The butterflies in her stomach fluttered with delight at the very thought of it. She'd been in love with him for years and for the last few months *he* had actually fancied *her*. All those misread situations seemed so silly and childish now.

'I was interested,' she said. 'But I didn't think you were and I didn't want to be some dopey cow mooning after you. I really thought you were oblivious to how I felt.'

'I was. For a long time. I didn't realise you'd any feelings for me until that night in the restaurant. When you got so annoyed at me for talking about Ellie, then I knew.'

She smiled. She couldn't bring herself to proper laughter just yet. The experience with Lane was still too raw.

Ray took her hand tenderly and caressed it. He knew it would take a while for Laura to bounce back.

There was a knock on the door and Tom popped his head around.

'Are we up for visitors?' their boss asked.

'Tom, speak to her, will you? She thinks she's going home.'

The inspector came in and studied Laura. She'd regained a smidgen of colour in her cheeks but still looked ghostly compared to normal. It wasn't the only noticeable difference. The inspector could see a shadow in Laura's expression that hadn't been there before, a doubt in her eyes, usually so open and friendly around those she knew and loved.

'They've treated my head wound, boss. We still have work to do.'

'No, you don't.' Tom pulled over an extra chair. 'Legs back in the bed, Detective.'

Laura chewed her lip, but swung back onto the bed, allowing Ray to pull the blankets up over her legs.

'They're beautiful flowers,' the inspector said, noticing the large bunch of lilacs placed in a vase on the bedside table. 'An admirer been in, huh? That chap you were going out with last year, was it?' It was his turn to smile as Ray and Laura both flushed crimson.

'I jest,' Tom said, not cruel enough to embarrass them for any length of time. 'Laura, that was some blow you took to the head. They need to keep you under observation for thirty-six hours. I just had a lovely little chat with the hospital administrator. Very helpful chap. So, even if you checked out of here, you wouldn't be allowed back to work.'

Laura sighed. Then she remembered.

'I'm so sorry about June. Ray told me. I can't believe it. How is Sean?'

Tom swallowed.

How was Sean? How could anybody be when he'd just lost his soul mate, the love of his life, in such horrific circumstances?

Willie had returned last night at Tom's request to bring their former chief home. Usually so stoic and wise, he'd turned up at the Reynolds' door blubbing like a baby and had only pulled himself together when it looked like Sean was actually going to have to do the driving.

'What can I do?' Tom had asked his friend, before he left. 'What can I do to make this easier for you?'

Sean had just shrugged. 'There's nothing,' he replied. 'Nothing that you won't do anyway. I just needed to tell you in person. I had to . . . I had to get out of the house. But you know what you must do now? Go into work tomorrow and get that bastard to talk. Find your missing girl. Then we'll bury June and the world will keep turning.'

Louise had made her husband go to bed for a few hours, but sleep had felt like an impossibility as he raged at the cruelty of the world. He must have dozed at some point. He remembered snatches of vivid dreams, June clutching his arm on the couch that day, an image that morphed into Laura, her mouth gagged as she mumbled incoherently and desperately.

'He's coping,' Tom answered Laura's question.

'When's the funeral?' Ray asked.

'Not for a little while. There has to be a post-mortem to establish for certain what happened.' The inspector swallowed.

'Anyhow, that's for another day. Laura, how are you holding up?'

He could see her stiffen at the question. She wrapped her arms around herself defensively.

'I'm fine. How many times do I have to say it?'

'I don't mean the head. After what happened – how do you feel?'

She shrugged.

'Like an idiot. What was I thinking going out there alone? I tried to ring him, but he didn't answer. I said in the voicemail I just wanted to chat about his time in Britain. I thought I was reaching – it seemed so far-fetched, but we'd nothing else to go on. No leads. But I guess I didn't think he was an actual suspect or I wouldn't have called out, certainly not alone.'

'Of course you wouldn't have,' Ray said. 'You were clutching at straws, like the rest of us.'

Laura looked up and met Tom's eye. She knew what he wanted to ask.

'He didn't hurt me,' she said. 'Not in that way. I don't think he sexually assaulted any of the women.'

'Did he speak to you? Say anything that could help?'

'Most of the time, I was just down in the cellar on my own. It was pitch black and I couldn't see a thing. When he spoke to me, he said he wanted to be stopped. But then he put me in the boot of the car. He drove around for hours, until we arrived at those woods. He didn't mention Fiona Holland the whole time I was with him.'

Laura relaxed once she'd got the words out and Ray squeezed her hand.

'Have forensics turned up anything at the scene?' he asked his boss.

'They collected a lot of samples,' Tom replied. 'Emmet is working through them as we speak, but he believes he's isolated blood and hair for Una Dolan. There's a lot of it, so they'll be working for a while. They have to discard Laura's, ours and Lane's, obviously.'

Laura shuddered. She'd never shake the horror of being down in that cellar where other girls had been held and had not been so fortunate. She knew she would have nightmares about it for the rest of her life.

'It will take time,' the inspector said, examining her face and reading her thoughts. 'But you'll recover from this. Don't try to bury it, though, Laura. Deal with it properly. You'll need to see the garda counsellor.'

'The only thing I need is for us to find Fiona,' she answered. 'I can't bear the thought of her being kept somewhere like that. I felt so . . . hopeless. And that was just for a day. She's been gone weeks.'

'I know,' Tom said. In his gut, he didn't think Fiona was still alive, no matter how much he wished it so.

On cue, the hospital administrator arrived at the door of the room.

'Inspector Reynolds, he's ready.'

Ray stood up with Tom.

'I don't think so,' the inspector said.

'What are you talking about?'

'You shot him, Ray. There isn't a hope in hell of you doing this interview with me. Michael is waiting downstairs. He's just as eager as you to nail this bastard.'

'Michael? What the hell? He was injured and you're still bringing him instead of me?'

'It was a flesh wound. His arm is in a sling and unlike Laura,

I have no medical advice telling me he can't return to work. Please, you need to stay here.'

Ray sat back on the chair, glowering.

'Is my company that bad?' Laura asked, her doing the comforting now.

The tension eased in Ray's shoulders and he smiled.

'I suppose if Tom is ordering me to stay with you, I'd better do it.'

The inspector left the fledgling lovebirds alone. Once outside the room, his features hardened again. He sent Michael a text and within minutes, the other detective arrived.

'Are you sure you're okay to do this?' Tom asked him, nodding at the injured arm.

Michael raised his eyebrows dismissively.

'I don't want this to affect my merit award chances, but they won't even give me the good pain relief, that's how little damage was done. Two shagging Solpadine is all I'm allowed. Anyway, I'm grand. Let's get this bastard.'

Tom clapped him on the good shoulder.

'Come on, then.'

Tom and Michael greeted the two guards stationed outside and entered the room.

The hospital medical staff had propped Lane up on pillows, making him as comfortable as possible. The left side of his body was covered with a large bandage and he was attached to various drips. Both hands were cuffed to rails at either side of the bed. The blood loss had been significant, but Ray had aimed well, considering how close he'd fired to the man's head. No major organs had been hit and Charlie Lane would live, the only legacy of the injury being some nerve damage in his arm.

Tom would have to get Ray down to the firing range to see if he really was as good a shot as everybody was now saying, or if the man in the bed had just been incredibly lucky.

Lane had refused the offer of a solicitor, so they were alone.

'Inspector,' he croaked, as the two detectives sat in the chairs placed beside the bed. 'It looks like you got your wish. Here I am, alive. And I suppose you're going to make sure my life is the hell I feared.'

'Let's be honest, now. Dead or alive, it was always going to be hellish.' Tom's voice was measured. 'Where's Fiona?'

'I remember you asking me that last night. I suppose I should have expected it. Will you believe me if I tell you I don't know?'

The inspector clenched and unclenched his fists. It was a calming technique that usually worked for him but on this occasion didn't seem to be up to much.

'I don't have time to play games with you, Charlie. Or should I call you Cormac? Which do you prefer? What did your grand-dad call you?'

The other man gritted his teeth.

'Animal. That's what he called me.'

Lane closed his eyes, his expression anguished.

There was a part of Tom that felt sympathy for the man who had once been the little boy. He had suffered a violent and abusive beginning, like so many offenders the guards encountered. But the inspector couldn't do anything for the child who'd witnessed horror at the hands of his grandfather. And he was angry because, of everybody, Charlie Lane knew how it felt to be locked up and frightened. Yet he'd inflicted that time and again on innocent women, and worse. He'd survived his ordeal as a child. His victims had no such luck.

'Why did you do it?' he asked Lane, curiosity getting the better of him. 'Was it to punish your mother for leaving you? Why didn't you find her and put her through what you'd experienced? The women you took had done nothing wrong.'

'I looked for her,' he answered. 'She was dead. I didn't want to punish her. I wanted to forgive her. But she denied me even that. They tracked her down – social services – soon after they found me. Told her what her father had done to me. But she didn't care. She was so far gone with her addictions that I didn't matter. He beat me every day and kept me in that cellar for weeks and she didn't care. But you're wrong, Inspector.'

'What am I wrong about?'

'Those women I took. They weren't innocent. They were all just like her. Sluts. Bitches. Women who didn't give a shit about anybody or anything bar themselves. I chose carefully. Their own neighbours told me what they were like. Sometimes, even their family.'

'No,' Tom shook his head. 'No, that's not true. They were just young women, living their lives. Maybe they made mistakes, but who knew what their futures held? You'd no right to take that from them. My detective – you know nothing about her life. And what about Pauline O'Hara? She was a victim of domestic abuse. She didn't party, or sleep with lots of men, or abandon a child. What had she done wrong?'

Lane flushed.

'Pauline. She . . . her death was a mistake. I was just driving around collecting fares and there she was, waiting at the bus stop. It was lashing rain and she was on her own. I pulled over, just to offer her a taxi on the cheap. She'd all those shopping bags. She got in. She was so like my mother. She had the same eyes, the same smile. Something clicked in my head. It was almost the anniversary of my mother leaving and it was like God had given her back to me.

'She was relaxed in my company. Chatty. She told me she'd been living in an awful situation but she was going to get out of it. I turned the car and drove in the direction of where I was living at the time. She laughed and said she couldn't leave right now. But then she got angry and I put my hand over her mouth. She was so scared, she just sat there quietly for miles.'

'Where were you living back then?'

'Just outside Waterford City. I kept her for a while. I didn't want to hurt her. I wanted to protect her. I wanted her to stay. But sometimes, all I could see was my mother and I needed her to know how much pain I'd been in. How frightened I was. She didn't understand. One day, she was screaming and yelling at me and I just placed my hands around her throat and squeezed until she stopped.'

Lane's eyes glazed over as he recalled the final moments of his first victim's murder. Tom wanted to look away, but he was transfixed.

'How long did you keep her?' he asked, when he found his voice.

'I . . . can't remember.'

That was a lie. Tom waited.

'I don't know. Maybe six months?'

'Jesus,' Michael spat.

'I didn't want to kill her,' Lane protested, as though that somehow excused his holding her captive for so long. 'I didn't. I vomited, after, when I realised what I'd done. I thought she'd wake up. I bought her a present – a little bracelet – and I told her if she woke, I'd let her go. I would rescue her, just like I'd been rescued.'

'But she didn't,' Tom said. 'The thing is, I can believe what you're saying, Charlie. And if Pauline had been your only victim, this would be a different conversation. But you went and did it again, didn't you?'

Lane blinked. He nodded, slowly.

'Not for a long time,' he said, his voice low. 'I didn't want to do it again. I moved away from Waterford, down to West Cork. Everything was – normal. But I couldn't stop thinking about Pauline. It was horrific, when she died. But after I accepted that she was dead – what I'd done – I felt calm. It was as though, with her death, something had been put to rest. For the first time in my life, I was at peace. But, as time went on, it started to slip away.'

'So the only way you could find peace was by kidnapping women and murdering them? Pauline, Mary Ellen, Treasa, Eimear, Una and now Fiona Holland. You kept them captive for a while, Charlie. So where is Fiona? Have you killed her already?'

Lane shook his head.

'I didn't take her. I understand why you think I did, I went after a girl last April. I'd been watching her for a while. But I made a mistake. I forgot to put the roof plate on the car and when I pulled up beside her and asked her to get in, she started screaming. Another car came up behind me, so I drove off. It was a sign. I had to stop.'

Tom shook his head in disbelief.

'Amazing,' he said. 'You were foiled in April and all of a sudden you have your urges under complete control? You dug up Una so we'd find her and stop you? Do you really expect us to buy that? You wiped clean every trace of your crime in the cellar in your West Cork house. Why do that if you wanted to be stopped? And now you claim it's just a coincidence that Fiona Holland, who lives a couple of miles away, went missing in exactly the same circumstances as your previous victims, just a few months later? A girl who fits the very profile you were targeting – young, a little reckless, leaves her child at home with her parents – in fact, everything that angered you. That was just a strange alignment of the fates? Absolutely amazing.'

Lane was getting agitated, his body starting to tremble, the cuffs clinking against the rails.

'I'm telling the truth,' he said, his voice shaking. 'When the police came to the house I was staying in in Cork, it scared the hell out of me. I wanted to keep going, back then. I had to kill Mary Ellen a few days after I took her and it didn't give me the same satisfaction. I knew I couldn't risk taking a woman again in a location where I lived.'

'This is a crock of shit,' Michael snapped. 'I don't believe you.'

'I'm telling the truth, I didn't take Fiona. I wouldn't be that stupid.' Charlie lifted his head off the pillow and raised his voice.

'You wouldn't be that stupid?' Michael snarled back. 'You attacked a garda detective and tried to kill her. You shot me!'

The door to the room flew open and a doctor strode in, followed at a pace by two nurses.

'Okay. That's enough, detectives. My patient's blood pressure is rising to dangerous levels. You need to leave.'

'His blood pressure is rising?' Tom retaliated. 'I'm about to blow a gasket. Where is she, Charlie? Where's Fiona?'

'Inspector, if you don't leave now, I am going to have hospital security come and remove you and your detective!'

Tom stood up. He kicked his chair back as he did.

'We'll leave,' he barked. 'I'm going to ask you one more time, Charlie. What have you done with that girl?'

'Inspector!'

'I didn't . . .' Lane panted, struggling for breath, the blood rushing to his face. 'I didn't take her. I swear it.'

'You sent us a letter. You told us you had her!'

'What? I didn't. I didn't send any letter.'

'Shit, shit, shit!' Tom slammed his hand against the wall in the corridor. 'We have nothing. They won't let us near him again today.'

Michael shook his head.

'Richard Holland keeps ringing headquarters,' he said, his voice brittle. 'He thinks we're hours away from finding his daughter. He thinks his family's nightmare is nearly over.'

Tom closed his eyes and massaged his temples, trying to keep the stress headache at bay.

'Okay. We'll go back to HQ and get everybody together. We're missing something. Another house, a burial site, something. We've a serial killer trying to convince us he suddenly has a conscience. He wasn't displaying any of it with Laura last night.'

'Does it happen?' Michael asked. 'Is there any possibility this is a coincidence? I don't believe he would have stopped, whatever he's telling himself – but is he telling the truth about Fiona?'

Tom shrugged.

'Stranger things have happened. But we're dealing with a pathological liar. Never forget that.'

Joe Kennedy was waiting for them back at headquarters.

'Tom – can I have five minutes?'

The inspector looked at his watch impatiently.

'I'm under pressure, Sir.'

'Please?'

Tom wavered, then nodded at Michael to start proceedings.

'I just want to check in with you,' Kennedy said, closing the door to his office. 'You've been through a lot in the last twenty-four hours. Can I get you something? A tea or coffee?'

Tom shook his head and sat upright in the chair. He'd cottoned on to his new chief's method – reel you in with concern and platitudes, then try to manipulate the situation. He would be alert for whatever was coming, this time.

'I'm fine,' he replied. 'Just eager to conclude this investigation.'

'Are you sure you're able to continue?'

'Are you doubting my abilities?' Tom asked, sounding far more relaxed than he felt.

'Well, look at it like this. You've done a superb job in tracking down and arresting Lane. Saving your detective in the meantime – nobody can deny that was excellent police work. Although, people will probably wonder why she was allowed to go out to his house alone in the first instance.'

Kennedy paused.

'They might,' Tom interjected. 'Of course, luckily for Laura, we knew immediately something wasn't right and launched a full-scale investigation into her disappearance. Otherwise, I can't imagine what might have happened. If we'd assumed, for example, that she just hadn't been arsed to turn up for work . . .'

Kennedy pursed his lips and pushed his glasses up his nose.

'As I said,' he continued. 'It was very good police work. And I will ensure that you are commended for it. I am concerned, though. The Hollands are desperate to find their daughter and we might need fresh eyes at this stage. You don't look like you've slept and I know you're dealing with a loss, too. You were close to Sean's wife, weren't you?'

Tom nodded brusquely. He wasn't prepared to give this man anything of his private life.

'That's a lot to deal with. Then there's your conduct in the hospital just now. I've had a complaint from the hospital administrator that you threatened to arrest him and then you nearly had to be forcibly removed from Lane's room. Is that true?'

'They were trying to prevent me interviewing the only man who might know where Fiona Holland is. I don't have a crystal ball. If that girl is in danger, we have no way of finding her unless he confesses.'

'And did he tell you where she was?'

Tom stared down at the table.

'No.'

Kennedy sighed.

'We're only having this conversation because I have your best interests at heart, Tom. All the good you've achieved in arresting Lane will be lost if you fail to find Fiona. And other things might come to the surface then.'

'Like what, exactly?'

'Well, like you casting aspersions on members of the force – and making accusations against Sergeant Healy.'

Something inside Tom snapped.

He was exhausted and he was grieving, and all of that he had to leave to one side while he concentrated on finding Fiona. But to be expected to cope with this arsehole and his self-serving agenda as well? No. That was too much.

'I don't want to argue with you, Sir,' he said, his voice low. There was an edge to it that even he didn't recognise. It sounded quite calm, but incredibly dangerous. 'But I am going to leave this room now and return to my investigation.'

'And if I stop you?' Kennedy said.

The words came out of Tom's mouth before he could censor them.

'If you try to stop me, you'll leave me no option – I will phone Assistant Commissioner Bronwyn Maher. I'll start by telling her my concerns regarding some of our colleagues around the country and their responses to missing women who fit a certain profile.

'And then, Sir, I'm going to tell her that I've reconsidered. That, in light of the success of this investigation, I've decided I am happy to be promoted. I want to ensure this force continues in the progressive vein pursued by the likes of Sean McGuinness and Bronwyn herself. And I'm not sure that there's anybody better than me to do that.'

Tom looked up and straight at the chief.

'Now, what job do you think she'll want to promote me to?'

Kennedy met his gaze, unblinking, but the colour had risen in his cheeks. Tom had hit on a sore point – the possibility of Kennedy being shunted out of his role to make room for the first choice for the job.

The inspector was expecting the other man to rage and threaten. Perhaps warn Tom he'd made a serious enemy. That sort of thing. But it was in his reply that Tom realised what the man's real talent was – an ability to see the writing on the wall and to adapt. Kennedy was clearly not yet as close to Bronwyn Maher as he'd like to be. And maybe he knew Tom had the backing of An Taoiseach himself.

It was too soon for him to go all out in a head to head with the inspector. He'd pushed too far, too early.

'I think you've misread this situation and are over-reacting, Tom,' Kennedy said, coolly. 'It's my job to assist you and make your role easier. I understand you're tired and feeling the pressure. Against my better judgement, I'm going to let you resume your role in this investigation. Afterwards, though, we will need to have a conversation about our professional relationship. If you do not respect me in this role, Inspector, that is an issue.

'And I want to leave you with this. I believe you have vastly underestimated the assistance I have provided in order for you to run this investigation unimpeded. Not once have I asked you to deal with the media during what has proven to be one of the most sensational cases in the history of our force. I've ensured you've had all the resources necessary at a time when budgets across other departments are hanging on by a thread. And not once have you thanked me for any of that. I promise you, we will return to this at a later date.'

'Let's do that,' Tom said.

He was trembling from the anger coursing through him. And more – he knew he'd given Kennedy what he wanted. The inspector had allowed the chief to provoke him into showing his best hand.

But he also felt chastened. Kennedy had thrown stuff back at him that Tom hadn't been prepared for. What he'd said was true and the inspector was annoyed that he hadn't even considered that side of things.

Worse still, Tom might have just created a situation where the only way he would be able to deal with this man was to actually take his job.

As good as that threat had sounded, it really wasn't what he wanted.

*

They went over everything again. Lane's financial details. His work record with the Hollands. They were in the middle of compiling a full list of all his deliveries in the last few years – no easy task considering the man travelled the country every other week. But Tom's team was looking for patterns. Lane might be renting somewhere with cash payments which would require recurring visits.

'We'll have to release his identity in the morning, if we make no progress,' the inspector told the team. 'See if anybody comes forward with information. A landlord we don't know about, hopefully.'

'Could he have been in league with Vincent Carney?' Bridget asked. 'Should we search his house again, see if there's something we missed?'

'It was a thorough search the first time and I can't see the two of them being in this together,' Tom answered. 'But we can't rule anything out so, yes, get a team out there first thing.'

'Are we still considering her boyfriend and, eh, the other person of interest we dealt with?' Michael asked, meaning Healy. His involvement still wasn't widely known.

'Yes. We will have to speak to them again tomorrow. Is there anything more from Emmet's team?'

'He's still working through the DNA,' Ray informed the room. He'd returned from the hospital earlier and got straight back into it. 'He's managed to isolate two unknown groupings. One of them could be Fiona's. He says his team will keep going through the night.'

'Good. Well, even though I'm inspired by their dedication to work, I think we need to call it a night ourselves, folks, and come in fresh in the morning. Go home and get some rest.'

There were grateful sighs around the room from the exhausted officers.

Ray approached Tom as the room was emptying.

'You're planning to stay, aren't you?'

'You know me so well.'

'Yep. Of all of us, boss, you need the rest the most. Why don't you tell me what it is you need done and I'll do it? I owe you one.'

'How's that?'

'You figured out Charlie Lane yesterday. If you hadn't . . .'

'One of you would have.'

Ray shrugged.

'I don't know. I think that's why you get the big bucks.'

Tom smiled.

'Okay. But I don't really know what it is I'm trying to figure out. My head is all over the place.'

'Wouldn't you feel better if you slept on it?'

The inspector rubbed his jaw.

'I don't know how to explain it, junior. It's just . . . there.' He reached out his hand like he was trying to touch something he couldn't see. 'I won't be able to sleep until I put my finger on it.'

'I get it. But where are you going to begin?'

Tom bit his lip.

'Come with me,' he said, throwing on his suit jacket.

Natasha McCarthy was still at her desk.

'Congratulations,' she said, standing up to shake their hands when Tom and Ray came in. 'That was some police work.'

'Thanks. Sorry to be disturbing you. Are you in the middle of something?'

'Paperwork. Yet another watertight file for the Director of Prosecutions. I really hope this one cops it good. He was raping both his daughters. Since the age of eight.'

'Jesus. Do you want us to leave you alone?'

'Shit, no. It's horrendous. Come in and distract me with something for a few minutes. A bit of serial-killer gossip, that'll be nice. What can I help you with?'

'Well, you probably know the score on our guy. He claims he didn't sexually assault his victims, he was just recreating what was inflicted on him as a child – forced captivity. He's swears Pauline O'Hara's death was accidental but that he killed the rest to emulate the feeling of calm he had after her murder.'

'Okay. Sick puppy. It's not really my area this, though. Would you not be better talking to Linda?'

'I spoke to her earlier. Lane fits the serial-killer persona perfectly. A complete split personality and serious mental instability with violent tendencies. Linda reckons he even truly believes that he wanted to stop. But he wouldn't have, of course. He'd have just kept going, getting more reckless each time. Maybe he did dig up Una to lead us to him, or maybe he just needed to increase the thrill factor.

'It's your area of expertise I want now, though. Sexual offences. We discovered in the course of the investigation into Fiona's disappearance that she was in a number of unhealthy relationships. One of her boyfriends was handy with his fists. The other – well, he's a guard.'

Natasha frowned.

'Hmm.'

'Are you surprised?'

'That there's a guard out there with a penis and no sexual

moral compass? Can't say I am. It's not like he's the only one. Guards, believe it or not, are members of the human race. There are plenty who abuse their positions for power trips and sexual gratification. The key thing for us is having the resources to weed out those who do and respond appropriately.'

Tom nodded.

'I agree. There's another player in the Fiona case. That guy whose name you got for Ray, the one with previous. Vincent Carney tried to attack her before and is a registered sex offender. What concerns me is that Charlie Lane is absolutely adamant that he didn't take Fiona and there are certain elements to his story that have me wondering if he's actually telling the truth. He claims he didn't go after women in his home area because it nearly came back to bite him in the Mary Ellen case. And he seemed genuinely bewildered by the letter we received.'

'I see. So you're wondering if Fiona was taken by somebody else – perhaps with a sexual motive?'

Tom shrugged.

'It's always possible, Tom. The abusive boyfriend might have gone too far. She may have been about to out the guard, so he silenced her. Neither of them have form for sexual assault, but that's not a prerequisite. And, let's be honest, the guard would know how to dispose of her body without being caught. Carney, though – well, he's your strongest suspect, I would have thought. Given he has prior convictions.'

'I've just thought of something, boss,' Ray said.

'Go on.'

'We searched Carney's property for somewhere he could have been hiding her. But what if he'd already buried her on his land? Maybe Healy was in on it – maybe he murdered her and got Carney to bury her so he could point the finger at him.

Who'd believe the local – what did he call him, a simpleton, wasn't it – over a guard?'

'The village idiot. That was the term he used. After his passionate defence of people with disabilities.'

Tom considered Ray's theory. It was plausible. They could start a search of the land around Carney's house tomorrow with that in mind. Bring in the dogs.

'Thanks, Natasha,' he said, shaking her hand again.

'For all the use I was to you,' she smiled. 'And now I have to get back to this appalling case. Families, huh? Completely screwed up. It's either love or hate, there's no in-between.'

'Wanna grab a quick dinner?' Ray asked. 'I can see your head is still buzzing. Louise won't thank me if I send you home in this state.'

'She's over in Sean's,' Tom said, glumly. 'I'm barred from joining her. She said I'm to go straight home to bed after here.'

'Well, then.'

'Don't you have a new girlfriend to visit? Those flowers are probably wilting in that hospital heat at this stage. Or there could be a handsome doctor chatting her up. With the amount of hits and misses you've had in this little love saga to date, I'm surprised you've left her on her own this long.'

It was Ray's turn to look down in the dumps.

'They won't let me in again. I already rang. Her family were there all day and they said she needs her rest now. I got the shop to send her up one of those giant "Get well soon" balloons.'

'Oh, she'll be thrilled with that. So I'm second choice, am I? Go on then, you can treat me. Let's go to the Italian in Blanchardstown. I can just about keep my eyes open for their vesuvio pizza and a glass of Barolo.'

They met Willie in reception and told him the plan. He gamely offered to join them, moaning that his wife was driving him to distraction.

'I got a bit teary over June McGuinness,' he said, 'and she's been trying to mollycoddle me all day. Turned up here with my lunch! How's about we leave the car, lads, and get a taxi down so I can have a few pints?'

'You don't want to drive?' Tom feigned horror. 'I'd always assumed we'd have to surgically remove those pedals from your feet if we ever suggested going somewhere and you not driving. But perhaps you're too traumatised after having your human rights breached today. Imagine, your wife bringing you lunch. The nerve of her.'

Willie raised a scornful eyebrow.

They didn't need to phone a taxi. Ian Kelly was down at reception and offered to drive them, Blanchardstown village being on his route home.

It was an offer he wouldn't be repeating. He spent the short journey being hectored and dictated to by Willie, the worst backseat driver in history.

'Never again,' he whispered to Tom, as the inspector closed the passenger door. 'He makes me nostalgic for Sunday drives with the missus.'

Tom waved him off and turned to catch up with his colleagues. The meal was a good idea. He was glad of the camraderie and the light relief after nothing but tension and pain for the last few days. It didn't make the fact of June's death any easier, and Tom felt a stabbing pain in his gut wishing Sean was here with them and June safe at home. But it was a little reminder that, as his old friend said, the world kept turning.

Sean still had his sons and daughters and grandchildren to hold himself together for and of course, he had Tom and Louise, who were almost as close as family. They would all be there for each other in the coming days and weeks.

Besides, if Tom had gone straight home, he'd have spent the evening in morose solitude, unable to sleep anyhow.

The inspector caught up with Ray and Willie as they were climbing the stairs to the restaurant. He was still ruminating on the conversation with Natasha and was distracted. An idea had planted itself in his head and he was trying to think it through.

The owner showed them to a table, bantering with Ray and Willie as he offered them the wine list.

'Tom knows what he wants, don't you?' Ray said.

His boss didn't answer.

'Tom. Hello?'

The inspector looked up.

'Sorry, what?'

'What wine were you after?'

'Oh. Sorry. The Barolo, please.'

'A pint for me,' Willie said.

'I only have Guinness or bottles of Italian lager,' the owner explained.

'Jaysus, nothing foreign. Guinness will do.'

'You're in an Italian restaurant, what do you mean, "nothing foreign"?' Ray quipped. 'What are you planning to eat?'

'They do steak, don't they?'

Ray shook his head.

They perused the menu.

'What are you thinking, boss?' Willie asked.

'Ah, it's probably nothing.'

'I was referring to the menu, but normally when you say that, it's something.'

Tom smiled.

'Well, just there I was thinking about those markings that Emmet found indented on the letter we got, allegedly from Charlie Lane. I feel like their meaning is on the tip of my tongue. It's like I've a bloody crossword clue stuck in my head.'

'Now, gentlemen, your wine and one Guinness. Who'd like to try it?'

'He's the expert.' Ray pointed to Tom.

The wine was perfectly drinkable, but it left a bitter taste in Tom's mouth.

Because as he sipped, it came to him as clear as day.

There was no hope of finding Fiona Holland alive.

They'd been idiots thinking that letter had come from Lane.

And it hadn't been from a crank.

Her killer had sent it.

# CHAPTER 41

Tom woke up feeling fresh and ready for what he had to do.

He turned on his side and watched Louise sleeping peacefully beside him. She'd arrived home late last night but he'd still been awake when she climbed into bed and snuggled up to him. He'd wrapped his arms around her and they'd fallen asleep like that, but somehow in the night their limbs had become disentangled.

Her auburn hair had fallen onto her face and he tucked it behind her ear, running his fingers tenderly over her cream cheek, bathed in the morning sunlight. She opened her eyes and looked at him.

'I know how lucky I am to have you,' he said, his voice throaty.

'Bloody right, you are.' She smiled, but with sadness. It didn't feel fair to be so grateful for each other when Sean was waking up alone this morning, yet again. But she knew it was only natural that Sean's loss would remind them of what they had.

'You've got to the bottom of it, haven't you?' she said, studying him.

'The case? Yes. How can you tell?'

'You look more relaxed. I can see the veil has lifted. Your eyes – they're peaceful. When you can't figure things out, they're distant, away off thinking. You're here, but not here. Do you know where she is, then, Fiona Holland?'

'No. But it's only a matter of time. She's not being held cap-tive, I'm afraid. Fiona's dead, I'm certain of it. I know who killed her. I'm going out to see him this morning.'

'You didn't go last night?'

'No. He thinks he's safe. He's not going anywhere.'

'Well, go tell him he's wrong, then.'

Tom nodded and kissed her, before throwing off the duvet and heading for the shower.

Ray was outside a half-hour later.

'Coffee?' Tom offered, putting a travel mug into the car's cup holder.

'Thanks. Right, let's go turn the screws on this prick.'

The inspector had filled him in on his theory last night over dinner and Ray had quickly come to the same conclusion.

They planned their line of questioning on the drive out to Meath.

'We have to make him think we have something absolutely concrete,' Ray said, as they turned in the direction of Trim. 'I can't see him caving just because we apply a little pressure.'

'I don't know,' Tom said. 'He might play into our hands.'

But he agreed. They'd massage what they knew to get the truth out of him, if they needed to. The irony of deciding to blur the lines, when he'd been so vexed by the errors of some of his garda colleagues in the course of this investigation, wasn't lost on Tom.

Caroline Holland opened the door. She was holding Fiona's son, who peered at the two men curiously. His red hair was brushed and soft after a morning bath, his skin pale in the sun-light. He was so like his mother and grandmother.

Caroline's eyes filled with hope when she saw Tom and then with sorrow when he slowly shook his head.

'I'm sorry, Mrs Holland, I'm not here with good news.'

'Oh. Well, it can't be long, can it? You must be able to make him talk. You caught him – I know you'll find my daughter.'

She beckoned them in, leading them to the room they'd sat in when they first visited the house.

'Is Richard at home?' Tom asked, holding the door open for her.

'Yes. I'll call him. Ah, there's Nikki. She helps with Cían. Nikki, will you take the baby and fetch Mr Holland?'

'Of course.'

Nikki's accent was French. God love her. She'd probably come to Ireland thinking she'd landed a handy au pair job with a nice family, and somehow ended up in the middle of this mess.

'Nikki, hold on,' Tom said. 'Mrs Holland, is Fergus about? He should be here, too.'

'Yes, he is. He and his father are going over some business. Richard hasn't been there lately, obviously. But now with Fiona coming back – well, he's making sure Fergus hasn't run us into the ground.' She laughed, the sound hollow and forced.

Nikki took the baby and went off to summon the two Holland men.

'I don't think I've told you before but this has always been Fi's favourite room,' Caroline said, sitting down on one of the chairs. 'It's the green. She finds it soothing. God, I can't believe what happened. That somebody we knew took her. Well, I didn't know him as such. I knew he worked for us. To think, we gave him access to our daughter. Thank God you figured it out.'

She closed her eyes and inhaled. The inspector could see that though she was still wound to a tight knot of concern, Fiona's mother's despair had been replaced with something else. Patience. She was calm, believing now that it was just a waiting game until her daughter was found.

Her hope made Tom hate even more what he had to do here, what was coming.

Richard and Fergus arrived together. Both men looked at the inspector questioningly, but Tom knew only one of them was concerned for Fiona's well-being. The other wanted to know what the detectives knew, what they'd come for.

'Thank you for seeing us,' he began. 'I'm sorry, as I said to Mrs Holland, that I'm not the bearer of good news. In fact, I'm afraid you might need to prepare yourself for very bad news.'

'Oh, my God,' Caroline wailed. 'Is she dead?'

Richard paled, his hand grasping his wife's.

'We haven't found her yet,' Tom continued. 'But I fear that, yes, she may be dead. I'm afraid also that we've been pursuing the wrong line of inquiry. I think it may be the case that Fiona has been dead all along.'

'Wait a moment,' Richard barked. 'You've caught him, haven't you? Charlie Lane. You said he kept the women for a while. So he can't have killed Fi already and if you haven't found her body yet – why are you saying this? Why are you upsetting us? I don't understand.'

'He didn't take Fiona,' Tom said, gently. 'I don't really understand this either. But I think your son does. Don't you, Fergus?'

The young man looked shocked for a minute. Then he scowled at the detectives, his face assuming its usual sulky pose.

'What do you mean by that?' he spat.

Richard and Caroline were looking from Tom to Fergus and back again, completely adrift.

'I don't understand how anybody could murder his sister and let his parents live through the hope that she was still alive,' the inspector explained. 'It seems particularly cruel.'

'What are you saying?' Richard jumped to his feet. 'How dare you accuse our son. Have you lost your mind?'

His wife's jaw dropped open.

Fergus stayed sitting, his face contorted with hatred.

'That's a disgusting thing to say,' he growled. 'What, just because you haven't found her body, you think you can start throwing the blame back at her own family? That's sick. You're sick, Inspector.'

'No,' Tom said. 'We know it was you, Fergus. You made a fatal mistake with the letter.'

'What letter?' Richard cried.

'We received a note. The sender wanted us to think it was from the serial killer. It claimed he'd taken Fiona and we wouldn't find her, so we should give up.'

'Well, then, you know it was him,' Caroline whispered, her voice small.

The inspector glanced at her. Richard Holland was railing against the accusations, but Caroline was hunched over on the sofa, her tiny frame huddled into itself as she tried to retreat from what Tom was saying.

She wouldn't look at her son.

A mother always knows, Tom thought.

'Why weren't we told about this letter?' Richard snapped. 'Didn't you think we'd a right to know?'

Tom held up his hand.

'We receive a lot of communication in an investigation like this, Mr Holland, and most of it is from cranks. We can't inform the family until we're certain the contact is authentic. And we weren't in this instance. It wasn't signed; there was nothing in it about the other murders which would have let us know he was the real deal. For example, he could have mentioned the bracelets he'd given to his victims. That information wasn't released to the public.' Tom turned his attention back to the young man, who was still glaring at the inspector. 'So, you wouldn't have known about that, Fergus.'

'If you hadn't sent the letter, we might never have figured it out. But you wrote it in your own notepad and we were able to pick up the letters and numbers that had been written a few pages beforehand. It took me a while to get there. I should have figured it out the day we went to see you at the garden centre. You had Lane unloading five hundred bags of fertiliser from a delivery truck. S-P, L. 500. F dash E, R. Supplies. Five hundred bags of fertiliser.'

There was a shocked silence for a moment.

Richard broke it. 'Now, this is just getting ridiculous. Charlie Lane worked in our garden centre. You said it yourself, he was unloading the damn things. Why couldn't he have written those letters and numbers? If that's even what the words are.'

Tom shook his head.

'Charlie Lane was just a delivery man and gardener. He wasn't in charge of your business. And we've more proof. The handwriting. Our experts looked at the note and they looked at the directions Fergus gave us to Vincent Carney's house that day. They match, even though he tried to disguise his handwriting. It doesn't fool the experts, Fergus.'

The inspector was stretching the truth about the handwriting analysis. Lying, for want of a better word. He'd no idea where those written directions had gone. He'd probably left them in Charlie Lane's car when it was clear the man didn't need them to find Carney's house. But it wouldn't be hard to get another sample of Fergus' penmanship.

For a while Tom had toyed with the idea that Fiona's father had sent the note. Fergus had referred that day in the garden centre to how he was in charge but his father was still overseeing the orders. But that hadn't meant he'd been writing the orders out – just ensuring they were correct. Ultimately, Fergus' insistence that day that the serial killer had Fiona and that she was already dead had given it away. Her parents, Richard included, passionately believed Fiona was still alive. You could see it in them. But there had been something in Fergus' eyes. He knew she was dead and it wasn't just that his hope was gone. It was because he had killed her.

'No,' Richard shook his head. Fergus remained remarkably calm and quiet. 'This is utterly ludicrous. What possible reason could Fergus have for killing his sister? He's been out on the searches with us! I'm going to have to ask you to leave, Inspector. The next conversation you have with us will be in the presence of our solicitor.'

'I'm afraid I can't leave without taking Fergus with me. And as for why he did it, I assume it's because she refused to listen to you, is that right, Fergus? When you asked her who was hitting her and she wouldn't tell you? You were sick of her, weren't you? Running around the village, screwing every bloke that moved. Probably your mates, too. You said it yourself, it was a nightmare having such a slut for a sister.'

'Stop it!' Caroline cried. 'Don't speak about her like that. She was not a slut!'

'Oh, come on!' Fergus snorted. 'Open your eyes, woman. On this – and only this – the inspector is correct. Your darling daughter would spread her legs for anybody who bought her a fucking vodka. She was a whore.'

The slap rang out sharp and clear. Richard Holland had lashed out at his son before any of them could react.

'Don't you ever speak like that about your sister,' he roared. 'She's worth ten of you.'

Fergus stood up slowly, recovering from the shock, his hand clasping his cheek.

'That's right,' he said. 'Daddy's little angel. You thought the sun shone out of her fucking arsehole. Even when she popped a bastard sprog, she was still the golden girl. She never lifted a fucking finger to help with the business but still you'd have chosen her over me if you had to, wouldn't you?'

'Is that why you killed her?' Tom said, standing too. There was an opportunity here that they had to grab. He and Ray had discussed whether they should claim that Fiona had been seen getting into Fergus' car, anything that might frighten him into confessing, but that would have been dangerous. If he'd picked her up somewhere remote, he'd have known they were reaching. But he saw now that they could rile the young man into confessing. He was a loose cannon, not a calculated killer like Charlie Lane. His role in her death would probably have come to light already, were it not for the Lane distraction.

Fergus laughed at him.

'Yeah. Yeah, right. I killed her because of a little bit of sibling rivalry. Your lot must have to deal with a massacre a day. Nice try, Inspector.'

Caroline Holland stood up and crossed the room. She pulled her husband aside and stood in front of her son, staring up at him.

Tom watched as she placed her hands on either side of his face, tenderly, like any mother would to comfort her son.

'Did you kill her?' she whispered, her voice imploring.

Fergus' expression shifted between anger and confusion.

'Do you think I'm capable of that?' he replied.

Caroline sighed.

'I gave birth to you, my darling. I carried you in my body for nine months and I laboured to deliver you. When I held you, my firstborn, I knew that I would always love you. No matter what. Do you hear me? No matter what. You were my baby. You stole my heart. You still have it and you always will. Fiona could be . . . difficult. I understand that. But did you hurt her? I need to know.'

Tears began to flow down Caroline's face.

Fergus swallowed and tried to pull her hands away, but she held him firm.

Richard placed his hand on her arm. She shook him off. There were only two people in the room – Caroline and her son.

'Did you kill her?' she asked again. 'I'm begging you. Tell me. I won't have any peace until I know. None of us will. It has to be said out loud before we can move on.'

Fergus' eyes began to well up. He bowed his head close to hers and a sob erupted from his throat.

The inspector barely heard the whispered, 'Yes'.

There was absolute silence in the room, then Fergus shrieked and pulled his face away from his mother. Five long slashes had been ripped down each cheek where she'd dragged her nails. He jumped backwards and she flew at him. Tom and Ray had to hold her back. Richard Holland was paralysed, unable to process what had just happened.

'Where is she?' Caroline screamed. 'Where's my baby?'

Fergus fell back onto the couch, stunned. For a minute he

said nothing, watching his mother strain against the strength of the two men grappling with her.

She wanted to kill him.

Defiance filled her son's face.

'You lied,' he snarled. 'You fucking lied. "You stole my heart." Sure. But only for a few years, huh? Until that bitch came along. I'll tell you what I did with her. What I should have done with her when she was born. What you do with any feral cat. I drowned her. I fucking drowned her. Satisfied now?'

Caroline howled and collapsed to the floor between Tom and Ray. Richard Holland stumbled back onto the couch, unable to stand, unable to talk.

'Fergus Holland,' Tom said, facing the young man. 'I'm arresting you on suspicion of the murder of Fiona Holland. You do not have to say anything, but it may harm your defence if you do not mention when questioned something you later rely on in court. Anything you do or say may be given in evidence.'

# CHAPTER 42

It didn't feel like a day for a funeral. In Tom's memory, every funeral he'd ever attended had complemented the mood of the mourners – lashing rain, dark clouds, freezing cold.

But this morning, the sun was splitting the stones and the birds sang in the sycamore trees dotted around the graveyard.

Maybe this was better, for June. After all, she'd been a sunny person. They'd played her favourite piece of music in the church and it hadn't been some maudlin number that made everybody weep even more. Louise had leaned close to Tom's ear and whispered, 'Isn't that from the horse racing? I didn't know June was into horses.'

'It's A Musical Joke,' Tom responded, then, seeing the confusion on his wife's face, added: 'That's the name of the piece. Sean's into all the serious, heavy compositions and June used to set up the CD player in his car so it would play that every time he turned it on. She said it made her laugh to think of him cursing and looking for his "morbid requiems".'

They'd both smiled, glad Sean was allowing his wife to have the last laugh.

Tom kept his arm gripped around Louise's waist in the graveyard, ostensibly to support her but more to comfort himself with the reminder that she was there.

There were more funerals coming. Lane's five victims would

be laid to rest one by one. And soon, the coroner would release Fiona Holland's body.

Once they'd charged Fergus, he'd quickly given up the location of Fiona's body. His parents refused to see him and despite his tough guy act, it was clearly affecting him. Perhaps he figured that if he cooperated, they'd forgive him.

He explained how he'd picked his sister up on the road just a half a mile away from their home. She'd been beaten and he demanded to know who'd done it to her. Instead of seeing his possessiveness for what it was – him, in his own way, trying to be a good brother – she'd thrown it back at him, accusing him of fancying her himself and being a sick bastard. Fergus had yelled at her and, while the car was still moving, she'd leaned over him to release the door locks, opened her side and jumped out.

He'd been driving slowly on the narrow road, so Fiona hadn't hurt herself. But something about her reckless action caused Fergus to crack. He chased her and dragged her back to the car. She bit him as he tried to force her in and that had made him snap. He dragged her back to the river they'd just crossed.

'I told her she was a filthy-mouthed bitch and I was going to wash her tongue clean,' he said. 'And I just held her head under until she stopped struggling.'

They'd found her body there, weighed down in the water with rocks, under the bridge not far from her home. She hadn't been found earlier because, due to the lack of resources, the search teams had only had one guard assigned to each to coordinate the efforts of the locals. Fergus had ensured he was allocated that patch. He'd given it the all clear and nobody had double-checked the bridge.

The last Tom had heard, Bart Healy had been up to see

Fiona's parents to confess that he'd fathered her child. The inspector didn't know what had motivated him – probably a misplaced sense of guilt. But things didn't augur well for the sergeant. The Hollands didn't want him to have anything to do with Cían and were seeking to have him dismissed from the force because of his relationship with their daughter.

Tom wondered if any of that would have come out if Fiona's body had been discovered earlier.

It was such a strange confluence of events, Lane living so close to the Hollands and working for them.

Would they have caught Lane at all if they hadn't met him because of Fiona's disappearance, something in which he'd had no hand, act or part?

The 'ifs' and the 'maybes' had kept Tom awake for the first few days after everything came to light.

But having spoken to Linda at length about it, the inspector had agreed with her assessment that most difficult cases were usually solved by just such a series of strange coincidences coming to light. That, and diligent, painstaking police work.

Tom sighed and Louise gave him a sympathetic glance. Today was the traumatic footnote to a very long few weeks.

He looked across to Sean, flanked on either side by his children. One of his many grandsons stood in front of him. Tom recognised him as the little football star, the one whose Sunday matches Sean had never missed, until he was too busy caring for June and couldn't attend any more.

Sean had his hands on the young lad's shoulders, his face resolute and controlled. He'd held it together for the whole service, even delivering the most beautiful oratory, filled with funny anecdotes from the couple's shared life.

He'd only spoken of her illness at the very end and even then just to say how well she'd handled it.

The priest finished speaking and indicated to the family that they should approach the grave.

Sean held a single yellow rose, June's favourite flower because it symbolised friendship. As he dropped it into the grave the big man crumpled, convulsed by great heaving sobs as his sons and daughters watched on in panic. They'd never seen their father be anything but strong – his abrupt, acerbic personality was the stuff of legend, even within their family.

Tom moved around the grave and took Sean's arm, turning his friend towards him and gripping him in a tight hug. He had to make true on his promise to June, the last thing she'd asked him to do. He had to take care of her husband.

'She's gone,' Sean choked. 'My darling is gone.' The raw vulnerability of his grief was the most devastating sound Tom had ever heard.

'I know,' he said, a lump in his throat. 'I know. Listen to me. She's looking down at you now and she's thinking, "That's right, you old codger. I knew you worshipped the ground I walked on." And she did, Sean. She knew. Even at the end.'

'Even at the end,' Sean repeated. 'Tom.' He leaned into the other man's ear and whispered urgently. 'She did it on purpose. There was no aneurism. She drove the car into the tree. She didn't want to lose herself. She didn't want to forget us and she didn't want us to see her dying inside.'

Tom pulled back in shock.

And in that moment he knew Sean was right.

*Maybe it's better this way.* That's what June had said. *The other way would have been so drawn out.*

She knew she was losing herself, so she took matters into her own hands.

Sean nodded, his face composed. It's okay, his expression said. I can cope. She wanted me to cope.

The inspector stood back as Sean's family took over, embracing him before they cast their own flowers into the grave.

Tom would stay at the ready, in case he was needed.

He'd be there.

# ACKNOWLEDGEMENTS

As always, my biggest and loudest thanks to my husband and children. Martin, Isobel, Liam, Sophia and Dominic, I love you all more than anything in the world.

To Stef, Hannah, Kathryn, Rachel and all the amazing team at Quercus and Hachette for being on top of their game and behind me all the way.

To the designers for providing me with amazing cover after cover.

All my extended family, my friends and neighbours – you've taken Tom Reynolds into your hearts and I love how much you love him. Especially you, Catherine Conway, for travelling over from Britain for every launch. Natasha Brennan Finnegan, for listening to my crazy plots on our exercise walks. And Martin Stynes, Pearse and Roisin Doherty, for making me feel like a more talented writer than I probably am.

Thank you to the reviewers and bloggers who've gone out of their way to support these books and tell people they're worth a punt.

The readers – especially the ladies (and man) from Warrenpoint Library – who will travel the country to buy the Reynolds books – you've made my writing experience truly wonderful.

All those who kindly offered up their names for *Sleeping*

*Beauties*. Well, more like begged, cajoled and harassed – you all owe me a glass of wine. Your names are famous!

And last but not least, my agent, Nicola Barr. When we Irish pair up, the world needs to watch out.

Thank you all.

Read on for a preview of *The Confession*,
the new standalone psychological thriller from Jo Spain

# THE
# CONFESSION

# Prologue

*Present day, 2012*

It's the first spray of my husband's blood hitting the television screen that will haunt me in the weeks to come – a perfect diagonal splash, each droplet descending like a vivid red tear.

That, and the sound of his skull cracking as the blows from the golf club rain down.

There's something so utterly shocking about that noise. I'd never heard it before and yet, the moment I did, I knew instinctively what it was. The crunching sound of a fractured head is strangely and horrifically unmistakable.

A few minutes earlier, the two of us had been watching a crime thriller on that television, now criss-crossed with blood. We were sitting separately in our armchairs – expensive black leather recliners. A particularly scary scene was playing out on the wide LCD screen. The killer in the show was on to his third victim and as he hunted her in deserted, creepy woodland I placed my hands over my eyes, unable to watch the inevitable. Harry laughed at me for being so girly.

That was when the stranger walked into the centre of our living room.

We hadn't even heard him enter the house.

A golf club dangled loosely from his right hand, but he didn't seem threatening, if you ignored the unexpectedness of the situation. A pair of jeans, a T-shirt. It was like he'd just strolled in off the golf course that sat to the rear of our property.

Harry turned to me, completely bewildered. Then my husband stood up, his body faster than his brain, a mammal reacting to this peculiar invasion of our space. His mouth was just opening to form the first indignant question when the man swung the golf club at him.

Harry buckled, momentarily winded. He was stunned but his eyes met mine and I saw him make a quick calculation. My husband has always been great like that. Throw him into any awkward situation and he'll negotiate himself out of it in minutes. Charm the birds out of the trees, my mother always says. Although, this time, it didn't look like words were going to work.

Harry is a strong, athletic man. He works out several times a week and one of those sessions is with a boxing coach. He's had a lot of stress in the last few years and there's nothing like laying into a punchbag to let off steam.

So when he pivoted to deliver a right hook to the man standing so nonchalantly in front of us, I thought, *This is it*.

Except it wasn't.

The man hit Harry again while my husband's fist was mid-air.

And again and again, and he's still hitting him.

Harry didn't stand a chance.

My husband is on the floor now, his attacker visibly sweating and grunting from his exertions as he brings the golf club down repeatedly. His knuckles are white on the iron, his arm muscles tense. Every time the weapon lands it makes a stomach-churning thumping sound, and each blow draws fresh blood, cartilage, saliva, teeth. There's vomit spewing out of Harry's mouth and a damp patch has spread down the leg of his beige trousers.

I'm still in my chair, watching all this.

I don't speak.

I don't run for my phone.

I don't launch myself at the stranger.

What I really want to do as all this is happening is cover my eyes. I want to block out the sight of the horror, just as I did with the thriller on TV.

At last the beating stops. The man releases his grip on the golf club and surveys the damage.

Harry is unrecognizable. There's blood everywhere. This is what they mean when they use the expression 'beaten to a pulp'. This . . . mess. A barely human form. Here lies the man I've known nearly all my adult life. A man who has held my hand, kissed my lips, lain beside me, been inside me – I know every inch of his body and recognize not a bit of it right now.

Then the intruder bends down to Harry's ear and whispers something, quietly, softly, like a lover's sweet nothing.

What? What did he say?

The man stands up and studies me. He has dark eyes – black, in fact. Black hair too. Not dark brown – coal-like. Thick eyebrows. Full, red lips. Younger than me but not by much, maybe ten years or so. He is good-looking. Even covered in my husband's blood.

I know what he is.

A reckoning.

We aren't perfect, Harry and I. All of us have our secrets, don't we? The little petty lies. The bigger sins.

But what has Harry done to provoke this?

My eyes are drawn back to his body, and I whimper. I've imagined Harry dead many times but not this . . . I never thought it would be like this.

Then the man turns on his heel and walks out of the living room door. Just like that, he's gone.

I dimly register the front door opening and slamming shut.

I'm alone, bar the bloodied and battered form on the floor inches from my feet.

That's when I finally do something, when my body throws itself into action.

I wet myself.

# Part One

# Julie

When I first met Harry, he told me he worked in finance.

What does that even mean? I asked. To me, finance was a title sharp-suited men gave to ambiguous jobs in new-build office blocks in the capital. They weren't *real* jobs. I grew up in a little village in rural Ireland. I was used to men in overalls, with calloused hands and bent backs, weather-beaten faces and an all-round lesser sense of entitlement.

In the early nineties in Ireland, 'finance' took off in a big way. The eighties had been bleak for our little country – mass emigration and unemployment, high taxes, politicians up to their necks in brown envelopes and dodgy deals. But in the nineties there was a shift. None of us knew it, but the state was about to embark on its Celtic Tiger journey. Wealth was flooding into Ireland and, Jesus, you've never met a nationality that could get comfortable with money faster. You'd swear we'd always had it.

My background didn't prepare me for what was coming. Dad managed a small farm long before the European Union made it profitable, and Mam stayed at home, rearing child after child. She'd missed the memo in the seventies that said nobody gave a shite any more what the Pope thought about condoms and what went on in the marital bed. Luckily, for me. I was the youngest of our large family. I was adored and spoiled, for all that you could be spoiled with what little we had.

But I was never content. Leitrim had nothing to offer. Thankfully, as the last of the brood, there were no expectations on me to hang around the farm or live close by. My older siblings carried all those responsibilities. I was allowed to finish school, and I worked hard − hard enough to earn myself *the* golden ticket: a place at Trinity College Dublin to study the arts. My plan was to become a teacher. I'd read Maeve Binchy's *Circle of Friends*. New pals, the capital, three months off every summer and a great pension? Yes, please.

Leaving the county was the first indication I was a breed apart. My poor grandmother almost had a heart attack when she heard where I was headed. Fair enough, it was the nineties, but she was of her age − eighty-five − and she'd had a number of rules beaten into her over the decades. Firstly, single girls didn't move from Leitrim to Dublin on their own unless it was to deal with an unpleasant and unwanted surprise in their bellies. Secondly, they didn't go to college unless it was to learn hairdressing or secretarial skills. And thirdly, if they were going to flout every rural tradition going, they certainly didn't go to Trinity, which was bursting at the seams with sneaky, superior Protestants. She still thought the college had its ban on Catholics.

Turns out, she was right. Trinity would prove very dangerous for me. Not the place, but the people I would meet there.

I first saw Harry McNamara at the college ball in my third year, 1994.

My date had got, as we country people say, langered, and it wasn't even midnight. My pal Grace had also abandoned me, in order to suck the face off a PhD biology student. Left to my own devices, I walked around the various old stone courtyards, my face changing colour every time I passed one of the multicoloured ground lamps strategically placed to illuminate Trinity's Victorian-era walls. I hoped I'd bump into one of my friends to finish the night in company. I was never comfortable being alone.

I heard a low whistle, followed by the words:

'Well, now, if it isn't Jessica Rabbit.'

Harry called out to me through a circle of people, all gathered around him, the centre of their universe. He was leaning casually against the wall of the provost's garden, holding court. His bow tie hung open around his neck and a cigar stuck out of the side of his mouth. He was, without exception, the most handsome man I'd ever laid eyes on. He was so *un*-Irish-looking. Thick, wavy brown hair framed a tanned, sculpted face, and his tux was expensive – perfectly tailored, the way a man should wear a suit. And tight-fitting enough for me to see he had the toned and muscular body of an athlete.

But his smile – oh, his smile was the clincher.

The group parted like the sea for Moses as he moved towards me, all of them envious at the newcomer who'd unintentionally and so easily won his attention.

'Are you addressing me?' I said, eyebrows raised as I looked around, pretending to check he hadn't intended the comment for somebody else. 'Is that your thing? Yelling sexist remarks at random women?'

I was well able for him, used to the attention of the opposite sex.

I'd been born with natural flaxen curls, sky-blue eyes and plump red lips. Attractive to most men, I guess. My curves, though, as Harry had so evidently noticed, were my selling point. I've always been petite (Polly Pocket, my older sisters affectionately termed me early on). But as soon as I hit my teens, I developed, big time. I was a 36DD by the time I'd turned eighteen. I'd gone from being 'Polly' to 'Dolly' in the nickname stakes. All the Ferguson girls were alike, blonde curls and pretty faces. But none of them got my chest. My sisters were disgusted.

The night I caught Harry's attention, I knew I looked sexy. I was wearing a tight emerald-green evening gown. It had started out as a cheap thing from Primark but had been transformed into something magical after Grace's mam got her hands on it and gussied it up on her sewing machine.

'Jesus,' Grace had said, green-eyed. 'Mammy, you wouldn't let me across the threshold in that get-up, and you practically stitch Julie into it.'

'I love you, petal, but Julie has a figure to work with,' Mrs Delaney had replied, giving poor Grace's two fried eggs the once-over.

'Everything I haven't got, I inherited from you, you horrible old woman,' Grace grumbled.

The dress would have been put to better use on my sex-mad friend. Unlike many of my peers in college, I wasn't there to find a man. I loved that our mam had always been home, but the thought of being a young, settled housewife sent me into a panic. And I certainly didn't want to end up with a bun in the oven before I had a ring on my finger.

I'd kidded myself into thinking I was Ms Independent.

I knew nothing about myself.

Harry had laughed when I snapped my retort back at him, then tutted playfully.

'Is it sexist to point out you're the best looking woman here? Honestly, I don't know who you came with tonight, but the man is a simpleton leaving you alone. Unless you figured that out yourself and it was you who abandoned him?'

I smiled, despite myself.

'He's . . . somewhere.'

'I see. So, while he's somewhere, I'm going to seize this opportunity to woo you, and I'll start by getting us some champagne. It's just not right, you gliding around, goddess-like, without a drink in your hand. And it can only be the best.'

'It's far from champagne I was reared,' I snorted. 'And did you just say "woo"?'

He blushed.

'I did, didn't I? It's your dress. It looks like it was made for you and your . . . eh, assets. I can't remember my own name, let alone what century we're in.'

'Wow. Tell me. Did you practise in a mirror before coming out tonight, or is this just you?'

'Seriously now – would you fake being this cheesy?' He lowered his head and smiled out at me from under his fringe, an adorable brown-eyed puppy. 'Please. Don't torture me any longer. That gang behind me are watching to see if I can pull this off and if you knock me back my reputation will be ruined, utterly. Can you even pretend you don't think I'm a total arse?'

'I would take pity on you, but you promised me fancy champagne and they're not serving it.'

'Well, now. I see light at the end of this tunnel you're making me crawl through. They have it all right. You just haven't been to the right bar.'

'U-huh. Just so you know, I can't be bought. Fizz or no.'

'Are you saying you're priceless?'

'Got it in one.'

I'm not a cliché. I didn't fall for Harry McNamara just because he was a smooth talker and happened to have a case of bubbles behind the bar reserved for the alumni of the college. And, even with him charming and me tipsy, there was no way I was jumping into bed with him. I was still a girl from a small country village – nowhere near cosmopolitan enough for one-night stands.

We talked and, as we did, I discovered that he was actually a former, not a current student, which explained his access to the alumni bar.

'Dear God, how old are you?' I asked. 'Is the college aware you're here, preying on young, vulnerable women? And what is your actual job – in finance, I mean?'

He was amused by that.

'I'm twenty-seven,' he said. 'I hope that's not too old for you. What are you – early twenties? Come on. I'm hardly a predator. And my job? I'm a banker. Of sorts.'

'Oh! Well, why don't you just say that? You work in a bank. Why does everybody have to use fancy terms these days like "finance" and "consultancy"? I'm going to be a teacher. Not a "provider of knowledge". What? What are you laughing at?'

'You,' he said, leaning in, until his long-lashed chestnut eyes were centimetres away from mine and I could feel his breath hot against my lips, mint and alcohol-flavoured. 'I could listen to that accent all night. It's melodic. Are you always so frank?'

'Oh. I thought you were laughing because I just want to be a teacher.'

He came close to my ear and whispered, 'Come on, now. You could never be *just* anything.'

I pulled back, blushing, alarmed at how much my body was responding to his. I was still a virgin but all I could think was *I want this man to fuck me senseless*. Turns out I was a latent harlot.

'Do you want to get out of here and we can get a drink somewhere more private?' he asked.

'No. My friends are here too. I need to find them. We have a policy – no woman left behind.'

'Ah, go on. Ditch 'em. The night is young. It's only . . . shit, it's not even light out yet. I'm not giving up on you.'

'Yes, well, I don't give up easy either,' I said. 'And I can see my pal Grace over there. It looks like she's come up for air. I have to go.'

Everything about Harry was an aphrodisiac. It wasn't just his looks – it was his confidence, the power he exuded, that assuredness. He was that little bit older and he was seducing me, but not in a sleazy way.

And there was something about him. Something . . . dangerous. Like he didn't play within normal rules.

I'd always been a good girl. Good girls are meant to go with good boys. But being the focus of Harry's attention was intoxicating.

In the end, there was more pulling me towards him than even I knew. I was an ambitious young woman but I was used to being loved. A large, tight-knit family will do that for you. I might have wanted to carve my own path in the world but I didn't want to do it alone.

And I think I sensed something similar in Harry. I'd learn, as time went on, that he wasn't as confident as he came across. He liked having people around him, lackeys and sycophants. But he'd never really had anybody who mattered. No family, I'd later find out, and no real friends. He let very few people get close.

The night of the Trinity Ball, I gave him my number.

Here's something I didn't know at the time.

Harry had come to the ball that night with a date. She wasn't with him when he saw me – maybe she'd gone to the loo or to touch up her make-up or something. Harry was gone by the time she got back.

You could say it was love at first sight and she was incidental to the story.

That would be the romantic interpretation.

Would it have mattered, anyway, if I'd known how easily he could pick up and drop women? Harry probably would have just spun it another way and I'd have most likely chosen to believe him. We were both good at that, but him especially.

Like when he told me that night that he was a banker – what he failed to mention, or at least correct me on, was that he didn't just work in a bank.

He owned one.

In his early twenties Harry had started his own bank; it dealt predominantly with funding up-and-coming property developers, headed by an up-and-coming financier. Here was a man well used to getting what he wanted.

I resisted him for months, which made the chase all the more exciting.

By that stage, I was head over heels for him and he with me.

You see us, don't you?

Young, innocent, hopeful, in love.

That was us at the beginning of our fairytale.

But here's the thing about fairytales.

Sometimes they're darker than you can ever imagine.

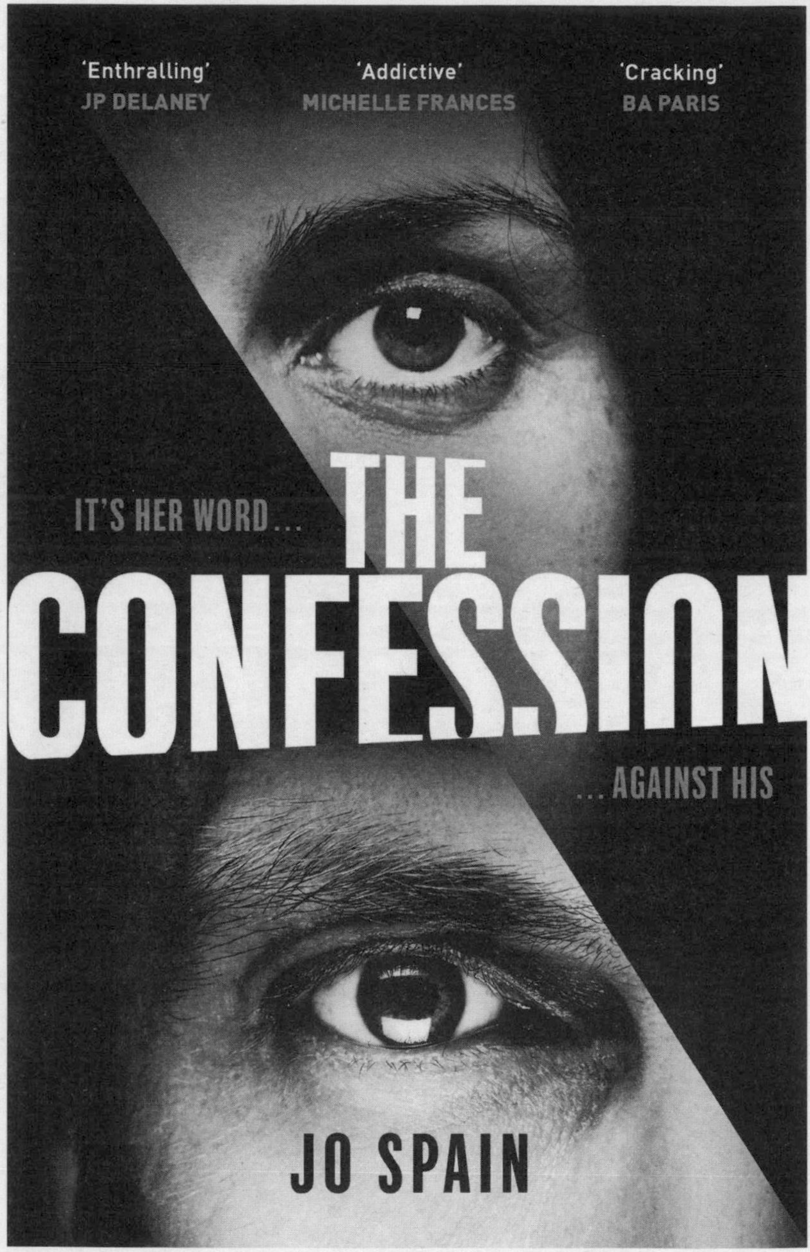


Available now